CHANGELING'S
FEALTY

BOOK ONE
OF THE CHANGELING BLOOD SERIES

CHANGELING'S FEALTY

FEALTY

BOOK ONE
OF THE CHANGELING BLOOD SERIES

GLYNN STEWART

**FAOLAN'S PEN
PUBLISHING**

faolanspen.com

This edition published in 2018 by:

Faolan's Pen Publishing Inc.

22 King St. S, Suite 300

Waterloo, Ontario

N2J 1N8 Canada

ISBN-13: 978-1-988035-55-0 (print)

ISBN-13: 978-1-988035-99-4 (epub)

A record of this book is available from Library and Archives Canada.

Printed in the United States of America

1 2 3 4 5 6 7 8 9 10

First edition

First printing: October 2017

Illustration © 2017 Shen Fei

Faolan's Pen Publishing logo is a trademark of Faolan's Pen Publishing Inc.

Read more books from Glynn Stewart at faolanspen.com

1

My introduction to the wonderful people of Canada was literally running into a large, leather clad, blond man who stopped unexpectedly as I crossed the parking lot of the bus station.

The man turned to face me, sniffing exaggeratedly, and bared a canine smile. "Well, lookie here; I think I smell something...*faerie*."

I raised my hands placatingly, wanting anything but a fight within an hour of my arriving in the city of Calgary. "Sorry, man, I didn't mean to run into you," I drawled quickly, only to see his grin expand. Somehow, the man knew what I was.

"I would think *your kind* would be more careful, little faerie," the man told me, and with a sinking feeling I realized the canine impression was more than just a passing fancy. A wolf shifter had decided to pick a fight with me, in a parking lot.

"I just got into town," I said as quickly as I could. "I didn't know this was your pack's territory."

That, apparently, was the exact wrong thing to say.

"*Pack?*" the man snarled. "I am *Clan Fontaine*, you punk. Not some animal to run in a pack!"

I didn't have time to apologize before the man swung. Normally, there are other tricks I can pull, but there were mortals in the parking lot. Unable to do more than stand there helpless, I took the massive fist in the stomach and folded.

A rough hand grabbed the back of my head, through the stolen hat, and kept me moving downward. I slipped on the ice and was introduced to the cold, frozen concrete.

The shifter's knee drove into the blade of my shoulder, pinning me to the icy ground as he shoved my face into the grit.

"You're new in town," he growled in my ear. "So, I'll let it go. Once. Your kind has a Manor north of here." He yanked my bruised face up and pointed at a blue-and-white bus just pulling into the lot. "You want that bus."

With that, my "welcoming committee" let go of my face, letting me drop back to the icy pavement.

———

I LEFT the south because I was sick of it. Down there, "my kind" has been set up for centuries, if not long enough to stop some of the elders' bitching about the "Old Country" and the "Old Ways."

Maybe it would have been better if they had actually *been* my kind. The old fae run the Deep South of the United States, so far as the supernatural goes, but I'm not true fae.

My name is Jason Kilkenny, and I am a changeling. My mother, whatever Powers are listening preserve her soul, was a mortal woman with the misfortune to have a one-night stand with a frisky fairy—my father. I was the result, and she never saw my father again.

It's not an uncommon story. Given the fae population of the Deep South, I'm surprised that changelings aren't half the damn population by now. But then, the old fae disapproved. Which is why I was there, freezing my half-human butt off outside the Greyhound station in a Canadian city as far from home as I could think of.

My mother passed on when I was nineteen, before I'd discovered what I was. On my twenty-first birthday, some jackasses made a comment about her, and I was too young and too drunk to take it.

Next thing I knew, I'd laid out four of the biggest bruisers in the bar and set the last on fire with my mind for good measure. For about a week, I thought I might be some kind of superhero.

Further encounters with people like my "welcoming committee", not to mention other fae, proved me very sharply wrong. This, again, leads us to me freezing in a Canadian winter, waiting in line for the indicated transit bus outside the Calgary Greyhound depot.

As fae go—hell, even as changelings go—I'm a pushover. I'm an Olympic-level athlete who never exercises, and I can conjure faerie fire —if I'm really angry, I can hurt someone with it. Most of the time, I'm lucky if I can light a cigarette.

Of course, even little changeling me could create a lot of havoc if I acted out in public, so everywhere we go, all changeling and fae check in at a Manor like the one the shifter had directed me to—neutral ground, a meeting place for fae. I assume other supernaturals have similar rules, and if they're looking for one of us, they come to the Manor and speak to the Keeper.

My bus finally arrived and I got on, passing the driver some coins from the sparse collection of Canadian currency I had on me. My collection of currency was sparse in general—dropping out of college to dodge assault charges left me without much means of making ends meet, and the old fae are not generous.

The Seelie Court—the good guys, as much as any of the fae are such a thing—had helped me bury my old past and forge some kind of new identity. I was too weak a changeling to be much use to them though, so I ended up drifting from town to town, Manor to Manor, bouncing off rule after rule, true fae after changeling.

I got sick of being the bottom rung in a highly formalized ladder, so when someone mentioned that Calgary, way up north, had a tiny and informal Court, I bid my home states an unfond farewell and started catching buses.

Ending with this white-and-blue Calgary Transit vehicle whose heating could not *possibly* be working. There was no way it could be that cold in a vehicle with working heat.

When the bus finally disgorged me by the bar, surrounded by hotels, that my welcoming committee pointed me toward and the surrounding fae-sign told me was the Manor, I couldn't feel my fingers, despite the heavy gloves I'd stolen somewhere in Montana.

A faded blinking neon sign announced VLTs and karaoke. Under that, a recently updated sign, barely lit by the streetlights, announced cheap draft of some beer I'd never heard of.

The wall behind that sign told me what I was looking for. Fae-sign, invisible to those without our blood, declared that this was a Manor, neutral ground, and that swift death awaited those who broke the neutrality of the Manor.

Walking in, I was almost stopped by a sudden blast of hot air. The inside was so warm, it took a minute for the noise to sink in. It was late on a Thursday evening, and the volume had been cranked on the bar's sound system.

A blonde girl dressed in a uniform that would have meant swift death in the winter night outside flowed her way around the handful of patrons in the bar to me.

"Can I get you something?" she asked, her voice helpful. My system still in shock from the sudden blast of heat; it took me a moment to realize she was true fae—a water nymph with a bewitchingly delicate beauty to break the hearts and minds of mortal men.

Being a changeling made the effect much less bewitching, though she was still very cute.

"I am a wayfarer in need of succor," I said softly, the ancient words sounding strange in my slow Southern drawl. "I must announce myself before the Keeper of the Manor and Lords of the Courts."

I'd spoken quietly enough that I was sure no one other than the girl had heard me, but she quickly glanced around anyway, and then grinned at me in a way that made me regret my immunity to her kind's power over men.

"Everyone here tonight is one of us," she told me quietly. "I'm Tarva; have a seat and I'll grab you a drink and Eric."

"I don't know if I can afford the drink," I admitted ruefully.

"You're on succor," she answered. Which meant that for the first three days I was in town, all my food and lodgings would be covered by the Manor—it was a tradition I'd abused to survive down in the South. Normally, however, I'd get nothing until I'd announced myself.

"Then can you grab me a coffee, please?" I asked. After six days of bouncing from one bus to another, I wasn't sure I wanted to meet the Keeper and Lords without some caffeine in me.

"Sure thing!" she answered with another smile. She disappeared for a moment and then returned with a steaming cup of black coffee. "Eric will be right out," she told me.

The coffee was shit. I'd been spoiled by my three-day-long stopover in Seattle, where the Manor was an old independent coffee house that survived in the era of Starbucks by brewing *fantastic* coffee. Even realizing my bias, this was pretty bad coffee.

The bar was badly lit, so it took me a moment to realize just how short the man who came in from the kitchen was. In thick platform shoes, Eric stood just over three and a half feet tall. His hair was thick and white, and bushy eyebrows shadowed recessed eyes over a large hooked nose.

The gnome crossed the room to me and climbed into the stool opposite.

"I am Eric von Radach, Keeper of the Manor in Calgary," the gnome said quietly. "Announce yourself, stranger."

"I am Jason Kilkenny, changeling out of Georgia of no known fae parent," I laid out quickly. "I seek leave to settle and take up a mortal occupation, as my blood is not thick enough for me to serve the Courts."

Eric typed all of what I said into a tiny laptop that appeared from nowhere and vanished just as thoroughly a moment later.

"You've come a long way, Mr. Kilkenny," the gnome observed. "What brings you all the way up here?"

"A hope for quiet," I answered honestly, though my welcome to the town was now making me doubt that hope. Again. "I just want to live a normal life, and it's hard to remove oneself from the Courts in the South."

"A fair hope," Eric agreed. "I see no concern for us here. You will need to meet Lord Oberis, of course—I called him before I came out. He should be here"—there was a burst of wind as the doors opened and closed again—"shortly."

The man who entered was every inch a sidhe lord, fair and terrifying. Like everyone else in the room—including me—he wore his blond hair long to cover his ears, and it brushed against the shoulders of the heavy cashmere coat he wore. The tall fae walked across the room toward Eric and me, and I considered what Oberis would see.

I am tall for a human but short for a fae, at just under six feet tall. I probably looked scrawny and underfed to this perfectly chiseled specimen of inhumanity. My mixed brown hair was as long as Oberis's but due to lack of care rather than style. I was dressed in a mismatched mess of clothes stolen or purchased for warmth more than color coordination on the way north. Every possession I owned was in a backpack at my feet.

There was no way—*no way*—that the fae lord would have dropped everything to come meet the new changeling in town. Fae lords had *flunkies* for that. And yet...

"I am Oberis," he introduced himself superfluously when he reached the table. "Lord of the Court here in Calgary—there are hardly enough of us to justify two courts," he explained with a grin that somehow shattered the cold inhumanity of that perfect face.

"This, my lord, is Jason Kilkenny, changeling of no known lineage," Eric introduced me formally. "He wishes to settle and pursue mortal employment."

"Is that so?" Oberis regarded me, his gaze level but warmer than I expected from the winter outside. "Why mortal employment? There are few changelings here, even fewer than there are fae. We may find some use for you."

Well, if there were that few fae floating around this city, that would at least somewhat explain why his Lordship was here talking to the newcomer so quickly. It meant both that he wasn't busy and that, weak as I was, even *my* presence might be considered important.

"With respect, Lord," I answered slowly and carefully, trying to consider how to dodge politics without offending a fae lord in apparently desperate need of help, "my blood is too weak for me to be of much aid, and I desire more than anything to leave the world of Court and Manor behind. It has brought me little but grief."

Oberis nodded. "Very well. I grant you both succor and the right to settle. However, there is one last formality."

My sigh of relief stopped in mid-breath at his words. "What formality, my lord?"

"I am not the final authority here in Calgary," Oberis explained. "In this city, we all answer to the Wizard and his Enforcers."

"There is a Wizard here?" I squeaked. The last heirs of Merlin's teachings were few and far between in the modern world—I'd heard one old fae guess less than twenty remained—and were basically demigods that only traveled because moving the continents around to bring their destination to them was a bit too flashy.

2

"MAGUS KENNETH MACDONALD," Oberis answered as I caught my mental breath. "All in this city have accepted his authority and power, and so we accept his strictures. He insists on meeting all new supernaturals when they arrive in the city. Given his habits, the car for you should be arriving about...now."

The door opened again, admitting another gust of wind, and a man in a plain black suit and no winter overcoat stepped in. Wordlessly, he crossed to the table where I sat.

"Lord Oberis, Keeper Eric," he said flatly. "Is he ready to meet my master?"

"If you wish to stay in Calgary, you must," Oberis said simply. I looked at the mortal in the suit and nodded.

After all, what the hell *else* was I going to do?

I FOLLOWED THE SUITED MAN, who seemed totally unbothered by the cold. It didn't seem fair. From everything I could tell, the man was totally mortal, where my supposedly superior fae blood gave me no protection from the chill he completely ignored.

He led me to a black SUV with tinted windows. A small metal decal marked the windshield frame, a stylized silver K. I glanced at the windows and was somewhat relieved to realize the bruising from earlier had already healed. I had *some* benefits from my fae heritage, at least.

The suit, clearly oblivious to my self-inspection, gestured me to the front passenger-side door. Obedient, I got into the vehicle, grateful for the fact that he'd left the engine running and it was *warm*.

"Where are we headed?" I asked.

"The Wizard's Tower," he answered, and I could hear the capitals on the words. "Downtown," he added, after a moment's thought, apparently to decide if he could spare the vocabulary.

After that, he remained silent for the entire trip, not that I made much attempt to engage him in conversation. I hadn't expected to end up meeting a Wizard when I got off that bus, and if I'd known that was in the cards, I might have never left Georgia!

The wordlessly grim man in the driver's suit was a not-so-subtle hint that obedience was a wise choice tonight, however, so I sat in my seat quietly like a good little changeling.

It took less time to make it back into the city's downtown core than it had taken me to get out of it, and I tried to conceal a sigh of relief as we drove into an underground parking garage under one of the office towers. The garage was far from *warm*, but it certainly beat the frigid Canadian air outside.

The black SUV was now parked between matching vehicles in dark green and dark red, all with the stylized silver K decaled onto the window frame. Another man in a black suit, cast from the same mold as my driver though shorter and fairer-haired, exchanged nods with my driver and gestured for me to follow him.

He led me to an elevator, where he made a great show of pushing five buttons in a specific sequence. So far as I could tell, he was more concerned with hiding the small key he unlocked the elevator with than with which buttons he was pressing.

Whichever it was, all of the elevator buttons flashed once and then went blank as the elevator started its smooth ascent. The Wizard certainly didn't seem to have any issue with modern technology—or spending money. The elevator was wood-paneled and floored in black and red tiles.

The elevator was also fast, and it took less than a minute to reach the top floor of the building. The doors slid open, and my erstwhile companion gestured me through.

Being the good little changeling tonight, I exited the elevator into the lobby of a law firm. The same tiles as the elevator covered the floor of a good-sized front room, and a receptionist's desk faced the two elevator doors. A single door stood on the left side of the desk, and a dozen or so chairs were clustered around a small table and coffee station.

A sturdy-looking blonde woman, silverish tattoos tracing across both her cheeks and clashing sharply with a trim black suit identical to the men who'd brought me there, stood up behind the desk as I entered.

"Mr. Kilkenny," she greeted me. "We were expecting you, have a seat, the Magus is busy but he'll be with you shortly. Can I get you a coffee? It's from a local organic roaster; they're really good!"

It took me a moment to catch up with her rapid-fire delivery and confirm that I would like a coffee. She bustled me over to a chair, poured a cup for me and passed it over when I declined cream or sugar with a wordless nod.

To my surprise, the receptionist was right—it was good coffee. Not too hot, either; the pot was apparently kept at just the right drinking temperature. After seeing me settled, the woman returned to her desk, doing whatever mysterious work it is that receptionists do when men like me are stuck in their waiting rooms.

I'd just finished the coffee when she looked up from her computer and the door behind her popped open.

"The Magus will see you now," she told me. "It's the first door to your left."

"Thank you," I told her. "What was your name again?"

"Sarah," she replied.

"Well, thank you, Sarah. That *was* good coffee."

Passing the cup to her to be thrown in a dishwasher, I took a deep breath and walked into the Wizard's offices. The hall continued with the same black and red tiles, but here the paneling was waist height in some rich dark red wood.

The first door to the left was made of the same wood and was closed. I knocked.

"Come in," a firm voice ordered. I obeyed and took my first look at the Wizard of Calgary.

Kenneth MacDonald was, without any great effort, the centerpiece of attention in the room, even if I couldn't put my finger on why. The Wizard was of average height, several inches shorter than me, completely bald, and in every way utterly unimposing. Yet he radiated power in a way even a fae noble like Oberis couldn't match. Everything and anything else in the room faded in comparison to the certain knowledge that one stood in the presence of one of the heirs of Merlin, nigh unto a demigod made flesh.

"Lord Wizard," I tried to say formally, but fear and awe drew a mortifying squeak from my lungs in mid-word. In an attempt to regain some composure, I focused my attention on the outer wall of the room, which was a single giant window looking out over the city's downtown. Even this late at night, lights were on in many of the office buildings. From here, we looked down on most of them, including one narrow, needle-like tower that was probably *supposed* to be tall.

"Have a seat, Mr. Kilkenny," the Wizard said gently, apparently recognizing my discomfort, and gestured. A large soft armchair, one of four I now saw were set next to a table by a large roaring fireplace, floated across the room to drop in front of the Wizard's desk. I obeyed the unspoken order and seated myself in the chair.

"You are Jason Kilkenny," he continued once I'd sat down, "changeling of no known bloodline, born in Georgia to Melissa Kilkenny, a professor of Irish history recently immigrated to the state, twenty-four years ago. Identified just over three years ago on your twenty-first birthday."

"How do you know all that?" I asked, impressed and even more terrified. With a chuckle, MacDonald turned the large flatscreen monitor on his desk to face me and I saw a picture of myself attached to a page of text.

"I emailed a friend of mine among the Fae Council," he told me. "They have a file on every fae they know about. Yours is the shortest I've ever seen, to be honest."

"Oh," I breathed softly, not sure if I was reassured that his means had been mundane.

"What is your purpose in Calgary?" the Wizard asked.

"I'm looking to find a place to live and mortal work," I answered. "I didn't want all this hoopla; I just wanted to move in quietly and avoid politics and attention." I was whining. I *was whining at a Wizard.* Shit.

"This is, from the supernatural perspective, a backwater," the Wizard told me. "It is a backwater of some importance, for many reasons, but still an area with few inhumans present. I insist on meeting all of us, for my own reasons."

I nodded, remaining silent and regarding the heavy wooden desk and the wall of windows behind it that framed the Wizard. He stood and turned to look out the windows himself, eyeing the brilliant lights of the business towers and homes.

"My Order dislikes involving ourselves in inhuman politics," he said to the window, the reflection of his eyes watching me. "However, I accidentally created a power vacuum here some years ago and found myself forced to impose order.

"So, impose order I did," he continued. "You have met my Enforcers."

It wasn't a question, and I nodded agreement.

"They bear my seal," he told me, gesturing at the desk where I saw the front was engraved with the same stylized K as I'd seen on the SUVs. "Any man or woman who bears that seal speaks with my voice and will be obeyed as the law in this city. Do you understand me, Mr. Kilkenny?"

"Yes, sir."

"I do not care for mortal law," the Wizard said simply. "My Covenant with the inhumans of this city is simple: I keep the peace.

Murder, assault, rape—of mortal or inhuman alike—these will not be tolerated. Conflict between the species will not be tolerated. I will have peace to do my work. Follow these rules, and I will guarantee your safety. Now. Place your hands on my seal."

The order was unexpected, and it took me a moment to catch it and lean forward to place my hands on the seal burned into the front of the desk.

"Do you, Jason Kilkenny, swear to uphold this Covenant, to observe my peace, and do no harm while within my city?"

Oaths are not sworn to Wizards lightly. They have ways of punishing those who break them. I didn't have a choice.

"I do swear."

"Good." MacDonald conjured, and the door behind me swung open. "This audience is over. Speak with Sarah on your way out; she will assist you in finding your mortal employment." He eyed me over the desk. "Three days of succor won't do you much good if you're still unemployed at the end of it, and the job market in this city is a killer."

With a nod and a careful bow, I saw myself out of the Wizard's presence.

———

I ALMOST RAN RIGHT into the two men arguing in the hallway outside. One was huge, easily the largest man I'd ever seen. Dark-haired and full-bearded, he stood an easy seven feet tall and loomed like a human wall.

"His word is final," the other man told the giant, and I blinked as he came into focus. By any comparison except the man he stood next to, this man was tall, a few inches over my own six feet. He was shaven bald, and I could see lines upon lines of gold and silver runes tattooed up his neck and onto his bare head.

"You ask me to allow the creation of weap—..." The giant cut off in mid-sentence when he saw me, then returned his glare to the tattooed man. "We will continue this conversation another time, Winters," he snapped, and strode back towards the lobby.

The tattooed man—Winters—looked at me.

"You're the new changeling, I take it? My master mentioned you," he said softly. "Carry on." He gestured me toward the front door.

Accepting the dismissal as given, I quickly slipped out to see Sarah.

"Who were those guys?" I asked her, as quietly as I could.

"Gerard Winters and Tarvers Tenerim," she answered. "Winters is my boss—the Head Enforcer." Looking more closely at the blonde woman now, I realized that the silverish tattoos that traced around her cheeks were made of the same goldish-silver runes as Winters' tattoos had been. "Tarvers is the Alpha of Clan Tenerim—the senior shifter clan in the city—and the Speaker for the shapeshifters in town."

I nodded, trying to organize a mental picture of the balance of power and authority in the city. The Wizard was unquestionably at the top, with Winters as his right-hand man. Then Tarvers and Oberis, and I wasn't sure which of them would be regarded as more "senior".

"Magus MacDonald said you'd be able to help me find work," I told Sarah. "Something quick-ish, I don't know if I can make it more than a week or two after my succor runs out," I admitted.

"Well, let's see," she replied, tapping away at her computer. "What are your qualifications?"

"Umm...three quarters of a mechanical engineering degree and a lot of manual labor?"

"Hrm," she murmured, absently chewing on the end of a pencil. "Can you drive?"

"Yes, but I think my license has expired," I answered.

"Oh, right, that's not an issue," she answered, and picked a manila envelope up from the desk. "The Magus conjured this while you were in with him," she told me, and slid it across to me.

I opened it and found a passport, birth certificate and driver's license with my name, picture and age, but saying I'd been born in someplace called Winnipeg. Everything was complete, including—I checked against a light—all the watermarks and holograms. I could only assume they were correct as well.

Wizards scared me.

"Then yes, I can drive. Why?"

"I have a friend with a courier company who's desperate to fill a slot ASAP," she answered. "I can have him give you a call in the morning, if that works?"

"At what number... Oh." The last item in the envelope, which I was willing to swear *hadn't* been there when I opened it, was a top of the line smartphone.

"The phone's 'service plan' goes through a semi-magical relay that taps into everybody's network—you won't be getting cellphone bills," Sarah told me with a smile. "I'll have my friend—Bill Trakshinsky is his name—call you. Go get some rest."

Another suited Enforcer—this one in a shaven-headed variety with no visible tattoos—was waiting to take me back to the van.

I managed to stay awake, despite the apparently standard lack of conversation from the Enforcer—Sarah was the only one of them who'd seemed chatty—to make it back to the Manor. The dingy bar had emptied out, but Tarva was still there when I all but ran into the warmth of the building.

"You made it back intact, I see," the nymph told me with a smile that would have broken the heart of a mortal man. She handed me a key. "Eric wasn't sure how long you'd be at the Tower, so we booked you a room in the motel across the parking lot. He must like you," she added, cocking her head at me flirtatiously.

"Why?"

"He and Oberis agreed to extend your succor to seven days," she explained. "We don't usually stick to the three days of tradition, so that's not a lot more than normal, but we usually stick to five or six." She shrugged. "Your room is booked for all seven, and you have a tab here and at the barbecue place on the other side of the strip mall that Oberis will cover."

She was right. That *was* generous, which made me suspicious. I didn't think I'd made an overly good first impression, but apparently, I hadn't shoved my foot in my mouth too badly.

For a moment, I was content. Seven days, plus the cash I had on me, should get me through to my first paycheck if Sarah came through with the courier position. Then it all came crashing down with one horrific thought.

To get to the interview, hell, to even get to the motel room, I was going to have to go back outside into that cold.

———

THE MOTEL ROOM turned out to be worth the trip across the parking lot. It was nothing pretty to look at, but the heat worked, the bathroom was clean and the bed was soft. Three out of three on that list is two out of three better than a lot of places I'd stayed over the last few years.

I was woken in the morning by the ringing of the smartphone to discover that I'd barely managed to get my winter coat and gloves off before passing out on the bed. I groggily crawled across the room to grab the phone.

"Kilkenny," I croaked.

"Jason Kilkenny?" the voice on the other end asked.

"Yeah, that's me," I confirmed, rubbing sleep from my eyes with my free hand.

"Jason, it's Bill Trakshinsky from Direct Couriers," the man introduced himself. "A friend of mine said you're looking for work, and I'm desperate for a driver. Can you come into our office this afternoon for a test drive?"

"Of course!" I quickly agreed, trying to force enthusiasm through my exhaustion. "You'll need to give me bus directions," I added, "I'm new to the city and don't have a vehicle here yet."

"Sure," Bill answered cheerfully, and quickly reeled off a series of bus route numbers and landmarks that I carefully wrote down. "Two o'clock work for you?"

If I followed his directions correctly, it would take me an hour to get to his office. That would let me sleep for four more hours and still have an hour to get ready.

The sleep sounded amazing.

"Sure," I parroted back at him.

———

BILL MUST HAVE BEEN EVEN MORE desperate than the blonde Enforcer Sarah had implied. There were three delivery trucks sitting in their yard when I arrived, but I didn't see any drivers when I entered—just a very harried-looking redheaded receptionist. She flashed me a "one minute" finger signal when I entered the spartan office, dealing with a customer on the phone who was clearly complaining about a late package.

"Yes, sir, we'll do our best, sir," she concluded, waited a moment more, and then clicked the phone back onto its stand.

"I'm Trysta; can I help you?" she asked with a summery smile, a welcome spark of warmth in the chilly day.

"I'm Jason; I have an interview with Mr. Trakshinsky?" I told her.

"Of course!" Her smile flashed again, and I couldn't resist smiling back. "He's on a conference call right now, but if you can wait a minute, he'll be right with you. While you're waiting," she continued, apparently without breathing, "I need to run your driver's abstract. Can I borrow your license?"

Hesitantly, I passed her the license I'd been given last night. I presumed Sarah wouldn't have sent me somewhere where their IDs would get me in trouble, but I wasn't sure.

Trysta hummed a bouncy tune as she worked, apparently without much difficulty, to pull up a fictitious record of my driving history.

"There you are!" she announced brightly. "Looks like a clean record; that's good." She printed off a sheet of paper and handed it to me. "Take that in with you." She checked her switchboard board. "Bill is free; head right on in."

She gestured to one of four plain white doors leading off from the reception area. I followed her instructions and went in to meet Bill.

He turned out to be a crusty old fellow dressed in jeans and a faded blue dress shirt. I felt like he looked right through me as he looked me up and down, and I regretted the fact that clean jeans and a nice sweater were the best clothes I had.

"Hmph," he grunted at the sight of me, and took the driver's abstract. He glanced at the sheet of paper and tossed it on his desk. "Come on," he barked, walking past me.

"Where?" I asked.

"I don't care if you talk pretty, do I?" he asked. "I care if you drive safe. So, come on."

I followed him out to the delivery trucks, where he got in the passenger seat and gestured me into the driver's seat. With a deep breath, I obeyed.

———

BILL'S IDEA OF A "TEST DRIVE" turned out to be "I'll show you how the GPS works, give you an obscure address, and let you go find it." The GPS was easily five years newer than the truck it was mounted on, a quiet and accurate little piece of technology.

I found his first address quickly, so he gave me another one. I found that one. I handled one street covered in ice, at least three idiots I could *swear* were trying to kill us, and navigated to three addresses, each easily six or seven miles apart, before returning to the dispatch yard.

Bill pointed me to the stall we'd pulled out of when we left, and I neatly parked the van. I was a little impressed with myself until the old trucker grunted, "I've seen better."

"Oh," I responded, crestfallen.

"Check with Trysta for your details and paycheck setup," he continued.

"I got the job?" I asked, caught off guard by the sudden swing in tone.

"Yup," he answered gruffly. "Now go see Trysta."

The redhead happily rifled through my various identification.

"Is this your current address?" she asked, glancing over the driver's license and typing at blurring speed as she read everything.

"No, I don't have a permanent address here yet; I just moved into town," I explained.

"Not a problem; just let us know where you settle in when you have an address, if you could."

"Of course," I promised. She continued on her way down the form and then ran two copies off on her printer.

"Now, you get paid a week in arrears," she explained quickly.

"Start tomorrow, you'll get paid for half of this week next Friday. Works?"

"Works," I agreed, quickly skimming the HR boilerplate and signing both copies of the form. "When do I start?"

"Six AM tomorrow." The girl—she was a year or so younger than me, I thought—sounded disgustingly cheerful at the thought. "We all start then," she added.

I groaned but nodded acquiescence.

3

SIX AM THE NEXT MORNING, I reported to work and was promptly tossed into a van with Jake, the oldest driver at Direct Courier, to learn the ropes. He was on the edge of elderly, only a few years from retirement, with a thick accent and from somewhere in Eastern Canada I didn't catch the name of.

The two days I spent with Jake passed in an exhausting blur, but on the Friday of my first week in this frigid city, he pronounced me ready to go out on my own at noon. He helped me load up the packages Trysta gave us and sent me off on my merry way.

I delivered everything on time, got the necessary signatures, and returned to the office to Bill presenting me with a beer and a clap on the shoulder—I was now officially part of the team.

The rest of the tiny office gathered around and everyone hoisted a "the week is over" beer—Trysta, Bill, myself, Jake and the other two drivers. It wasn't much of a courier company, all told. But they'd offered me a job and a place, and I wasn't going to turn that down.

My weekend blazed past in a blur of cheap beer at the Manor and shitty motel TV—it wasn't like I had much else to do! My first week in the city had passed far better than I was expecting. I spoke to the motel manager and parted with over a third of my remaining cash to pay my room up to the end of the week and my paycheck.

Looking over the paltry remaining funds in my wallet, I budgeted out food for the four days between my succor expiring and my first paycheck. It just, barely, covered me going out and buying a knee-length heavy gray winter jacket.

With that, and the new job, I managed to settle into a routine by Tuesday—get up at oh-Powers-o'clock, get out of the motel and down to work by bus, scrape in the door for six, and be out by six fifteen in the van. The job was pretty simple, pretty easy to be good at. Trysta greeted me with bright smiles each time I came back, and when Friday rolled around, there was Bill with the beer again, and this time, paychecks all around.

"Hey, Jason," my new boss interrupted me as I was leaving. "You have a place yet?"

"I'm still living at the motel," I admitted. "Need to save up for rent."

"There's a place near here," Bill told me. "My sister owns it, wants a handy man to rent. Can front you the deposit and you pay me back over the next coupla months. Sound decent?"

I blinked at him. Bill hadn't been any less gruff or terse with me since he hired me. I hadn't expected this. I guess the generosity fit with the man; it was just in contrast to his usual demeanor.

"Can I take a look at the place first?"

"Sure. Can take you now," he offered.

"Okay."

We trooped out to Bill's aged red Chevy pickup truck and drove over to the apartment. It was within walking distance of the dispatch, really—not that I'd want to do that in the winter; the weather remained utterly frigid. It was a short little four-story brick building, and Bill's sister—a stocky older woman with graying brown hair—was waiting for us.

"So, this's Jason?" she asked, and Bill responded with an affirmative grunt. She offered her hand. "I'm Rhonda; come take a look at the place."

"You can make it home yourself?" Bill asked. I nodded. One of my smartphone's many features was an ability to plot bus routes. "All right, places to be," he said shortly, and returned to his truck as Rhonda led me down the stairs into the basement of the apartment building.

The tour of the apartment didn't take very long. It was basically one big public room with a kitchen off of it and a bedroom tucked away out of sight. Walled in plain white drywall, floored in worn-but-solid dark blue carpet.

Rhonda quoted me a rent figure that was a bit under half of what I expected to be bringing home from Direct. Certainly more than I currently had to pay.

"My brother and I talked, and he's agreed to front me your deposit and half your first month's rent, and take it off your pay for the next few months," she told me, "to give you a chance to get settled right away."

"When do you need to know?" I asked, finally, unsure if I was willing to accept *that* degree of charity from my boss.

"Let Bill know on Monday and we can sort things out," she told me. "I can throw in a mattress too, but that's about all I can do for furniture, sorry."

"I'll have to think about it," I answered awkwardly. "I'm not sure how comfortable I am taking charity."

"Hardly charity, boy," Rhonda laughed at me. "It's Bill's way of making sure you keep working for him!"

I shared the laugh, but I was still feeling awkward at the thought as she walked me back up to the apartment building entrance. Walking outside, I stopped in sudden shock.

In the half hour or so we'd been inside, the temperature had skyrocketed. It was still not warm, but it was getting dark, and I was now quite comfortable inside my heavy winter jacket.

"Ah, the chinook finally came in," Rhonda observed.

"Chinook?" I asked.

"Warm winds over the mountains—give us a boost of warmth in the winter. Are you okay to get home?" she asked.

"This is the warmest it's been since I got here," I told her. "Hell, I can *walk* home in this. Thank you kindly for the offer, ma'am; I will think on it and let Bill know."

"Sounds good," she agreed. "Enjoy your weekend, Jason."

She walked over to her new silver sedan and I settled my jacket carefully on my shoulders and queried my phone for a walking route back to the motel. It looked like about forty-five minutes' walk, which wasn't too bad in the actually non-frigid night.

The walk took me north to one of the major roadways through the city, with several bars along the stretch I had to walk. I'd just passed one of these when I heard the sound of a scuffle on the other side of a fence along the road. For a long moment, I paused, not wanting to get involved.

Then I heard a girl scream, then stop in mid-sound. The next thing I knew, I'd run halfway up the fence, grabbed the top and was vaulting over to land in the deserted alley on the other side.

I headed toward the scream, jumping two backyard fences and coming into a deserted residential side street. A petite girl, hair dark in the shadows, backed away from her three attackers, one hand pressed against her throat.

The three attackers were my size and closing in on her. They moved with an odd grace—very similar to the inhuman grace of the fae, but not quite there.

One of them grabbed the girl's arm and yanked her to him. "Why struggle, baby—it'll hurt less if you don't—you may even enjoy it."

I had a quick sensation of cold air as I charged, and then I was next to the thug and pulled his arm off the girl.

"I don't think so, motherfucker," I told him, and introduced his face to my fist. The thug stumbled backward several feet, his nose broken and spewing blood.

"You'll pay for that, food," he snarled, and long white fangs flashed in the streetlights. Vampires. Nobody told me this city had a vampire problem.

I wasn't quite sure where the girl had got to, but I kept myself between the three vampires—and I quickly confirmed all three were vampires, now that I knew what to look for. This was going to suck.

One of the non-bleeding vampires came for me from the left. He was an amateur, telegraphing a wild haymaker that I managed to easily deflect, only to stumble back in pain as his unexpected snap kick caught me in the stomach. Okay, so he wasn't the only amateur in this brawl.

They had speed on me, but I was stronger, so I grabbed the feeder before he got too far away and dragged him in close. He tried to bite me, the bastard, so I headbutted him. Hard. His eyes started to glaze, so I did it again. He stumbled backward, and I kicked him in the nuts.

Each of them was faster than me and almost as strong. I didn't have time to play fair. As it turned out, the other two had been closing while I grappled the other one, and I paid for the first vampire's kick to the nuts with a sledgehammer blow to the side of the head.

I half stumbled, half dodged sideways and avoided the kick from the third vampire, shaking my head to clear my vision as they closed in. I faked a jab at the feeder on the left and then bodily charged the one in the middle, the one I'd junked a moment before. With him still dazed, I managed to drive him back a step or two and toss him to the ground, but then a deathly cold hand grabbed the collar of my jacket and yanked me back from him.

Panic flared, and familiar warmth flowed through me. Hoping that I could convince the girl to stay quiet afterward, I let the feeder drag me back until I could see him. Then I grabbed his arms with both hands and called faerie flame.

The feeder screamed as green fire seared up his arms, burning away his clothes and roasting his already-dead flesh with a sickening stench of burning pork. He scrambled back from me and snarled again.

A moment of silence followed, broken by the characteristic *thunk* of a shotgun being pumped, and I turned to face the vampire I'd punched in the face to start the brawl. His face had healed, and he held a sawed-off pump shotgun pointed at me.

"Fucking faerie," he spat. "End of the line."

"Suck it, motherfucker," I answered with an obscene gesture, and he lifted the gun to aim at my head.

Then a hundred and something pounds of screaming wildcat slammed into the side of his head and the shotgun went flying. The vampire screamed as claws tore his skin, the wildcat shapeshifter returning the favor of my rescue attempt.

One feeder out of the fight, but that left two more, and the one I'd burned had regenerated his arms and found a knife somewhere. Even from a few feet away, the knife felt wrong—cold-forged iron.

I was changeling, not a true fae. That didn't make my kind's ancient bane much less effective on me. It just made its touch crippling, not instant death.

While I was busy staring horrified at the knife, however, the third vampire was sneaking up behind me and slammed both his fists into the small of my back, his foot into the back of my right knee, and his knee into the back of my head as I crumpled.

I hit my knees, my head spinning as I saw the vampire with the knife approach me, a sick grin on his face. From the corner of my eye, I saw the girl, back in human form and in torn clothes, get pitched away from the feeder she'd jumped. A silver blade glittering in her shoulder explained why she'd shifted back.

The vampire she'd fought rose to his feet, an aura of darkness gathering around him as he called on the blood powers of his kind to end the fight I'd foolishly joined.

Then he vanished, replaced by the front of a black Hummer. There was a blur of motion, and the vampire with the cold iron knife was suddenly in pieces, replaced by one *pissed the fuck off* grizzly bear.

The third vampire ran, and the bear growled. Even through my spinning head, I caught the note of command, and I saw a tall fair-haired man *shift* into a wolf and leap off after the feeder. If feeders deserved pity, I'd have pitied it.

The bear was gone, I realized, and the burly black-haired giant from the Wizard's Tower replaced it, kneeling by the shifter girl, gently removing the silver knife. I felt a hand fall on my shoulder, but before whoever it was could say anything, I collapsed, pitching face forward onto the pavement.

4

I woke up to the feel of a warm, wet cloth being used to gently clean my face. For a moment, I had no idea where I was or what had happened, then I jerked upright at the memory of the vampires beating on me.

"Hey, hey, take it easy," a female voice told me, and I found myself face to face with the wielder of the cloth. Bright green eyes looked directly into mine, atop an adorable button nose and a scattering of freckles. "You took quite the beating."

"I heal quickly," I answered slowly, relaxing back slightly and taking in the rest of the petite redheaded woman—enough to recognize the girl I'd leaped to the rescue of in the street. "What happened?"

"I have a panic pager and I hit it when they caught up with me—before I even knew they were feeders, to be honest," she told me. "I wasn't expecting Tarvers himself to answer—or for you to show up."

"And we're all lucky you did, changeling," a deep bass growl interjected, and I looked up to see the door to the small bedroom I'd been placed in filled with the hairy form of the leader of the shifters in Calgary. "Our girl here might have managed to escape if you hadn't shown up, but we would have lost the feeders then. This way, everyone wins."

The bear shapeshifter crossed the room to me and offered his immense hand. "I know your kind don't heal as quick as us shifters, so I brought you back with us so we could treat your wounds. We owe you a debt, stranger. I am Tarvers, Alpha of Clan Tenerim, and I and my clan are in your debt. What's your name?"

"Jason Kilkenny, sir," I answered politely.

He snorted. "Don't call me *sir*, Jason," he ordered. "Now, listen. I had our doctor check you out, and he says you'll be fine by morning but you shouldn't move much till then. So, you're a guest in this house till this morning and a friend of the clan for your actions. If you have need of us, call. Now, rest!"

With that final barked command, the sheer presence of the man faded as he strode from the room, and I looked back to the girl I'd saved.

"What's your name?" I asked. "If I almost got myself killed for someone, I'd at least like to know their name."

She giggled. "I'm Mary," she told me. "Also of Clan Tenerim. I'm the younger of two lynx shifters in a clan of wolves and bears, so they all treat me like their baby sister. And the Alpha overestimates my chances of escaping—I'd have been toast if you hadn't intervened."

Mary inspected me critically, and leaned in to wipe off a last speck of dirt and gravel from my face. She kissed me on the cheek, softly.

"Thank you," she said quietly. "Now, Dr. Clementine said to let you rest, so I'm going to get out of your hair." She smiled. "I took the liberty of programming my number into your phone."

With that implied hint and a brush of her fingers against my cheek, Mary left the room, leaving me in the dark room with some healing bruises and her scent.

———

I BARELY MANAGED to open the room's door in the morning before it was yanked out of my hand and I was urged gently back into the room by a shaven-headed young man with a stethoscope around his neck. He was built quite similarly to Mary, and I presumed some relation.

"You don't move one more step until I check you out," he told me firmly. "I'm Clementine Tenerim, Mary's brother. Now sit down."

Somewhat bemused, both by the energy everyone in the Clan seemed to bring to everything and the care they were showing, I obeyed. Clementine poked and prodded, listened to my heart with the stethoscope and flashed a light in my eyes. Then he apologized.

"Sorry, but most of the folks I work with and on are shifters," he told me. "Even silver wounds, like that stab Mary took, will heal almost immediately once you abrade the silver out. Even with another inhuman, I have to be a bit more careful."

"Thanks for the worry, doc," I told him. "It's appreciated."

He nodded, and gestured for me to follow him out of the room. The front room of what turned out to be some sort of townhouse was occupied by Tarvers and three men who were almost as large.

"Have a seat, Jason," the bear Alpha asked. "We have some questions about last night, though we're waiting on one more."

A car pulled up outside and a door slammed. A lean man I recognized as the wolf shifter from last night stepped up to the door, his hand going inside his open jacket. He relaxed at the sight of the man on the other side of the door, and opened it to reveal Oberis.

I bowed my head to the Lord of the fae Courts. I hadn't seen him since my first night in Calgary, and I was quite content to avoid his attention if possible.

"Per our Covenant with the Wizard, I can only ask you questions with a leader of your Court present," Tarvers rumbled, gesturing Oberis to a chair by mine. "Welcome to the Den of Clan Tenerim, Lord Oberis."

"I am grateful for the invite and the welcome, Alpha Tarvers," Oberis replied with the instinctive grace and charm of a fae noble. "Kilkenny, are you all right?" he asked me directly as he sat.

"I'm fine; these gentlemen took good care of me," I answered quickly. I didn't want to get tied up in the politics of inhuman factions. Avoiding them was why I was *in* Calgary.

"He protected one of our own, at risk to himself and with no call for reward," Tarvers rumbled. "You should be well pleased with your man, Lord Oberis."

"So it seems," the fae Noble replied, impenetrable even to me. I hoped that meant he agreed. I didn't want to be in trouble with Oberis right now.

"I need to ask you about the vampires, Jason," Tarvers told me. "Did anything about them stand out? Any tattoos or symbols?"

"Um." My response was hardly the most eloquent of answers, but I had to think. "Didn't you have a better look than I?"

"There wasn't enough left of the bodies to really examine," the big shapeshifter answered, his voice somewhat self-satisfied.

"I didn't see any symbols," I answered, thinking carefully. "But I did notice... I burned one of them pretty badly, and he healed it almost instantly. They had to be very well fed. And one was beginning a blood working when you hit him."

"Not a lot of vampires can actually work their blood magic," Oberis interjected grimly. "Most feeders use up most of their power just staying alive and enhancing their bodies."

"So, well-fed, well-taught vampires," Tarvers concluded grimly. "A cabal has entered our city. I guess we have to tell the Wizard."

"I will accompany you and speak for my changeling's words," Oberis agreed. Hopefully, his doing so got me off the hook of seeing the Wizard again!

"Now, Lord Oberis, I ask you to stand witness," the bear Alpha told my lord. Tarvers stood, looming to his full seven feet in height and removing a length of gold chain from a pocket. He crossed to me and draped the chain around my neck.

"By my word and the witnesses here, I acknowledge a debt owed," he said formally. "Jason Kilkenny is named friend and ally of Clan Tenerim, and is owed a Boon. Call upon us at your need, and we will answer in payment for the life that you saved."

I inclined my head, accepting the debt. "Thank you," I said quietly. Boons were a big deal among inhumans—it was more than your life was worth to refuse a Boon without a good reason. I couldn't have refused the Alpha if I'd wanted to.

With that business concluded, Oberis stood and gestured for me to follow him to his car. I traded a firm handshake with Tarvers, watching my hand vanish in his giant fist, and followed the fae noble out.

I got in the passenger seat of the car, and Oberis handed me an envelope. It crinkled familiarly, and I opened it to be absolutely sure.

"Why?" I asked, eyeballing a sum of cash that was easily two months of my courier salary.

"I make a point of rewarding those of my Court who make my life easier," Oberis said dryly as he started the car. "The Clans are the dominant force in this city after the Wizard, and you just wiped out a year or more of slowly growing irritation with us in a single moment of selfless bravery. Tarvers is as deadly serious about the Boon as any of us would be—but this is your reward for your service to the Court, not to the Clan."

I'd learned a long time before not to argue with generous fae—and to count the money very carefully when they'd moved on. I bowed my head in acquiescence. After all, this was money I'd earned, and that meant I didn't need to borrow from my boss to pay for the apartment.

Apparently, stupid chivalry was rewarded well in this city. If you survived the vampires, that was.

5

I TALKED to Bill after work the following Monday. He seemed somewhat disconcerted by my suddenly having money, which I explained to him as "a relative passed on and left me a little money, not much but more than I was expecting."

He and Rhonda still managed to take me by surprise by the speed with which they handled the transaction. He had me back at the apartment complex that night, signing the lease and trading Rhonda my damage deposit and first month's rent for the keys to the basement apartment.

The next step was picking up my—paltry few—belongings from the motel and checking out. By the end of the night, I was moved into my new place. And very aware I needed to go shopping, as all I had was the single mattress and base Rhonda had provided for free.

The next evening was spent opening a bank account—my first in several years—using my Wizard-provided fake identifications. It turned out I had a credit history. Wizards scared me.

Once I had the bank account and had deposited my funds into it, I went furniture-shopping. I didn't need much, but the apartment still looked much more like home with a table, a desk and a proper bedframe in it. A computer was bought on Monday, and a quick stop into Eric's acquired a modem that would link me to both the Internet and Fae-Net—the closed distributed network the fae used to keep in touch.

It was less than five minutes after I'd set up my connection to Fae-Net that I heard movement in my apartment. I turned to find myself facing a statuesque woman with raven-black hair that hung to her waist over a neat blue business suit who should not have been there.

I didn't have a chance to ask what she was doing before she grabbed my hands and *stepped*.

My apartment was replaced with an inky black nothingness, lit by a slight glow coming off my kidnapper's skin.

"Sorry," she said quickly, her voice hitting buttons in the back of my head as I blinked at her. "My presence in Calgary must be kept secret."

"Um," I gaped. The woman was familiar, and heart-stoppingly beautiful enough to distract me from the void around us. "Where are we?" Regaining some of my composure, I demanded, "And who are you?"

"We are Between," she said simply. "The space between worlds. You survive here by my power, or the void would take all life and warmth and breath from you, leaving you a lifeless corpse.

"As for who I am, I am disappointed," she told me sternly, and all my breath rushed from me in one horrifying instant of recognition. "I am Mabona. Do you not recognize your Queen?"

Mabona.

Mabona. Queen of the fae.

Mabona, Mistress of Seelie and Unseelie alike. Lady of the High Court and all others. Queen in Ireland before men ever walked there. Mother and Queen to *all* of my kind.

I don't remember consciously sinking to my knees, but I knelt before her. The Queen of the fae was like unto the Wizards—a true Power made flesh in the world.

"I am sorry, my Queen," I answered her. "I was surprised, and I did not expect to ever lay eyes upon you in person." The Queen was *never* seen by most fae—even among the noble fae like Oberis, they usually only saw her once, if at all. She acted through her Vassals—entire bloodlines of fae, almost always noble, bound to her service.

"I have need of your service," she told me, and I cringed. I was hoping it wouldn't be that. I could refuse her; it just wasn't *wise*. "I need eyes and hands in this city, but the Covenants between the Powers forbid me to walk in a Wizard's marked domain."

"Isn't Lord Oberis your..." She didn't let me finish the sentence.

"Oberis serves his Court," she snapped. "He serves the Court that answers to him, and then he serves the Seelie Lords and Ladies, and only then, at a distant third, does he serve me. I have need of a Vassal in this matter."

There was no doubt in my mind on one thing—Queen of all fae or no, I was *not* signing on for *that*. Agreeing to Vassalhood bound me and all my descendants to her service.

"Lady, with all respect," I said carefully, "there are many others in this city worthier of such an honor."

"Who said anything about honor?" she answered with a cold smile, and my heart stopped at the quiet power in her voice. "By your father's blood, Jason Kilkenny, *you are mine*."

That voice ran along my nervous system like fire, yanking me to my feet to face her as she willed. Her words rang in my very veins and I *knew*, in my bones and my blood, that she spoke only truth.

Shit. Somehow, some way, *I was a Vassal of the Queen*. Shit.

"Lady," I said slowly, trying to let the fire of her words fade out of my body. "I did not know. I would not have thought one of my weak blood would be such." I hid behind the formality of the words. It wouldn't do to show gut-wrenching fear in front of the Queen. Not that I thought I fooled her.

"You have not yet come to your full birthright," she told me, "but you will serve me regardless. You have encountered the vampires in this city."

I nodded, not trusting my voice at the moment.

"They are part of a greater plan—a full cabal has moved here, and done so without the Wizard knowing." The Queen looked at me, and I tried and failed to avoid her gaze. She locked eyes with me and held me in her burning, inhuman, gaze. "There is a plot afoot to destroy the

Magus MacDonald. You will find this plot. You will locate its perpetrators. And you will, by your hand, or Oberis's, or MacDonald's, whatever is necessary, see them destroyed."

I swallowed. The void around me pressed in, cold and unforgiving and warning of the fate of those who defied the Queen.

"I am yours to command," I said slowly, unwillingly accepting the burden she laid upon me. "If I may ask one question?"

"You may, but many answers are worth more than you can pay," she told me bluntly.

"If my father was your Vassal, who *was* he?"

"He was mine, as are you," she replied. "More it is not yet time for you to know. Go."

She *pushed*, and I fell out of the Between, back into my apartment. I breathed quickly, trying not to hyperventilate.

The Queen of all fae had Marked me as her Vassal, one of the ancient bloodlines that served her. It made no sense. Those bloodlines were noble fae, or near enough for power. I was...nothing. I'd presumed my father was minor fae of some kind—a will-of-the-wisp or something similar.

And as her Vassal, I had a mission to prevent the murder of a Wizard—a demigod made flesh, a Power that walked the world.

I needed a drink.

6

I WENT TO THE MANOR, Eric's. It's a tradition of our kind that the Keeper is like the theoretical old Catholic priest—completely neutral and bound not to tell others what you told him. In a city with two Courts, it was the Keeper who was the intermediary. In Calgary, I was just hoping that I could talk to him without the story spreading.

I was shivering with the cold when I came in—new warm coat and gloves or not, the "chinook" had fled again and it was way too cold in this city.

"Hi, Tarva, can you get me a beer and let Eric know I need to talk to him?" I told the nymph waitress with a smile as I slid onto a barstool. She nodded and slipped away into the back.

It was a Wednesday night, and the bar was half-full. Not all of the patrons had the feel of fae or other inhumans, so I had to be careful what I said in public. Shortly after Tarva vanished into the back, I saw the door swing open and Eric glanced out, making the same assessment as me. He wasn't as noticeable as some inhumans, but he was still better off not wandering around in full view of the mortal public.

When he looked at me, though, his eyes widened at something, and he immediately gestured for me to come back into the kitchen. I grabbed my beer, got up and followed him.

"Come quickly," Eric ordered, moving faster than I thought the little man had any right to. He led me to a door off the side of the kitchen, and then down a spiral staircase into the storeroom under the kitchen. We dodged around boxes and bottles to another door, which led into a well-lit, gorgeously furnished basement apartment.

"Have a seat and drink your beer," he told me, gesturing to an overstuffed dark purple couch. It looked like the apartment was walled and floored in bare concrete, but it was hard to tell. Voluminous drapes covered the walls, and thick rugs had been laid in an attractive interlocking pattern. A tiny kitchen was tucked against one wall, and a solid oak door presumably led to Eric's bedroom.

The Keeper returned to the lounge with a snifter of brandy and sat in a chair in matching purple to the couch I was in.

"I told Barry I wouldn't be back up tonight," he told me quietly. "As soon as I saw you, I knew something was up. I think I know what, I've seen this before, but tell me in your own words."

I took a long drink of my beer and marshaled my thoughts. "Long story short, Queen Mabona came to visit me, informed me that I was of one of Her Vassal bloodlines and belonged to Her, and gave me a mission," I told him succinctly.

Eric emptied the brandy snifter in one swallow. He picked up the bottle, refilled his snifter, and offered it to me. I shook my head no.

"I thought I recognized the sign on you," he said quietly. "Mabona. The Queen of all fae."

"How fucked am I, Eric?" I asked bluntly.

"Um...both a lot and just a little?" he answered. "You are Marked as Her Vassal. Any Keeper in any Manor in the world can see that, and we owe our fealty to the Queen as well."

"Wait, the Keepers owe fealty to the Queen?" I interjected. I always thought the Keepers didn't owe loyalty to anyone except the fae race.

"And through Her to all fae," he answered. "Like you now. We Keepers are charged to aid Her Vassals in any way we can; we share the joint mission of preserving the fae race rather than any specific Court or faction."

"That doesn't answer how fucked I am," I observed.

"You are pretty fucked, so far as getting out of it goes," Eric said bluntly. "She's in your blood, in your powers. She has Marked you as Her own, and you are Hers. However, it's not all bad.

"You now serve only Her and the High Court, for example," he continued. "You stand outside the normal systems of Court and Fealty. While I wouldn't recommend testing the theory, you technically don't answer to Oberis anymore. You are protected, as Her Marked Vassal, from interference by the other Powers. She rewards and protects those who serve Her well."

"And is utterly merciless to those who betray Her," I suggested aloud.

"Yes, but Her Vassals don't really have that *option*," Eric reminded me. "When I said She was in your blood, it wasn't a metaphor. Even if you tried to avoid completing whatever task She gave you, you'd find yourself doing it as you went about your business, only realizing what you'd done afterwards. It's a dangerous way to go, though; I disrecommend it."

I could see many ways that trying to investigate a plot against the Wizard without realizing what I was doing could prove dramatically fatal.

"It just doesn't make sense to me," I told the Keeper. "I always understood that Her Vassal bloodlines were all noble or near-noble fae. But I'm one of the weakest-blooded changelings I know of. Am I misjudging Her bloodlines, or am I a late bloomer or something?"

"I know of late-blooming changelings," Eric said slowly. "One gentleman I knew didn't come into his mother's gifts until he was almost forty. There's only one problem—how long ago did you first manifest?"

"Three years, give or take," I replied.

Eric nodded, taking a slow sip of his brandy. "Every changeling I've ever known of has manifested their powers over a year and a day," he told me. "You have every power you will manifest from your blood."

"I assumed my father was a weak will of the wisp or something," I admitted. "I don't see how he could possibly have been of Mabona's Vassal bloodlines."

"Wait," Eric said, holding up the hand not holding his snifter, and suddenly examining my face with a new energy. "That rings a bell. A Kilkenny and a will o' the wisp... What was your mother's name again?" he asked.

"Melissa," I replied, now very confused as he continued to examine my face.

"Melissa," he repeated slowly, getting up and begin to pace back and forth on the rug, his brandy forgotten in his hand. "Little Melly Kilkenny—redheaded woman, Irish and a historian, right?"

"Yes," I agreed slowly, watching the gnome pace, wondering if he'd seen the same file MacDonald had. "How do you know my mother?"

"I worked with Melly on a dig in the early eighties. We were investigating one of the old tomb sites in Ireland for the High Court," he answered.

The High Court was the joint Seelie-Unseelie court that ran Ireland's fae and, in theory, that all Courts answered to. Made up of nine Powers, the High Court was led by Queen Mabona and rarely, if ever dealt with mortals.

"They hired a mortal historian?"

"No," Eric said quietly, stopping and locking his gaze with mine. "They hired a *changeling* historian—Melly Kilkenny, daughter of Soria, one of the strongest will o' the wisps I ever met. Your mother was a changeling."

"That's impossible," I disagreed. "She would have said *something*."

"I don't know why, Jason," the Keeper told me, "but she fled Ireland under a cloud of political discontent and foreswore all things fae. You have the gifts of a wisp's child through her."

"But a wisp's gifts are all I have," I told him.

"You have not yet come to your full birthright," he answered me, echoing the Queen's words earlier that night. "Every gift and power you have shown so far is from your *mother's* blood, not your father's. We have no idea what gifts you may still command."

"Great," I said quietly. "So, I have the downside of a Vassal bloodline—service to Mabona—and not one drop of the power or strength I should have to complete Her mission."

The Keeper nodded and finished the second glass of brandy.

"What was your mission?" he asked finally. "I am bound to help you in any way I can."

"She said there was a plot to kill the Wizard," I told him. "I am tasked to find it and stop it."

"I take it back," Eric said dryly. "You *are* fucked."

"Thanks."

"I'll keep my ear to the ground," the Keeper promised. "If you find anything, let me know, and I'll see if I can track down more on any leads you find."

"Thanks," I replied, somewhat more sincerely this time. Now that I thought about it, the shifters might know something, and Mary had programmed her number into my phone.

"So, um, Eric," I said slowly, hoping the subject change would work, "what is the policy on fae dating outside the Court here?"

He laughed. "I heard about you and the shifters over the weekend," he told me. "Well done, by the way.

"But yes, that's okay. It's not like we have to worry about half-and-half babies, after all," he continued. "For whatever reason, most of the inhumans are cross-fertile with humans, but none of us are with each other. So, go ahead, call the girl.

"Her Clan may have some idea about the Queen's warning," he added, echoing my own thought.

————

My work the next day was a chaotic blur. One of the other drivers called in sick, so those of us who were left were running around twice as much, moving our own packages and taking care of his. I was over an hour late back to my apartment.

I threw a microwave meal into the appropriate appliance and reflected that after half-living on the streets for a few years, even bachelor living and a six AM to four PM job seemed like a huge step up. That thought and dinner gave me the energy to grind up some coffee and fill a coffee press. The local organic coffee roaster that I'd been introduced to in the Wizard's Tower was growing on me. The one I was drinking was named after some resort or mountain or some such nearby—it had a picture of three mountains on it.

With half a hot cup of coffee in me, I booted up my computer and began to skim the Internet and Fae-Net to see if there were any obvious clues about a threat to the Wizard. Just like humans, we have our message boards and conspiracy sites.

A half hour's trawl came up with nothing definite in the slightest. Not on a threat to the Wizard, anyway, though from the hints I saw, there was *definitely* a vampire cabal in town, which worried me.

Nobody liked feeders. Vampires weren't the only group of them—wendigo, banshees, and a few others fell into the category—but they all ate people. Blood or flesh or souls, they devoured people one way or another and left corpses in their tracks.

I didn't like that they killed people—by and large, I *liked* humans. I also understood that most inhuman authorities *hated* risks of exposure. All of us, including the humans, were happier with the current deal. I had the suspicion that it was only collusion with mortal authorities who agreed with us that allowed us to keep the secret.

But there were enough worried comments, enough possible sightings combined with my own encounter to be very sure that the Queen was entirely correct. A cabal had moved into Calgary. Seeing as how the Wizard had known I was there, and I was a nobody, that must have taken a lot of skill.

There was a threat. I could already see that MacDonald was the key to the stability of this city and his death would cause chaos in the inhuman world. By the time the dust settled, a cabal could be fully settled in, entrenched enough to force its inclusion in the local Covenants. It had happened before.

Feeling a little guilty for planning on using her as an information source as much as anything, I pulled up Mary Tenerim's phone number in my phone and told the phone to call her. It rang three times, and then her voice came on the line.

"Mary speaking," she answered briskly.

"Hi, Mary, it's Jason Kilkenny calling," I said. "You told me to call you."

"So I did," she replied, her voice brightening. "Thank you again for the rescue."

"It was nothing," I told her uncomfortably. "I was there; I couldn't walk by."

"I don't know if it was nothing," she said with a laugh. "You probably saved my life. I'd like to make it up to you if I can."

"What did you have in mind?" I asked carefully.

"How about I buy you a drink and we talk about that?" she offered. "I know an *adorable* Irish pub downtown that has nothing to do with *anybody*."

She didn't leave much doubt as to what she meant by *anybody*. A pub with no connection to any inhuman sounded like a perfectly safe place to meet a pretty girl for a drink.

"That sounds great; when?"

"I can be there in about half an hour," she said eagerly.

I looked at my computer. I might find more online, but I could find that as easily tomorrow. Besides, well, it had been a *long* time since my last date of any kind.

"Works for me," I agreed. "So, how do I get to this place?"

I told her roughly where I was and she gave me quick transit directions.

"I'll see you in half an hour," I promised. Hanging up, I then promptly started panicking over what to wear. I still didn't have a lot of clothes, but with a bit of effort I found a sweater that I'd actually cleaned and a clean-looking pair of jeans.

Throwing my heavy winter coat over that, I ventured out into the bitterly frigid night to catch a bus.

7

THE PUB TURNED out to be completely subterranean, in the basement under a photo shop with only a doorway and a sign on the main street level. With no windows, it was lit only by a series of hanging globe lights that cast a stark pattern of light and shadow over wood paneling and furniture that was probably older than I was.

Some of the tables had been cleared away to make a stage, and a very Irish-looking lass was crooning into a microphone in Gaelic while playing a guitar softly. It was softer background music than I was expecting of a pub on a Thursday night, and most of the bar patrons had clustered around her stage, enjoying the music.

Mary had grabbed a table in a back corner. She was sitting on the edge of it, watching for me, as the back end of the table was almost invisible in shadow from the stairs. She saw me and waved me over.

"Hi, Jason," she said cheerily. "Grab a seat, take a look at the menu and let me know what you want to grab to drink. I already ordered us some nachos."

Her cheerfulness was infectious, and I found myself returning her brilliant smile as I slid in across from her. I glanced at the beer menu for, oh, five seconds, and then ordered the same locally brewed traditional ale I'd ordered at every bar in Calgary since Tarva had served it to me my first night.

"Sorry for needing directions," I said, flailing about for something to say. "I'm pretty new to the city."

"Calgary can be confusing if you don't know the setup," she nodded. "When did you get here?"

I actually had to think about it for a moment. "Three weeks, give or take a few days," I told her. "Came in on the Greyhound."

"That's awesome," she said, and I returned her smile. "Where did you come from?"

"A lot of places, really," I said slowly, glancing around to make sure none of the other patrons were close enough to overhear. "Georgia, originally, but I wasn't raised as fae. It was a shock to discover I was a changeling, and I did a lot of bouncing around before deciding to come up here."

"Damn." She was quiet for a moment, sipping her beer. "I always knew that I was a shifter—I was raised in Clan Tenerim."

I found myself somewhat envious of Mary in that moment—being raised not merely knowing you were supernatural but among others who knew and understood just what that meant sounded like a dream to me.

"Clementine's and my mother married into the clan, though," Mary continued. "We're Métis and Tenerim on Dad's side, but an Irish shifter clan on Mom's. No one was quite sure what *kind* of shifter Clementine and I would turn into." She sighed. "Dad was a lynx shifter, which Clementine and I got. Sadly, I think a lot of people were hoping we'd inherit Mom's shift—she was an Irish dire wolf, and *nobody* got on her bad side!"

I had seen pictures once of the old, semi-magical dire wolves. They only lived on in the shifters who could take their form these days—but only bear shapeshifters could challenge them for size or sheer physical strength.

"I can see why she'd be...well respected," I agreed. "Is she still with you?"

"No." Mary was back to being quiet, and I mentally kicked myself. "She died in the fight with the last cabal that came to Calgary. We bore the brunt of that fight until MacDonald intervened—it's why no one likes to think of a new feeder invasion."

Another couple was shown to the table next to us, and we swiftly moved on to other topics. "So, you're Calgary-born, then?" I asked.

"Yeah, that side of the family was here long before there was a city. I was raised and went to school here."

"University?" I asked.

"I have a two-year accounting diploma," she answered with a laugh, cheering up slightly from my ham-handed reminder of her mother. "I keep the books for Tarvers. My brother, of course, is a doctor, which gets him a lot of respect from the...family. What about you?"

By *family*, of course, she meant the Clan. It made sense. Someone with the physical prowess and dexterity of an inhuman and full medical training would be an amazing doctor and highly valued, even by a group whose members regenerated *almost* any wound.

"I got about three quarters of a mechanical engineering degree, back before things changed." I couldn't say more than that with the couple sitting next to us. I didn't need to, either; she nodded understanding.

We kept the conversation to small things like that as we finished our beers and nachos. Eventually, convinced that the continually drunker and louder couple next to us weren't planning on leaving, Mary paid the bill and we wandered out into the night.

It had got colder. I kept thinking the city couldn't *get* any colder, and then it would prove me wrong.

"We're on the same bus," Mary told me as we left the pub. "We can grab it just over here."

I followed my redheaded native guide through the frozen downtown, watching for patches of ice.

"Did Tarvers learn any more about the cabal?" I asked her, finally getting to my second, not nearly as fun, reason for meeting up with her.

"Nothing I'm aware of," she admitted, shivering a bit as she checked the time for the next bus on her phone. "Damn, the next bus isn't for twenty minutes."

"I've heard some hints they may be in something...bigger," I explained as I moved closer to her, trying to share some body heat. She unhesitatingly leaned against me. There were enough layers involved to make it horrendously unintimate, but the gesture still set my heart racing.

"Why so curious?" she asked.

"My Court asked me to investigate, since I'm so junior no one will notice me asking questions," I answered semi-honestly, sliding an arm around her. She snuggled in as we leaned against the bus shelter and each other.

"I'm in much the same place," Mary told me. "I'll keep my ears open if it means I get a second date," she added with a wink.

Even through the utterly frigid night air, I felt my cheeks flush. "I think that's a deal," I told her. "Though you would probably have gotten the date without it," I admitted, with what I suspected was an even deeper blush.

"I'm feeling around as best as I can, and I'm new enough people will write awkward questions off to that," I explained quietly. "That wasn't why I called you, but it is high in my mind—I'm *way* too junior to want to fail the Court."

"I'll ask some folks quietly," she said. "But I can't be sure of much."

"That's more than I hoped for; thank you."

She snuggled in against me and turned her face up toward mine. I started to involuntarily lean towards her...

And then the bus screeched to a halt next to us, plowing slushy wet snow all over our feet.

8

I HAD BARELY MADE it into the dispatch office the next morning when Trysta waved me over to her desk.

"Jake's wife just called in," she told me quickly, her voice strained. "He slipped on some ice and fell leaving the house this morning—the paramedics have rushed him to hospital. He's definitely broken a leg and they think he may have smashed a hip."

"Shit." Jake was the oldest of the drivers, and he'd done his best to help mentor me even after he'd finished training me.

"Yeah, Bill is on his way to the hospital right now, and that takes our two bonded drivers off the roster for today," she told me. "Bluntly, you're the only driver I've got left without a possession charge on their record. That, of course, doesn't matter for much of anything—except the airport delivery. Fill out this form," Trysta ordered, passing me a sheet of paper.

"What's this for?" I asked cautiously.

"Bonding, basically insurance that covers us if you break airport security or something dumb," she explained. "They won't let courier drivers in who aren't bonded. I'm getting it rushed through."

Nodding in acceptance, I quickly finished the form and handed it back to her.

"What do I do?"

"For now, I've got a light load for you to run out, and by the time you're back, everything should be good to go for you to head up to the airport," she said, handing me the standard signing form for a load of packages. I signed for it and went out back to grab a pallet jack.

The GPS led me efficiently around my route, and I had just delivered my last package when my smartphone went off, advising me I had a text.

It ordered me to meet the sender—an "Enforcer Michael"—at a given Starbucks location, and was closed with his name and a symbol I didn't think most cellphones could produce—the stylized K of the Magus Kenneth MacDonald.

I checked in the GPS. The Starbucks was right on the way back to the office. Somehow, I wasn't surprised. They'd made it very clear on my first night that anyone using that sigil was to be obeyed and had access to at least some of the abilities of the Wizard himself.

I sighed and went to the Starbucks. A fair-haired and tanned man in a black business suit, looking like he'd been cast in the same molding machine as every other Enforcer of MacDonald's I'd met, stood by the front door. He spotted me and offered his hand.

"What's going on, Michael?" I asked the man, taking his hand. It was better to be polite with these guys. While what I'd been told led me to expect that I could probably take the tattooed human apart with ease, he was backed by a Wizard.

"Let me buy you a coffee," he said instead of answering the question. "I know you can't spare much time, but it's the least I can do."

"Fine," I responded. "Venti white chocolate mocha, whipped cream." That monstrosity of sugar and caffeine wasn't even something *I* drank, but I'd heard Trysta order it for herself, and it sounded like she was going to need it today.

While we were waiting for our coffees, the Enforcer turned to look at me and carefully flashed a ring he wore on his left index finger—the same stylized K as in the text message.

"The Wizard has need of your services," he told me.

"I presumed as much," I said dryly. "What do you want?"

"Your employer has rushed a bonding for you and advised airport security you will be making a courier delivery to the airport today." Michael picked up his plain black coffee and sipped carefully.

"I have two packages that will go in with your shipment," he continued. "One you will deliver to a man in the loading dock; the other you will place with the rest of your packages for shipment out." He raised a hand to block me arguing. "There will be no cost or risk to your employer; we just want to avoid this package showing up on any official manifests."

"Why all the secrecy?" I asked, exaggerating my slow drawl to buy myself time to think.

"That's not really your business, Mr. Kilkenny," the Enforcer replied. "The Magus MacDonald requires this of you. Consider it partial payment for your identity papers and other assistance you have been provided."

I picked up my mocha to cover my concern, and Michael quietly rapped that ring on the counter. I didn't really have a lot of choice. The Wizard could end me with a thought, and refusing his people's requests was likely a quick way to get him angry at me.

"All right, where are the packages?" I asked in agreement.

Michael gestured for me to follow him and led me to a silver sedan. He pulled two packages, looking identical to Direct Courier's standard boxes, from the backseat and handed them to me.

"This box," he said, hefting the larger of the two—the size offices bought printer paper in, "you will keep with your shipment and send out—it is already labeled for shipment. This one,"—he showed me the smaller box, about the size of a shoebox—"you will leave with the head loader, Bryan Filks."

"Your service is appreciated," he told me, and I answered with a grunt before taking the boxes and leaving him standing there in the freezing winter air. Served him right.

I tucked the boxes under my seat and headed back to the office, where I promptly handed the Starbucks confection to Trysta.

"I figured you could use the extra time to sort out the bonding or whatever it was," I told her with a wink as she gratefully accepted the gift. "How's Jake?"

"Bad," she admitted. "From what Bill said, he's fractured his shin and his thigh bones, and has broken his hip in at least four places. His kneecap is intact, thank Goddess, but he's going into surgery for them to try and fix his hip in about two hours."

"Have Bill pass on my best wishes," I asked her, and she nodded agreement.

"The bonding is done," she said, trying to be all business, though the fact that her eyes were trying to match her red hair caused her to fail at least a little. "You're cleared for the airport shipment. The GPS has the security gate you'll need to go through loaded into it and the offloading dock you'll head to from there."

"Thanks, Trysta," I said. I reached over to squeeze her hand. "I'm sure Jake will be okay, so let's get this handled so he doesn't yell at us all when he gets back."

That got a weak smile from her. I don't think anyone in the company had ever heard Jake so much as raise his voice.

———

I LEFT the shoebox under my seat and loaded the bigger one into the truck before pulling up the two pallets of boxes and loading them in on top of it. I carefully shifted the box so it was about a third of the way back in the truck, and then filled everything else in over it.

The entire drive up to the airport, I worried that something about the two boxes would attract some sort of additional attention, or get me arrested, or something similarly horrific. By the time I pulled up to the security checkpoint, I had mostly managed to put my fears aside— it wasn't like the Wizard's people had any reason to try and screw me over.

I was still aware that being a changeling and sharing much of the fae's lack of ability to sweat was the only thing keeping me from nervously sweaty palms, and I couldn't help glancing at the guards' holstered weapons as two of them walked out to check out the van.

"You're the temp driver for Direct?" the first guard greeted me.

"Yeah," I told me. "Not sure how temp, either—Jake managed to bust himself up pretty good." I gave the guard the quick summary of Jake's injury.

"Poor guy, always seemed nice enough," the guard said with a groan of sympathetic pain. "Can you open up the back of the truck and step out, please?"

"Is this normal?" I asked carefully as I stepped down to the ground.

"Yup," the guard said cheerfully. "We run you and the packages through chem sniffers, looking for bombs. Always got to worry someone will blow up a cargo plane, after all," he added with a wink as he ran a metal detector over me, picking out the metal buttons on my jacket, which he quickly checked, and my belt buckle.

The two guards checked me and the van out quickly and efficiently, probably motivated by the freezing cold outside.

"All right," the guard doing all the talking told me as his companion retreated to the warmth of their security booth. "You know which dock?"

"The GPS does," I said, pointing at the gadget on the dashboard.

"Cool." He waved me forward as the other guard hit a button to open the gate. The GPS promptly resumed spitting out directions, and I followed them into the commercial zone of the airport.

A few minutes later, I pulled up to an offloading dock. A smoking man in coveralls guided me, and when I stepped out, his nametag revealed him to be Bryan Filks.

"Give me a moment; I'll grab a couple of guys to help you," he told me.

"Wait up a sec," I said. "Bryan Filks, right?"

He checked his nametag. "Yup," he grinned at me.

"This is for you." I passed him the box, and the grin faded as fast as it had appeared. "I was told you'd know what it was."

"I do," he said flatly, and something about the way he said it suggested asking more would be unwise. He took the box quickly. "I'll grab you that help," he told me, and vanished into the building.

For several minutes, I shivered in the cold, and then Filks and two more guys in warm-looking coveralls arrived to help me start unloading boxes. We worked quickly, but even the work wasn't enough to keep us warm. When the last box was loaded, we closed the van up, and the airport guys looked me over.

"Come in for a minute and grab a cuppa hot chocolate," Filks told me. "It's fucking freezing out here."

I nodded agreement—there'd be no argument on that point from me in this city! A minute or so later, they dropped a steaming cup of hot chocolate into my half-frozen hands. I wanted to cuddle up to the thing and never let go, but a tiny voice in the back of my mind suggested that these guys might know something about how the vampires got here, even if they weren't inhuman.

Filks vanished as I took my first sip of hot chocolate, and I eyed the other two—Tom and Harry.

"You guys only ever work on the shipping side?" I asked.

"Nah," Harry replied. "Other than Filks, most of us working here are those on workers'-comp 'limited lift weights'—Tom and I are normally heavy cargo receiving, but we both managed to gum up our backs within two weeks of each other. I'll be done here in two weeks, though."

"Lucky shit," Tom grunted. "Docs say mine won't ever be what it was—I'm on light or semi-light for life, it sounds."

"You must see everything come through here," I said. "What's the weirdest thing you ever saw?"

"Dinosaurs," Tom laughed. "A few years back, the zoo updated their animatronics display, so we had these crates with full-size fake dinos in them come through. One of them got 'accidentally' turned on —no fucking clue how; they don't have batteries, after all—but you should have *seen* the reaction around here when a T. rex roar, right out of *Jurassic Park*, came blaring through the main cargo hangar."

"Almost as spooked as when that load of cadavers came through," Harry agreed, with a shiver as he mentioned them.

"Load of cadavers?" I drawled questioningly. That sounded promising.

"About nine months back," Harry said, thinking slowly. "There was a special refrigerated cargo container came in on an express cargo flight from Philadelphia. Some of the paperwork got fucked up, so security checked it out—it was full of corpses. Thirty of them. It was two days before everything got sorted out and some muckety-muck from the med school at the U came over to grab them."

"People were *really* spooked," Tom agreed. "Kelly thought he saw one of the corpses walking around the airport the night before the doc came for them. Like I said, spooked."

"Who was the doc?" I asked, trying to fake passing curiosity and drinking more hot chocolate.

"Sigurdsen? Sanderson?" Harry shrugged. "Something like that."

"Oh, for *really* fun loads, though, you should have seen the day they were shipping in a load of tank parts to send up to the base in Edmonton," Tom said with a grin. "Soldiers *everywhere*."

I quietly drank my hot chocolate, listening to their stories, but no clues beyond a box of cadavers—one of which had walked!—coming into town nine months before.

Maybe I should look into this Dr. Sigurdsen, or whatever, after work.

————

WHEN I MADE it back to the dispatch office, Bill was there with Trysta, wiping sweat off his forehead with a dirty rag.

"Hey, Jason," he greeted me. "How was the airport delivery?"

"Cold," I replied. "Otherwise, no problem."

"Good," he grunted. "It looks like you'll be doing it for a bit. Jake'll be down for about four weeks, the docs say."

"But he's okay?"

"Yeah, the surgery went off without a hitch."

I breathed a sigh of relief. "Four weeks on airport duty, huh?"

"Yeah," Bill confirmed. "I *can* do it, but I prefer to be the backup, not the one and only."

"Understood, boss."

Bill grunted, and wordlessly gestured Trysta and me out of the office—it was closing time. The redheaded receptionist bundled herself up tightly in her winter coat and followed me out.

"What are your plans tonight?" she asked me as we walked to the bus stop.

"I have research to do," I answered with a smile, "and a girl I should be calling back."

"Oh," she said, and went suddenly quiet.

"Yourself?" I asked.

"Nothing much," she said shortly, and the rest of the short trip to the bus stop passed in silence and me wondering just what I'd said wrong.

I worked it out *just* after her bus pulled away. With a sigh of "oh, Powers, I'm dumb" I boarded my own never-quite-warm-enough public transit.

9

It didn't take much time on the Internet to find the phone number for the University of Calgary's med school, and one of the advantages to starting at six in the morning was that most places were still in business hours when you got home.

I decided to bite the bullet and called them.

"Good afternoon, Cumming School of Medicine," a cheery young male voice answered.

"Hi, I'm looking to make an appointment to see a Dr. Sigurdsen," I told him calmly. "It's to do with a shipment he signed for some months back."

"Hold a moment," the young man told me. It wasn't much longer than a literal moment before he was back.

"I'm sorry, we don't have a Dr. Sigurdsen here," he said. "We did have a Dr. Elisse Sigridsen here, but my files show she left the faculty about a year ago. Are you sure this shipment was to do with the medical faculty?"

"There was some mix-up with the paperwork, and the airport asked me to look into it," I lied, hopefully smoothly. "They said it was headed for your faculty—I was advised it was a cargo of donated cadavers."

"Um…" The man on the other end swallowed. "I believe"—he paused again—"that we meet all of our needs for that…resource from donations in the local region. Let me check, but I don't think we've received a shipment in a while." There was silence on the line for a moment, broken by the sound of a keyboard.

"Yeah, that's correct," he finally continued. "We last imported cadavers two years ago."

"There must be some confusion, then," I allowed. "Thank you for your time."

"Yes, of course. What was your name?" the man asked, but I hung up as he finished the question.

An Internet search quickly confirmed what the receptionist had told me. Dr. Elisse Sigridsen was a pathologist, with a specialty in rare human parasite strains. She'd worked for the U of C's Health Sciences Centre for ten years, including many research trips around the world for research.

Some of her paper titles were *very* interesting: *A Pathological Study of Human Mutation. Human Genetic Strains and Supernatural Myth. Rare Variations in Human Physiology.* This was the kind of woman who'd *love* to meet an inhuman—so she could dissect them.

But she hadn't been working for the U of C when she'd signed for that container, and it had never gone to the university, either. So, who had she been working for, and where had it gone?

Boxes of cadavers were suspicious when investigating vampires in the first place, but now this was starting to stink to high heaven.

Curiosity itched, though, so I threw her name into Fae-Net as I grabbed my phone to call Mary. The results came back instantly, and I dropped the phone with Mary's number undialed as the red text flashed up on my screen:

WARNING: Supernatural Hunter. This individual possesses an unknown degree of awareness of the supernatural, and has reacted hostilely to all known encounters.

More details scrolled across the screen as I viewed a Fae-Net warning notice. Sigridsen was confirmed responsible for the death and —my earlier thought proved correct—dissection of five true fae and one changeling. Three more changeling and several fae murders were suspected. The warning notice concluded that she was *definitely* aware of the fae vulnerability to cold-forged iron and of most if not all of its limitations.

This woman had spent ten years bouncing around the world, hunting inhumans. Driven, from what the mortal Internet articles had suggested, by nothing more than an insatiable curiosity, she had killed and dissected half a dozen people—and I only had definite information on the confirmed fae murders. Anything outside of the Courts wouldn't be solid enough for this sort of file.

If Sigridsen had been offered some of the answers to the riddles she was clearly willing to kill to resolve, she would almost certainly have been willing to abuse her name and credentials to sneak a container of vampires into the city.

Which, I realized with a sigh, did me no good whatsoever, because I still had no idea where she'd taken the container, nor any way to do so much as contact her.

———

AT A DEAD END on my own, I called Mary.

"Hi, Jason," she chirped cheerfully into the phone when she picked it up. Call display ranked somewhere slightly above wizards on things that made me uncomfortable most days.

"Hi, Mary," I said lamely. "How's my favorite wildcat?"

"The only other wildcat shifter you know is my brother," she told me laughingly. "He may be offended after stitching you up."

I laughed with her. She had a point.

"I'm good," she answered. "Work is boring, and a friend left me asking all sorts of uncomfortable questions around."

"Where do you work?" I asked. "I was lucky and found a courier job right after I hit town."

"You'll laugh," Mary told me. "I work at the local geek central—it's a giant board-game, book and anime store right downtown. You'd be surprised how many inhumans are gamers."

"I'm not sure I even know what you mean by the term," I admitted.

"Role-playing gamers," she explained. "Dungeons and Dragons, that sort of thing. It's fun; you should come out for our weekend gaming group at the store—we're playing tomorrow."

"I may do that," I said. Given the near kiss the other night, I figured time spent with Mary was a good thing. "I'm sorry if my questions caused issues."

"Tarvers told me to tell you to be careful," Mary said bluntly. "Then he asked for your email and said he'd be in touch with whatever he learned. Something along the lines of 'I don't tell fae where to dig their own graves.'"

"I appreciate his vote of confidence," I said dryly.

"Clementine examined what was left of the bodies, but nothing came of that," she continued. "The most intact was the one Barry chased down, but we shifters don't leave a lot behind."

I still had vivid memories of the one Tarvers had taken apart, and I couldn't see how one of the large shifters *could* leave much behind.

"Does the name Dr. Sigridsen mean anything to you?" I asked. The line was silent for a long time. "Mary?"

"Yes," she said flatly. "I'm not allowed to explain that, though. Look, are you okay entering Clan territory?"

"I woke up in it on the weekend," I reminded her.

"I'm going to call Tarvers," she told me. "The equivalent to your guys' Manors is the Lodge. The one in Calgary is a sports bar named Victor's in the northeast. Meet us there in an hour."

"Okay," I agreed slowly. She gave me the address.

"Sorry for the mysteriousness," Mary said quietly. "You'll understand once Tarvers explains, I promise. See you soon."

She hung up, presumably to call Tarvers, and I put my phone down, feeling more than a little confused. Apparently, the shifters there *had* dealt with Dr. Sigridsen. And the only way I was going to find out more was to head to the Lodge and meet with Tarvers.

I sighed and grabbed my coat. It was a Friday night, and I suspected it was cold outside.

———

I MISSED NOT JUST one but two bus connections on my way to the northeast and ended up taking over an hour and a half to get to Victor's. It wasn't quite what I was expecting—I was figuring it would be a biker bar or something similar, with brawly tattooed men smoking outside by the rows of motorbikes. Instead, Victor's was a quiet sports bar buried in a residential strip mall.

There was a row of motorbikes but also a moderately full parking lot of cars. Two young men, one the fair-haired shifter from the other night who Mary had called Barry, loitered outside the entrance. From the way the one I didn't know moved before Barry waved him to relaxation, both were carrying.

"Tarvers is waiting for you," Barry told me. "Booth at the end on the left."

"Thanks." I nodded to the shifters and entered the bar.

The inside was plain but solid. The booth tables were heavily mounted wood, and even the freestanding ones looked bolted to the floor. The bar looked like it had started life as one giant tree—presumably from somewhere not Calgary—and been hacked into shape. The lights were just dim enough to hide what I was sure were permanent stains on the bar.

Two giant flatscreen TVs hung above the bar, showing the progress of a hockey game and holding the attention of most of the bar's patrons. I don't think I saw a single human in the bar, though.

I followed Barry's directions and found the two shifters waiting for me. Mary looked up at me with a bright smile, and Tarvers simply grunted and gestured me to a seat, sliding a whiskey on ice across the table to me.

"You'll want the booze," he said grimly as I sipped at the whiskey and coughed as it burned its way down.

"How did you come across Sigridsen?" the leader of Calgary's shapeshifter population asked.

"You know what I was asked to investigate," I told them. That I hadn't been asked by Oberis was a detail they didn't need to know, and I was more comfortable not telling them. "I asked some questions up at the airport and was told a story about a cargo container of cadavers coming into the city about nine months ago—and Dr.

Sigridsen signed for them for the university. Except no one at the university knows anything about this, and she hasn't worked for them for a year."

"No, she hasn't," Tarvers said, a grim satisfaction in his voice. "We're pretty sure she knows that if we find her, she's dead."

I looked at him, surprised. Most inhumans generally ignored the human populace half the time and looked down on it the rest. We weren't much noted for specifically trying to hunt down mortals.

"Maybe you should start at the beginning," I suggested.

Tarvers nodded and took a gulp of his beer.

"Clementine was the first of us in a while to go through higher education," he told me. "While we have more control when we change than myth tends to suggest, it's still risky to spend that much time in purely human company."

"Barry's younger brother Abraham followed Clementine in," he continued. "He's a wolf shifter, so it was a bit riskier, but Clem had shown us it could be done. The year Clem graduated as a doctor, Abraham entered pre-med. One of his first teachers was Dr. Sigridsen. We didn't know, then, that the fae Courts had issued a hunter warning on the bitch.

"Abraham made it into his second year without an issue, and then something—we're not sure what—went wrong," the big bear shifter said quietly. "Sigridsen got suspicious and started stalking him. She was good—the bitch hunted fae, after all. It was around this time I mentioned what was going on to Oberis, who warned us that there was a hunter at the school.

"It was too late." Tarvers drained the remnants of his beer and gestured for the waitress to bring him another. "Abraham had mentioned to us that he was starting to feel nervous, so when Oberis told me about the hunter, I took five good men and rushed to the campus. We found his dorm room destroyed—every sign of a struggle.

"We found later that Sigridsen had taken him by surprise and injected him with a silver nitrate–laced tranquilizer. He almost killed her regardless, and she almost killed him with the tranquilizer, but in the end, she took him alive."

Mary hadn't said a word the whole time Tarvers had been talking;

now she laid a hand on her clan leader's shoulder and squeezed, sharing a sad smile with me.

"It took us two weeks to find who had taken him and where," the big Alpha finally continued, his voice quiet and pained. "She nailed him to a table with silver and dissected him. And then, when he regenerated, she did it again. And again. And again. She was *studying* him, like he was an animal, only worse. No animal could have survived what was done to him. A human, an animal, even a fae would have died by the end of the first day. She repeatedly dissected him and studied his regeneration for *two weeks*."

"Powers," I cursed softly.

Tarvers lapsed into silence, and Mary squeezed his shoulder again and then continued the story for him.

"I was on the strike team that went in after him," she told me. "One of my first tasks for the Clan, actually, was scouting out the site. We hit her house in the middle of the night, trying to capture her, but it turned out she'd trapped the place. Barry was badly injured, as were several others, and she escaped—but we got Abraham out. But...she broke him, Jason," Mary said, her voice tired. "Broke his mind like a twig—he'd been repeatedly tortured for *weeks*.

"That was a year ago," she continued. "Sigridsen vanished, though we don't think she left the city. Abraham is only now starting to show some improvement under continuous care and therapy."

"If we find that bitch, she is dead a thousand times over," Tarvers growled. "From what you said, she's now dealing with feeders. But in a year of searching, all we've been able to be sure of is that she's in the city. We have police and government contacts, but she hasn't registered a change of address since we destroyed her house.

"So, yes, Jason, we know who she is," he continued. "I don't know how much use knowing what we know is to you—we haven't found her. But if you do..." He paused. "If you can't get us there, understand that she is *far* more dangerous than a human should be and utterly without comprehension of us as people. Kill her first. Kill her hard."

With that, Tarvers finished his beer and stood up, leaving Mary and me alone at the table. She switched around to slide up next to me.

"It wasn't a story I could tell over the phone," she said quietly. "Even if I didn't need Tarvers's permission."

I looked at her, meeting her green-eyed gaze and taking her hand in mine.

"I don't know how," I admitted, "but I will find her. In the Queen's name I swear it."

This human had tortured a kid into insanity and murdered over half a dozen people, simply because they weren't human as she understood the term. And for her *curiosity*. I knew that when I met her, I'd have anger enough to fuel an inferno.

But no one had seen her and there was no official address; how could I *find* her? I stiffened as the answer struck me, accidentally pushing Mary away.

"Sorry," I muttered. "I just thought of a way to find her. I'll see you at your game thing tomorrow?" I asked, sliding out of the booth.

She looked up at me, her eyes unreadable. "Okay," she agreed.

I gave in to temptation and leaned in to press a quick kiss to her forehead.

"I'm sorry, but I think I need to act on this now," I told her as she smiled sadly at me.

There were no official government records of her address—but I worked for a *courier company*.

———

UNFORTUNATELY, I didn't actually have a *key* to the office, though I did at least know the alarm deactivation code. Fortunately, the semi-industrial area Direct Couriers was headquartered in was utterly deserted at nearly midnight on a Friday night, and the superior senses and reflexes of a changeling had made learning to pick locks a breeze during my years of disreputable wandering in the South.

Needing to take my gloves off to do it hurt, but at least I was fast.

I opened the door quickly and stepped in to the sound of the beeping security alarm. I'd been given the code to activate it if I was the last to leave, and the same code calmly disarmed it. Trysta's computer was turned off, and I booted it up, watching the door nervously in the darkness. I didn't need a light, and the dark helped conceal me from any passers-by.

I'd picked up Trysta's password almost by accident, watching her keystrokes one morning, and I quickly typed it in once the computer booted up. The computer rejected it, and I cursed aloud. She'd changed it, but what to?

It was one of those "include a capital, a special character, and a number" passwords, and after a moment, I tried again—switching out the 4 at the end for a 5.

It worked. With the computer booted and logged in, I fell to searching for the archive I knew existed—a list of every name and address we'd ever delivered to.

If I was very, very lucky, we'd delivered something to her. When I found the directory, I searched for *Dr Sigridsen*, but I got no hits. Tried again with just *Sigridsen* and started to figure I was out of luck, until I figured to try one last thing.

There were four *Elisse*s in the directory. Two had full last names, one was *Elisse R.*, and the last was *Elisse S.* A scattering of deliveries across the years Direct had been active, and an address change for the first package less than a year old.

I wrote down the new address and shut off the computer. I slipped out of the office as quietly as I'd come in, reactivating the alarm and locking the door as I left. Bill would be confused when he looked at the alarm records showing the deactivation on Monday, but there were no other signs I'd been there. I could live with a confused boss.

It was too late to take the bus and too cold to stay out much later, but I didn't want to wait. This woman was actively involved with the cabal, a key to the mission the Queen had given me, and a potential threat to anyone who encountered her.

I checked the address, shrugged, and called a cab.

———

THE CAB DROPPED me off outside a small detached home in a newly built suburb in the central north end of the city—I think the sign had called it Panorama Hills. I paid the cab driver cash and pulled my coat around myself, scoping the house out from the outside.

Nothing suggested this was the home of a university professor turned serial killer. The front lawn showed neatly kept in the light from the streetlamps. No light escaped from the house, though as I walked toward the front door, I realized that was because every visible window was completely covered in heavy drapes. There was no way light could leak out.

It was quite possible there was someone home, and I was starting to wish I'd picked up a weapon somewhere. Sparks of anger in my veins and a warmth in my hands said I wasn't defenseless, but I figured it would probably be easier to just shoot someone.

I stopped outside the door and sent Mary a quick text. "If I don't call by dawn, check out this address."

That sent, I tucked the phone into my back pocket and kicked the door in. Brilliant yellow light spilled out into the night as I walked into the house. A sudden sense of danger hit me, and I dove sideways as a shotgun blasted through the space I'd been standing in. I hit the ground and rolled back up to my feet. A steely gray-haired woman was running toward the front of the house—but the shotgun had been triggered by a laser tripwire and didn't look to have a second shot.

"Who the hell are you?" the woman demanded, yanking an ugly-looking pistol from a cabinet behind the wall.

Before she'd lifted it to fire, I'd crossed to her and quickly broken her wrist, sending the pistol careening against the wall—thankfully still on safe; I could *feel* the cold iron in the clip. I barely even noticed the surprise on her face at my speed.

"Dr. Sigridsen, I presume," I said calmly, breaking her other arm as she tried to hit me, and shoving her back into her living room. She stumbled and landed on a couch.

"You're one of *them*," she spat. "One of those fucking monsters."

"Monsters, huh?" I said. "One of the people in this room tortured a nineteen-year-old boy. It wasn't me. Can you say the same?"

"I was *studying* it, not torturing," she spat. "Anything that abnormal should be studied, to understand it, use it."

"Studying involves kidnapping a student and repeatedly attempting to kill them?" I snarled as I advanced on her.

"That monster shouldn't have been among real people," she told me. "I saw it—it would have turned on them eventually. It looked at my students and saw *food*."

"I've never known a shifter who saw people as anything but people, actually," I said conversationally.

"What did it matter?" she demanded. "It had a solution. What happens to you, *monster*, if I were to inject you with cancerous cells?"

I froze, just out of reach of her. That explained...a lot. "They'd die," I said flatly.

"Well, they didn't do that in me," she snarled. "I could have found a cure, saved *millions*, but you monsters had to interfere!"

"It doesn't work that way, I'm afraid," I told her. "Nothing you could have learned by torturing that boy could save you. And those that could would never help a murderer."

"Hah! There was one who could," she answered. "What do you know?"

"I need to know what you did with the container of vampires you brought into this city," I told her bluntly, and she laughed in my face.

"So, you know how I first served." She laughed. "What makes you think I'd surrender my saviors?"

"Because, Dr. Sigridsen, your 'saviors' eat people to live," I told her, a sinking feeling in my stomach. Blood magic could cure cancer, easily. It also left the "patient" almost entirely enthralled to their healer.

"Tell me where they are."

"What can you do to me?" she laughed in my face. "There's nothing they can't fix. You can't stop them, and they will heal me again and again and again."

Sigridsen was insane. And she had the key information I needed.

I took the final step to her and slammed her back into the couch by her shoulders.

"*Tell me*," I snarled in her face.

She laughed, and pain seared through me as the echoing crack of a pistol rang through the room. The bullet ripped through my stomach and sent me stumbling backward as she lifted another pistol she'd pulled out of the couch with her freshly healed arms and bared her fangs at me.

The vampires hadn't cured Sigridsen's cancer with a blood working. That would have been too easy for me…

"They made you a vampire in payment," I gasped, feeling for the wound. It wasn't cold iron; it would heal. It wasn't a fatal wound to me—for that, she'd either need the gun she'd left in the hallway, or to be a much better shot.

"I will not betray my new brothers and sisters," she crowed, raising the gun to shoot me again. I dodged, lumbering to my feet and feeling the bullet whiz past my head. Fire flared through my right hand, scorching the gun and misfiring the ammo with heat. Sigridsen dropped the gun as it half-exploded in her hand.

Her eyes glittered with madness as she pulled a short, heavy knife from somewhere. It wasn't cold iron, but there were lots of wounds I couldn't regenerate from.

"What can you do to me?" she said in a hiss. "They have made me immortal!"

I stood, willpower and power driving away the pain as I conjured faerie flame in my hands.

"I can burn your body to ashes, bitch," I snapped, and threw the flame at her. It burned up her arm, forcing her to drop the machete, and I stepped forward, throwing more flame as she went for the gun in the hallway. I caught her in the side, but it didn't stop her from sliding into the hallway and grabbing the ugly pistol with its cold iron rounds.

I didn't conjure flame fast enough, and the heavy cold-hammered iron round tore into my shoulder. Pain tore through my body, driving me to my knees, and she fired again. Another bullet ripped through my chest, and I coughed up blood as she closed.

"Why aren't you dead?" she snapped. "I thought this shit killed you fucking fairies dead."

"I'm not true fae, bitch," I said, coughing up blood with my words. "I've more human left in me than *you* do!"

Anger and pain flared through me and out my extended right hand. A burst of green flame, an inferno like I'd never conjured before, flashed across the room. Sigridsen screamed as the gun literally melted in her hand, the bullets exploding and flying off wildly. One of them might have hit her, but I would never know—the tendril of flame kept going clean through her, incinerating half of her body and burning a huge hole in the wall behind her.

Normal, yellow flame began to lick around the edges of the hole as I stumbled out. I caught a glimpse of a familiar black Hummer screeching around the corner of the street, breaking at least three traffic laws, before the blood loss and cold-iron poisoning caught up with me and I collapsed.

10

I WOKE UP TO PAIN. My entire body ached, and the two cold-iron wounds burned like fire.

"Shit, he's awake," Clementine snapped in a voice sharp with panic. "We *can't* use anesthetic for this; someone put him out!"

Cold, cold hands touched my temples, and I felt a flare of power, and then the world was gone.

———

WHEN I WOKE AGAIN, my body ached, but none of my wounds burned. I couldn't pinpoint the bullet wounds, which told me someone had cleaned the wounds of cold iron. Which would have fucking *hurt*, hence them keeping me knocked out.

I opened my eyes to the same spartan room I'd been left in when I first was taken to Clan Tenerim's Den. I wasn't alone, but this time it wasn't Mary or one of the shifters who was in with me. A tall dark-haired woman in a black skirt suit sat cross-legged on a chair by the door. Her gaze locked on mine as I looked at her.

"Good, you're awake," she said briskly. "I am Laurie. Oberis sent me."

I could feel her power across the room. She was fae, not quite Noble but strong enough for that. She stood, and to my eyes her visage shimmered, and I cursed mentally. A single glimpse through the glamor she'd woven around herself revealed the true nature of the woman. She was still tall and dark-haired, but her skin was withered with centuries of wind and sun, warped by birth and age. I was sharing a room with a hag.

Hags wielded great magical power, though physically most would barely be a match for me. I knew who'd kept me asleep while Clementine had abraded cold iron from my flesh.

The thought led me to toss aside the blanket over me to examine my wounds. They'd been bound up, but the bandages were clean and not bloody. I touched them gently and could feel the flesh mostly closed over.

"How long was I out?" I asked Laurie.

"It is Sunday morning," she told me. She passed me a bundle of clothes. "Dress," she ordered.

"Can you at least leave the room?" I asked. The hag was creeping me out.

"No," she said flatly. "I am not to leave your presence until I have delivered you to the Lord of the Court. I am your guard."

"My guard?"

"I have discussed this situation with Alpha Tarvers," she told me. "You have lied to the Clan and used the goodwill of the court to your advantage. Also, you have threatened the Covenants."

She tossed a newspaper on the bed in front of me as I began to dress. The headline blazed:

NORTHWEST FIRE LEADS TO DISCOVERY OF SERIAL KILLER

In the aftermath of a fire in the northwest of Calgary Saturday morning, police have found the remains of no less than six people in the basement of the burnt-out home. Identifications have not been confirmed, but police believe them to be the bodies of several missing persons reported in the area.

"Damn," I whispered.

"Had you passed your knowledge of Dr. Sigridsen's location on to the proper authorities, we would not have been at risk of the discovery of a vampire by mortal authorities," Laurie snapped. "We are lucky that *her* body was sufficiently destroyed that they will not be able to identify her as inhuman."

"Now," she continued mercilessly as I pulled on shoes, "are you going to cooperate, or will I have to geas you?"

"I will cooperate," I said quietly. This wasn't good. As a Vassal, I technically didn't answer to Oberis, and it was a tossup whether Laurie would be *able* to geas me—but from the way the Queen had phrased her orders, I didn't think she'd appreciate *them* learning that.

I followed the hag from the room, avoiding the glances of the shifters as I passed through the Den. When we reached the front door, however, Tarvers blocked it. Laurie turned her glare on him.

"We agreed to this, Alpha Tarvers," she said coldly.

"I will speak with him," the big shapeshifter rumbled.

"My orders are clear," Laurie responded. "I am not to leave his presence."

"In private," Tarvers told her.

"I have my orders," the hag said flatly.

"You have my word, as Alpha of Clan Tenerim, as Speaker for the Clans of this city, and a signatory to Calgary's Covenant, that he will be surrendered to your justice," the Alpha told her formally. "Now give me a minute."

They held each other's glares for a long moment until the tall hag nodded sharply and stepped around him.

Tarvers turned his cold gaze on me.

"Thank you for what you did," he said flatly, "but I need to know something."

"What?" I asked, my voice small as I studied his feet. This was not how I'd envisaged seeing Tarvers after taking on Sigridsen.

"Look me in the eye," he ordered, "and tell me why you lied to us."

Slowly, I raised his gaze to look into his eyes. It was the first time I'd looked into the Alpha's eyes, and I realized for the first time that it was not size or strength or blood right that made Tarvers Tenerim master of Calgary's shifters. He looked into my eyes and through them into my soul, and I knew, in that moment, I could no more deceive him than myself.

"I did not lie to you," I said quietly, sure that he knew I spoke the truth. "I did not tell you everything, and I cannot tell you now what I did not tell you then, but I did not lie to you."

"Huh," he grunted. He held my gaze for a long moment before he finally allowed me to look away. "I will accept that, Jason Kilkenny. Know that my Clan owes you two boons. I will try to convince Mary you didn't lie to us," he added, "but I don't know if even success will help you."

"Why?" I asked.

"You will be barred from seeing the Clan," Tarvers told me bluntly. "Your Lord is rightly angry in his belief that you have used his name falsely. Even if only by implication." He winked at me and offered his massive hand.

"You have done us all and the Covenants a service," he told me as I shook his hand. He pulled me in and whispered in my ear. "We got the bitch's computers out before the fire took everything. I will let you know what we learn...discreetly."

He released me and opened the door.

"Good luck, Jason," he told me.

"Thanks," I drawled slowly, taking in everything he'd said. "Good luck yourself."

He nodded and gestured me out of the Den toward my guard.

———

LAURIE WAS WAITING OUTSIDE, standing by the door of a dark blue SUV. She wordlessly pointed me to the passenger seat, and I obeyed just as quietly. The key turned itself in the ignition as she got in, and the car shifted into gear as she placed her hands on the wheel.

Show-off.

The drive through the city was painfully slow. Laurie, like many hags, was apparently completely anal about rules. Every stop sign was stopped at for *exactly* three seconds. Every yield sign was slowed for. She even slowed down to a stop when the lights turned yellow!

This being the real world, this meant we got passed by almost everyone, honked at three times, and flipped off once. We passed that last car again several minutes later, the driver having gone off the road and slammed into a retaining wall. Someone was standing by the vehicle, talking frantically into a cell phone, but I couldn't tell if the driver was okay.

Laurie had a vicious little smile on her face as she drove by at precisely the speed limit, and I shivered. It was certainly within the hag's abilities to hex a driver into crashing, and it was a potent reminder that hags were *Unseelie* fae. They didn't tend to be nice people, and it seemed Laurie was no exception to *that* stereotype.

Thankfully, that was the only incident on our way, and she eventually pulled us into the parking lot of a midsized hotel and conference center in the southwest quadrant of the city. A central tower stood by the road, proudly proclaiming its western-themed name, with one wing stretching along the major road and one stretching away. On the base of the large green-and-yellow sign, I readily recognized the delicate script of fae-sign, invisible to mortal eyes.

This was the joint Seelie-Unseelie Court. The physical home of fae authority in Calgary. The place I had consistently avoided even learning the location of since I got there. Also, and most important today, here was where Oberis, fae Lord in Calgary, would pass judgment on his subjects.

Laurie pulled into a STAFF ONLY parking spot and stuck a plastic parking pass on the SUV's rearview mirror.

"Let's go," she ordered, the first words she'd spoken since I came out to meet her. She led the way, and I followed her into a lushly decorated lobby done tastefully in dark blues and greens. Display signs behind the reception counter announced the bookings for conference rooms A1 through C6. All of the C-block conference rooms were booked by "Callahan Enterprises".

"C wing is always booked," Laurie told me as she led me toward the door with its two security guards. "We change the name every few days, but we don't let mortals in—it's the permanent Court."

Apparently, she was aware I hadn't been there before, and I was grateful for the unexpected explanation. Maybe she wasn't *all* bad.

The two guards shifted slightly as we approached, and I realized what they were with a shock. Both were gentry—the second highest class of Fair Folk, physically equal to the nobles but almost lacking in the mystical gifts that made Laurie, for example, so terrifying.

Of course, "physically equal to the Nobles" meant "faster and tougher than human tanks," so the gentry were plenty terrifying in their own right. At the sight of Laurie, both bowed slightly and stepped aside.

The door swung shut behind us, and it was suddenly very clear we'd entered a region mortals didn't enter. The lights were dimmer, calibrated to the fae's superior vision. Gentle murals of forest landscapes covered the walls, and if you looked at them out of the corner of your eye, you could swear you saw animals moving.

The carpet didn't change immediately, but as we moved farther into the Court, the dark blue fabric of the lobby carpet gave way to a thick mass of dark green moss, warm and comfortingly moist on the feet. The air in there, a space belonging to the fae, felt more alive than anywhere I'd been in a while.

I breathed deeply. For all that I avoided the politics of the fae Courts as best as I could do, even I could not deny that being there was more relaxing than walking in the mortal world outside.

Finally, Laurie stopped at a set of double doors and gestured, swinging open both sides. With a deep breath, I preceded her through, and she allowed the doors to swing shut behind us.

"My lord, I present the prisoner," she announced loudly, and the mutter of conversation in the room ceased, leaving me to study the people I'd been brought before.

The Court of the fae in Calgary resembled a business conference more than anything else. Twelve large tables filled the room, with half of them empty and small meetings going on at the others. The twelfth, the largest table, stood on a raised platform at one end of the room, and Oberis himself sat at it, looking down over his people.

Maybe two dozen people were in the room, mostly true fae with a scattering of changelings like myself. This was, as I understood it, about a third of the fae in Calgary. There was easily enough space in the room to hold all of the eighty or so of us in the city.

"Bring him before me," Oberis ordered.

I didn't wait for anyone to enforce the order—if nothing else, both

Oberis and Laurie could theoretically force me to obey by puppeting my limbs. I suspected that they couldn't do so through the geases being the Queen's Vassal had left on me, but I also knew that revealing that would be a bad thing.

"Jason Kilkenny," Oberis said flatly as I reached the space directly in front of his table. "You stand accused before this Court of risking the Covenants of this city, of pursuing vigilante justice against the best interest of this Court and of falsely using the name of this Court to support some quixotic quest against this cabal of vampires you believe has infiltrated the city. What do you have to say for yourself?"

I took a deep breath. Getting out of this without pissing off Oberis enough to get myself killed, or revealing *why* I had been hunting the cabal, was not going to be easy.

"It is not a belief," I started. "I now have seen proof that a group of vampires, in slumber and refrigerated to give the appearance of being corpses, was brought into this city nine months ago. I do not believe that pursuing this cabal, by its nature a deadly threat to our Court and this city's Covenants, is against our best interests."

"Even if you are correct in your belief," Oberis barked, "there are avenues and authorities this information should have been passed on to. It is *not* your mandate, child, to hunt down feeders in their homes and wield fae power in a way that risks our secrecy. It is not even within this *Court's* mandate to hunt feeders in this city.

"If there was truly a cabal in this city," he continued, "the Wizard would know and would have dispatched his Enforcers to deal with them. That is *their* mandate and authority, not ours."

I wondered how much that pissed him off. It was not in the nature of fae lords to submit easily to external authority, even that of the higher Courts, let alone a Wizard's.

"You lied to Clan Tenerim and have embarrassed this Court by stating you had orders from us," Oberis said, his voice cold. "By such, you have risked our reputation and authority in this city—reputation and authority won with sacrifices you don't seem to comprehend!"

"I did not state I had orders from this Court," I said quietly. "Nor were they from this Court."

"Then who were they from?" he demanded. "*I* am the authority for the fae in this city!"

"I cannot answer that question," I told him, staring at the moss carpeting the ground. This was where things were going to get awkward.

"You *will* answer the question," Oberis told me, his voice low and dangerous. "You claimed to the Clans that you had authority no one in this Court gave you. If this was *not* a lie, then who gave you that authority?"

"I cannot answer that question," I repeated.

"You appear to be under the illusion, child," the fae lord said, his voice approximating ice in temperature, "that you are allowed secrets from me. You are not. You *will* answer the..."

Oberis's ice-cold rant was interrupted by the double doors slamming open and the small figure of Eric von Radach stomping in. For all that the gnome was less than half the height of the doors he had just come through, he was suddenly the center of all attention in the room.

Eric was the Keeper. The Keeper was the neutral arbitrator in fae affairs, the keeper of secrets, one whose word that something was true would be taken, even when the secrets themselves could not be revealed. It was tradition that a Keeper did not enter Court *except* in that capacity.

"I claim Right of Confidence on this trial," the gnome said simply into the silence that had descended. "We have passed beyond—*far* beyond, my lord," he noted pointedly, "affairs that should be public knowledge of the Court."

For a moment, Oberis looked torn between having Eric thrown out and ordering everyone *else* out, both of which would be possible but...unusual. Finally, he sighed.

"Fine," he said. "You and you"—he pointed at me and Eric—"follow me."

He pushed his chair back from the table and stalked toward a door in the corner of the banquet hall cum courtroom. I hurried to follow, after a quick glance to make sure Eric was coming as well.

The door led back out into the moss-carpeted hallway with the conference room exits, and Oberis strode confidently down the hall while Eric and I hurried to keep up. We quickly left the conference center and passed into a—still moss-floored and hence fae ground—hallway of offices. On a Sunday, they were all empty.

Oberis led us into the office at the end, which turned out to have been re-walled in stone-and-mahogany paneling. A massive black walnut desk occupied pride of place in the small room, and the stones that made up the bottom half of the walls had been carved into bookshelves—every one of them full of well-worn copies of books on a thousand topics. Oberis's library covered everything from quantum physics to electrical engineering to philosophy, and I didn't doubt he'd read every one of the thousands of books in his office.

Other than the chair behind the desk, there was no seating in the office, and he looked to Eric as we entered.

"Keeper, if you would be so kind," he said, gesturing to the empty space in front of his desk, his voice suddenly tired.

Eric nodded and promptly pulled two chairs, copies of the ones I'd seen in his apartment, out of thin air and sat on one. Gingerly, I took a seat on the other and faced Calgary's fae lord across his desk.

For all of the medieval trappings of the office, the computer that sat on the desk looked like something out of science fiction. Any CPU casing was presumably hidden inside the desk, and the monitor was paper thin—turned off as it was, I could actually see through it. There was no visible keyboard, though I recognized a box at the base of the monitor as the projector for a laser one. A black mouse, textured to look like a piece of obsidian, was the only other item on the desk.

"I think I have all the pieces now," Oberis said quietly. Here, in private, he sounded much less powerful and more tired than he had in public, and I suddenly wondered just how old he was. A noble fae could easily live over a thousand years, and many of the older ones found dealing with the pace of modern politics and power difficult.

"I'm left with one question for you, Kilkenny," he continued. "Which one?"

"Which what?" I asked, confused.

"One of the High Fae entered my city via the Between," Oberis told me patiently. "I can only assume, now, that they came to visit you for Powers only know what reason. This High Fae would be the source of your orders and why you did not actually say this Court had given you your task—making you neither an embarrassment to this Court, if we can confirm this to the Tenerim, nor a liar to the Tenerim. So, I have to know which of the High Court commands you."

There were nine members of the High Court of the Fae—the Powers who ruled our kind. The Queen ruled them, but the Horned King, the Lord of the Wild Hunt, the Ladies of the Seasons, and the Seelie and Unseelie Lords were all Powers—demigods like the Magus who ruled Calgary.

"I am a Vassal of Mabona," I said quietly. There wasn't much point in lying to him now.

He looked over at Eric. "And this is true?" Oberis asked.

"Yes," the Keeper said quietly. "He is marked to those with eyes to see, like the Keepers. By blood right, he is a Vassal of the Queen, and She has claimed him as such."

"Damn," the fae lord whispered, eyeing me as he rested his head in his hands. "Do you have any idea how fucked up you're making my life?"

He sighed, pulled something out of his desk and tossed it to me. I caught it—it was a small burlap bag, about the size of a sandwich ziplock.

"Take a look at that," he told me. "That is what everything in this city is about."

I opened the bag. Inside was a mix of dust and small stones, all the same shade of dark gray. I sniffed and realized the stone was giving off a faint cinnamon-like aroma.

"What is it?" I asked finally.

"Heartstone," Oberis told me. "It's a by-product of the oil sands production, it all flows through Calgary, and the Wizard has a complete lock on it. Ninety percent of the world's production comes from here, and everyone wants to control it."

"Why?" I asked, passing the bag back to him. It smelt nice and looked odd, but it was hardly the first unusual material I'd seen since being dragged into the world of the fae.

"Mixed with gold, it is orichalcum, the alchemist's key and a requirement for any magical artefact and much of a Wizard's higher powers," Eric explained, eyeing the bag on Oberis's desk. "Mixed with mercury, it is quicksilver—an extraordinary drug for our kind that can make us stronger, faster, more powerful. Mixed with human blood, it is lifesblood and can temporarily allow a vampire to be, in almost all ways, truly alive.

"And mixed with silver," Oberis finished grimly, "it is bane, instant death to any shifter, and capable of shattering any non-Powers' magical constructs.

"It is through control of the flow of heartstone that the Wizard commands this city," he continued. "He deals with the shifters to limit it, with us to supply it, and with wizards and fae elsewhere for it as well."

"Everyone wants it," I said quietly, "and the shifters want to leave it where it is. And mortal politics?"

"Inhuman politics have *always* had their reflections in the mortal world," Oberis said with a nod. "You are correct: the designs of the various factions have shaped the politics around the oil sands in the human world."

Oberis looked me in the eyes.

"The Court has been censured for your actions," he explained. "Our supply of heartstone has been temporarily reduced in punishment, though as you did not break the Covenants, your punishment is left to me.

"Understand that you *have* embarrassed this Court, and I cannot let that pass," he continued. "While I understand that you are bound to obey the orders of your mistress, I must demand that you do so more discreetly in future. It is within the limits of my authority over one such as you to demand that you do not interact with the other groups in this city, and so I lay that restriction on you.

"If you need aid in your task, turn to Eric or myself," he instructed. "You will *not* make contact with Clan Tenerim or the other shifters, do you understand? This is *my* will and this is *my* city, so you *will* obey."

I bowed my head in agreement. I couldn't really argue—Vassal or no Vassal, Oberis could still kill me with a word.

"For the rest, I will regard your wounds as punishment enough," he continued. "Is this satisfactory, Keeper?" He turned to Eric.

The gnome nodded. "You are within your rights," he said simply.

Oberis hit an intercom button. "Laurie, attend, please."

The hag entered the room after a minute or so.

"Take Mr. Kilkenny home," the fae lord instructed. "The Keeper and I still have matters to discuss."

———

LAURIE DROVE ME HOME, exactly as precisely obedient to traffic laws as when she drove me to the Court. When we pulled up next to the apartment, she locked the door before I could get out.

"It appears my lord has chosen to be lenient with you," she told me, and for the first time since I'd met her, she fully dropped the glamor. Old, old black eyes glared at me, and I shivered as the full force of the hag's attention hit me.

"I have seen the aftermath of your stupidity," she continued. "Leave these affairs to those better suited for them, or perhaps next time I will not bother my lord with the affairs of troublesome children. Do you understand me?"

I nodded, fear having frozen my voice. She unlocked the door, and I was almost shoved out, standing on the sidewalk, watching her drive away.

Just to add to everything, Oberis's pet hag had taken a disliking to me. I had no doubt that if she decided "not to bother" Oberis, my life expectancy would then be measured in minutes.

With a sigh, I went into my apartment building. Discretion was now doubly necessary, but I had no illusions about my ability to defy my Queen. Or even keep Her from knowing what was going on, as was pointed out to me when I logged onto Fae-Net.

I didn't even know the email client I used for the Fae-Net *had* the ability to mark a message as "high priority", but I had one marked as such. There was no return sender, and it was signed merely *M*.

You have done well, she started. *Events are moving quickly, and you have achieved more than I had hoped.*

Sigridsen's capture would have been preferable to her destruction, as

Oberis or the shifter Alpha could have forced her to reveal more, but the circumstances were beyond your control.

I request that you attempt to avoid being as drastically wounded in future. I have arranged for certain supplies to be delivered to your apartment. Use them wisely.

M.

A suspicion in my mind, I looked around my apartment. I was correct—a black hard-cased briefcase had materialized on my table at some point since Friday evening. I'd missed it coming in, since I hadn't expected there to be anything in my house I hadn't put there.

I opened the briefcase. The left half was occupied by a neatly folded cloth package. The right half contained one of the smallest pistols I'd ever seen. The receiver was marked with a cleanly filed flat space that *should* have held a serial number, and the text IWI LTD COMPACT JERICHO 941.

Two ten-round magazines filled the space around the pistol, and two twenty-round boxes rounded out my "care package". I pulled one of the bullets out of the box and shivered at the touch. I'd seen these rounds before, in the hands of fae security—it was a modified hollow-point carrying a mixed silver, cold-iron and garlic distillate payload.

It wasn't enough of any of the three to prove fatal from one round, though the 9 mm rounds would do a good chunk of damage on their own, but three or four of those in just about any inhuman would give them a very bad day.

Returning the bullet to the box, I pulled out the cloth package. It was a plain, dark gray undershirt. Running my fingers down it, however, I could feel lines of impact-resistant gel capsules, and turning it inside out, I saw someone had inlaid a series of what looked like runes in a goldish metal that I suspected was the orichalcum Oberis had mentioned.

Apparently, the Queen preferred me alive and not shot to pieces. Who would have figured?

11

In the morning, however, it all seemed faintly ridiculous. I was *not* going to be the only courier in the city driving around carrying a firearm! I left the Jericho and its thoroughly lethal ammunition in the briefcase.

Of course, that didn't stop me putting the armored vest on. If nothing else, it turned out to be very warm, and I wasn't sneering at that in the weather Calgary had boasted since my arrival. That I was sure the Queen's gift would stop anything short of tank rounds helped as well.

I made it into work exactly on time, to the usual hustle of Trysta and Bill sorting everyone out with their loads for the day.

"Hey, Jason," Trysta greeted me. "You're on the ten AM airport run, same as yesterday, but I've got a load for you to run out beforehand."

"Works for me," I agreed, and then groaned as one of the other drivers accidentally elbowed me.

"You okay, man?" he immediately asked.

"I broke up a fight on the weekend," I explained quickly. "I'll be fine. Just watch my chest, if you can."

"Are you going to be good to drive?" Trysta asked when I turned back to her.

"Yeah, I'll be fine," I repeated. "Just bruised." She nodded and handed me the clipboard for my morning deliveries.

I was half-expecting the text that arrived as I was halfway through my trip, instructing me to meet Enforcer Michael at a different Starbucks location from last time, this one on my way back to the office from this trip.

"Is this going to be a regular thing?" I asked as I met him in the parking lot. This time, he had the mocha I'd ordered last time waiting for me. I took it gratefully, the cup warm in my hands amidst the frigid air.

"It is convenient for us to have an inhuman that can make official courier deliveries," he said quietly, passing me a single box. "This is for air shipment," he instructed. "Include it in your drop-off."

"You could try booking through the company rather than all of this cloak-and-dagger," I told him. "I can't say I'm overly enthused with putting my employers at risk."

"Measures have been taken so there will be no risk, fiscal or otherwise, to your employers," he replied calmly. "We will see to it that they are compensated for any minor loss due to your service to us. We have the ability to have them added to the preferred courier list for several significantly sized companies in the city. I calculate that the gains from that addition would far outweigh the few minutes of your time we require."

"Fine," I grunted. "But if anything happens to harm them, I will take it to the Court and have my lord file a complaint under the Covenants. Are we clear?"

"Perfectly, Mr. Kilkenny," he accepted calmly with a slight bow of his head.

I took the package. Unless I was willing to take my concerns to Oberis—and right now, I didn't want to remind him that I *existed* —there was nothing else I could do.

———

THE REST of the day passed smoothly, with the Enforcers' package vanishing without a trace amidst the rest of the outbound shipment.

Trysta was noticeably more businesslike with me than usual, without nearly as many of the bright smiles I'd grown used to receiving.

There was nothing I could do about that situation, however, so I accepted it with a sigh and continued on with my job. The workday ended with me walking home on my own through the freezing weather, thankful for the extra warmth of the Queen's vest.

The weather fit my mood pretty thoroughly. On the one hand, the woman who I had been interested now likely believed me a liar who'd used her for information. Even if she didn't, I was forbidden to deal with the Clan now.

On the other, one of my coworkers was apparently interested and somewhat upset that I didn't return her interest, which might become uncomfortable in the future.

On yet a third hand, I'd followed the link through the airport as far as I could, and that trail had ended in a fiery mess when I accidentally burnt down Sigridsen's house. While the shifters might get something from her computers, I would never know—I couldn't contact them to find out.

As if to demonstrate how frustrating the situation was, it promptly started to snow. I quickened my pace as visibility began to decrease and the temperature slowly dropped around me. I was two blocks from home, and the snow got thicker fast.

After a few minutes, I couldn't see more than five feet in front of me, and even fae vision couldn't keep me from risking getting very lost. I kept putting one foot in front of another, leaning into the wind and pulling my hood down lower to try and protect my face.

A dark figure materialized out of the white like a ship breaking through a wave. A heavy coat covered them from neck to toe, and a thick scarf and a pair of ski goggles protected them above the neck. None of their skin was bared to the snow—or to the sun that had been shining a few minutes before.

You hunt too well, a voice sounded in my head. *We do not need to be enemies, child.*

"Who are you?" I tried to say, but the wind stole my voice. The figure shook its head, suggesting that they could hear me.

Silly, silly child, the voice said. *I would not reveal so much just yet. I am...connected to those you hunt so virulently. You know so little about the situation and are so weak. Why risk yourself?*

"Because they're *feeders*," I said with feeling. I figured that it didn't really matter if I could even hear myself—which was good, because I couldn't. The wind was brutal, and the snow was now falling sideways almost as much as down.

Such emotion, mmm, the figure purred inside my head. *I'm told your kind are sweet to the taste; did you know that? Human enough to feed on, fae enough to be a heady drink.*

I tried to summon faerie fire to defend myself, but the wind and snow snuffed it out. A pealing laugh resounded in my head, and the figure pointed.

There is your home, little changeling, the voice told me. *You are not food tonight. But watch your step, for you walk in shadows without understanding who casts the light. Leave well enough alone, little changeling, and you will live.*

The shadowed figure stepped back into the snow and was gone. After a moment, I followed where it had pointed. Within ten steps, I found myself on the front porch of my apartment complex and leaned against the wall.

Someone had just gone out of their way to warn me off as impressively as they could. I may not think I was getting anywhere, but that someone obviously did!

———

AT NO POINT in the night did the snow slow, and by morning, the city was buried under more than a yard of snow. I woke up to Bill calling me to let me know he'd shut Direct down for the day—even if we managed to make it into dispatch, he wouldn't feel comfortable letting us take the trucks out on the streets.

I went out to check the front door of the apartment complex, not quite believing Bill's description of the city as buried. Apparently, the snow had drifted with the wind, because the front door of the complex was glass, with full-length windows on either side, and it was *completely* covered in snow.

After weeks of being at work disgustingly early, I was very awake at six in the morning. A quick search revealed a snow shovel in a closet off the main hallway, so I grabbed my winter coat and got to work.

An hour later, I'd managed to clear the building's front patio and a pathway down to the road, which had not been plowed. My "pathway" resembled a canyon, but I'd packed in the sides so it would stay up. Hopefully, the still-blowing snow wouldn't fill it in too badly before the plows came to dig us out.

Assuming the plows came to dig us out. After a week worrying about the orders of the Queen, vampires and conspiracies, the prosaic worry of merely being completely snowed in was somewhat of a relief.

I took a quick stock of my groceries and started making breakfast. Given the state of the streets, I was more than a little surprised when my door buzzer rang. It took me a minute to put aside pans and spatulas and get to it, and by then it had buzzed again.

"Yes?"

"It's Eric," the intercom told me. "Can you let me in? It's bloody freezing out here."

Bemused, I hit the button to allow the old gnome entrance and, a minute or so later, opened my door to a knock. The gnome stood in my hallway, dripping wet, a pair of snowshoes as tall as he was leaning against his shoulder. For a moment, all I could do was stare at the incongruous sight before I finally managed to stand aside and let him enter my apartment.

"I can't say I was expecting company," I told him as I gestured to my couch. I grabbed my computer chair—the only other place to sit in the apartment—and turned it to face him.

"Good," he said gruffly. "If you weren't expecting me, and with the weather outside, we can assume no one else figures I'm here or will ever know." He pulled a small gold pyramid inscribed with runes in the goldish silver I was learning to recognize as orichalcum, and placed it beside him on the couch, studying the runes for a moment.

"What is that?" I asked.

"This is one of my most carefully guarded secrets," he told me.

"There are very few ways to block the Sight of a Wizard without him knowing that it has been blocked, and this is one of them."

"The Sight?" I asked, realizing with a sigh that it would be another morning of questions.

The gnome shook his head. "How do you think that MacDonald knew you were here? That the Enforcers always seem to know what you're up to? Wizards see like you and I, but they also See—they can perceive everything within the areas they have marked as their own. MacDonald has marked Calgary and the oil-sands projects as his territory; he Sees everything."

"Then how did the cabal sneak in?" I asked in my slow drawl.

"That's the question, isn't it?" Eric told me quietly. "Some of the Enforcers have been given a portion of his Sight; it allows them to operate without pestering him with questions. Even if he somehow missed the feeders, they should have seen them. Somehow, this cabal not merely snuck into the city undetected but has evaded detection since."

"With one of those?" I pointed at the pyramid.

"Something similar," he admitted, "but not one of these—they are the mostly closely held secret of the gnomish smiths. I have only been permitted to make three. Oberis has one for when he absolutely needs it, I have this one for moments like this, and a third conceals my workshop, just in case.

"But what I miss, Jason, and what I fear is key here, is how they could conceal *every* vampire *all* of the time. You tracked Sigridsen by purely mortal means, really. The Enforcers should have known where she was the moment she was turned."

"You think some of the Enforcers have been corrupted?" I asked. That was a nerve-wracking thought. Wizards were supposed to be all-knowing within their area—the Sight Eric mentioned. Deceiving one enough to betray him...well, *I* wouldn't try it.

"It's at least possible," he said grimly. "I don't know how to investigate that, but it's something for you to consider, a link you need to watch for."

"Honestly, I feel like I'm grasping at straws, and they keep setting themselves on fire," I admitted. "I've lost my best sources through the Clan, and I'm not sure how to go forward."

Eric nodded. "I have some more information for you," he told me. "I've called in some favors, and one of my contacts has agreed to meet with you—he works for the Calgary Police, so he has access to databases we don't."

"That's more than I had," I said gratefully.

"His name is Aheed Ibrahim," Eric continued. "He's not human, but he's not a breed of inhuman you've met before. He's a djinni."

I blinked. "I thought they really were only a myth."

"Very little is only a myth," the gnome reminded me wryly. "However, the djinn are very rare—unlike most inhumans, they are only fertile with each other. They are also quite powerful—Aheed is easily the equal of a lesser noble of the Court. He, his wife and their two children, however, are a tenth of the djinn in North America.

"Aheed drives hard bargains, and djinn are tricksters by nature," Eric added. "Like in the old stories of them granting wishes, anything he does or offers will have a price—make sure you know what it is before agreeing to it. He's mostly a good guy, so it will rarely be huge, but be careful what you agree to."

"When do I get to meet him?" I asked.

Eric shrugged and pulled a second set of snowshoes out of thin air.

"I was thinking after breakfast?"

———

SNOWSHOEING through the buried city with Eric was a humbling reminder of where my physical prowess ranked against one of the true fae. I picked up the tricks and knacks quickly but was still hard pressed to keep up with a man slightly over half my height.

The sad part was that I could tell he was holding back, as much to avoid notice from the handful of people digging their way out around us as to let me keep up. He had more practice with the 'shoes and was faster and stronger than I was. On his own, Eric could have made the several-mile trip to Aheed's small inner-city bungalow in maybe fifteen minutes.

It took the two of us a little under an hour, which was still better time than we would have made driving in the mess of snow and slush the city had become. Snowplows were out, and people with heavy trucks were out driving repeatedly through the snow, packing it down for others who didn't have four-wheel drive.

Between the city workers and the gusto with which many of the city's people had thrown themselves into opening up roads and clearing pathways, I would be surprised if the city wasn't mostly open by evening. I was impressed.

Aheed's bungalow was one of the ones where the owner had clearly been out as early as I had. The driveway and front paths were cleared, but snow had drifted down over the course of the day to provide an inch or so of surface cover.

Eric strode confidently over the new snow and rang the doorbell. The door was swiftly answered by a woman who looked in her early twenties. She was dark-haired and dark-skinned, clearly of Middle Eastern extraction.

"Ah, Mr. Eric," she greeted the gnome. "And this would be your friend you wanted to introduce to my husband? Come in; get out of the cold."

"Jason Kilkenny, be known to Nageena Ibrahim," Eric told me as he led me into the warm bungalow. It was easily twenty-five, thirty degrees Celsius in the bungalow. Somehow, it didn't surprise me that the djinn kept their house at a level most of the city's other occupants would regard as eye-meltingly hot.

"Mr. Kilkenny, welcome." Nageena inclined her head to me and then turned to Eric. "My husband is downstairs. You know the way. I will bring tea."

Eric nodded to her and led the way for me through the bungalow. It was decorated with small Arabic-style hangings, all looking hand-woven.

"They're all Nageena's work," Eric told me when he saw me eyeing them. "Remember that she is over seventy—she's had a lot of time to make them, and a lot of time to get good at it."

It was easy, dealing with inhumans, to forget how old we all were. I didn't look any older than when I'd manifested at twenty-one, and I didn't expect to noticeably age for another forty or so years—and I was half-human.

Nageena and her husband were well past "retirement age" for mortals but still looked like young parents—too young, in fact, to have the adult children I knew they had. To look as old as Eric did meant the gnome was probably well into his third century at least.

My ruminations on Eric's age were interrupted by our entry into Aheed Ibrahim's underground computer lab. There was no way to describe it. Five separate computer towers were hooked into a bewildering array of monitors and cables and speakers. Despite the best efforts of what looked like industrial cooling units standing by what I realized was a commercial-grade server rack, it was even warmer down there than upstairs.

"Master Eric, Mr. Kilkenny," the dark-haired man sitting on a chair in the middle of all that technology greeted us. He turned to face us and rose to his feet, offering me his hand. "I am Detective Lieutenant Aheed Ibrahim," he introduced himself with a clipped, vaguely British accent.

"Good to meet you, Detective." I shook his hand and then took the seat he gestured me to. For all of the computers in the room, the two chairs other than Aheed's own looked like recent additions. "Thank you for agreeing to see me."

"I owe Eric a multiplicity of favors earned in several manners over some years," the djinni told me. "An opportunity to repay him is not something I will pass up lightly, and my position with the CPS provides me with access to information you would not otherwise be able to review. These computers"—he gestured around him—"are linked through secure connections to the CPS and Interpol servers."

"So, what information does Eric's favor get me?" I asked. "I am looking for—"

"Information on a group of vampires you believe entered the city some months ago," he interrupted me. "Eric advised me of the situation and I have done some research."

He turned back to the computers and fiddled for a moment, and a chart popped up on one of the monitors. "This is the missing-persons reports for Calgary, by month, for the last two years."

There was a sudden, sharp increase and Aheed pointed to it. "This surge started nine months ago—approximately when your vampires are believed to have arrived, correct?"

"Yeah," I agreed, eyeing the chart. If I was reading it correctly, missing-persons reports had doubled over a three-month period, stabilizing at twice their earlier level.

"These reports are a useful tool for looking for vampires," Aheed told me. "They are hemovores; they have no choice but to feed. Only the very strongest of them can feed and not kill.

"Unusually," he continued in his precise fashion, "several of our missing persons have resurfaced. While a portion, certainly, were ordinary cases, it is likely at least one or two are something...else."

"But they'd be obviously vampires," I objected. "Even to humans, they'd stick out."

"I would agree," he replied with a nod, "except that one of our reappearing persons went missing again a couple of weeks ago. His court-ordered therapist hasn't heard anything from him since a Saturday several weeks ago when, as I understand it, you and Clan Tenerim dealt with a group of vampires."

A click of Aheed's mouse threw a picture of a dark-haired young man up on another screen. "Recognize him?"

I looked at the picture long and hard, mentally hollowing out cheeks and adding the shadow of a moonlit night, and then nodded.

"He was one of the vampires who attacked me," I confirmed. He'd been the one who'd come after me with a cold-iron knife.

"And so, he was a vampire," Aheed said with satisfaction, and then brought up another picture of the young man. "This is Mike Russells two days before you and he fought," he continued. "Note that this photo was taken in daylight—this is a still frame taken from the police station security cameras."

Russells looked perfectly alive in the picture, shading his eyes from the sun as he calmly entered the police station.

"How?" I asked.

"Lifesblood," Eric said quietly. "Human blood mixed with heartstone would allow a vampire to do that. It would allow them to sustain a legal identity, one the cabal could use to buy property and vehicles."

"Did this Russells buy anything?" I asked.

"No," Ibrahim said, shaking his head. "He was too poor and broke for large purchases to be immediately justifiable. If he had survived, he would likely have 'come into some family money' and used it to open a front business of some variety. One of our other returned missing persons may still do that."

"So, none of them have?" I checked.

"No," he admitted.

"But they have to already have some base of operations," I told the two other men. "Have you discovered anything on that?"

Aheed brought up a map of the city with tiny red dots on it on another monitor—he hadn't turned any of them off yet. "If you analyze the distribution of missing-persons reports in the last nine months," he said, gesturing at the new image, "you'll note that they are disproportionately in the northwestern quarter of the city. The northwest is generally regarded as being a higher quality and is often disproportionately lower in missing-persons reports.

"That still, however, leaves you a full quadrant of the city for possible locations," he added, "including the entire university campus."

"That's not hugely helpful," Eric observed. "I expected better for one of my favors."

Wordlessly, Aheed passed me a USB stick.

"This drive contains all of the information I retrieved on our six remaining reappeared missing persons," he told me.

Aheed's comment on the university reminded me, and I looked at him.

"Which of these are the cases that turned out to be Sigridsen's murders?" I asked.

The djinni looked at me, surprised, and then fiddled for a moment, turning a grouping of the dots blue. "Those."

I stood and walked over to the monitor to look at it more closely. The blue grouping was off-center from the main grouping, more central-north, where most of the missing persons were scattered evenly over the northwest.

"She sticks out," I observed. "But she's how they got into the city.

She had to have prepared something. Do you know if she purchased any property—for that matter, what name was the house she was living in owned under?"

"I don't know," Aheed admitted, sounding surprised. "I can find out, though."

I turned toward him and pointed a finger at him as his fingers flew to the keyboard.

"Yes, but what will it cost me?"

The djinni stopped, his fingers suspended over the keyboard. For a moment, he tried to fake a shocked expression, and then he broke out into deep laughter.

"You warned him well, Eric," he told the gnome. The djinni turned his gaze on me as his wife came down the stairs behind me, the smell of tea suddenly filing the warm computer room.

"There is always a price with a djinni," Aheed told me. "You are quite right to ask what it will be. In this case..." He eyed me. "In exchange for everything I can discover about Sigridsen, properties she owned or was involved with that may lead you to the cabal, I want a blood sample."

"No," Eric snapped instantly. "I can call in another favor."

The djinni held up a hand. "You are not the one bargaining, my friend. My hobby is analyzing inhuman DNA," he explained to me. "Much of our nature is bound up in things that science cannot explain, but blood still reveals many secrets. In trade for one small vial of your blood, I will track down what connections Sigridsen had."

I looked at Eric, who shrugged helplessly. "It's a fair trade—*if* she had connections that can lead us to the cabal," he directed at Aheed.

The djinni shrugged in turn. "You are bargaining for my services, not for guarantees," he told me.

I considered it for a moment. My blood wouldn't, unless the djinn could do something I wasn't aware of, give Aheed any huge power over me. It was a minor thing, really.

"Done," I agreed.

"Good; now, if that's settled, can you three drink your tea?" Nageena instructed us as she set her tea tray down on a small table clearly kept down there for the purpose. "While you're doing that, I will grab my needles."

I sipped at the tea as Aheed turned back to his computer and went to work. A few minutes later, Nageena returned with a tray of sterile-looking medical equipment and a folding table. She quickly and efficiently laid my arm on the table and drew the one tiny vial of blood. A tiny ouch, a minor gross-out, and I had finished my side of the bargain.

"Sigridsen hasn't owned anything in her own name since the shifters burned her out last year," Aheed told me. "At least, not real estate property in Calgary. One house in Africa. Some shares, none of them enough to give her a noticeable say in any company."

"That's not very useful," I observed.

"No, but it does tell us that the house she was living wasn't held in her name," the detective said absently, scrolling through multiple databases as he switched between screens and monitors. "Ah, here. Sneaky woman."

"Oh?"

"Her full name was Dr Elisse Laura Sigridsen," Aheed told me. "However, according to this, she was married for five years when she was younger. For that time frame, she was Dr Elisse Laura *Marshall*. Being a sneaky woman, she managed to keep *Marshall* as a legally existing name when she went back to her maiden name.

"The house was owned by E. Laura Marshall," he concluded. "It has been for two years. There are, however, no other properties under that name."

"Damn," I cursed.

"Do not be so hasty," the djinni told me. "I agreed to trace all connections, and I have found one. Laura Marshall is one of the founding shareholders of a small investment trust operating in Calgary —a *real estate* investment trust. I have a list of apartments, a few warehouses—it's approximately eighty million dollars in property, with over seventy percent purchased in the last nine months even though the trust has been operating for three years."

"So, the company was originally hers, but the vampires took it over?"

"Almost certainly," he nodded. "May I have that again for a

moment?" Aheed took the USB stick away from me and plugged it back into the computer.

"Very well. I have added all the information I could find on both of her identities and on the Sigrid REIT. Their head offices are in the northwest, as are a significant portion of their properties."

"Somewhere to start," I agreed. "Thank you."

"The deal is kept," Aheed said in formal tones.

12

———

"WHAT ARE YOU GOING TO DO?" Eric asked me once we were outside again.

"I'm not sure," I admitted as I strapped myself into the snowshoes. "Check out the offices tomorrow night, late enough that any mortal staff should have gone home?"

"Want a suggestion?"

"I'll take one, sure," I admitted to him. "I'm still trying to get past flailing around lost, but I'm not sure how successful I'm being."

"Call Oberis," Eric said simply. "Jason, you're dealing with powers and factions and politics you know nothing about—and no one knows this city's inhuman politics better than our lord."

"Still don't want to trust the Enforcers?" I asked.

"If we need to bring them in, that should be Oberis's call," the gnome told me. "And if he makes it, he'll go straight to the Wizard. We can't do that."

"Will he help?" I asked. I had, after all, just caused Oberis a lot of trouble.

"You are fae; he is your lord," Eric said as we snowshoed our way across the still-buried streets. "Even if you weren't a Vassal of the

Queen, he would help. Now he knows what you are, he is *bound* to help by his fealty to the Nine."

Eric borrowed my phone and dialed the number for me before passing it back. The phone rang once, and then Oberis answered.

"What is it, Jason?" he asked abruptly.

"I have word on my task," I told him. "The Keeper advised that I bring it to you. We have a lea—"

"This is not something to discuss on the phone," Oberis cut me off. "Stay where you are."

He hung up, and I looked at Eric in confusion. "He said to stay here; I'm not sure why."

"So I can find you," a familiar voice said behind me, and I turned swiftly—only to tangle my feet in the snowshoes and crumple to the ground.

The Seelie lord laughed and helped me back to my feet. He hadn't bothered with snowshoes, simply standing lightly atop the thick drifts of snow in a pristinely white suit. Even compared to the chill of the winter day, his gloves were cold.

"Do you trust me, Vassal of my Queen?" he asked me, and offered me and Eric each one of his hands. The gnome took it unquestioningly, but I looked at him for a moment and then breathed deeply.

"I did call you," I admitted, and took his hand.

There was a flash of cold, cold *nothingness*, and then warmth wrapped itself around me. We stood in a featureless black expanse I recognized as Between, where the Queen had taken me to tell me of exactly what I'd been born to.

"Between," Oberis confirmed as he saw me glance around. "We are in a bubble of warmth and air sustained by my power. Here, unless a member of the Wild Hunt has followed us, we have perfect privacy."

I nodded. "I don't suppose Eric could conjure us some chairs?" I asked, with a glance at the gnome.

"Not here," he answered. "My 'conjuring', as you call it, is actually retrieving objects from a storage space I keep Between. I can't access it from here."

"You said you had word on your task from the Queen," Oberis said quietly, his white suit and fair skin seeming to glow in the dark of the

Between. After a moment, I realized it wasn't an illusion. The light we were seeing each other by was emanating from the noble's skin. "I assume this means you have learned something about the vampires."

"We have learned that they have turned at least one person taken in the city, and returned them to the population to act as their agent," I explained. "He used lifesblood to appear alive and interact with mortal authorities."

"Damn," he murmured. "Lifesblood—you're sure?"

"I saw the footage of the man walk and breathe as if alive, and yet it was barely a day later when we *know* he fought Jason here as a vampire," Eric confirmed. "Heartstone is the only way."

The fae lord turned away from us. "This is bad," he told the darkness beyond his circle of life and light. "It also explains how the vampires snuck into the city."

"Some of the Enforcers have betrayed the Low Covenant," I said quietly. The Low Covenant was the one that bound together every faction in a given city and laid out the laws they would function by.

Oberis nodded. "Our Covenant laid out exactly who got how much heartstone. So, either the heartstone is being funneled back into the city by one of the known recipient groups, which is unlikely, or it is being siphoned off at the source. By the Enforcers."

"Wouldn't the Wizard know he was betrayed?" I asked.

"He should," my lord answered grimly. "And yet clearly he *has* been betrayed and knows nothing of it. What else have you learned?"

"Under the name she owned the house I found her in, Sigridsen owned significant holdings in a real estate investment trust," I explained. "It owns apartments and condos all through the northwest, where the disappearances of people have been concentrated. The trust also owns several warehouses, and has an office near the University.

"Most of the property was bought since the vampires came here," I finished.

"Good enough reason to believe they are funneling money through this trust," Oberis agreed. "We need to act on this evidence ourselves," he told me and Eric. "If we could trust the Enforcers, I'd bring them in, but with evidence of corruption among their ranks, I must have enough evidence to go directly to Kenneth."

"What do you need of me?" Eric and I asked, almost simultaneously.

"Of you, Eric, nothing," Oberis said gently. "If you can do your best to keep the Unseelie quiet until this is resolved, I would appreciate the effort, though.

"Of you, Jason, patience," he continued. "You are the representative of our Queen in this, so I would have you present, but it will take me time to quietly assemble the arms and people for such a task. If I acted today, all I could send would be you and Laurie.

"Give me three days, and I can assemble a strike team of gentry and major non-noble fae," he told me. "You will primarily go in with them as an observer, but you will accompany them. Acceptable?"

I thought about it for a minute. "You can't act yourself?" I asked. Oberis on his own would be far more comforting support than a dozen gentry or "major non-noble fae"—like Laurie.

"I am bound by the Low Covenant myself," Oberis reminded me. "I cannot become personally involved in things without talking to Kenneth first. So, we will need a chance to assemble a team. Keep your head down until then, all right?"

"Okay," I agreed. "It makes sense. Thank you," I added.

Suddenly, the three of us were standing in my sparsely furnished living room.

"I will do what I can," the Seelie lord told us. "It is in everyone's interest to see the feeders driven from the city. Enjoy your snow day," he instructed, and *stepped* back Between, vanishing from my apartment.

———

IN THE MORNING, Bill called and asked if I wanted a ride to work. I gratefully accepted the offer and was delivered to the dispatch office before anyone else had arrived. I followed Bill into the back, thinking I'd help him set up the pickup loads. Instead, to my surprise, he pointed me to a chair.

"We have about ten minutes before Trysta gets here, and I wanted to talk to you," he told me gruffly. "There's a camera in this office," he said bluntly. "I'm not sure *what* you were looking up on our computers that late at night, and I know you didn't steal anything, but I'm still not overly impressed with you breaking in here."

For a moment, I was too shocked to say anything. My boss waited patiently until I got my composure back, then I met his gaze and shrugged helplessly.

"Dead to rights," I admitted in my soft Southern drawl. "I didn't know there was a camera, and I know I didn't damage the lock. I just needed to look up a customer for...personal business."

Bill nodded. "Look, I know Sarah is involved in something," he said quietly. "I assumed you were too when she sent you to me. I don't give a shit if it's drugs, the mob, or gunrunning—but it stays out of this office. No harm done this time, but if my business gets dragged into whatever you're messed up in, I will break you."

All of this was said in the same quiet, perfectly level voice. I could feel his disappointment as a physical thing in the room with us.

"It won't happen," I promised. Like I'd told Michael, I didn't want Direct to get stuck in any of the messes I was involved in. It *wouldn't* happen, no matter what it took.

"Good," he grunted. "Let's set up the loads."

The rest of the morning passed in companionable silence until Trysta showed up. She cheered up the office with a bright "Good morning, boys!" and then set to work with us.

By the time the rest of the drivers showed up, we had the first morning loads and pickup routes set up and ready to go. I checked my own schedule and headed out to my truck to program in the GPS.

When I got the text from Michael telling me to meet him, I'd already finished programming the appropriate Starbucks into my GPS. I got there to find him, once again, waiting for me with a steaming cup of coffee.

"You're going to have to be damn careful about that promise of yours," I told him sharply as I took the coffee. "My boss is aware that I have 'connections' to something, and he does *not* want that spilling over onto them."

The Enforcer shrugged his shoulders. "We will do the best we can," he said. "That is all I can offer; you know that."

He pulled a small box and a plain white mailing envelope out of his car and passed them to me.

"For the airport again?" I asked, not realizing until I took the envelope that it was unaddressed.

"Not this time," Michael said, shaking his head. "The envelope is for you—consider it our payment for your services so far. The package has an address on it—Ink Quill Industries; they're in the northeast near the airport, so delivering there shouldn't be a problem."

I glanced at the address on the label. My slowly growing awareness of the locations of things in the city agreed with his assessment of the office's location. A faint whiff of a spicy scent I couldn't quite make out caught my nose before the cold wind swept it away.

Sliding the package into my truck, I opened the envelope. It contained cash—crisp, clean twenty- and fifty-dollar bills totaling about a week's worth of my salary.

"A bribe to keep my mouth shut?" I asked.

"Compensation for services rendered," Michael disagreed. "We reward those who work with us, Jason."

If everyone rewarded those who worked with them like the Enforcers and Oberis, I almost didn't need to work for Direct!

I pocketed the money and shrugged. "All right, I'll see your package delivered," I told him. He nodded and returned to his gray sedan with the stylized K symbol decaled onto its wing mirrors.

With a sigh, I got back into my truck, turning the heat up to beat back the city's vicious cold. On one hand, vampires and fae lords, and on the other, a day job and a "police" force all too eager to exploit said job for their own purposes.

If the vampires didn't kill me, job stress might.

INK QUILL INDUSTRIES turned out to be a midsized building that looked like it contained a factory, a warehouse and an office, buried in the middle of a small industrial and warehousing district south of the airport. The name of the company was on the side of a large quill-pen logo with stylized drops of red ink on the tip.

The parking lot was all but empty and it looked like the factory was shut down. I pulled in next to a blue compact car and eyed the snow that covered the parking lot. Someone had gone through at some point with a snowblower and cleared off most of it, but it still looked frozen and slippery.

With a sigh, I pulled my gloves on and grabbed my clipboard and the delivery package. Whatever else moving up to Calgary had taught me, it was teaching me a little bit of tolerance for cold.

Not that said tolerance would stop me bitching about the cold anytime soon, and I was cursing under my breath as I half-ran across the slippery parking lot to the office door and ducked inside.

The heavily tinted glass with its silkscreen quill pens had kept me from realizing it was one of those two-door setups, with an interior door a secretary has to buzz you through. Of course, to add insult to confusion, the inner doors were also silkscreened and heavily tinted, and I could barely see through well enough to tell that there was no one at the front desk.

There was a buzzer by the locked inner door, however, and I hit that. I heard it sound on the other side of the glass, faintly. I waited a minute or so and pushed the buzzer again.

I was about ready to hit the buzzer for a third time when I finally saw movement on the other side of the glass. A figure, heavily blurred by the tinting, walked up to the front desk and hit a button. The door in front of me clicked and I entered the building.

A young, fair-haired man stood behind the desk in suit pants and a dress shirt. He waved me forward into the office.

"Sorry, I was in the back, *trying* to set up a print job," he said cheerfully. "Most of our guys and gals are *totally* snowed in; they're not getting anywhere till something *radically* melts this snow."

"I have a package for Ink Quill," I told him, passing him the clipboard.

"*Awesome!*" He took the clipboard in one hand and offered me his other. "I'm James Langley, the VP of operations and one of *only* three of us who made it through this *spectacular* snow dump."

The man's enthusiasm shone through even bad news, and I

couldn't help returning his smile as he dashed off an extravagant signature on the clipboard and passed it back to me.

I handed him the box, and he took a quick glance at it.

"I've been *waiting* for this," he said. "*So* glad you could make it through this *total* wreck of a city. Want a tour of the presses? It *totally* doesn't look like we're getting much else done."

Somehow while he was enthusiastically proclaiming, the box managed to disappear into the desk.

"Presses?" I asked.

"Yeah, we're a *totally radical* small independent book-binding and print shop, man," he explained. "Take special orders for some *amazing* folks—pamphlets, self-published authors, those sorts of *radicals*. Helping *change* the world in our own small way."

"I'd love to see the place, but I have to get back to our dispatch," I told him. "Like you said, the city is a bit of a wreck, but the deliveries must go through."

"'Neither snow nor rain nor heat nor gloom of night stays these couriers from the swift completion of their appointed rounds,'" Langley quoted at me, and then laughed at my somewhat blank return look. "I guess that's the US post service, isn't it? And it's just an inscription anyway, if a *totally* awesome one. Powers speed you; drive safe."

"And may They guard your hold," I answered automatically before I realized this theoretically mortal human had just used an *inhuman* blessing. He winked at me and buzzed the door to allow me out.

"Like I said, we work for some *amazing* folk," he told me, and allowed me to flee to my courier truck, where I found myself huddling in on myself for warmth as it warmed up and I thought.

There *were* humans who knew about the inhuman world—I was pretty sure that was part of how we kept our presence secret—but I'd assumed most were like Bill. Bill knew *something* was going on and was not unwilling to help if favors were called in, but he didn't know or want to know everything.

Langley was clearly sufficiently "in the know" to either know or guess that I wasn't human, and to know a blessing most inhumans would respond to instantly. I guess even our world needed its books and pamphlets, and a small print press would be the perfect size for the sort of quantities we would need.

I started the truck into motion, both intrigued and somewhat disturbed by the thought of a world that had never even occurred to me existed—one of humans recruited into supporting the inhumans and given enough knowledge to be able to do so.

It was a surprisingly strange thought.

13

THE REST of the day passed in the calm frenzy inevitable when the roads were horrible and your job mainly involved driving from place to place. I passed at least five separate accidents, but thanks to my fae reflexes and the high quality of the delivery truck's tires, I made it through my delivery routes an hour or so late but perfectly safe.

I returned home through now mostly clear streets to an email from Oberis, letting me know that he was coordinating several people, and that I should come to the Court tomorrow for five PM. I dashed off a quick reply letting him know I would be there, and moved on to other emails.

The second of these was from Tarvers.

I know you are forbidden to contact us, he began, *but nobody has been stupid enough to tell me I can't contact you.*

We've dug into the files in Sigridsen's computer. They're all majorly encrypted and some pile of gibberish my tech boys fed me to explain why it's taking so long to get any useful data out of them. From what they have got, we've managed to track down two of the cabal's members—both outsiders brought into the city.

Neither was overly cooperative and both are now dead. One, however, had a quantity of lifesblood in his apartment—if you don't know what that is, suffice to say it has an ingredient that is highly controlled by the Enforcers.

We are backtracking the feeder's movements and dealings as best we can, and we think we have some clues as to where he got the 'blood. I'm going to see them followed up, and I will email you again once we know more.

I will be in touch. And call Mary. If anyone counts that as contacting the Clan, I'll claw them into silence.

I reread the email twice. At least *someone* was getting somewhere productive with this whole mess. The fact that the shifters had found lifesblood confirmed the suspicion Eric and I had shared. Hopefully, they could track it back to its source.

If we could identify the specific Enforcers who had broken the Covenants and provided heartstone to the vampires, we could get the Magus to punish them. That kind of proof would shake up the whole city, but it would also see the guilty punished—which would probably lead us to the cabal and whatever conspiracy against MacDonald the Queen wanted me to pursue.

Reading the email a fourth time, I decided to obey his last instructions and called Mary. The phone rang several times, and I was beginning to fear I'd either called at a really bad time or she didn't want to talk to me after all.

Then she answered the phone.

"Hi!" she said breathlessly. "Sorry, you caught me in the middle of something."

"I can call back later," I offered, suddenly worried I'd caught her with a guy or something. That thought triggered a spark of an anger and unexpected spasm in my chest.

"No, I was, um, just thinking about you, actually," Mary said awkwardly. "I wasn't sure I'd ever hear from you again; Tarvers told me you'd been banned from contacting the Clan."

Not quite sure what she meant by that, I answered her second comment.

"Tarvers told me to contact you," I told her. "He said he'd 'claw into silence' anyone who counted it as contacting the Clan."

She chuckled quietly. "I guess he likes you," she said. "I think he threatened to claw the last guy I was interested in into pieces if he didn't go away."

I swallowed. Somehow, the concept of Tarvers as overprotective patriarch of the women of his Clan was...very plausible.

"I do have to ask one question," Mary said, and her voice was suddenly colder. "Were you only seeing me to use me for information?"

"No," I said instantly. "That you could help me made it easier to work up the nerve to do so, but it was hardly my only reason. And I never lied to you," I added.

"So Tarvers said." Her voice was suddenly warm again. "He said you looked him in the eye and said that, but that you couldn't explain why not."

"I have orders from *a* fae Court," I said simply. "Just not Oberis. I really can't say more."

"I guess," she answered, and was quiet for a moment. "I'm still pissed at you."

"I don't suppose I can blame you," I said after a moment, feeling small.

We were both quiet for a long moment, and then a hunch struck me.

"Can I buy you dinner to make it up?"

"Good boy," she said with a soft laugh. "Yes, yes, you can. There's an Indian restaurant—Namskar's—about fifteen minutes' walk north of you. Meet me there in an hour?"

"Tonight?" I asked, surprised by her sudden shift in mood.

"Why not? I had no other plans!"

I mentally shrugged.

"In an hour, then," I agreed. "I need to change; see you then?"

"Me too," she said. "See you."

Shaking my head, I hung up the phone and went looking for some of my nicer clothes.

———

I'D DONE a little bit of clothes shopping since being employed and collecting a few payouts for various services, so I managed to come up with nice slacks and a dress shirt to wear underneath my heavy winter jacket.

I quickly showered, shaved and threw on said slacks and shirt before heading out. It was likely to be faster to walk than wait for a bus, but it was a chilly night. Walking briskly through the foggy dark lit by streetlights and car headlights, I managed to stay somewhat not-frozen until I reached the red brick building that contained the restaurant Mary had suggested.

Stepping inside, I found the restaurant was quiet enough that I quickly secured a table for two and managed to shed my winter coat. Looking less like the Calgary winter default of a puffy marshmallow, I settled into my chair and ordered a tea while I waited.

Five minutes after the hour she'd suggested, Mary arrived. Her small form was entirely lost in a padded blue winter coat that hung all the way to her ankles. She saw me and joined me at my table with a brilliant smile that I nearly lost myself in before regaining wits enough to stand up and take her coat.

Under it she wore a tight red sweater and black jeans that accentuated every single curve of her body, and I swear I simply ogled her for a good few seconds before hanging up her coat and accepting her hug hello.

"It's good to see you," she said as we took seats opposite each other. "With everything that went down, I wasn't sure you'd be willing to see me again."

"Powers, no," I admitted. "The only reason I hadn't called was because I was forbidden to talk to the Clan."

She smiled at me and then glanced down at her menu. We both went through them in companionable silence until we found what we wanted, and put them aside to wait for the waitress.

"I'm sorry for using you for information," I said quietly after we ordered. "I don't have a lot of contacts in this city, or I wouldn't have."

"We lean on the friends we have," she told me. "It's not like you weren't up-front about what you were asking for. Are you having any luck on your end?"

"Some," I said cautiously, looking around the restaurant full of humans. "Not sure how much I should talk about it in public—or at all."

She nodded acceptance of that. "All right, then, tell me about you!"

"What do you want to know?" I responded, fumbling for some acceptable answer.

"Well, tell me about your parents," she decided.

"My mother was a historian and apparently a changeling, though I didn't know that till after she passed on," I told her, speaking quietly enough when mentioning the inhuman parts, I was reasonably sure no one else heard me. "I was raised on a university campus, for all purposes."

"I'm sorry about your mom," Mary said impulsively, reaching across the table to squeeze my hand. "How did your dad take it?"

"I don't know," I said. "I've never known him—no idea if he's even alive or not. About all I know is that he was true fae."

The redheaded girl across the table from me shook her head, and I realized she hadn't let go of my hand. A slight shift on my part and we were holding hands across the table, which she met with a brilliant smile.

"The whole changeling thing is hard for me to grasp," she admitted, also speaking quietly so we wouldn't be overheard. "Shifter...genes, for lack of a better word, are much more dominant—any child of a shifter is a shifter, end of story. One reason why there's so many of us, I guess."

I nodded. Fae, *including* changelings, worldwide only had about three quarters the numbers of the shifters, and between fae and shifters, we made up almost two thirds of the inhuman population of the world.

Of course, said population was around a hundred and fifty, maybe a hundred and sixty thousand people all told—a tad less than a quarter of one hundredth of a percent of the world's population.

Our dinner arrived, interrupting that line of discussion. I finally released Mary's hand so I could eat, and dug in with ravenous hunger.

After a few minutes of both of us thoroughly demolishing our food —both of our species had highly active metabolisms, after all—I eyed

Mary across the table and snuck my hand out onto the table. I didn't quite take hers, but I definitely offered mine.

She quickly slid her hand into mine with that same brilliant smile.

"What about you?" I asked. "What's your family like?"

"Well, there's Clementine, the doctor, who *everyone* in the Clan looks up to," she started. "There's Mom, the dire wolf shifter from Ireland—I've mentioned her. She passed on when Clementine and I were still kids."

She was quiet for a moment, probably reflecting on the similarities to how her mother had died and the current situation with the vampire cabal.

"What was your father like?" I asked to break that chain of thought.

"He was the lynx shifter who fell in love with and earned the love of a dire wolf," Mary said simply. "What he lacked in power he made up in charisma, wisdom and the willpower to stand up to anyone. I remember, when I was younger and Tarvers was a new Alpha, my father arguing him down from some of his more dangerous plans.

"It was my father who negotiated the Covenants between Tarvers, Oberis and MacDonald," she told me. "I think that was when he managed to convince my mother he was worth her time. He had the will and wisdom to talk three powerful men into working together instead of staying at loggerheads."

"What happened to him?" I asked softly.

"Car accident," Mary said, her voice equally soft, and I squeezed her hand comfortingly. "One of those freak things that can happen to anyone—he was hit by a semi, crossing the street. There is damage even shifters can't heal—he was killed instantly."

The arrival of the bill distracted us from the morbid tone of the conversation, and I quickly paid it. Dinner sorted, Mary rose from her seat, offering me her hand to pull myself to my feet.

"Walk with me?" she asked as we pulled on our coats.

I nodded and followed her out of the restaurant. We walked a bit of the ways down the street, shivering against the cold until we'd passed out of sight of anyone in the foggy night. Once the fog had enwrapped us in glittering whiteness, Mary stopped and turned into me.

My arms came up around her almost without thinking, and for a long moment, we simply stood in the night, sharing warmth and holding each other. I couldn't say which of us moved to kiss the other first, but heat warmed me from the inside as our lips touched.

We stood there like that, warming each other, for a long moment, and then a cold breeze swept through the fog and we both shivered, breaking apart slightly.

"Mary, I—" I began, but she laid her finger on my lips.

"Jason," she said quietly, "if you were about to suggest *anything* other than going back to your apartment and continuing this in warmth, don't."

14

As it turned out, Mary had neither experience with nor enthusiasm for the idea of waking up at five o'clock in the morning. Her response to my alarm going off was to tighten her arms around me. Since we were both completely naked, this was more than a slight distraction from my plan to get up and ready for work.

It was with more than a little regret that I squeezed out of her embrace and began the process of getting ready. Shared blankets were *warm*, and the basement apartment was cold first thing in a winter morning.

I showered and shaved and dressed for work, and then sat back down on the bed next to Mary and leaned in to kiss her gently awake. She didn't move for a moment, then slowly opened her eyes and returned the kiss.

"I have to go to work," I told her quietly. "I take it you don't get up this early."

"Not really," she admitted sleepily, the blanket falling away from her and exposing a very nice view.

"The door locks from the inside, if you want to sleep a bit longer," I told her, leaning in to kiss her again. "I do have to go, though."

She pouted adorably for a moment but then nodded.

"I'll make sure everything's locked up," she promised. "Are you free tonight?"

"No," I said sadly. "I have some Court business to deal with after work."

"Okay," she murmured, sliding back down into the bed. "Call me when you can; let me know when we can hang out, 'kay?"

I carefully tucked the blankets up around her and claimed one last kiss.

"You bet on it," I promised. She smiled sleepily at me and I quietly left the room, turning the light back off as I did.

The morning chill seemed minor and unnoticeable as I walked to work. Part of that was my frame of mind, and the rest was that the temperature had clearly risen. A check of my phone showed we were going to have highs around freezing, instead of twenty degrees lower than that, for the rest of the week.

I drifted in to work with a cheery smile on my face and immediately fell to helping everyone get set up for the day. With everyone's loads and pickups established, I left a few minutes early, heading out on my route.

Halfway through my morning run, I got a text from Michael telling me there wouldn't be a pickup today. Meeting him had become such a regular thing that I had to take the most convenient Starbucks out of the route my GPS was calculating to get me back to the office.

The day passed quietly. The lack of more snow after the snowstorm meant the roads were now almost completely cleared. Many places were still accessed by narrow canyons of cleared path through waist-high banks of snow, but everywhere had managed to dig themselves out by day three after the storm.

I was honestly impressed. I'd never seen a snowstorm like the one that had struck, and I'd expected it to take more than two or three days for everything to return to mostly normal. Everyone had spent the first day digging out of their homes, the second day digging into their workplaces, and the third day acting like nothing had happened.

I finished my routes exactly on time and checked quickly in with Trysta before grabbing a cab. For all that it was warming up in the city; I still wasn't planning on trying to take transit to get to the hotel that doubled as the fae Court for this city. It was cold out, the roads, while improved, still sucked—and I did *not* want to be late to meet Oberis.

The cab delivered me to the hotel and I paid in cash, entering the building just over five minutes before Oberis had told me to arrive. I followed a young man in a dark gray suit with long blond hair into the lobby and checked the conference board.

"Talisman Energy" had booked the C wing today, I noted, and then I walked to the doors to that wing of the hotel. The blond youth I'd followed in had beaten me there and was shaking hands with both of the guards.

One of the guards noticed me and gestured me forward. I joined them and the newcomer in front of the security doors.

Now I got a closer look at the newcomer, I saw the resemblance to Oberis immediately. His hair was cut almost identically and was the same shade of gold. His eyes shared the lord's tawny gold and his chin followed Oberis's sharp lines. There were differences as well, but this youth was clearly closely related to the Seelie lord.

The guards waved me through and the noble youth followed me into the hallway. We walked forward until the carpet turned to moss in silence, and then he eyed me sideways.

"So, you're the changeling who's been stirring up such a ruckus?" he asked. "Jason, right?"

"I guess so," I admitted in my slow Southern drawl. "And you are?"

"Talus," he answered. "I'm normally Oberis's representative up in Fort McMurray, but he called me down here to help deal with the commotion you've raised."

"Which you shouldn't be discussing in public." Laurie's cold voice cut into our conversation as the hag stepped out of a door to join us in the hallway, tucking a cellphone away in a pocket of her conservative business suit as she did. "Lord Oberis is waiting for us; let's go."

With a shrug at me, Talus fell into step on one side of the hag while I joined them on the other, allowing her to lead the way for all three of us.

She led us down the same hallway Oberis had led me down after my first visit there, and then into Oberis's office. Oberis was sitting behind his desk, watching us enter, his fingers steepled on the desk in front of him.

Two men and one woman, all with the neatly perfect features of the gentry, were seated waiting for us alongside three empty chairs. Without being instructed, I took one, as did Talus and Laurie.

"I'm glad you could join us," Oberis told Talus. "I hope my call didn't interrupt anything up north?"

"Naw," Talus replied. "We just finished the semi-annual audit of the heartstone production. Speaking of which—" He pulled a folder of papers out from under his suit jacket and tossed it on Oberis's desk.

"What's the summary?" the Seelie lord asked, glancing at the folder without picking it up. "It may be relevant to this whole affair."

"We checked and double-checked after you warned us about lifesblood in the feeders' possession," the young noble told us all. "None of the known production is going astray, and we've got enough agents and contacts in the projects to be certain there's no hidden production.

"In short, if heartstone is going missing, it's after it reaches Calgary, not at the source," he concluded.

"So, from the Enforcers or one of the Covenant's authorized receivers, then," Oberis said grimly. "We have reviewed our own stockpiles, and the Clans destroy their share. It's not coming from us or them. But there are receivers outside the city, so it could be any of them."

The Seelie lord shook his head and eyed us all over his hands.

"For those who don't know," which I suspected was only me, "Talus is my nephew and the Court's senior representative up at the oil sands projects in Fort McMurray, where he watches over heartstone production to be sure none goes astray and that we get our fair share.

"Given what he just told us, it looks like our best bet for finding the heartstone source is to track it through the vampires, which is why you all are here," he continued.

"Thanks to Jason here"—he nodded toward me—"we now know of a company, a real estate investment trust, founded by the doctor who helped the vampires enter the city. Review of its records show that its investment base has dramatically increased in the last nine months— since the time we believe the vampires entered the city.

"Much of said investment is through shell companies and holding agencies," he added. "This makes it difficult for us to track down what properties are owned, but we *can* find the offices of the REIT itself.

"You six are going to raid said offices," he told us. "You are operating under my sanction, so tell any Enforcers that give you difficulty to refer their issues to me. You are sanctioned to use whatever force necessary against any vampires you encounter—I would prefer prisoners, but I'll settle for corpses over free vampires, clear?"

I nodded in grim acceptance, and so did the others in the room.

"Humans involved, I leave to your discretion," Oberis said quietly. "Minimize injuries or fatalities if possible, but do what is necessary. Remember that most of the employees will have no clue what is really going on; that is why you are going in at night. However, some will be fully aware of their employers and what they're involved in."

"Though they may not know the rest of us exist," Talus interjected. "Vampires recruiting humans tend to try and pretend they are the only part of the supernatural that exists—trying to draw on the *Twilight* influence and similar 'vampires are our friends' tripe."

Oberis nodded. "Exactly," he said. "You are all capable of taking on any humans involved; the only real threat is vampires on site.

"I want prisoners if possible, records regardless," he said. "Paperwork, property deeds, invoices, entire hard drives—clean them out. Don't let the police get called.

"Talus is in command," he finished. "Good luck."

With that, we were dismissed and followed Talus out of the office and back deeper into the hotel. We headed downstairs, into the basement of the hotel, where the moss and wall murals faded away to bare concrete marked with fae-sign.

Talus led us to a solid metal door guarded by a fae in a security uniform and unmarked by fae or human signs. The guard checked Talus's security card against a reader and then a clipboard list, and then finally stood aside, allowing us into the Calgary fae Court's armory.

I tended to forget, given how few members the Court in Calgary has, just how pervasive the finances and influence of even a small joint

Seelie-Unseelie Court like Calgary are. The armory drove the truth home, though.

In a country where hunting rifles were difficult to acquire and handguns almost impossible, the Court's armory had hanging coat racks of body armor in every size. Cabinets of long arms, from assault rifles to automatic shotguns, lined one wall, where the other had neatly organized rows of handguns, machine pistols, and submachine guns. The far wall sported a small number of machine guns and rocket and grenade launchers, but the centerpiece of the entire armory was two massive oak wardrobe-like standing closets.

The oak they'd been built of was almost black with age, and they had no handles or locks, only intricate patterns of runes that would open the doors to the right words and uses of power. Inside were the prizes of any court—the orichalcum-enhanced and rune-empowered magical weapons forged by the gnomes, and often passed down through families for generations.

Talus went straight for the machine pistols, pulling out concealed holsters and tossing them to each of us.

"Put these on and grab one of the machine pistols," he instructed.

I quickly examined the holster, which had been modified slightly to take the different size and bulk of a machine pistol from an ordinary handgun, and then grabbed a gun. It had the T shape familiar from popular media of an Uzi, but was only half again the size of the small pistol I had left at home—an IWI Ltd. Micro Uzi, according to the neat labeling on the case I removed it from.

For all the neat and detailed labeling, and the readily available preloaded twenty-round magazines that I collected five of, the serial number on the weapon had been neatly filed off. How the gun had made its way from its manufacturer in Israel to the armories of a supernatural organization in Western Canada was a mystery to me, and hopefully would remain a mystery no matter what happened to the weapon in question.

Laurie was eyeballing everyone's size and passing out vests. These were plain Kevlar, no runic enhancements that I could see, but I put the one she gave me on over my shirt and the runic armor I wore under it regardless.

It took us fifteen minutes to pass out weapons and ammo and put on the vests. We then all put our heavy winter coats back on, their bulk easily concealing the body armor and hidden weapons.

Then Talus went around again, sticking a radio/microphone earpiece on everyone and double-checking all of our gear one final time.

"Everyone ready?" he asked, and we nodded. "Let's go."

———

THE YOUNG FAE noble led us out the back of the hotel, to a dark green SUV with tinted windows. Night had reclaimed the city as we'd prepared, along with a chilly fog that diffused the light from the streetlights and left the city a glittering white wonderland against the shadow.

We introduced ourselves in the SUV as we drove through the city. Two of the gentry on the team turned out to be a brother and sister, two redheads in formfitting body armor named Dave and Elena. The third was an overly serious fair-haired youth named Robert.

Robert was carrying a black briefcase containing a laptop and some other tools I hadn't caught sight of when he was loading them. Listening to him talk to Dave and Elena, I quickly realized that he was even younger than me. Gentry lived a long time; it was easy to misjudge their ages.

With the snow and fog and traffic, we were easily an hour getting to the offices for Sigrid REIT. The last ten minutes or so of the trip passed in silence as everyone checked equipment and weapons.

This was the first time in my life I'd ever headed into a situation where I presumed there would be violence. I spent most of that last ten-minute silence checking there were bullets in the magazines I was carrying for the Micro Uzi.

"First time expecting trouble?" Dave eventually asked me, causing me to realize I was checking the magazine in my gun for the third time.

"Yeah," I admitted. "Most of my encounters have been...surprises."

"Well," he said slowly, "to be blunt, you're slower and weaker than everyone else here. Hang back, shoot at anything that comes right at you, and let us deal with any major threats. Elena and Talus and I have worked together before, and we all know Laurie and Robert as well. We'll be fine."

I nodded, and slotted the magazine pack into the machine pistol as Talus slowed the van.

"We're here," he said quietly. He turned to look back at us. "Robert and I will go in first and deal with the security system. You four move up and secure the entrance. Corral anyone who tries to leave. Don't kill anyone you don't have to."

I followed Elena and Dave out of the car, and Laurie quickly stepped in to cover the rear as we moved to cover the main doors of the ten-story office building as Talus and Robert went inside.

"Door is locked," Robert reported over the earpieces, and then the door popped open in front of him. "Not an issue; no alarm here."

The two figures vanished into the building, heading for the stairs down.

"No security on this floor I can sense," Talus said quietly into the radio. "There's enough iron in the building I can't sense if anyone's in above us."

"At the security office, hooking in," Robert said, almost talking over him. "Looks like all the cameras are being fed offsite. Cycling through them all now."

There was a pause, and the four of us standing outside shivered, waiting.

"There's no one in the building," he told us, and a huge weight slipped off my shoulders. "Which is weird," he continued. "There should be at least one security guard. Looping the feeds; you're good to go in—but watch your backs. This doesn't smell right."

Dave moved forward first, opening the doors while Elena covered him.

"Remember," Talus said over the radio, "just because the cameras didn't see anyone doesn't absolutely guarantee there's no one up there. Watch your step. We'll join you at the stairs."

We reached the stairwell door, which was sealed by a keypad and magnetic lock. Laurie gestured the rest of us out of the way and laid her hand on the door. A moment later, she pulled her hand back and the door opened with it.

Talus and Robert were on the other side, and the fae noble gestured us up the stairs before leading the way. Sigrid REIT was on the eighth floor.

Eight floors passed quickly and in silence, Talus stopping us at each floor so he could scan the floor with his sixth sense. Reaching the eighth floor, though, he didn't even slow down. As soon as he reached the door, it clicked unlocked and swung open for him.

"Show-off," Laurie muttered over the radio.

"Quiet," he ordered. "Search the floor, check for hard drives and paper..." He trailed off at the end of the sentence as we walked out on to the floor and saw the state of what *had* been Sigrid REIT's offices.

"It didn't look like this on the cameras," Robert said quietly, as we surveyed the chaos.

Someone—or a group of someones—had swept through the office like a hurricane. Filing cabinets were overturned. Computer desks rearranged. Several computer towers looked like someone had taken an ax to them repeatedly. Feeble sparks still glowed in the pile of ashes that looked like it had been a foot-deep pile of papers.

Laurie stood still in the doorway, still mostly in the stairwell. "What the hell?"

"The place has been cleaned out," Elena said briskly. "There may still be something around we can retrieve; let's take a look."

The gentry and Talus started moving forward, and my teeth started to itch. The sensation was familiar, and I focused on it for a moment as I followed.

Cold iron! I could feel cold iron somewhere around. The others presumably sensed it too, but Talus and the three gentry seemed unbothered, starting to separate and move apart. It wasn't a big chunk of cold iron, just little bits. Lot of little bits. Lots and lots...

"EVERYBODY DOWN," I yelled, and dove forward, tackling Talus and slamming him down to the ground as the first claymore mine detonated.

Cold-iron ball bearings ripped through the room at waist height, and a second claymore detonated. I could feel the iron whizzing across my back, and then suddenly Talus and I were falling. The floor beneath us vanished in a burst of fae Power and we dropped.

Only moments later, another explosion rocked the floor above us as more explosives, these not the cold iron–filled claymores but more traditional charges, shattered structural beams and blew out windows.

We kept falling, wrapped in a glowing nimbus of force as Talus blasted his way through each floor in turn, more explosions echoing above us. We hit the main floor with a shock I felt reverberate through my bones and flesh, even with Talus cushioning us.

The fae noble was on his feet before I even processed that we'd stopped falling. He grabbed me by the collar of my jacket and dragged me across the floor as he pulled me out of the building.

He got us clear and turned back to look at the building. The top three floors of the office were just *gone*, the last support pillars collapsing inward as I watched the growing inferno consume the last clue I had to fulfilling my Queen's mission.

Then I spotted motion out of the blaze, and a black figure leapt from the sixth or seventh floor; I couldn't tell which with the smoke. They plummeted half the distance to the ground, and then Talus had his hand outstretched, slowing and stopping the fall, pulling the figure toward us.

He guided Laurie to a soft landing on the snow pile. All glamors lost to the flames, the hag bore every ounce of her true hideous face, and I doubt Robert had ever seen anything so beautiful. The young gentry lay broken in her arms, one of his legs sheared clean off, and I could *feel* the burn of the cold iron that had done it as Talus and I rushed to him.

"He's dying," Laurie coughed through the smoke. "I don't know how much iron is in him. I think he missed the claymore blasts, thanks to your warning."

"Enough," Talus said shortly, then looked at me. "You can sense cold iron?" he demanded.

"I thought everyone could?"

"No," he told me flatly. "It's rare. I can't." He paused, looking down at the moaning boy, and then back at me. "And it can save him. Do you trust me?"

For three years, I had learned never to trust the noble fae. I had learned my kind were capricious and callous and often cruel. And even Robert was true fae, almost noble.

And it didn't matter. A boy was dying on the snow in front of me, red blood staining the stark white beneath him.

I gave Talus my hand and, for the first time in my life, shared minds with a noble of the fae.

15

"I AM NO MORE prepared to risk my son than the humans are," a voice boomed. "The way the Germans keep going, there won't be much *left* of London by spring!"

I peeked through a crack in the door, watching my father and mother argue. A bomb had fallen close to the house last night, and many of my schoolmates, fae and human, had been sent into the country. Few who could manage to be elsewhere were still in London.

"But to Canada?" my mother demanded. "It's so far, and the sea isn't safe."

"Calebrant has offered to carry him Between with the Wild Hunt, with the other children of the Courts," my father—no, *Talus's* father; I was seeing his memories, ones the current circumstance brought to the forefront of his mind—said. "They will carry our future to safety. We can walk the paths ourselves to visit if time allows, but bombs pay no more dignity to our kind than to humans. I *must* know the heir to my clan is safe." Talus's father softened his voice, and his pain leaked in. "I must know Talus is safe, now that we've lost his brother."

THAT WAS the last time Talus had seen his parents, at the age of twelve. He'd been taken aboard the personal mount of Lord Calebrant—the Wild Hunt's master, a dark-haired twig of a fae, slightly built and short for a fae lord at less than six feet tall—and carried through the darkness to Canada.

Two weeks later, his father's words had been proven true. A bomb had destroyed the ancestral home of his fae family. After the Blitz, Talus had never returned, raised in Calgary by his uncle Oberis.

Older and wiser now, Talus looked to the gentry of the city for the closest thing to equals, to their children for his hope for the future. He'd watched Robert grow up. Always from a distance. Never from close up.

Close up, someone might see the resemblance between the gentry boy and the fae noble who could never admit to being related to him for risk of censure to them both. Someone might realize what secret Robert's gentry mother had taken with her when she'd died in childbirth, and never named the boy's father.

———

I OPENED my eyes and looked into Talus's, and saw the pain he could never reveal. The truth he could never admit about the young gentry whose life the cold iron stole away second by second.

I saw his pain, felt it through the link between us, and gave him my power. I felt our strengths merge, and for a moment, I could feel the world the way Talus felt it, see it as he saw it—in strings and lines and bars of power and energy, to be touched and changed at a moment's whim.

We followed my sense for the cold iron and found the strands and pieces working their way into his son's flesh. We wrapped tiny lines of force around each one and carefully, ever so carefully, for our power does not work well with cold iron, pulled each one out of Robert's flesh.

An eternity passed in a moment, and then the last of the iron was gone, and Talus released my hand and the link, both of us panting feverishly.

"Sirens," Laurie told us. "Can he be moved?"

"The iron is out," Talus said quietly. "We have no choice; we can't be found here. Dave and Elena?"

The hag simply shook her head.

Talus grunted and picked Robert up easily, leading the way quickly back to the SUV. Fire trucks and other emergency vehicles began to arrive as he slipped us away into the night. I held my breath for a moment, afraid that one of them would see us and stop us, but we eluded detection as we fled the scene.

We didn't drive far before Talus pulled us off the road and put the SUV in park. Leaving the engine on for heat, he rejoined Laurie and me in the back, checking on Robert.

The hag had sat by him the whole way, a tiny trickle of power helping the wounded gentry to heal. "He's going to be okay," she told Talus.

"Hold up," he told us both. "I need to check in."

The noble stepped out of the SUV, taking his cellphone out into the cold with him. I turned back to trying to bandage up Robert's still seeping but now slowly healing wounds. I could see Talus outside in the snow, talking on his cellphone and gesturing wildly with his free hand.

Finally, he turned the phone off and got back in the vehicle.

"We're heading to meet my uncle at the doctor's," he told us. "He's arranged for some of our people to make sure Dave and Elena's bodies are quietly shuffled out of the mess. Poor bastards."

I nodded. There wasn't anything I could say. Unlike Talus, I had only just met the two gentry who'd just died. From my glimpse into his memories, they'd been his friends for longer than I'd been alive. Friends who had been wiped from the world in a single moment of fire.

The cabal had been warned we were coming. Not just that someone was coming but that *fae* were coming, or they wouldn't have used cold iron in the claymores. I didn't want to think of the amount of effort cold-hammering something resembling the thousands of ball bearings in the mine represented. Effort put into trying to kill us—kill *me*. I *liked* not being killed.

———

IT WAS a short drive to the house of the doctor the fae Court kept on retainer. He was waiting for us when we arrived, already dressed in scrubs and standing by a stretcher with a young woman.

The girl was a platinum-haired changeling, but the family resemblance between doctor and assistant was striking. I found myself wondering, as she helped me load Robert onto the stretcher, what kind of fae her mother had been.

The father and daughter rushed Robert into the house, and we followed them in. It turned out that they had turned what had probably been a main-floor office or something similar into a—totally concealed from the outside—brightly lit and fully functional operating theater.

I barely had enough to see that before the changeling daughter closed the doors to the operating theater, leaving Talus, Laurie and me standing in the living room. It was a neatly furnished room, with two chairs, a couch and a loveseat, all in a starkly sterile white.

"I guess we may as well sit down," Talus suggested.

"I'm going to go have a smoke," Laurie said.

"Don't leave," Talus ordered. "My uncle is on his way; he'll want to debrief all of us."

She nodded and left, heading for the front door, leaving Talus and me alone in the sitting room, watching the door past which Robert was being operated on. We both sat for a long minute, just staring at the doors.

"Who knows about Robert?" I finally asked. I didn't need to say what about Robert—he knew I'd been in his head when we linked.

"My uncle," Talus answered. "His grandfather, Raphael. Dave and Elena knew too, but I guess that's irrelevant now."

"That few?" I was surprised.

"Noble fae aren't supposed to have affairs outside of the nobility," he said. "Or, at the very least," he continued drily, "we're expected to avoid having or acknowledging any children that come of said affairs."

"Like Robert," I said quietly.

"Like you," he pointed out. "A Vassal? Your bloodline is more noble than mine, changeling."

"Keep that quiet," I asked. "Eric and Oberis are the only ones who know."

"A wise choice," he said with a nod. "I will keep your secret if you keep mine, Jason."

"Done," I said without hesitation. I wasn't planning on blabbing about anyone else's parentage; that much was for sure. I knew too little about my own, and I knew *that* was dangerous.

"Thank you," Talus told me, but any further conversation on secrets was cut off by Laurie's return, a haze of acrid cigarette smoke offending sensitive fae noses.

The hag took a seat on the loveseat, facing the chairs where Talus and I were staring at the OR door. Silence hung in the room for several minutes, to be interrupted in the end by Oberis stepping out of Between into the middle of the room.

"I was delayed," were his first words. "I had to arrange for our people's bodies to be removed so we can give them decent burials in our own way. Stay seated, you three," he ordered as I started to rise.

The fair fae lord took a seat on the couch, focusing his gaze on each of us in turn. The room was silent, the tension thick enough to be cut with a knife.

"What happened?" Lord Oberis finally asked.

"They were expecting us," Talus said bluntly. "They'd looped footage so we didn't see anything before we got up to the floor, and then cleaned the office out."

"They destroyed any papers or computers they couldn't take with them," I added. "It looked like a pretty thorough job."

"There was some kind of ward over the bombs," the noble fae continued. "I didn't sense them. Jason did"—he nodded at me—"because there was cold iron in the claymore mines they used as the main trigger. I didn't know he was an iron-seeker."

"I didn't know that was *special*," I said. "Not that it was enough to save Dave and Elena."

"Iron-seeking is not uncommon among the fae, but not truly common either," Oberis told me. "I am an iron-seeker, but Talus here, who shares many of my gifts, is not. So, you warned Talus. What happened then?"

"If he'd just warned me, Uncle, I would be dead," Talus said quietly. "Dave and Elena didn't have time to duck. Robert only survived because he was blown back into the stairwell, which Laurie hadn't got out of yet when we triggered the bombs. Jason *tackled* me and knocked me to the floor. Without that, I'd have been in the path of the cold iron."

"I think you repaid the favor," I told Talus. "You got us through the floor and to the ground safely despite the bombs."

"Yes, one of my people in the fire department did mention an interesting hole that the fire thankfully destroyed before more than one or two of them saw it," Oberis said softly. "It seems I am in your debt, Mr. Kilkenny, for the life of my nephew, and that you two are even."

"We were lucky," I said. "Those bombs could have killed us all."

"We lost two good people," Oberis told me. "That is never lucky. But I understand your point. This cabal has picked an enemy, it seems."

As the import of those grim words sunk in, the door to the operating room opened and the doctor, stripped of gloves and face mask, stepped out.

"Dr. Lacombe, how is he?" Oberis asked.

"It was touch-and-go for a minute," Lacombe said simply. "If you'd been any slower at getting the cold iron out, I think the damage would have spread too far for me to do anything.

"As it is, I've stopped the bleeding, both internal and external, and have stabilized him on an IV. He's still borderline," the doctor said quietly, and looked at Oberis.

"My lord, I'd like permission to add a small dose of quicksilver to his saline," he continued. "It would guarantee his survival and speed his healing dramatically."

"How much?" Oberis asked.

"Less than a milligram," the doctor said immediately. He'd clearly been expecting the question.

"Do it," Oberis ordered. "But watch him afterwards. One dose shouldn't cause addiction—"

"But it's better to be careful," Lacombe finished for him. "Your will." The doctor returned to the operating room, letting the door swing closed behind him.

The Seelie Lord of Calgary looked around at the three of us, still armed and armored under our winter coats, and sighed.

"This was fucked beyond all recognition," he told us. "You walked into a trap and walked out. You saved Robert's life, unquestionably. All of you, go home. Return the gear to the Court at a later date."

A tiny hand gesture suggested that I should stay for a moment as Talus and Laurie drifted out. I crossed to the couch and stood next to Oberis.

"I am sorry, Vassal of my Queen," he said quietly. "We find ourselves further from completing your mission, when we expected to gain ground."

"Two people *died*," I answered, equally quietly. "I'm more sorry for them."

He nodded stiffly and gripped my shoulder.

"I can feel in these old bones that the Queen's warning is true, and that something deeper is going on here," he told me. "Keep the gun and vest. I have the feeling the day will come when you will need arms and not have time to turn to me.

"Now go rest," he ordered. "We will find them, Jason, I promise you. For your oath to our Queen, and for the sake of our dead, I promise you that."

———

TALUS DROVE ME HOME. Given that the weather had yet to improve in the slightest, I was grateful, but we spent the drive in near silence. I had no idea what to say to a man who had lost two people he'd been friends with for longer than I'd been alive, and he was willing to keep his own peace.

I turned my cell phone back on shortly before we arrived at my apartment. I had a single message, a text from Mary asking me to call her when I could.

I put my phone aside and looked over at my driver.

"You going to be okay?" I finally asked as we pulled in next to my building.

"My son will live," the fae noble said quietly. "Dave and Elena won't. That's going to take some wrapping my head around. I'll have a better idea tomorrow, I'm afraid."

"Drive safe, man," I told him, offering him my hand. He took it and I squeezed. He nodded in acknowledgement, and I left him in the SUV.

I made it down to my apartment and then collapsed on my couch with exhaustion. After a long, long moment, I realized I was way too hot with the coat on, and took it off. With that done, I had to take the concealed holster off to be comfortable.

The Micro Uzi and its holster ended up on top of the black briefcase containing the Jericho, tucked down the side of my computer desk. The heavy Kevlar vest got tossed over the back of the couch, incongruous against its cheerful orange color.

The armor and weapon discarded, I collapsed back onto my couch, pulled my phone out and called Mary. It wasn't until after the phone had rung three times that I realized it was almost midnight, and then the phone went to voice mail before I could hang up.

"Will someone *please* think of the cat girls?!" Mary's voice demanded from the recording. "You've reached Mary Tenerim, I'm not available right now, please leave a message."

"Hi, Mary," I said awkwardly once it started recording. "Just letting you know I got your text and called; forgot how late it was when I got home. Call me tomorrow if you're free to hang out?"

The message left, I slowly dragged myself to my feet, stiff and sore from an eight-story fall, however cushioned it may have been by a fae noble's magic. I had to be at work in a little more than six hours.

16

THE NEXT DAY followed my normal routine. It was so normal, after the day before, as to be almost painful. I did my first rounds of drop-offs and pickups, and met Michael for my Enforcer pickup. He had a package for the airport and clearly didn't know that I'd been at Sigrid REIT the night before, or I'm sure he'd have said *something*.

My airport delivery trip, including the extra delivery, went seamlessly, and I made it back to the office just in time for lunch and Mary calling to check up on me.

"Hey, are you okay?" were the first words she said when I answered the phone.

"I'm fine," I said slowly. "Why do you ask?"

"When you tell me you have 'Court business,' and that night a building explodes and rumor in the community says a Court strike team were inside when it blew, I do have to wonder," the shifter girl told me dryly.

I sighed. "You're too smart for your own good," I told her. "Yes, I was there."

"Shit," she said flatly. "Are you okay?"

"Barely," I admitted. "I can't say much more at work."

"Fair enough," she said. "Should I come over and cook you dinner and you can tell me about it?"

"You may have to order in," I warned her, her offer bringing a smile even through my continuing weariness. "I don't think I actually have enough pots to cook with."

"That's probably good," she replied with a laugh. "I'm a *terrible* cook. I'm off at five; should be at your place at quarter to six?

"Sounds good," I agreed.

I walked back out in the office, aware that Trysta was watching me. I returned her gaze calmly, and she glanced away. Sighing to myself, I went to load up my afternoon truck. I was pretty sure I knew what her issue was, and there was nothing I could really do about it.

———

BY A QUARTER TO six that evening, I'd managed to clean up my apartment, clean all the dirty dishes, put away all the clothes, and generally make the place look less like a bachelor pad. I'd also checked my email and discovered that Oberis had organized a funeral for Dave and Elena on Monday afternoon.

I bounced an email to Bill letting him know I would need to get off work early that day, and then found myself looking at the two guns sitting beside my desk. The Jericho's black carrying case would pass as a briefcase, but the Micro Uzi and its shoulder rig were a little harder to conceal, as was the Kevlar vest.

Both ended up being bundled into my closet as the buzzer for the front door of my building rang. I closed the closet door and made it back to my intercom as the buzzer rang again.

"Hello?"

"It's Mary," she told me cheerfully. "Its freezing out here, so can you let me in?"

"Of course!" I buzzed her in immediately and had to keep myself from racing to the door like a horny teenager. I still opened it while she was still halfway down the hall, and she greeted me with a brilliant smile as she closed the distance and kissed me very thoroughly.

"Good to see you," she purred, snuggling into me through her heavy winter jacket, which, it finally processed, was *really cold.*

"Let's get you inside and out of that coat," I said, gently drawing her through the door and closing it behind her.

She quickly shed the coat and curled up, cat-like, on my couch. Smiling at me, Mary patted the couch next to her. As soon as I sat down, she uncurled slightly to snuggle up to me as I slid an arm around her.

For a minute or two, we cuddled in silence, and then she gave me a quick kiss and pulled back to look me in the eyes.

"So, what happened last night?" she asked.

"We were investigating a lead we had on the cabal," I said quietly. "I think..." I paused, not sure if I was certain of what I was about to say, and then went gamely on ahead.

"I think someone told them we were coming," I told her. "They destroyed too much rather than moving it for it to have been a planned move; they did it on short notice. And they knew it was fae coming, too—they used cold iron-loaded mines to start their explosions, to make sure any fae in the office were dead."

"But you made it out," she said, taking my hands in hers and squeezing gently.

"By luck, and timing, and the power of a fae noble with just enough warning," I said, squeezing her in turn. "Two of the gentry who went in with us didn't, and a third was badly wounded."

"Damn," Mary whispered. "I'm sorry."

"It wasn't even a fight we could win," I whispered. "We were expecting that, initially. It was just a trap. Someone set us up and killed two good fae in the process."

"Who?" she asked, although she had to know the answer in advance.

"I have no idea," I told her. "I'm not even sure who knew we were going other than those of us who went, and all of us nearly died.

"I'm going to find out," I continued grimly. I was sure that between Oberis and me, we could manage it. And then someone was going to pay.

Mary squeezed my hands again, hard, bringing me back to the moment.

"Relax," she told me. "You will find them. For now, let it rest for a bit and come here." She pulled me to her, just wrapping me in her arms and holding me, letting me focus on something other than memories of explosions and blood.

After a while, she started kissing my neck, causing me to focus on something else entirely for a while.

————

MARY LEFT QUITE LATE. I insisted on calling her a cab, though she refused to let me pay for it.

"Call me in the morning," she told me, kissing me on her way out the door. With a sigh, I went to bed.

Morning came way too soon, and two late nights left me fuzzy with fatigue that coffee only took a slight edge off. Nonetheless, I struggled into the Queen's enchanted armor vest and work clothes, and headed in to the office.

I traded vague pleasantries with Trysta and Bill while setting up my morning loads. I knew I was noticeably slower than usual, but neither of them commented.

Bill did call me aside when I was done.

"I got your email about the funeral," he said quietly. "What happened?"

"There was an accident," I told him. "They died together, a brother and sister."

"Friends?" he asked.

"Members of my home community I was working on a project with," I answered. It was close enough. "The accident was related, so I feel obligated."

"It's not an issue," he told me firmly. "I'll have Trysta note not to schedule you for an afternoon trip. You seem tired," he added, "are you okay?"

"I'm fine," I told him. "I, um, have a new girlfriend...I think."

He laughed. It was actually the first time I'd seen the man laugh, and it was a resounding, deep belly laugh that echoed around the office for a moment.

"You think, eh?" he said. "Yeah, that's about the way of it with women. Enjoy it while you can, son, and try to avoid the messy divorce at the end, eh?"

I nodded, blushing slightly. He gestured me out to get started on my route.

Halfway through my morning run, I got the normal text from Michael to meet him at a Starbucks. For once, this Starbucks wasn't exactly on my route home. Apparently, the Enforcers gifted with part of the Wizard's Sight were not *totally* omniscient.

There was another Enforcer waiting with him when I arrived. They all seemed cut from the same press—the same black suit, the same rough build, the same orichalcum tattoos. This new one was a black-haired version I hadn't met before.

"Mr. Kilkenny," he greeted me, offering his hand as if it was balmy and warm outside instead of fifteen degrees below zero. "I am Enforcer Percy; Michael works for me. I handle all of our deliveries and out-city shipments. I wanted to meet you in person."

I shook his hand. He may have been totally oblivious to the cold, but *I* was wearing gloves, which made it mostly tolerable.

"I always like to know the people I'm using for deliveries," he continued silkily. "We have two packages for you to deliver today. One is for the airport outbound flight; the other is for Ink Quill again."

"All right," I said. "Give me the packages."

"I must say that we do appreciate your willing assistance," Percy told me. "It's always preferable to not have to force cooperation."

This guy really needed to work on his small talk.

"If you tried, I'd go to the Court," I replied, trying to keep my voice as calm as his. "There are always limits."

He smirked. "Of course." He gestured for Michael, who'd remained silent throughout the entire exchange, to pass me the packages.

One got slightly squished between us, and we quickly double-checked the box as Percy stood there, watching us. It didn't look too damaged, though I got a noseful of a strong, spicy scent—cinnamon or something like that. Powers only knew why the Enforcers were shipping cinnamon, but the one I worked for wasn't overly talkative.

Michael and I loaded the boxes into my truck. Percy leaned against the blue sedan, watching us, then got in and started the car while waiting for the junior Enforcer.

"I'm sorry," I told Michael as we lodged the box for Ink Quill under three other pickups.

"For what?" he asked.

"You having that douche for a boss," I said dryly.

Michael tried *valiantly* to glare repressively at me, but the clear agreement in his eyes totally undermined the effort.

17

My airport drop-off went without any issues, all of the packages loaded up and ready to make their flights. Somebody in a rush to make sure he made *his* flight, however, was in an accident while I was offloading the packages. The entire road on my route to Ink Quill was blocked by emergency vehicles, and out of two lanes each way, only one lane was getting through.

I was running over an hour behind schedule by the time I made it through the accident, and was cursing out the Enforcers for adding this extra stop to my route. I pulled my courier van into Ink Quill's parking lot and parked next to a giant black Hummer.

In more of a rush than was probably good for me, I grabbed the package and pushed through the outer doors into the office, only to stop at the sight of the *inner* door halfway off its hinges with its glass paneling shattered.

The scene inside the office had frozen as I burst in, and I looked in at it in complete shock. A security guard was lying groaning in the corner, his broken arm lying at an impossible angle and a pistol lying at his feet in two pieces.

A secretary with long blond hair was cowering behind the

remnants of her desk, which looked like it had been broken by having someone slammed into it. Repeatedly.

A very large, very ugly semiautomatic pistol was being pointed at me by a gentleman I recognized as Barry Tenerim, one of the wolf shifters who seemed to follow Tarvers everywhere. Two more dark-haired men with the angular features I'd come to associate with the Clan stood behind him.

The final element of the frozen tableau was Tarvers standing there with James Langley held two feet off the ground by the collar of his expensive dress shirt, blood leaking from the human executive's clearly broken nose.

"Help!" Langley squeaked when he saw me. "These men are totally *insane!*"

I walked in slowly and carefully, stepping around the debris while mostly ignoring the pistol trained on me.

"Tarvers," I greeted the big man in my slow, soft drawl as I lay the package I was carrying on the floor next to the shattered desk. I looked from the Clan leader to the sobbing receptionist and laid a hand on her shoulder.

"It's going to be okay," I told her. "He's just a big teddy bear unless you piss him off." Still squeezing the receptionist's shoulder, I looked back to the Tenerim Alpha and the print shop VP, still half-frozen in tableau, and sighed.

"Tarvers, would you care to explain why you have the man I'm delivering packages to floating in midair?" I asked. It seemed that unless I said something, everyone was just going to stand around like statues.

"I told you we were tracking the lifesblood," the Alpha growled in answer, his face inches from Langley's face. "We traced it, all right. The heartstone came from here; we're sure of it.

"And this mewling prick knows something," he continued.

"I don't know..." Langley trailed off as Tarvers met and held his gaze. The human met the angry glare of an Alpha. It took a *strong* will to lie to an Alpha.

"Tell me," Tarvers growled.

"I don't even know what heartstone *is*," the VP whimpered.

"Dark gray stone or dust," Tarvers explained helpfully. "Smells like cinnamon."

Even as the poor human slumped in mute admission, Tarvers's words struck a chord, and I grabbed my package back up and sniffed it.

"Shit," I whispered, and tore the package open. Inside the shoebox-sized delivery box, packed in bubble wrap and Styrofoam, were three small velvet bags. With the box open, the distinctive smell of cinnamon with a metallic tang I now realized was heartstone drifted through the air.

"The Enforcers had me delivering it to him," I told Tarvers. "What for?"

"We use it in *ink* for special books for them," the printer exec exclaimed.

"All of it?" Tarvers asked, locking gazes with the man again. He didn't answer. The human had caught on to the only way to avoid incriminating yourself when speaking to an Alpha.

The big bear shifter shook his victim like a bear shakes a fish.

"All of it?" he repeated his demand.

"No," Langley whispered, his voice broken as he slumped in Tarvers's hands.

Before anyone could say or do anything in response to the human's admission, the outer doors to the office flung open again to unleash a flurry of activity.

In a blur of motion, four men in black suits carrying bullpup assault rifles hit the ground in a kneeling row, the muzzles of the odd rectangular guns sweeping the room and settling in to each cover one of the shifters.

Two more Enforcers followed them through, flanking the door and covering me and the security guard. I realized that at least some of the bullets in the guns were cold iron, and I slowly stood up, raising my hands above my head.

A seventh man, his head shaven bald and the second-tallest person in the room after Tarvers's giant frame, stalked into the office. Orichalcum tattoos wove across his visible flesh as he stepped through the firing line of his men.

"Tarvers," Winters said flatly. "Put him down or my men will shoot you. The guns are bane- and cold iron–loaded. You *will* die before you reach them."

"This man has dealt with vampires," Tarvers growled. "By the authority of the Covenant, I claim the right to interrogate and judge him."

"And I will point out that he is an employee of the Enforcers and hence of the Magus, and under his jurisdiction," Winters, leader of the Enforcers, told the Alpha calmly. "Put. Him. Down."

Tarvers dropped the human and turned to face Winters fully.

"I have traced lifesblood found in the possession of a vampire to this man," he told the Enforcer. "This matter has nothing to do with the Enforcers. Leave."

"As I said, this man is employed by us and hence under our jurisdiction," Winters replied. "I will investigate your claims and advise you of our findings. Please leave; at this point, your presence will only impede the investigation."

"One of your employees is passing heartstone to *vampires*, and you expect me to walk away?" Tarvers demanded.

"The authority to investigate these matters and deal with this alleged Vampire incursion falls to the Magus under the same Covenants you appealed to," the Enforcer said. "I have the jurisdiction here, not you."

"The Covenants don't even mention you, you arrogant shit," Tarvers told Winters. The distance between the two seemed to be shrinking without either of them noticeably moving. "The Wizard has *failed* in his obligations. I will investigate this attack on my Clan. Either stand aside or have the Wizard himself speak to me."

"You aren't worth the Wizard's time," Winters responded, his voice never changing from the same flat, level tone he'd been using since arriving. "That's why we Enforcers were created, so that the pointless troubles of the lesser creatures of this city would not be carried to him.

"I will investigate your allegations," he continued, "but right now, the only thing I have proof for is that you assaulted someone under the Magus's protection. There will be sanctions leveled for this action."

Tarvers laughed, literally in the Enforcer's face. "You are a piddling little man," he growled at the human. "The Magus signed the Covenants as one among equals, and you are nothing but servants. By relying on you, he has failed in his charge, and so I will tell him.

"We are done here; get out!" the massive shifter bellowed.

The image would forever be burnt into my mind. Six armed Enforcers, carrying weapons that could put down most of the other people in the room with a few shots, covered everyone in the room. Three wolf shifters faced them, their every muscle tensed as they readied to spring into action. A handful of humans and me, scattered around the outside watching the confrontation in horror.

And in the center, Tarvers, a bear shifter and a giant of a man, faced Gerard Winters, a smaller, shaven-headed man whose golden tattoos glowed gently on his flesh.

I could never say who struck first. One moment, the two men were still, facing each other amidst their followers, and then they were a blur of motion. Fists and claws slashed, and I could see Tarvers begin his transformation as the other Enforcers' guns started to aim.

He never finished it. Before the Enforcers could open fire, the fight was over. Winters stood, panting slightly, with his suit jacket and shirt torn from his frame but his tattooed flesh unmarred. Tarvers's body lay on the floor; his severed head dripping blood from Winters's hands.

A glittering silver short sword was now visible in the Enforcer's right hand, slowly dripping blood from its blade of bane. The other Enforcers' guns snapped instantly back to the other shifters, cowing any further attack before it started.

Winters tossed the shifter's head onto his corpse and turned to look at the other shifters.

"Take this carrion and get out," he ordered.

18

For a long moment, no one moved or did anything. Then I took a deep breath and stepped forward, aware that at least one gun barrel was following me as I moved, and carefully hooked my hands under Tarvers's shoulders. I pointed with my chin for Barry to take the Alpha's feet.

My movement started the shifters into motion as they quietly obeyed the orders of the man who'd just murdered their leader. I led them out, carefully avoiding looking at Winters. I don't think I could have done so and stayed calm enough to continue this course.

The three shifters were in shock, but their reaction if that faded would be violent. Unless I kept them calm, I knew Winters would add more bodies to the count for today.

"Load him into the car," I told them, my voice catching in midsentence. "Then follow my van."

Barry nodded wordlessly, the shifters obeying me in silence.

I stepped away from them and started my van, checking to be sure that the black Hummer followed me out of the parking lot. I didn't drive far, just enough to be completely out of view from the Ink Quill and any route the Enforcers would likely take to leave, and then pulled over.

"Why are we stopping?" Barry demanded, stepping out of the Hummer into the cold as I pulled my cellphone out.

"I hate politics," I said aloud. "I don't *like* it, I don't *understand* it—and it just fucking killed a man I liked. We need help, and there's only one other person at Tarvers's level left."

Gesturing the wolf shifter abruptly to silence, I called Oberis.

I got Laurie.

"What do you want?" the hag demanded.

"I need to speak to Lord Oberis," I told her.

"He's busy; you can speak to me," she informed me.

"No," I told her harshly. "I must speak to Lord Oberis."

"You don't get to decide that," she said coldly. "Tell me what this is about and maybe I will let you talk to him."

I hate politics.

"Alpha Tenerim is dead," I said flatly. "I need to speak to Lord Oberis."

"Oh," she answered. "I'm sorry, Lord Oberis is simply not available," she continued, her voice somewhat more polite now. "I will pass on your message as soon as I am able."

She hung up on me, and I stared at my phone for a minute. Not available for the news of a major player's death? That was a pretty spectacular level of "not available."

I looked at the three wolf shifters from the Clan Tenerim, all of them looking like very lost, very *dangerous* puppies. Oberis was the leader of my Court; who the hell else was I supposed to talk to when everything went to hell?

I hate politics. Then, I realized that Eric, if nothing else, could probably get ahold of Oberis! I dug his number out of my phone and called him.

"Eric, we have a situation," I said quickly when the gnome answered his cellphone. "Tarvers Tenerim is dead. Gerard Winters killed him. I can't get ahold of Lord Oberis. What do I do?" I asked plaintively. I was lost, completely out of my depth, and left hoping that the Keeper would have some idea how to help me.

"Fuck," Eric said simply when I finished. He was silent for a moment. "Fuck," he repeated. "Call Talus—I don't care what Oberis is involved in; Talus will know and be able to interrupt. Here's his number."

I quickly scribbled the fae noble's number down.

"Thank you, Eric," I told the Keeper. "I had no idea who else to turn to."

"Call Talus," he repeated. "Powers keep you safe."

I did. After a couple of rings, Talus answered.

"Who is this?" he demanded.

"It's Kilkenny," I told him. "Eric gave me your number; we have an emergency."

"Okay," he said. "What's going on?"

"The Tenerim Alpha is dead; I need to speak to your uncle," I explained.

"Shit." Silence on the other end of the line. "He's in a teleconference with five other Lords." A moment of more silence. "Stay on the line," Talus instructed.

I heard Laurie's voice in the background. "You can't go in there!"

"Who are you to tell me what to do?" Talus said, his voice suddenly flat, cold, and angry—a tone of utter command I hoped no noble ever had cause to use on me. I heard a door open.

"Uncle, Kilkenny is on the line," the noble told Oberis. "It's an emergency."

"Gentlemen, excuse me a moment," I heard Oberis say, and then soft footsteps before the fae lord spoke into the phone.

"I just put off five of the most powerful fae on this continent for you," he said simply. There was no menace in his voice. It would have been redundant. "What is it?"

"Tarvers Tenerim is dead, murdered by Enforcer Gerard Winters," I told him in a rush, relieved to have finally reached him. "Laurie told me you were unavailable, so I called Talus—I'm sitting here with a dead Alpha and three shifters about to go critical."

"I see." His voice was flat. "Laurie, we will discuss this," he said, away from the phone but I heard the words clearly. "Talus, make my apologies to the Lords. Now, Jason, where are you?"

I told him, and he hung up without responding. Moments later, before I could even start panicking at being hung up on again, air *twisted,* and Lord Oberis stepped out of Between to face the vehicle full of shifters. With a wordless gesture, he called me to his side. With a sigh, I obeyed, walking slightly behind him as he approached Tarvers's vehicle.

Barry and the other two shifters stood outside it, ignoring the cold as they faced the fae lord sullenly, angrily. Oberis returned their gazes levelly.

"Show him to me," he asked them, his voice gentle. Barry nodded and led the fae lord to the back of the vehicle, opening it up to reveal Tarvers's body.

"Winters had a bane sword," the wolf shifter said quietly, his voice choked. "But he was so fast, so strong—I would never have thought a human would last a second against an *Alpha.*"

"Winters is no longer human," the leader of Calgary's fae told the shifter quietly. "He is much changed by the Wizard's runes, more a construct of magic now than a man."

"Twisted and evil," I muttered. I'm sure everyone there heard me, but no one commented. I'm not sure anyone disagreed.

"What happened?" Oberis asked.

"We followed a lead on the lifesblood we found on a vampire," Barry explained slowly. "It led to this print shop, so we started questioning the guy running the joint. He freaked when we asked about it, and tried to have a security guard evict us.

"After that, we started asking questions forcefully and Jason showed up and was being helpful," the wolf shifter continued, "until the Enforcers showed up.

"Winters told us we had no jurisdiction, that the man was under the Enforcers' protection, and that they would 'investigate our allegations.' He and Tarvers argued, then fought. He killed Tarvers."

"It wasn't even a fair fight," I said quietly. "I never thought I'd see Tarvers that outmatched."

"Thank you," Oberis told us all. "This is not acceptable, but I am not sure what to do about it yet." He sighed. "Take Tarvers home; I'm sure Clan Tenerim has affairs they must deal with. You did the right thing by waiting for me—I and I alone can take this to the Wizard until a successor as Speaker for the Clans is selected."

The shifters drifted into the car and drove off, looking like they were in a daze, and Oberis looked at me.

"You have a knack for trouble," he told me.

"I came here trying to *avoid* this shit," I complained, aware that this was *not* the time to whine but unable to help myself.

"And the Queen has bound you to try and find it," the fae lord reminded me. "There are too many pieces in play; I am not sure I understand what is happening. I need time to assess."

"What will happen next?" I asked.

"We will mourn Dave and Elena," he said quietly. "By Monday, I should know. Until then...we honor our dead."

"We all have our jobs to do," Oberis continued. "Deciding what to do about this is mine, not yours."

"Jobs," I said slowly. "Shit. I'm going to be so late back to dispatch."

———

I WAS. I spun a tale to Trysta about a restaurant I'd stopped for lunch where the service had been atrocious and they'd kept me waiting for my bill, and she'd laughed sympathetically and helped me load up my afternoon load.

I finally returned the truck to the parking lot over an hour late, with the office already deserted. With a sigh, I offloaded the next day's delivery parcels myself before locking everything up and starting the walk home in the cold.

Moments after leaving the office, my cell phone started to ring.

"Hello," I answered wearily.

"It's Mary," she said quietly, her voice choked. "I just found out about Tarvers. You were there?!"

"I was," I said, feeling the ache of weariness, a good chunk of grief, and a huge amount of guilt settling into my bones. "I saw it all."

"Are you okay?" she asked.

"Terrified," I admitted. "I have the feeling that things are starting to fall apart around us."

She was silent on the phone for a long time.

"Me too," she finally said. "Tarvers was a father to all of us. I'm scared."

"Can I see you?" I asked after a long moment, realizing what both of us wanted and neither of us wanted to seem weak by asking.

"I don't think I should leave the Den," she told me. "But you can come here. I'll make sure you get in. Things are...hectic here right now."

"I'll grab a cab; I should be there in twenty minutes or so," I promised. "Take care of yourself."

"You too," she told me.

I hung up and called the cab company.

———

THE TENERIM DEN was a townhouse complex of what had originally been twelve separate homes. At some point, they had all been bought out by the Clan, and the renovations had begun.

Now it was a warren of interconnected bedrooms, kitchens, media rooms, storage areas and armories that served as the home to over half of Clan Tenerim's forty-odd members and as a de facto home base for the shifters in Calgary.

Unlike the Lodge, which was neutral territory, the Den was definitely Clan Tenerim's turf. Other inhumans came there on the Clan's terms, and it looked like tonight, a lot of them had.

The Den's parking spots were full and the street outside was lined with cars. A dozen or so burly-looking men and women, mostly wolf shifters with a couple of bears and one individual, who after looking at them for a good ten seconds I realized was a *tiger* shapeshifter, lounged around a propane area heater in the yard between the Den and the street.

I recognized none of them, and only one or two were Tenerim, from their features. All of them moved with the ready tension of soldiers and guards, and as I approached the complex, several of them drifted over to me, attempting and failing to appear casual.

"This house is closed, changeling," one of them, a tall dark-haired man who I'd identified as one of the bear shifters—mostly by his height—told me. His tone was polite but firm. "We mourn one of our own."

"I know," I said gently. "I'm here to visit a child of Clan Tenerim, Mary."

"I'm sorry, this house is closed," he repeated.

I glanced up to the house, about to pull out my phone and call Mary, when the front door opened and Barry Tenerim hurried out.

"Not to Clan-Friends, Kal," Barry told the hulking bear. "Nor to those who stood by us when our Alpha was killed. This is the changeling who was there."

At the blond wolf shifter's words, the change in the demeanor of the guards out front of the Den changed instantly. They went from politely threatening to casually respectful, stepping back to give me space and offering nods of greeting.

The young shifter offered me his hand, and then took mine in both of his when I took it.

"If you hadn't been there, we would have attacked the bastard," he told me. "And there would be three more sons of Tenerim being mourned tonight. You did the right thing, and you saved my life.

"Thank you," he finished simply, then stood aside and gestured me towards the door, where Mary stood, waiting for me.

I barely made it to the door before I had every inch of my wildcat shifter girlfriend wrapped around me. For a moment, I froze under the impact, and then I wrapped my arms around her and held her gently while she sobbed into my shoulder.

Eventually, she let go and led me into a crowded living room. A growl from Barry that I barely heard vacated one of the loveseats, and we took a seat, clinging to each other for comfort.

Mary was crying. Nothing dramatic, nothing attention-seeking, just soft, quiet tears.

"He was more than our leader," she told me through her tears. "He was our patriarch, our Alpha. He was a father to us all in so many ways. It's hard to accept that he's gone."

I held her in silence. There was nothing I could say. I had known Tarvers a matter of weeks, not the years and decades of his Clan. He had been a good ally, a source of help and wisdom and, yes, a good friend.

"He *was* Clan Tenerim," Barry said quietly. "It's hard to describe, but this Den feels empty without him."

Mary continued to weep, and I continued to hold her. The room was very quiet, and as I looked around, I saw we weren't the only couple clutching each other for support, and no one else was talking.

After several long minutes, a man stood and crossed to me. Native by his features and coloring, his black hair was woven into long braids that fell to his waist that were tinged with gray. His skin was worn with time and sun, yet his eyes were bright, touched with an edge of felinity and carrying the full power of an Alpha's gaze.

The cougar shifter was *old*, and given how shifters aged, it was easily possible this man had been born before Columbus set sail. He had seen a world of change, and the pain written in his eyes and face told of its prices.

"I am Enli," he told me. "Folks around here call me Grandfather, as I am the oldest living shifter in this city." His eyes bore into me. "I was the oldest shifter when MacDonald came here. I am Alpha of what remains of the Enli Clan—and yes, it is named for me."

I bowed my head in respect. "What do you need of me, Grandfather?" I asked quietly. I doubted that the oldest Alpha in Calgary had come to see me just to introduce himself. While he didn't speak for the Clans, I doubted any shifter had ever made a major decision in this city without talking to him.

"I am sorry to interrupt," he continued, laying a gentle old hand on Mary's shoulder. "All of us grieve for Tarvers, but you were there when he died. I have heard Barry and the other boys' story. Now I must hear yours. I must understand everything that happened."

"Why?" I asked frankly. I didn't really want to talk about the Tenerim Alpha's murder yet.

"Because if I do not understand, I may talk my grandchildren into a war that should not be fought," the old shifter told me quietly. "With no Speaker, it is to me they will look for judgment on the actions of the Wizard's dogs."

I nodded, and sighed. "All right, I will tell you what I can," I told him, my drawl quiet in the near-silence of the Den.

The story wasn't easy to tell. Mary sat next to me, holding my hand throughout. I was stunned at how angry I found myself growing as I told the old cougar what I had seen, what I had heard, everything that had led to a servant of the Wizard killing the leader of the shifters.

Grandfather listened well, the fruit of centuries of practice, I suppose. He said little, a grunt here and there when needed to encourage me to speak, a pointed question to bring up details I hadn't thought of. He managed to wheedle more details out of me than I had thought I knew.

In the end, the story ran out, and I found myself weeping—half from grief and half from rage. The old Alpha laid one of his hands on my shoulder and the other on Mary's.

"This is a harsh time," he told us. "It is through the strength of individuals and their bonds to each other that we will survive. Draw on each other's strengths and those of those around you. Only as a Clan, only as a people, only as friends and lovers and family will we survive."

I bowed my head over his hand, holding tight to Mary. Enli squeezed both of our shoulders and then stood, as there was a commotion outside. Men shouted; I heard Kal's voice among them as an argument clearly proceeded.

It ended with the door to the house being flung open, and two men in the black suits of Enforcers stepped in. They hadn't drawn weapons, and I was amazed they'd made it through the guards outside without being torn to shreds.

A sudden rippling shift of motion and a dramatic increase in tension led me to realize that I was probably the only person in the room who *wasn't* armed, and one wrong word could start the war Enli had said he wanted to avoid. A war that would represent a *huge* failure of my attempt to protect the Wizard!

"This house is closed to outsiders," said a man I didn't recognize, though he shared Tarvers's bulk and features. "We mourn my father. *Your* kind are especially not welcome," he snarled at them.

"We are here to deliver the verdict of the Magus," the lead Enforcer, a dark-haired man of much the same mold as every other Enforcer I'd seen. He had no visible tattoos, but I was sure they were there.

"Speak your piece," Tarvers's son growled.

"A group of members of this Clan attacked an Enforcer-protected human business without provocation," the Enforcer said flatly, apparently oblivious to the slowly growing rumble of growls around the room.

"Inhuman gifts were used in full sight of humans, two of whom were badly injured, and a business and production facility in service to the Magus has been forced to temporarily close its doors.

"For this, the decision of the Enforcers has been to apply production sanctions—"

"Be silent," Enli snapped, and the Enforcer stopped in midsentence at the sheer power of command in the old man's voice. So did the low growling.

Grandfather stood, straightening to his full height and somehow overshadowing the many taller and bulkier men in the room.

"I have a piece for you to deliver to the Magus," he said flatly, and a dropped pin would have echoed in the silence that followed. He held the Enforcer's gaze, and it was clear the man could no more have looked aside than he could have sunk through the floor.

"The *murder* of Alpha Tarvers Tenerim, Speaker for the Clans and Signatory to the Covenants," Enli said slowly, the words falling one by one like hammerblows, "while he was pursuing an investigation of the presence of a vampire cabal—as authorized by the Covenants—by one of Magus MacDonald's *dogs* is an unquestionable act of war.

"In the interests of avoiding bloodshed," he continued, his voice colder than ice, "the Clans will accept a payment in blood and gold as reparations. The details of said payment will be decided by the new Speaker once he has been elected.

"If, *however*, further provocations come to pass"—Grandfather's tone was harsh, and I could *see* the Enforcer trying to melt away under his penetrating gaze—"such as, for example, unjustified sanctions on heartstone production levied as an attempt to falsely justify this murder," he continued dryly, "the Clans would be forced to see this as a sustained campaign against us and would hold emergency elections for a War Speaker to lead us in open war against the Magus MacDonald and his dogs."

The threat hung in the air like bared steel.

"Crawl back to your master, *dog*," Enli growled. "Tell him the Clans will no longer deal with his minions. If there are to be negotiations for blood price for this murder, he will come to us himself.

"Get. Out."

The tableau was frozen for an eternal moment until Enli released the Enforcer from his gaze. The man all but ran from the building.

19

THE ROOM WAS quiet for a long time after the Enforcers left. It felt different now, though, the grief now mixed with a slowly bubbling cauldron of rage. Grandfather had vented it for a moment and likely saved the lives of the two Enforcers he'd sent running, but the blood of the Clans was at a boil.

Some conversations continued, though Mary and I were silent as we held each other. Enli wasn't the only Alpha in the room—six of the other older men in the room were as well. In fact, unless I was severely mistaken, every living Alpha in Calgary was sitting in the Tenerim's living room.

The quiet conversations continued, but eventually Mary led me out of the living room and to her room. There, away from the politics and the talk of others, I held her as she wept out her grief for the man who'd raised her as his own.

"Can you stay the night?" she eventually asked, leaning into my shoulder.

"Not really," I admitted gently. "I have to be at work early tomorrow."

"Okay," Mary said quietly, and I kissed her. "You should probably get going, then," she told me. "It's getting late."

She was right. Slowly and regretfully, I pulled away from her, and with a final kiss, she led me down to the front door, where I called a cab.

I spent the cab ride home deep in thought. On the one hand, the Queen had charged me to track down the cabal, and the current conflict with MacDonald's Enforcers had grown directly out of that. On the other, my main charge was to prevent a plot to attack and murder the Wizard.

Any attacker would find it much easier to strike at MacDonald now that the Enforcers would have no support from the Clans, the strongest inhuman faction in Calgary. There was a good chance that war was coming, and that sort of conflict would *lead* to attacks on the Wizard.

None of this brought any of us any closer to finding and destroying the cabal and undoing whatever plot had allowed them into the city. The Covenants that bound the inhuman community in Calgary together lay preventing such incursions at the feet of the Wizard, and he had failed. His failure was the key to the wedge driving everyone apart and weakening not just his position but everyone's.

Someone was playing a long game, and I was afraid the growing division amidst the inhuman population was not merely something they'd allowed for in their plans but something they wanted and had helped create.

That thought suggested that the corruption in the Enforcers might stretch higher and wider than my worst fears—if Winters himself was involved... But that was impossible. If a Wizard's right-hand man was betraying him, surely a Power in his own right should be able to detect that?

There were only three major political leaders in Calgary among the inhuman community—the Lord of the fae Court, the Wizard, and the Speaker for the shifter Clans. Tarvers was dead, murdered by an Enforcer. The new Speaker wouldn't have his experience or the respect he'd earned from the Wizard and Lord Oberis. The political balance would shift—inevitably toward the Wizard and his Enforcers.

Was it as simple as that? The presence of the cabal used as a catalyst to weaken Court and Clan, allowing the Wizard to seize power? Or maybe *forcing* the Wizard to seize more control, distracting him away from another factor, exposing him to an attack on a level only Powers could understand?

The politics of Powers left the bodies of mere men and inhumans in their wakes, and I had been drawn into the orbit of not one but two of those mighty creatures. If a third Power was involved, an enemy of MacDonald's seeking to use all of this as a distraction to allow a strike at their level, I was so totally outclassed, it wasn't even funny.

But I was used to that. Most supernaturals were out of my weight class. It wasn't like I had to *fight* whoever was coming after MacDonald; I just had to expose them.

On that happy thought, the cab pulled to a halt outside my apartment building. I paid the driver and got out, shivering in the cold. A bitter north wind had swept into the city while I'd been at the Den, and I was grateful for the winter coat that warded off *some* portion of the chill.

A fog was beginning to settle in, and the cab quickly vanished in the shadowed white of the city's winter night as I headed toward my apartment. A shadowy figure appeared out of the white mist, and I had a moment of déjà vu before a fist caught me flat in the center of the chest.

The Queen's armor absorbed much of the blow, but it was still enough to stagger me and leave me open. A second blow smashed into my face, sending me collapsing backward, blood bursting from my nose.

Shadows whirled around the figure, masking and concealing features and motions. It lashed out with a kick that I rolled to avoid and come back onto my feet. My right hand flashed forward, and I pitched a bolt of green faerie flame at my assailant.

A whirl of shadow absorbed the flame, and then a tendril of darkness lashed out at me. It hit me in the left shoulder with a hammerblow the armor only barely kept from breaking bone.

Pain rippled out from my shoulder, and I focused on it, channeling it into my flame. I swung at my attacker, and to my surprise, a whip-like tendril of green flame flashed into existence around my hand, slicing through the shadows to a grunt of surprise from my assailant.

Unlike *any* flame I'd conjured before, the whip didn't fade, taking a physical presence in my hand as I slashed it at my attacker again. It wrapped around the figure's waist, holding them in place for a moment.

Then a blow of pure telekinetic force smashed into me, picking me up and throwing me half a dozen feet backward. The shadow glamor shattered, as did my flame whip, and Laurie advanced on me, all glamors faded and her full true features exposed.

"What the fuck?" I demanded, rising to my feet, and the momentary distraction allowed her to unleash another hammerblow of force. This one caught me in the same shoulder as the first shadow tendril, and this time bone *did* break. Excruciating pain radiated from my upper arm, where her strike had landed.

"My Lord's orders were clear," she told me, brushing aside a burst of flame I managed to conjure from my left hand. "You were to avoid Clan Tenerim."

I sensed the next force strike coming and rolled sideways, coming up to my feet facing the withered form of the hag.

"He himself was there; he knew why I saw them," I snapped at her. "What the hell is this?"

Another hammerblow of kinetic force slammed into my chest, but the armor absorbed much of the impact again, and I managed to stay upright, though I still stumbled back.

"He did not authorize you to walk into their Den and utterly flout his restrictions," the Unseelie fae told me. "He respects you, but you cannot flout his authority like that and not expect consequences."

Anger burned within me now. Oberis's precious *authority* was more important than Mary's grief? After the service I'd freely provided, working together with his people, and even his knowledge that I served the Queen, he was *this* petty? I obviously didn't know the Seelie Lord as well as I thought!

Pain mixed with the anger and drove me upright. I let my left arm hang where it fell, and raised my right to a ready position, letting my anger fuel the flame of my mother's gifts.

"Don't be a fool," Laurie snapped. "Accept your punishment; you cannot face me."

The mix of pain and anger drove me, and with a snap of my fingers, I re-conjured the vicious whip of green flame and lashed out at her. Fire hammered into her cheek, and I *smelled* her flesh burning as the whip seared her flesh.

"I'd like to test that theory," I told her. "Bitch."

20

Even as I faced the hag through the gathering fog, conjured flame in my hand, I knew this was not one of my smarter ideas. Physically, we were about equal. She, however, had far more Power and more ways to *use* said Power.

Anger and adrenaline rushed through me, and I advanced on Laurie, slashing the whip at her again. She managed to dodge this time and conjured tentacles of shadow, stark and black amidst the fog and the snow that was starting to fall.

I cut the whip through the tentacles, snowflakes vaporizing as they hit it. The tentacles broke apart as the flame hit them, and I carried through to bring the whip flicking back around to wrap around Laurie's arm as she raised her right hand to conjure something.

The hag screamed as the flame struck her flesh again, but it wasn't merely pain. My ears rang with the echoing noise of her voice, and I used the whip to jerk her toward me so I could punch her. My fist collided with her jaw, and the scream cut off.

However, that left Laurie mere inches from me, and more black tentacles suddenly flashed out. One drove into my broken arm, the pain making me cringe away from her. A mass of blackness encased and snuffed my whip as other tendrils of darkness grabbed my wrists and legs and tried to hold me in place.

I channeled the pain from the pressure on my broken arm, and for an instant, I was utterly encased in green faerie flame, glowing like the will of the wisp who'd been my grandfather.

The shadows that held me burnt away in the green light of the fire, and I stumbled backward, trying to break free enough to conjure more flame.

Laurie didn't give me the time. In my moment of focus as I burnt away the darkness she'd shackled me with, she loosed another hammerblow of force. I was too busy trying to get distance to dodge, and it slammed into my left leg, just below the knee, with a sickening cracking noise.

I fell. Another blow of telekinetic force hit my right leg, just above the knee, with another sickening *crack*. With three broken limbs, I collapsed into the half-packed snow, pain rendering me incapable of thought, let alone motion or fighting back.

She knelt by me, the glamor of a pretty young woman I'd first seen her in flickering into place around her.

"I told you," she said sympathetically. "You brought much of this on yourself." The hag surveyed the snow I lay in and the snow falling.

"I'd leave you here," she said bluntly, "but my Lord ordered you left alive. Like I said, he respects you. You just can't defy his authority like that."

Pain swept through me again as she scooped me up. She made no attempt to be gentle as she walked through the doors of my building like they weren't there and carried me down to my apartment. Once there, she casually dumped me in the middle of my living room floor, totally ignoring how my broken bones fell.

I couldn't prevent myself from whimpering in pain, and she looked back at me as I lay helpless in pain.

"I told you, you brought this on yourself," she told me. "Obey my Lord's orders, and I won't have to do this again." She eyed me as she paused judiciously and then concluded, "Bitch."

At some point after she left, I passed out from the pain.

———

BLURRY PERCEPTION RETURNED, pain dominating the world.

"I can't stay," a female voice said softly, my ears hurting at even that volume. The voice was familiar, but I couldn't place it. "If the Seelie lord did order this, he cannot know I was here—and I can only conceal myself from him for so long."

"I will heal him," another voice, also female but totally unfamiliar, promised.

"Good," the first voice answered. "I do not like where this is going, and he is my only Sight into this mess. I need him."

I had a sensation of motion, and then pain screamed back into my world, dragging me back into unconsciousness.

———

I WOKE a second time to even blurrier perception but less pain. I was on something soft, and I had a vague impression of a blonde woman leaning over me. She saw that my eyes were open and smiled gently before laying a hand on my forehead.

Sleep, not unconsciousness, claimed me in gentle arms.

———

THE THIRD TIME, I woke to soft female voices talking at the foot of my bed. I was conscious enough to realize I was in my bed this time and to compute that there was at least one person sitting on the end of my bed.

I slowly opened my eyes and blinked against the harsh brightness for a moment. Then I realized that the room was actually very dimly lit, only a lamp in the corner turned on, as my eyes slowly adjusted to any light at all.

I recognized one of the voices now and croaked her name.

"Mary?"

The conversation stopped, and I suddenly had two women at the head of my bed. Mary all but threw herself on top of me, hugging and kissing me. My limbs responded slowly, stiffly, but eventually I got an arm around her.

"Give him a moment, m'dear," the blonde woman told Mary, her voice carrying a thick Irish accent. "Only his right arm really works right now."

The stranger's words reminded me, and I tried to move my other limbs. They were stiff, slightly unresponsive and painful to move—but they moved. They weren't broken. Mary helped me sit up, and I looked questioningly at the stranger.

"I think I owe you thanks, but who are you?" I asked her.

"My name is Niamh," the stranger told me. Her eyes were a stunning green color, and she had tied her blonde hair up in a braid that wrapped around her head rather than falling to the ground. "Our Queen brought me here to heal you."

"You did this?" I gestured down at my surprisingly not broken body.

"I am like you," she told me, "a Vassal of the Queen but not noble. My father was a middling-ranked noble and a Vassal, but my mother was a mere dryad. I have some of both of their gifts, including healing, but I am beneath most noble fae's notice."

"I suspect you manage that avoiding notice better than I do," I groaned, slowly, with Mary's help, raising myself to a sitting position.

"So it seems," she agreed. "Your upper left arm was shattered, both of your shoulders had multiple hairline fractures, your right leg was broken in four separate places and your left kneecap was actually sheared in two. I don't think you avoid attention very well."

"You healed all of that?" I asked, impressed.

She nodded. "That and a dozen or so minor fractures in your ribs," she added. "You are *very* lucky you were wearing the armor the Queen gifted you. Without it, I judge your ribs would have been crushed and your lungs and heart likely pierced with bone fragments. I cannot heal the dead."

I winced at her description of my actual injuries—and how much worse it could have been!

"How did the Queen know?" I asked.

"You are Her Vassal," Niamh said simply. "She is at least vaguely aware of what happens to all of us, wherever we are. You are on a task for Her, so you are higher in Her thoughts."

"She's afraid Oberis did order this, isn't She?" I asked softly, remembering the half-heard conversation. "What does it mean if he did?"

"He ordered an attack on a Vassal of the Queen," the other Vassal said quietly. "The High Court will *not* approve. He will find them unwilling to take his calls for a time and their support lacking until he has re-earned their faith.

"Aiding you in defeating this cabal and this plot upon MacDonald will go a long way towards that," she continued, "but that presumes you are willing to *let* him."

I looked at Mary, who was now cuddled up to my side, and I squeezed her gently. I saw the worry in her eyes at Niamh's words and smiled as reassuringly as I could through the pain.

"I don't think I have a choice," I said quietly. Then a sudden horrified thought struck. "Shit, I have to get to work!"

"You'd look rather silly going in today, dear," Mary told me quietly. "It's Sunday."

"I kept you mostly unconscious," Niamh explained. "It was easier to heal you that way. It still took two days. Your work did call your mobile on Friday; I told them I was a nurse in the ER and you had been in a minor car accident but would be fine by Tuesday."

She fixed me with a steady glare.

"And you aren't going anywhere until then," she told me. "I need to return home tonight, but you are not going *anywhere* until Tuesday. Bed rest or, if you *have* to go anywhere, you're going in a wheelchair. Understand?"

"I don't have a..." I trailed off as she pointed. An expensive-looking unpowered wheelchair was sitting in the corner of the room.

"Much of the healing process is not yet complete," she explained. "You *will* be fully healed soon, but you must give the magic and your body time to work. Do not walk till Monday night at the earliest."

"I'll stay with you," Mary promised. "Clem has agreed to let me borrow his car, so I can take you to the funeral Monday."

I gave her another gentle squeeze in thanks.

"How are you getting home?" I asked Niamh.

"My half-brother is a member of the Wild Hunt," she told me. "A group of the Hunters is in Seattle today on other business. He will detour on his way back and take me Between to Ireland with him.

"Now," she said firmly, putting her hand on my shoulder and gently pushing me back down on the bed. "Rest. You are still healing."

————

I woke up later to a series of gentle kisses across my forehead and a giggling Mary. Half-consciously, I reached up to grab her and then stopped, wincing in pain. Muscles and tendons pulled and complained, and I slowly opened my eyes to look up at her expression of concern.

"Sorry, sweetie," she told me quietly. "Niamh told me to wake you; I didn't think."

"It's okay," I assured her. And it was. For all the aches and pains, I couldn't think of a better way to wake up than with a gorgeous woman kissing you. "What does she want?"

"Her brother is here," Mary told me. "She wanted to talk to you before they left. Can you make it to the wheelchair on your own?"

I nodded firmly in response, slowly and carefully swung my stiff legs around and off the bed. Equally slowly and carefully, I stood and took two stubborn, shaky steps toward the wheelchair. I then proceeded to fall halfway to my knees before Mary managed to catch me and help me make it the rest of the way, shaking her head at me.

"Thank you," I told her as we eased me into the chair. It had been a *long* time since I'd been wounded badly enough that it had taken more than day or two for me to heal. Fae, even changelings, healed quickly, after all. If I was still this weak, even after Niamh's healing, I must have been nearly dead.

The stunning blonde healer was waiting in my kitchen, sitting across the table from a gentleman who put her to shame. Easily three or four inches over six feet, the man was whipcord thin and visibly muscled. His eyes, green like his half-sister, seemed to pierce to my very soul. The silver-hilted sword he'd casually leaned against my table was unnecessary to demonstrate that this was not a man to trifle with—this was a Rider of the Wild Hunt.

He faced me with a smile and inclined his head slightly.

"Kilkenny," he said quietly. "I am Oisin, son of Liam, and I am pleased to make your acquaintance."

We shook hands after Mary rolled me up to the table, and I looked at Niamh.

"Thanks for your help," I told her. "I doubt I'd be around to complain if you hadn't come."

"The Queen asks, and we serve," she said simply. "You are welcome. Take this," she instructed, passing me a small black pottery vial. "I don't approve," she continued, eyeing the vial with distaste, "but the Queen insisted."

"What is it?" I asked, examining the vial carefully. A leather thong was threaded through a loop on the side, and I slung the vial around my neck. I was unsurprised that it hung just low enough to be tucked inside the armored shirt the Queen had given me.

"Quicksilver," Niamh said simply. "The Queen said to tell you to use it the next time you decided you had to fight someone outside your 'weight class,' as She put it."

I tucked the vial, precious beyond its weight, inside my shirt.

"How do I use it?" I asked.

She shrugged. "Pop the stopper and drink it. Be very careful, Jason," Niamh warned me. "Quicksilver is a huge surge of power; it will help you defeat an enemy, but it is also *highly* addictive. It is our kind's cocaine but with an actual use as well."

"Some of the weaker Hunters are known to use it to make up for perceived shortcomings," Oisin told me. "It is powerful. Which is, of course, a part of why it is so addictive."

"Thank you," I told Niamh again. She smiled and stood to leave, but Oisin didn't rise, instead staring intently at me.

"Have we met before?" the Hunter suddenly asked. "You seem very familiar."

I paused, looking very carefully at Oisin. The tall blond with his pointed ears and green eyes was of a type not uncommon among the noble fae. Nothing about him screamed familiarity at me, though. I was pretty sure I'd never met him before.

"I don't think so," I told him. "But I have bounced across many of the courts in the southern US; we may have met then."

Oisin laughed.

"Kilkenny, how old do you think I am?" he asked.

I looked at him, puzzled. A noble fae was likely older than he looked, but Oisin did look very young.

"Sixty?" I hazarded a guess.

"Add a century," he told me. "I have lived a hundred and seventy-one summers upon this world and spent the last hundred of those among the Hunt.

"By blood and by my Vassalage to our Queen, I have the right to leave the Hunt," he continued, "but if I did, I could never return. While I am bound to the Hunt, my ability to travel apart from it is limited, and the Hunt travels outside Europe rarely and never as a whole.

"I have not set foot in the southern United States since Calebrant led us, some two score years ago," he explained. "So, no, I have not seen you in the Courts of the South. And yet you are familiar." He shrugged and finally stood to join his half-sister.

"You are a mystery, changeling and Vassal of my Queen," he told me. "Someday, you and I may work out the answer to that mystery, but as I said, my movements apart from my duties to the Hunt are limited. I must return my sister and myself to the Old World."

"Pass my respects and thanks to the Queen," I told them, somewhat grudgingly. I was grateful She'd saved me, but if She hadn't dragged me into being a Vassal and trying to investigate this plot She feared, I wouldn't have been beaten on in the first place!

"We will," Niamh promised, and then laid her hand on her brother's arm. Oisin bowed his head to me, *stepped* Between and was gone.

21

THE REST of Sunday passed quietly. Still stiff, bruised and dizzy, I wasn't up for much. We threw in a movie and cuddled, talking of inconsequential things. To be more precise, Mary talked of inconsequential things—growing up in Calgary, putting up with her brother becoming a doctor, working in a gaming store, that sort of thing.

Every so often, her talk would touch on Tarvers, and she would be quiet for a while, both of us pretending to only pay attention to the movie. There was nothing I could really say or do about the Alpha's death. I could only hope that something in my investigation into the whole mess with MacDonald would turn up details or evidence I could use to punish Winters for the murder.

In the end, exhaustion from healing claimed me, and Mary helped me to bed, where I promptly passed out.

In the morning, I called my boss.

"How are you doing?" were the first words out of Bill's mouth. "I called your cell and got an ER nurse; she said you'd been in an accident and she wasn't sure when you'd be back at work."

"Stiff, bruised," I told him honestly. "I got bounced off the front of a car," I lied, "nothing broken in the end, but I am beaten to shit."

"You're a lucky fuck," he told me. "Look, take today and tomorrow off; come back in Wednesday. We can do without you for two days, and I'd rather you didn't make things worse."

"I should be fine to come in tomorrow," I insisted, knowing that with my natural healing, I would be.

"Did you get the idea this was arguable?" Bill told me with a grunt. "Get off the phone and go rest. I'll see you Wednesday."

I thanked him and returned to cuddling Mary. The rest of the morning passed in a gentle fog of cuddling and quiet conversation.

Eventually, however, the time came to go to the funeral for the brother and sister who'd died because I hadn't warned them fast enough.

Mary helped me into the wheelchair and then to the car. We drove to the small chapel that the Court apparently maintained for their own purposes, like this. The parking lot was mostly full as Mary pulled into an empty stall.

"Let's leave the wheelchair behind," I told Mary. "I'd rather not appear weak in front of the Court," I admitted.

"All right," she said after eyeing me for a minute. "But I'm not leaving your side, and you'd better lean on me if you need me."

Still stiff and sore, it took me a minute or so to get out of the car, which allowed me a few good long looks at the black SUV parked next to us—and the stylized K decal in its window.

At least some of the Enforcers were there.

———

LEANING SOMEWHAT ON MARY, I made my way into the chapel. As soon as we passed through the doors, I knew that no mortal had ever set foot in the building—it would be hard to conceal from the inside that it was probably four or five times as large inside as out and was in no way, shape or form the Christian place of worship it appeared from the outside.

Six hundred feet from entrance to nave, the temple inside shared the same shape as the chapel outside, but that was the end of its resemblance to a mortal church. Unlike the chapel whose shell it occupied, the temple had no internal walls. The entire space was open, four steps leading down to the massive, thirty-feet-on-a-side balefire pit. Today the fire in the pit blazed high and hot, flames licking ten or twelve feet into the air, almost reaching the level of the entrance.

Nine alcoves were cut into the walls on the top level, each centered on a statue and containing a hanging banner. The statues and banners were identical to those in every similar temple in the world, carved and woven to designs that had existed when Rome was born. Each honored one of the Nine, the High Court. We didn't worship the Powers, per se, but they stood head and shoulders above the rest of us.

As I understood it, none of the High Court were the original holders of their titles, and the statues were of the original Nine. Certainly, the statue in the Queen's alcove bore no resemblance to Mabona, though the stylized silver tree on the blue banner seemed just *right* to something in me.

The hall looked half empty, but after a moment's glance around, I realized that almost all of Calgary's less than a hundred fae were in the building. A dozen or so shifters other than Mary, presumably friends of Dave and Elena's, stood on the third level, looking down at the slightly denser crowd on the second level.

The first level was almost empty. Oberis stood closest to the fire, and Talus and Laurie stood next to him. I caught myself glaring at the trio and controlled myself with an effort. It wouldn't do to betray my current anger at the fae lord in public. Besides, this was neither the place nor the time.

Two more fae, male and female older gentry, stood on the first level with the Lord and his two courtiers. From the family resemblance, they were Dave and Elena's parents.

The only other occupants of the bottom level of the Hall were two stone biers, each carrying the cloth-wrapped body of one of the two we had come to mourn. I was a little surprised there was enough left of them for that—they had been very close to the claymores when they had detonated.

Mary and I slowly made our way down to the second level, where the fae and changelings gathered. The fourth and topmost level was empty except for a few new arrivals arriving behind us; the third held the shifters and a single pair of black-suited Enforcers. I recognized

Percy, Michael's boss, as one of them and wondered if he'd actually known Dave or Elena, or if MacDonald had just picked names out of a hat to send as a gesture.

When we reached the second level, I caught a few mutters at Mary's presence—this level was supposed to be limited to fae only. Between my current aggravation with fae protocol and my need to have her to physically lean on, I found the mutters easy to ignore.

I settled into one of the plain chairs that encircled the level with a carefully concealed groan of relief. From one or two sharp glances my way, it wasn't concealed enough. None of them said anything, though, and the arrival of Eric a moment later silenced any comments anyone would have made.

The gnome paused at my chair for a moment, long enough to squeeze my shoulder in sympathy, and then joined the quintet on the lowest level. Oberis inclined his head to the Keeper and looked up to survey the levels above him.

Oberis obviously felt that everyone who was coming was there, as he killed the lights in the uppermost level with a gesture of his hand. All of the electric lights dimmed, and sparks flew from the balefire to light rows of candles on the edge of each level. After a moment, the balefire and the candles provided the only light in the Hall.

"We are gathered here, in this place that stands outside the world, to honor and remember two of our own," Oberis said softly, his voice carrying to every corner of the hall.

"Dave and Elena Cunningham served me loyally and well for years," he continued. "It was in this service that they fell. While investigating reports of a vampire cabal in our city, we were betrayed, and Dave and Elena, along with several others, were led into a trap. A devious combination of old and new was used to attack them with cold iron, killing them before they even knew they were under attack."

The fae lord let silence hang in the Hall for a long time before finally speaking again.

"They died in my service, and there are obligations to be paid," he said, facing the Cunninghams' parents. "Any service you would ask," he told them, his voice even softer than before. "Any Boon I can give. Ask what you will, and it will be done."

The Cunninghams nodded, bowing slightly in acknowledgement of the debt. Mr. Cunningham stepped forward, cleared his throat and began a clearly prepared speech, reciting memorized words.

"Our children believed from a young age that the gentry had a duty, a responsibility, to help maintain order in our world," he said slowly. "While no parent believes their child to be truly perfect, Dave and Elena certainly tried their hardest to live up to that belief. All their lives, they were there for those in need, choosing service over themselves.

"Both of them sacrificed so much," he said sadly. "Neither had much in terms of relationships; few lovers or friends could compete with their steadfast devotion to duty. But they made a difference. Here, and elsewhere where they went on their business, people are alive who otherwise would be dead.

"They spent their lives protecting others, and died doing what they chose to do," he finished, choking on his tears. His wife didn't say anything, simply quietly weeping.

Eric stepped forward, glancing around the levels above him and those watching from there.

"We ask anyone with memories of Dave and Elena to share them," he told the crowd quietly. This was tradition. We saw too many of the realities behind humanity's myths to really believe in an afterlife. All that remains of us once we pass on is the memories we leave behind.

One of the shifters stepped to the balcony before any of the fae moved, and Eric gestured to him to speak.

"I will never forget the day I met Elena," the shifter began, his voice rough with emotion. "A rogue hippogriff had just wiped out a small human farm, and I was hunting it through the Rocky Mountains. It surprised me, and I crashed my van. I was wounded and alone, and the beast was hunting me. I thought I was dead, and then Elena arrived. She'd been hunting the same creature, and her timing was perfect. I'd have died that day without her."

The shifter sat back down, and one of the fae stepped forward, with a story of a fight with vampires in Winnipeg, where he'd stood shoulder to shoulder with Dave.

The stories that followed all had much the same theme. The process made the siblings' father's comments about their choice of lifestyle clear—all of them were of people being saved, battles being fought. No stories of jokes, or pranks, or lovers. Just of them as protectors and warriors. That was the life they'd chosen.

Eventually, even those stories died off, leaving only silence. Eric waited a few more moments, to be sure no one else was going to speak up, and then turned to the balefire.

"We commit the bodies of our friends to the eternal fires of the hearth, which shall never go out," he said loudly. "Let the smoke join the air of the world, let the ashes join the earth of the world, let the fire raise them up and may the water know them. Let them return to the world that birthed them."

The Keeper nodded to Oberis, who gestured. Slowly, the two stone biers lifted up, carried by his power to the balefire at the heart of the hall. The biers slid into the flame and lowered, the flame wrapping around them and slowly igniting the wrappings around the bodies.

The wrappings were soaked in herbs and spices, obviously, as the scent that came from the burning flesh wasn't the burnt-pork smell I remembered from the night of the explosion but a mixed scent of woodsmoke and what was probably sage.

The balefire of a faerie hall was hotter than a natural flame, and the bodies of our fallen were consumed quickly. When the last of the scent of sage and slight tinge of burnt pork faded into the clean woodsmoke smell of the fire, Oberis faced the north side of the hall—where the Enforcers sat.

"There is one last thing we must address today," he said harshly, his voice loud and no longer soft. "Dave and Elena died at the hands of a vampire cabal. The prevention of the arrival of these creatures in our city was part of what was promised as the guarantees for which we conceded authority to the Magus MacDonald under the Covenants of this city.

"Yet a cabal is here," he continued. "Dave and Elena are the only inhumans we know to have fallen to them, but we know of many human deaths we can attribute to their actions. We know how they arrived. We must assume that, like all feeders, they are hostile to us.

"What we do *not* know is how this came to pass," Oberis said grimly, and I didn't envy Percy having that stone gaze turned on him. "Our Covenants say that the Magus will prevent this. Our Covenants say that the Magus will investigate and destroy any vampire incursion into the city.

"But the cabal is here, and MacDonald has not acted," he concluded. "Humans are dying, and he has not acted. Our people"— he gestured to the balefire—"have died, and he has not acted. So, we have acted ourselves."

"And yet, despite the Magus's lack of action, when investigations into these vampires by an ally of ours—*by a signatory to the Covenants*— clashed with his Enforcers' daily operations, those Enforcers murdered Alpha Tarvers, Speaker for the Clans, in cold blood.

"*This is not acceptable,*" Oberis snarled, and the temperature in the room dropped. Despite the fire in the center of the Hall, and the candles throughout, I shivered at the sudden chill.

"I, like Tarvers Tenerim, signed the Covenants with Magus MacDonald," Oberis continued coldly. "And I know what was agreed to."

"So, Enforcer Percy Harrington," he said, addressing the senior Enforcer, "I have a message for you to bear to your master. As of *now*, he is on notice that he has violated the Covenants."

The room was silent. The balefire burned with an occasional *pop*, but I don't think the rest of us were even breathing. I know I was holding my breath as I waited for Oberis to continue.

"He has, per the Covenants, five days to respond to this notice," he finally said. "If we do not see some action by him against the vampires, *and* some response to the cold-blooded murder of Alpha Tarvers by Enforcers, I will approach the High Court for sanction upon him."

I swallowed, remembering Niamh's warning that Oberis would find the High Court unresponsive to his calls for some time. Did he forget so readily what he'd done? Was ordering a man who had aided and helped him beaten to the edge of death such a minor thing to him that he didn't realize it would cause a clash between him and the High Court?

"Tell your master, dog," Oberis continued icily, his gaze still locked on Percy, "that the *least* I will accept is the beginnings of a good-faith effort to dissolve the Enforcers—and the surrender of Gerard Winters to the Clans' justice.

"Now get out," he ordered. "You were here to bear witness, and you have borne witness; now leave this to the friends of the fallen—not those who have marked themselves their enemies!"

————

WITH THE CREMATION complete and the Enforcers evicted from the chapel, the silence in the hall was unbroken for what seemed like forever. After what was probably less than a minute, however, Dave and Elena's father directed everyone up to the top level, where a few gestures from Oberis folded tables down from the walls and spread white tablecloths over them. Several refrigerators that I had missed in the darkness were opened up, and several tables of drinks and appetizers quickly took form under the swift ministrations of a few fluttering pixies, glowing slightly in the still somewhat dim light of the hall.

Leaning as discreetly on Mary as I could, I followed the crowd up to join the wake. With the massive balefire in the center, the hall was not merely warm but hot. It took a conscious effort of will, given my current abused state, to keep myself from stripping off clothing and showing weakness in front of the Court.

It was almost as much of an effort not to glare at Oberis as the fae lord nodded genteelly to me. He walked with the Cunninghams, his attention for the day clearly focused on the parents of those who'd fallen in his service.

Mary gently but pointedly guided me to a table with food on it. I took the hint and slowly began loading up a plate. After I started to eat, Mary grabbed a plate of her own and began to take food. As I ate, I surveyed the hall and the crowd gathered.

The group of shifters mostly kept to themselves, though several of the fae who clearly knew them stopped by and stayed for a few minutes each. Even in this united Court, I could see clear dividing lines among the fae—Seelie clustered with Seelie, Unseelie with Unseelie. There were other groupings, but that was the clearest and most obvious, marked to my eyes at least by the groups Laurie and Talus each moved in—the hag an Unseelie, the noble a Seelie.

Talus spotted me looking over at him and appeared to excuse himself from the conversation and head my way. I sighed inwardly— after Laurie and Oberis, Talus was probably the person I least wanted to deal with of everyone here. While I doubted he'd known of Oberis's order, he still stood at the right hand of a man who'd ordered me beaten.

Nonetheless, in every other way, he was a man I'd normally regard as a friend, so I didn't quite have it in me to be rude and turn him away as he came to join me. He smiled at Mary and started grabbing a plate of food.

"I wanted to thank you again," he said quietly. "There is no doubt your warning and help saved Robert's life. I owe you."

I shifted uncomfortably. I'd shared this man's thoughts, knew what barriers lay against him acknowledging his son. I couldn't know that and not act to help.

"It was nothing," I told him.

"Hardly," the noble said dryly. "But you should also know—Robert healed far faster than Lacombe expected, and Lacombe knows our kind *very* well. He has begun to manifest the powers of a noble fae, and questions have been asked in Court that I could not avoid. I have officially acknowledged him as my son."

There was pain in his words. I couldn't imagine what it would feel like to have that kind of intensely personal moment and admission forced before the body of the Court, both Seelie and Unseelie. Taking into account the fact that fae nobility weren't supposed to breed outside the nobility, it could not have been an easy day.

"How did he take it?" I asked when Mary squeezed my hand after a moment of silence.

"Not...well," Talus said simply, and there was more pain in his voice. "He understands, I think, but he is very, *very* angry with me. I understand that, and he understands why I had to keep it secret, so I think we will work out our relationship over time."

"It will just be painful for a while," I said sympathetically.

"My uncle has had to punish me for public consumption," Talus told me, his voice still quiet. "I am being at least temporarily exiled from Calgary—I am to return to Fort McMurray and my duties there, with no permission to return to the city for some time."

Well, at least I wasn't the only one Oberis seemed to feel obliged to punish beyond all reason. I squeezed Mary's hand in turn and eyed the fae noble.

"Are you going to be okay?" I asked him.

He nodded, and there was something...odd about his eyes. He didn't look nearly upset enough for what he'd just told me. He was being punished because something his uncle had already known had become public—I would have expected him to be far angrier.

"I have to leave first thing in the morning," he told me and Mary. "Would you two do the honor of joining me for dinner tonight? I would enjoy less...prejudicial company than I've had recently."

"I smell a rat," I told him bluntly. "What's on your mind?"

Talus glanced around him quickly.

"I want you to meet someone," he explained. "I'll tell you more at dinner—mostly, I do just want company."

I was pretty sure he still wasn't telling me the whole truth, but something in his face warned me it was better not to ask there.

"All right, where?"

"The Stadium Park Steakhouse," he told me, and then gave quick directions. "I've reserved a table for four." He glanced around the wake. "I have to go be social. I will see you tonight at seven."

With that, he parted, leaving Mary and I to look at each other in concern.

"He's not telling us everything," I whispered to her.

"I don't think it's dangerous," she replied, and I nodded in agreement.

"I guess we'll find out tonight."

22

———————

"Tonight" wasn't a whole lot later. The wake for the Cunninghams lasted until just after six, at which point it was a rush for us to get across town to the restaurant in time. While we'd been closed up in the stifling hot ceremony hall, it had started to snow again outside and traffic had crawled to a standstill.

We made it to the restaurant shortly before seven and found ourselves facing a crowded line. Even on a Monday night, the restaurant was packed this close to the holiday season. I managed to squeeze through the crowd.

"We're meeting a man named Talus," I told the hostess. "He said he had a reservation; I don't know if he's here yet."

The elegantly dressed, cleavage-exposing, clearly underage brunette at the little podium checked her list, read something, and visibly swallowed.

"If you can come with me, please?" she asked, her voice somewhat shaky. "I'll take you to your table."

I was going to ask just what was wrong, but she took off almost before she was finished talking. I traded looks with Mary and shrugged, then followed the girl. She led us expertly through the dimly lit restaurant and around a large gas-fed fire pit in the middle of the restaurant to a door tucked away in a corner.

She opened the door and gestured through.

"Your reservation is in the private room, sir, ma'am," the girl said, standing aside to let us in.

"Thank you," I gave her a tentative smile and then entered the private room with Mary one step behind me.

The room on the other side was paneled in aged oak and held a single large conference table that looked older than the building. All of the furniture and decorations were to a far higher standard than the outside, and the chairs looked luxuriously soft under their leather coverings.

Talus, clad in the same subdued black suit he'd worn to the funeral, and a slim auburn-haired woman in a dark blue business skirt suit were seated at the table across from us, and the fae noble gestured for us to sit.

"Welcome to my private room here," he told us. "I use it for very discreet business, and I would prefer to keep what passes between us tonight *very* private."

"Why all the cloak-and-dagger?" Mary demanded as I sat. "And how the hell do you get a private room in a chain restaurant?"

"You own the franchise, the building it rents and their primary food supplier, and are the guarantor of the manager's immigration visa," the business woman told us crisply. "Of course, all of those are through various intermediaries, shells and numbered companies, but the management here is under no illusion who actually owns them."

"Jason and Mary, be known to Shelly Fairchild," Talus told us, giving the woman a small smile. "My realtor, girlfriend and sometime lawyer."

"I thought it was lawyer, realtor and sometime girlfriend?" the object of his smile teased him. "When did I upgrade to full-time?"

Talus's smile expanded marginally, and he took her hand affectionately.

"Please, go over the menu," he told Mary and me. "We are in no rush, and I want to be sure we aren't accidentally overheard by the staff. I trust them—they are all mortal and unaware of our politics, if nothing else—but some things should stay as secret as possible."

As if to prove his word, a waiter with short-buzzed steely gray hair entered the room to ask us for our drink choices. Mary and I reviewed the menu, both of us selecting steaks when the waiter returned again.

"To repeat Mary's question," I said to Talus when the waiter left with our order, "why all the cloak-and-dagger?"

"Oberis and I have realized that we are being betrayed at the highest levels of the Court," he said bluntly. "Shelly and I kept identifying targets, and I kept taking teams out to them to find them stripped."

"No shit, Sherlock," Mary snipped. "I could have told you that after the damn bomb."

"We suspected then," Talus admitted. "But it is now far past any possible doubt. The revelation of my son makes some options available that weren't before."

"Like what?" I asked.

"Officially, I am being exiled back to my office in the oil sands to continue supervising the heartstone operations and get me out of everyone's sight," Talus explained. "No one really thinks I'm being punished, but it helps everyone if I'm out of sight and out of mind, so it isn't being questioned."

"And what's *actually* happening?" Mary asked.

"I am returning to Fort McMurray," Talus answered. "There, I am going to quietly reassess the backgrounds and loyalty of my personnel, and put together an operations team from the gentry and higher fae I have there—one I trust completely, and, most importantly, had no one involved in the prior operations. The only overlap will be me."

"So no one here can possibly betray it," I said slowly. "Except Oberis or the three of us in this room."

"And no one in this room other than me knew of every operation, and they were all betrayed," Talus told me. "So, even if I didn't already think I could trust you all, you also couldn't have been the mole."

"You wouldn't be telling us this if you didn't want us—want Jason —to do something," Mary said. "So, what's the point?"

"Jason is the only person involved in this that I fully trust," Talus told us. "My uncle wanted to use Laurie, but I think we needed to use someone who is a newcomer to the community and still mostly an outsider to the Court. He left the decision to me."

Well, that explained how things went from Laurie kicking the shit out of me to me being dragged into super-secret Court black ops, I reflected. The left hand wasn't talking to the right. For a minute, I was tempted to ask Talus if he knew about that and really expected me to still be trustworthy, but then sighed aloud.

I'd help Talus if he asked, because he was a good man, and having been in his head, I *knew* that. Even if I didn't know that, it served the Queen, so my blood bond and Vassalage left me no choice either.

"What do you expect from me?" I asked.

"I can put together and equip a team from my people and resources up at the oil sands," he explained, "but I can't identify targets from up there. I need you to work with Shelly, and—if possible—the Clans"—he nodded at the two ladies in turn—"and find another facility. We ran out of Sigrid REIT properties, but those vampires went *somewhere*—find it for me!"

"Do we have any leads?" I asked.

"One," Talus said grimly. "I've called in a favor I didn't want to call. This individual isn't pleasant to deal with, but if anyone knows what the vampires are up to, he will."

"What's so unpleasant about this guy, and how would he know anything about the feeders?" I asked.

"Because he *is* a feeder," Talus said bluntly. "He's a wendigo—a flesh cannibal who lives in the city under sufferance from MacDonald as long as he sticks to eating carrion. He works in a morgue and steals internal...well, bits, prior to the bodies being formaldehyded, for food.

"He owes me, big time, and if anyone knows about the feeders, it's him," the noble concluded. "He knows you're coming, but he isn't happy about it, and you may need to be convincing...one way or another."

"How long do we have?" Mary asked. "I can pull help from the Clan, but things will be disorganized until a new Speaker is named at Tarvers's funeral on Sunday..." She paused. "Shit, that's when Oberis's deadline is up, isn't it?"

"Intentionally so," Talus confirmed with a nod. "If nothing has been done, Oberis will declare MacDonald in breach at Tarvers's funeral and ask the support of the new Speaker in sanctioning the Wizard."

"What can the Clan and Court *do* against a Wizard?" I asked. Even Oberis, a full fae lord, paled in comparison to the abilities of a full Magus, a Power in his own right.

"Not a lot," Talus admitted. "We can remove the Enforcers from the equation very quickly, though—their authority has always come from us being unwilling to irritate the Wizard rather than any virtue of their own."

"Damn," I said quietly. "So, in other words, we have until the funeral?"

"If at all possible, I want to drag the battered and silver-chained body of whatever feeder leads the cabal into the funeral and toss it in the face of whoever MacDonald sends," Talus told me. "That is Sunday night. I want to bring my people into town Saturday morning and strike during daylight."

"So, we have till Friday," Mary said quietly.

"I hope that through Karl—the wendigo I mentioned—you'll have info sooner, but yes," he agreed, "by Friday I *must* have somewhere to strike."

"Or we face open war," I said. Open war against the Wizard, which would make the assassination plot I'd been called upon to prevent so much easier. Someone was pulling strings here, and I was starting to feel like a puppet.

"Or we face open war," Talus confirmed.

And on that grim note, our food arrived.

———

LATER, after we had parted ways and Mary had dropped me off at home, I stared at Shelly's card where I'd dropped it on my table. The mortal lawyer worked for the fae Court, helping provide a fae noble with the power and wealth he needed to function in modern society.

She was a volunteer who'd chosen to involve herself in fae politics.

Talus was a noble, born and raised to play that vicious game. Each found this game of deception and investigation their element in their own way. I didn't think either would have turned away from it, given a choice.

And me? I'd come here because I found the politics of the South, the constant give-and-take between Seelie, Unseelie and other inhuman groups, the lies and the games, too much to deal with. There, I would only ever be a pawn in someone's game. Too weak, too young, too unimportant—to the Seelie lords, I was expendable.

I had no idea what had caused Queen Mabona to claim me as Her Vassal now. I'd really thought I'd run far enough that I could find somewhere where there was no quiet cold war between the fae courts. That there, in the hinterlands of inhuman society, in a city with less than two hundred supernaturals—not including Enforcers or however many vampires there were—I could stay out of the games.

But Mabona's arrival in my life had changed everything. She had commanded, and whether I agreed or not, I had no choice but to obey. Obedience had carried me to the inner circle of fae society and power in this city—of Oberis and his two main lieutenants, one was almost a friend, and the other two appeared to hold me in some disregard, but they knew me. I knew barely a dozen fae in the city, but I knew the rulers—because of the Queen.

I had been forced into that inner circle of power, and now it seemed that, somehow, I had to save the Wizard from an assassination attempt, destroy a vampiric cabal, and prevent open supernatural war in Calgary's shadows.

So much for staying out of politics.

———

RETURNING to work on Wednesday morning was a bit of a shock to the system. A day's rest barely seemed like enough after the weekend I had, but the return to work was adorably mortal and mundane.

They had a get-well card and Trysta had baked a cake. Everyone took a few minutes out of getting ready for the day's shipments to make sure I was okay.

I ended up repeating the lie about the minor car accident and only being a little bruised in the end a lot. It wasn't like I could explain to them, "I got beaten to the edge of death due to politics and healed by magic over the weekend." It sounded a little insane even to me.

Sliding back into the more mundane frame of mind of my job, after a weekend wrapped up entirely in the world of my other life, was hard. It was helped by Bill clapping his hands sharply after a few minutes of everyone clustering around me.

"Come on, people, we're all glad Jason is okay, but can we be getting to work, please?" he told us, to general laughter. He harried us all into getting to it and loading up our trucks, and then stopped me as I was about to get into mine.

Whatever he wanted, I hoped it was quick. The weather was continuing what I was told was an unusual cold streak—everyone kept expecting another one of their "chinooks" to roll in. I was just hoping to avoid freezing to death.

"Do I want to know what really happened to you?" he said bluntly.

I swallowed, turning to face him fully. "I'm not sure what you mean," I lied.

"'Minor car accident,' my ass," he snapped. "You don't drive outside of work, Jason, and pedestrians don't *have* 'minor' car accidents. So, what happened?"

I sighed and stepped down from the step of the truck, leaning against it and shivering in the cold as I looked him in the eye. "You want the short version, or the one you won't actually believe?"

"I know you're into shit I don't want to know about," he told me. "I'm figuring organized crime, but as long as you don't cause problems for me or mine and do your job, I'm going to let that slide. But I also need to know what's going to come back on me or mine—and you're one of mine now, got it?"

I was touched. There was no other way to put it. Bill had no idea what was really going on, and had made some assumptions that made me look a lot worse than the truth did—organized crime in this city was mostly drugs, so far as I could tell—but I worked for him, so he was willing to take my side.

"It's not crime," I told him quietly. "I'm not going to tell you what it is," I continued—telling him would do him no favors right now, with a supernatural war about to explode under his nose, "but it's not crime.

"The long and the short of it is that someone beat the shit out of me, but not as thoroughly as they thought," I explained. "I don't like it, but I'm not in a position to do anything about it yet, either."

My boss eyed me over. He stood silent and apparently immune to the chill setting into my bones.

"*Yet*, eh?" he answered.

"Probably never," I admitted. I didn't see much coming along that would make it possible for me to get back at Laurie, let alone at Oberis.

"Well, don't expect to get the day off if you get beaten up in your off hours again," he told me gruffly. "I prefer my people not to get into fights."

"I'll see what I can do about that," I promised. I knew what I could do about avoiding fights: not bloody much. If the Queen commanded, I obeyed. It wasn't like I had a choice.

"Now get in that truck while you still have your fingers," Bill ordered.

I obeyed.

23

FIFTEEN MINUTES out of the office, I got a text message, and the politics of the supernatural came crashing back into my life, just as I was hoping to have a quiet, mundane day.

It was from Michael, telling me to meet him at a Starbucks to pick up packages. I left it unanswered for several minutes, making two deliveries while I mulled over what to do in response. The leader of my race in Calgary had demanded that the Enforcers be dissolved. I doubted that helping them out was on Oberis's list of things he wanted us to do.

In the end, I sent a single-word text back. No.

It took less than a minute for my phone to ring.

"What do you mean, no?" Michael demanded. "You can't just refuse the Enforcers."

"Yes, I can," I told him quietly as I maneuvered the heavy truck to the side of the road so I could talk to him.

"When you entered this city, you agreed to aid the Enforcers in any way we needed," he reminded me. "Do you want to know what the penalty for breaking that is?"

"I know that my first oath is to the leader of the Court in this city," I said quietly. "Oberis has laid sanction against the Magus MacDonald, under the Covenants of this city. All fae are forbidden from offering aid or succor to the Enforcers or the Wizard."

"What?!" Michael snapped. "What bullshit is this? I haven't heard anything like that!"

A chill rippled down my spine. It had been formally announced—hell, the witness sent back to the Wizard had been Michael's *boss*.

"Notice was given to the Enforcers yesterday," I told him, trying to stiffen my voice. "MacDonald is being sanctioned for Winters's murder of Alpha Tarvers, and the Lord of the Joint Court has demanded the dissolution of the Enforcers. I'm sorry, but I am not allowed to help you."

There was silence on the phone for a moment, and then a beep as my phone informed me that Michael had hung up.

I sat there in the truck for a long moment. Notice had been given to the Enforcers Monday of what Oberis had demanded, but an Enforcer of moderate seniority like Michael didn't know a thing. I had assumed that the news would have spread quickly in such a tight organization, through the rumor mill if nothing else.

If Michael didn't know, who else didn't know? Had Percy told *anyone*? Or had Magus MacDonald ordered it kept quiet while he did damage control—Powers alone knew what damage control he could manage.

The most terrifying thought that occurred to me, just as I was putting the truck back in gear, was to wonder if Percy had told the Magus at all.

———

SHELLY CALLED me shortly after I got home that evening. It took me a moment to recognize the number on my phone, and I didn't remember giving it to Shelly. I guess Talus had, which made sense—she was the one who could contact Karl, the wendigo we expected to give us whatever clues came next.

"Hi, Jason," she greeted me. "How's life?"

"A ticking time bomb; how's yours?" I asked, and she laughed.

"About the same," she admitted. "On top of all my normal workload for Talus, plus my other clients, I now get to worry about an impending war in which I would be acceptable collateral damage. My best holiday season ever."

"The point is to avoid the war," I reminded her. "Good to hear you're in good cheer."

"I'm a lawyer," she told me. "If I can fake believing my client is innocent, I can fake good cheer."

"You do criminal law?" I replied. She sighed over the phone.

"Not anymore," she said. "And having to defend people I didn't think were innocent is why I don't." She let that sit in the silence for a moment, and then continued, "I spoke to Karl today. He isn't any happier about this than Talus said he would be. I had to remind him of his debt. And of the fact that if I revealed that he was eating bits of the bodies in his case to his employers, being fired would be the *least* of his worries."

"He knows something?"

"He was evasive on the phone," Shelly told me. "I think he was too upset to be called on his debt to not know something. He agreed to meet with you as Talus's representative."

"Where and when?" I asked.

"Tonight, at the morgue at the Foothills hospital," she told me. "Six thirty."

"Thanks Shelly," I said. "I guess I'll go call a taxi, I don't have a lot of time."

———

THANKFULLY, the cab took long enough to arrive that I could change into a fresh shirt and jeans. I hoped, vaguely, that a dark blue shirt and black jeans would somehow make me more intimidating. I wasn't really sure what a wendigo even looked like, or what it would find scary.

The cab delivered me to the hospital ten minutes before I was supposed to meet Karl. I intended, for about twenty seconds, to try and sneak in unnoticed. Then I realized I had no idea where the morgue *was*, and headed for the reception desk.

"Hi, I'm supposed to meet a Karl Redding here," I told her, emphasizing my slow Southern drawl, hopefully to make her take pity on the newcomer to the city. "He said to just come down to the morgue, but I don't know where it is."

"Trust Karl not to tell you half of what you need to know," the petite blonde said with a laugh and a toss of her hair. "It's not an easy place to find; I'll call him up for you. What was your name?"

"Jason Kilkenny," I told her.

She nodded, picked up the phone and dialed. "Karl? There's a Mr. Kilkenny up here to see you. Can you come collect him?" She listened for a moment and then nodded. "Thanks, he'll be waiting."

The receptionist hung up the phone and turned back to me. "He'll be up in a few minutes."

"What did you mean by 'trust Karl not to tell me' things?" I asked.

"Oh, nothing much," she said with another hair flick. "He's just an odd one, always a little out of it. Most people find him pretty intimidating."

I started to ask why and then spotted the man coming down the hall and let the question die unspoken.

Karl Redding wasn't the tallest or largest man I'd ever met, but then, I'd known Tarvers Tenerim. He towered four inches or so over my own six feet and looked easily four feet across the shoulders. He was heavily built, muscles clearly visible even through his hospital scrubs, and his hair was done in pure white dreadlocks. His skin was deathly pale, and only when I met his eyes and saw the Native American cast to his face did it hit me: he was an albino.

"You'd be Kilkenny, then," he said to me when he reached reception, his voice soft and warm, not at all what I was expecting from his imposing visage. "Come with me." He glanced aside at the receptionist. "Thanks, Jenny, I'll take care of him."

With a grunt and a shoulder toss, he indicated that I should follow him. There weren't many people that we passed in the hospital corridors in the evening hours, but all of the ones we passed quickly stepped aside for me and my human-iceberg guide.

He led me through various hallways and eventually down a set of stairs out of the normal way, to a clean and sterile concrete basement and a security door. A security badge emerged from the pocket of his white lab coat and he swiped in.

"Take a seat," he instructed, gesturing to a glass-walled office in one corner of the chilly room with its rows of metal doors.

I obeyed, grabbing one of the chairs in the tiny room. A moment later, Karl joined me, carrying a steaming Tupperware. "Threw this in the microwave before I came to get you; timing was perfect," he told me."

The scent of stroganoff sauce wafted though the morgue office, though I realized that he'd closed all the doors, and a ventilation system in the corner whirred away. It was *probably* enough to keep the morgue outside sterile. Then I caught the scent of the meat in the microwaved dinner. Pork. And I remembered what wendigo ate.

"That's human?" I asked, feeling slightly sick.

Karl grinned and nodded, taking a forkful of the pasta dish. "Want some?"

"No," I said flatly, eyeing him as he continued to blithely eat. "Are you doing that to see if it bothers me?" I asked after a moment.

"No, I'm eating because it's my dinnertime," he replied. "Of course, I invited you here at my dinnertime to see if it would bother you," he added.

"Of course," I repeated, and pointedly turned away to look around the small office. A plain gray metal desk that was likely older than I was dominated the room, with filing cabinets taking up most of the rest of the space. A pair of plaques on the wall declared Karl Redding a certified morgue technician, and a Kacy Miller as an MD and certified forensic examiner.

"I was told," I continued, looking back at Karl, "that you would be able to help us find the vampires in the city."

The big albino Native sighed and took one last bite of his long-pig stroganoff before replacing the lid and sliding it to one side.

"So, you can wipe them out," he said flatly. It wasn't really a question, and I couldn't argue the point with him, not really. "The fae's response to feeders always tends towards extermination first. I'm only breathing because my Clan is long known to the Courts, and we have always lived on carrion.

"Do you think I have a choice?" he demanded suddenly. "Do you think I *want* to eat people?"

I thought about it for a long moment, taking a long look at the man and considering him. I couldn't see someone *choosing* a diet that left them horrendously exposed in both the human and inhuman worlds.

"No," I finally admitted.

"We don't have a choice—*feeders* don't have a choice," Karl told me harshly. "Our bodies don't process other foods properly—without our diet, we die. Do you somehow expect the vampires to just lie down and die?"

"They kill," I said simply. "Whether it's their choice or not isn't really relevant—you don't kill."

"I have sixty years of cultural acclimation by my family, and a thousand years of tradition," he told me. "I was born wendigo, and my family raised me to fight the urge—and part of me still thinks that fresh, live human would taste so much better than carrion. And I'll never be rid of that urge, understand?"

The image his words conjured in my mind wasn't pleasant. Wendigo were rare enough that Karl would have grown up with mostly humans, and every day, his body told him humans were food. It would be horrible.

"What's your point?" I finally asked. Horrifying as his existence was, it still didn't help me find the vampires.

"The vampires don't have that upbringing or that tradition," Karl said quietly. "They are turned as adults, and all they know is that they *must* feed. For too many of them, their state is not their fault.

"They have no choice in what they do and never had a choice in what they are."

"They are monsters," I reminded him. "Whether murderers by choice or need, they are still murderers, and every day they are in this city, more innocents die."

"So simple and black-and-white for you, is it?" he demanded, slamming his fist into the desk as he glared at me. "Even though they never chose this, they are just monsters to be killed—pests to be exterminated?"

I returned his glare flatly. I couldn't really disagree with his point—vampires really didn't choose their fate.

"As long as they choose to kill to live, yes," I told him bluntly. "Are you going to help me or not?"

Karl broke the desk. Both of his fists slammed down with enough force that the metal bent and sheared under his fury. The sound of crumpling metal echoed in the tiny office, and his pink eyes were alight with anger.

"Remember yourself, *feeder*," I barked at him. "One phone call and you're done at this hospital," I reminded him. "We gave you sanctuary, a safe place, helped you meet your dietary need. Now the debt is called."

Power, both physical and spiritual, rippled along the wendigo's body, and I realized I was standing, facing him in the tiny room as sparks flashed over his flesh, and his white dreadlocks began to glow and whip around with a life of their own.

"Remember yourself," I snapped again, facing him head on and meeting his fiery glare. I was unarmed, but I felt the heat of my faerie flame gathering in my fingertips. We held that moment for what seemed like an eternity, and then the power and rage seemed to drain from him, and he collapsed back into his chair.

"You're right," he admitted, staring at the damage he'd done to his desk. Power still sparked over him, and he laid his hands on the dents. The remaining energy flowed from him, gently reshaping and repairing the metal.

"I owe a debt," he said, looking me in the eye, and the fight was gone from him. "But tell Talus this isn't payment of that. It's for the innocents. For the ones who will die—and for the ones who were turned and, on at least some level, would rather die than live on as they have."

I nodded slowly. That was, of course, the other side of his argument that some of the vampires were innocent. Not that it had occurred to me while I was busy trying to strong-arm him.

"I don't know a lot," he admitted. "But I do follow the sources of our bodies, and unlike every other morgue tech or coroner in the city, I know what to look for. They were scattered all over—I would guess that they'd spread out to avoid detection."

That fit with the pattern I'd been told of with the Sigrid REIT properties—small apartments and condos mostly, scattered across the city, mostly in the northwest.

"Where are they happening now?" I asked.

"I've seen most of the recent ones that show the signs myself," he said quietly. "They're coming from downtown—they'll have made some kind of den."

"Any idea where?"

Karl shook his head. "I can't say for sure."

"Any guesses?" I asked. Just the way the feeder had said he wasn't sure sounded like he still knew more.

The wendigo sighed, slowly, and nodded.

"Not so much where," he said, his voice now very tired. "But they're pack predators, in the end, so they'll follow certain patterns once detected—the same patterns any other feeder would.

"They'd spread out first, trying to reduce the risk of detection," he continued. "Now that has failed, they will concentrate for protection— you'll find the entire cabal in one or two locations. I can tell you they're downtown somewhere.

"They'll have found somewhere people won't go but that has plenty of space—an abandoned office or hotel. Probably close to a homeless shelter or some other source of easy food," he concluded, "and with easy access to sewers, though that's not hard to come by in a modern city."

"I assume," he said dryly, "that you have a lot more access to real estate records and on-the-ground knowledge than a morgue tech."

"We can probably work it out from that," I agreed. "Thank you for your help," I told him. "You saved lives tonight."

He grunted. "Not those of the feeders I just set up for you to kill," he told me. "You've got what you want, fae. Get out."

I gave him a slight bow of formal thanks and then obeyed the very clear instruction.

———

ONCE I WAS out of the hospital, I called Shelly.

"I think we've got something," I told her. "He suggested looking for an abandoned building near downtown, close to a homeless shelter or something similar."

"Won't they have scattered?" she asked.

"He doesn't think so—he says they'll concentrate for protection now they know they've been discovered."

"That may make things messy," she said quietly. "I can think of a place or two off the top of my head. If I run up a short list, do you think you can scope them out later in the week?"

"Yeah, I guess," I agreed. My phone beeped at me. "One second." I checked it, and it told me I had an incoming call, though I didn't recognize the number. "Excuse me, Shelly, I have another call."

"I'll be in touch; good night," she replied, and I switched over to the new call.

"Kilkenny here," I answered. "Who is this?"

"Jason, it's Clementine Tenerim," the caller told me. I didn't even know Mary's brother *had* my phone number.

"Hi, Clementine, what's up?" I asked.

"I need a favor," he answered, his voice slow and drained. He sounded exhausted.

"What's going on?" I demanded. I'd never heard the shifter doctor sound that tired before.

"I need you to meet me and Mary at the Lodge; I'll explain there," he told me. "You know which pub that is?"

"Yeah," I replied. I wasn't supposed to talk to Clan Tenerim, but I wasn't going to refuse Clementine, either. I owed him too much—and at this point, I owed Oberis nothing.

"I was there with Mary on our second date."

"All right. Please, come quickly," he asked, and then hung up on me.

24

WONDERING what the hell was going on; I directed my cab to the Lodge when it arrived. The yellow cab pulled into the parking lot of Victor's Sports Bar about ten minutes later. The cabbie had apparently picked up on my mood, because other than telling me the price at the end of the trip, he barely said a word to me.

I paid him and stepped out into the crowded parking lot. Cars of every size and description filled the lot to capacity, far busier than it should have been on a Tuesday night. As I approached the pub, however, I saw a sign out front proclaiming that the building was closed due to flooding.

The four large, burly men, one of whom I recognized as Barry Tenerim, out front gave the lie to that claim, however, as did the chaos of people coming and going through the front and back entrances.

"I'm sorry," one of the guards I didn't know rumbled as I approached. "The bar is closed."

"Wait, he's okay," Barry told the others. "Jason is a Clan-Friend of Tenerim; he's welcome here tonight."

"Clementine called me," I told Barry. "I wasn't expecting this kind of chaos; what happened?"

Barry glanced around, and then leaned closer to me.

"Ask someone inside," he half-whispered. "We're trying to keep things quiet. Talk with Clementine."

Confused and rapidly getting even more worried than I already was, I stepped through into the "flooded" bar. The inside was even more crowded than the outside parking lot—mostly because a good third of the bar had been roped off and turned into an impromptu emergency room. Treating shifters mostly involved bandaging them up, feeding them, and letting them heal their own injuries.

The rows of pub tables put into service as impromptu hospital beds, covered in duvets and cushions probably "acquired" from the department store just down the street, holding barely moving bodies, stood at odds to that normal treatment.

A number of young men and women, apparently impressed as nurses, moved up and down the tables at Clementine's direction, checking on patients and applying salves and hypodermics at the doctor's direction.

When Clementine saw me, he gave some final instructions and came over to me.

"What the hell happened?" I asked.

"Tenerim Den is gone," he said bluntly. "Someone firebombed us just over three hours ago. We got all the people, all the pets, and I *think* all the important gear out, but the Den is gone. Mary's okay," he continued, forestalling my next question. "She was one of the ones who went back in to pull out the explosives, and got hit pretty hard by smoke inhalation. She's sleeping it off over there." He pointed toward a corner.

"Smoke doesn't bother us too much, and we can heal minor burns pretty quickly, but major burns are bad even for us," the doctor explained quietly. "We have over twenty sets of third-degree burns, and those will take even our people a few days to heal."

"Damn," I said softly. Tenerim Den *gone*? Over twenty *shifters* badly hurt enough to put them out of commission for several days? "Why? Who the hell would do this?"

"Don't know who," Clementine said quietly, taking a seat in one of the bar booths. "But the why is politics—whoever Tenerim chooses as its new Alpha would have a foot in the door to become Speaker, even though they'd be the most inexperienced Alpha—Tenerim is the strongest clan, and the last Speaker was ours. But now we've been shown to be weak, unable to defend ourselves. Tenerim will not be the next Speaker."

"They did this"—I gestured around the impromptu burn recovery ward—"to make sure Tenerim wouldn't be in the running for Speaker?"

"We don't play politics gently," Clementine said sadly. "Fire and bullets and knives can't kill us, after all. This sort of thing is worse than usual, but it's a difference in scale, not in kind."

He sounded very tired. I suspected that this was the first he'd sat down since everything had gone to hell. Even through that, though, something didn't sound quite right in what he was saying.

"I'm hearing a *but*," I said quietly.

"Yeah," he agreed, resting his head in his hands. "There are four more days until the vote, at Tarvers's funeral. If we're starting off this bad, there's a real risk things are going to get worse. Most of our elections see a dozen or so duels with steel knives to sort out differences. If we're starting with firebombing, I don't think we're going to calm down."

"Any ideas who it could have been?" I asked.

"There are three Alphas in the running," he told me. "Darius of Clan Fontaine, Joseph of Clan O'Connell, and Thomas of Clan Smith."

"Clan Smith?"

The shifter doctor shrugged. "They're all family names originally," he reminded me. "I wouldn't think any of the three would stoop to this level of violence, but none of the other four Alphas have a chance unless those three were to die—and I haven't heard of an assassination in shifter politics anytime in the last few centuries."

"What about the...Grandfather, I think he called himself?" I asked, thinking back to the old Native shifter who'd cursed out the Enforcers.

"Enli Tsuu'Tina," Clementine said with a nod. "He isn't in the running—by choice. If he wanted the job, Tarvers would have stepped aside for him to have it—and the other Alphas would do the same now. Enli doesn't want the job."

I nodded, looking around the bar. It looked like Clan Tenerim had mostly moved into the Lodge for the moment.

"Are you going to stay here?"

"Just for tonight," Clementine told me. "I and Tarvers's two boys have access to the Clan accounts. Jim and Bryan are busy booking hotel rooms across the city right now, spreading out the Clan as much as we can as we set up to find a new Den."

"What was the favor you wanted?" I asked, remembering why he'd called me here as the full reality of the situation sank in. "Any help I can give Clan Tenerim, I will," I promised.

"The Clan will survive," the doctor said simply. "I am the only shifter doctor in the city, so I am mostly untouchable. *Mary*, however, is just as weak as I am by shifter standards and lacks that protection. I want you to take her out of here and let her stay with you for the week."

"I may not be the safest place to be hiding this week," I warned him. "Fae politics are...causing me issues."

"Nowhere in this city is safe," Clementine said bluntly. "I want her out of the line of fire of Clan politics, and I know you'll take care of her."

"Fair enough," I agreed. It was hardly like I was going to complain about having my girlfriend staying with me for a week. I just worried that some of the fallout from my duty to the Queen, or my apparent ability to piss off the fae Court, would fall on her.

"Let's go wake her up," I suggested. Clementine nodded and led me back to a darkened corner of the bar, where a dozen or so shifters had been covered with blankets and sleeping bags.

I saw Mary and knelt down next to her, gently shaking her awake. She blinked her eyes open and smiled broadly when she saw me. I almost missed it in shock at the state of her eyes. Even after several hours of regeneration, her eyes were still red and puffy from smoke.

"Jason," she said softly before pulling me down to kiss her. "When did you get here?"

"About fifteen minutes ago," I told her. "Clementine called me. He's filled me in on what happened."

"It was awful," she admitted quietly. "We had to make sure the guns and explosives were out of the house—the fire will be bad enough without the authorities wondering why the house blew up like an ammo dump."

"You had that many guns in the basement?" I asked. I'd assumed they had some—all the inhuman groups had long-standing arrangements to have illegal firearms—but enough to cause a noticeable explosion?

"Two hundred assault rifles and submachine guns, about twice that in various handguns, half a ton of plastique and a million or so rounds of ammo," Clementine said from behind me. "We have armored trucks in the lot full of the shit."

That would have been an explosion to bring down the authorities. *Ammo dump* was an accurate description.

"Mary, I've asked Jason if you can stay with him for the next few days," Clementine told his sister. "I want you out of the way until the damn vote is over."

"What?" she demanded, glaring at both of us. "Do *I* get a say in this?"

"Yes," I answered instantly. I wasn't stupid, after all. "I'm hardly locking her in my apartment, Clementine," I told the doctor.

"Mary, I have to stay with our people and make sure they're okay," he told her. "Otherwise, I'd be finding my own place to hide. You and I don't have the strength or power of other shifters; if we get caught in the politics we'll get crushed. Please?"

After a long moment, Mary nodded. "Can we take your car?" she asked.

Clementine chuckled. It was a quiet, rather pathetic excuse for a laugh, but it was a laugh, and Mary smiled at him.

"Yes, you two can take the car."

———

BY THE TIME we made it to my apartment, Mary had passed out again from sheer exhaustion. As gently as I could, I carried her downstairs and put her to bed. Not wanting to wake her in the morning, I then went to sleep on the couch.

I slipped out of the house in the morning after checking on her. She was still sleeping like the dead. I left her a short note on the night-stand, letting her know when I'd be home, but that was all I could do.

With everything going on, I was horrendously distracted at work. Thankfully, my various coworkers had grown somewhat used to my moods at this point and gave me a bit of slack. We got my truck loaded up, and off I headed.

Shortly after my third stop, my phone buzzed with a text message.

It was from Michael, the Enforcer who I'd been meeting every morning to pick up packages, and it simply said, MEET ME. IT'S NOT ABOUT WORK. He gave a specific Starbucks, and for once it wasn't conveniently on the way.

I left the text message unanswered as I made my next two deliveries. Bill likely wouldn't be happy with me for the delay, though he'd give me some slack, knowing something had gone down last weekend. I wasn't supposed to be helping Enforcers at all, though that order came from Oberis.

Plus, Michael had generally been straight with me, and he'd been honestly confused when I'd told him I wasn't allowed to help him. With a sigh, I texted him back.

CAN'T TILL WORK IS OVER. MEET ME BY THE OFFICE?

His response was just OKAY. I was left wondering just what was up until my day rolled to an end, and the Enforcer's blue sedan pulled up outside my dispatch office. Michael popped the side door.

"Get in," he told me.

Hesitant, and wishing I was armed, I obeyed. As soon as I was in the car, he took off.

"Where are we going?" I asked.

"Nowhere," he told me, a shadow of a grin crossing his face. "The more we keep moving, the less my brothers can track us. They don't have a full Magus's abilities, and movement confuses their scrying."

I blinked. *That* was a weakness of MacDonald's minions I hadn't been aware of.

"Should you have told me that?" I asked carefully.

"No," he admitted wryly. "But if I can't be honest with you right now, I am fucked."

I looked carefully over the Enforcer. He was as neatly dressed as every other Enforcer had been each time I'd seen them, but there was a set to his stance and features I'd never seen before. He was stressed. He was...afraid?

"What's going on, Michael?" I finally asked.

"I tried to go to the Magus about what you told me yesterday," he said quietly, his eyes focused on the road. "I've been an Enforcer for ten years. It's not *easy* to see MacDonald, but it's always possible. Just a few months ago, I managed to get into his office just to get him to sign a birthday card for Percy."

"And this time?"

"I was blocked at every turn," the Enforcer said quietly. "Doors that are normally open are locked. His phone goes straight to voice mail. His receptionist says he's in a meeting, yet no one has come to the Tower to see him."

"He could actually be in meetings," I said dryly. "He did just have a ticking time bomb dropped on him."

"That's the thing," Michael continued. "I tried to tell Winters or get Sarah to pass what you said onto him, and they told me that he was aware of it and that I wasn't to tell anyone else. 'The situation is under control but very delicate. Please keep this under wraps, or you may be disciplined.'"

"That's...not good," I told him. "The situation is *not* under control." The situation was rapidly spiraling even further out of control, with the Clans bombing each other, and the Court preparing for open war.

He nodded. "That's what I was afraid you'd say."

"So, why come to me?" I drawled back at him.

For a moment, Michael was silent, focusing on the road as he ran us through a random selection of clear-ish side streets.

"I am afraid that the Tower has been corrupted," he finally confessed. "I fear that at least some of my fellow Enforcers have not merely failed in the charge given to us by the Magus but actively betrayed it."

"From where I sit, I'm not seeing how that changes much for anybody," I told him.

"It should change a lot," he snapped. "Don't you get what I'm telling you? The *Enforcers* have betrayed the Covenants—and, I'm afraid, the Magus. MacDonald has nothing to do with this and probably doesn't even know Tarvers is dead."

"I've heard a lot about Wizard's Sight in recent weeks," I said slowly, trying to internalize what he was saying. "How is that possible?"

"There are ways to block Sight, to fool it, and who knows those ways better than the Enforcers?" Michael asked. "No one I've spoken to has seen MacDonald in about a week. I'm afraid he's been imprisoned—there are ways to contain a Wizard, and who has a better chance to use them than his own bodyguards?"

I stared at the road in front of us as pieces began to fall into place. I didn't have all the information yet, but the basics were there.

Someone—probably the vampires—had co-opted senior members of the Enforcers, probably including Winters, to their plan. The vampires had then played provocateur, sparking conflict, drawing the Clan and Court into action while the co-opted Enforcers kept their master inactive and in the dark.

Then Winters had acted, murdering Tarvers to create an intolerable provocation and ignite tensions between the local inhumans and the Wizard. Chaos was following. Conflict. And in the anarchy, the Queen's fear—MacDonald assassinated.

The scale was massive, the effort huge—and yet, Wizards were untouchable. Undistracted, they were unbeatable. Even if one was killed, three more would descend upon the murderer and annihilate him and everyone connected to him. But in the middle of the kind of chaos forming in our streets, who would they blame? Who would be held responsible?

With the Wizard's former employees to stir up the pot and spread confusion, either there would be no target, or there would be a false target, with either the Court or the Clan suffering the wrath of the students of Merlin.

"We can't let this happen," I said aloud, and turned to face Michael. "What do you need from me?"

"I'm not sure yet," he admitted. "I just had to make sure someone outside the Tower knew what was going on. I'm going to investigate, ask more questions. I'll keep in touch."

"And if I don't hear from you?"

"If you don't hear from me for more than a day, go to Lord Oberis," the Enforcer said grimly. "Tell him what I told you, and that I am likely dead. If you don't hear from me"—he paused for a moment, taking a deep breath and hesitating before he finally continued—"the Tower has truly betrayed its charge."

We pulled up outside my apartment. "Done," I promised him. I didn't want to face Oberis yet, but if things were that far gone, I would have no choice.

"Thank you, Jason," he said quietly. "I will be in touch."

25

I GOT HOME to find Mary in the process of leaving. I almost bounced off her in the stairway leading down to my floor, her hair up under a black toque and her winter jacket on.

"Plans?" I asked carefully. She and I hadn't had a chance to discuss how this whole situation was going to work, so the *last* thing I wanted to do was make her think I was being jealous.

"Sort of," she said. "I just got a call from a girlfriend of mine; she's in trouble."

"Related to this whole mess about the Speakerhood?"

"Yeah," Mary admitted. "She isn't Tenerim—she's Clan Fontaine— and she was being threatened."

"So, you're going to go charging right back into the fray?" I asked dryly. "Why won't her Clan help her?"

The whole point of Mary staying with me was to keep her *out* of this fight. Of course, looking at her now, I wondered if Clementine had realized just how completely futile trying to keep this woman out of any fight she chose was. She was his sister, so he probably did.

"She didn't say, but she's my friend and I'm not going to hide in this basement until everything blows over while people I know are in danger," Mary snapped. "I'm not asking for your help and I don't need your permission."

"No, you don't," I agreed quickly. No twenty-first-century male, half-human or not, was dumb enough to push that point. Mary was as capable of taking care of herself as I was. However, in the world of the supernatural, well, neither of us was very capable.

"Do you *want* my help?" I asked.

"I am not helpless, Jason," she snapped. "I can handle my own affairs. I don't need to be nursemaided and coddled."

That was...not quite the reaction I was expecting.

"Wait," I told her, pausing to think for a moment. "I don't know who you're angry at," I continued slowly, "but I don't think it's me. I'm just offering to help."

She took a deep breath and then laid her hand on my arm with a heart-melting smile—a huge difference from her snappish tone of a moment before.

"I'm sorry," she said quietly. "I'm so used to being regarded as the weakest member of the Clan, to be coddled and protected. I see it even where it isn't."

"I'm a *changeling*, Mary," I reminded her gently. "I understand being assumed to be weak. Hell, *you're* probably more dangerous than I am!"

She smiled again at that.

"I tend to forget that," she admitted. "Is that offer of help still open?"

"Of course," I told her with a smile. "Just let me grab a gun. I'd rather be over prepared than under."

———

WITH THE TINY but still lethal compact Jericho pistol the Queen had given me tucked away in its concealed holster under my heavy winter jacket, Mary and I piled into her brother's car and headed off to check in on her friend.

It was snowing again, rapidly turning the roads into a slushy nightmare. There was just enough slush and muck to make them slippery, and just enough snow coming down to reduce visibility. Mary drove us through the mess with a skill and confidence I envied—necessity had taught me how to drive in the snow, but I wasn't nearly as confident about it as she was.

She took us downtown and pulled in to the visitor spot of one of a dozen apartment buildings on the west side of the core. We walked around to the front door and Mary buzzed her friend's apartment.

There was no answer.

"She said she'd wait at home for me," Mary told me. "She should be here."

"Can we get in if she doesn't buzz us in?" I asked.

"I don't have a key or anything," she said. "It's a magnetic lock, so I can't even pick it. Can you do anything?"

I eyed the door, with its magnetically activated lock. If I had the telekinetic powers common to higher-order fae, this would be a cinch. Unfortunately, I didn't. I wasn't sure I could get through short of melting part of the door.

"Make sure no one walks in on me?" I asked her, and then knelt by the door, inspecting the lock close up. It was a pretty simple mechanism, when you get down to it. A trigger upstairs sends a signal to the lock, switching off the electromagnet and allowing the door to open. I could, theoretically, warp the switch with heat and break the connection for the power.

It might not lock again afterward, but it was more likely to than if I burnt the lock out of the door.

"When I say go, push the door," I told Mary, and then laid my hand on the door opposite to the box with the electromagnet. Tiny tendrils of green flame streaked out from my fingers, burning neat little holes in the glass and then in the casing of the electromagnet. Hoping I'd judged the location of the switch correctly, I took a deep breath and focused on heating it up.

"Go," I told Mary, moments before the door clicked as the heat popped the switch. She pushed the door open, and I released the flame. "If we're lucky, it will lock behind us," I told her, stepping through the door.

She let the door swing shut and crossed to the elevator. "She's on the eighteenth floor; we'll have to take these," Mary told me.

"Can you call her?" I asked, double-checking my gun as we waited for the elevator. I had, thankfully, picked up some normal bullets to go with the tiny automatic pistol, as given what I'd been told about shifter politics, I probably didn't want to be shooting people with silver tonight.

"If she's not answering her intercom, and she's here, I probably shouldn't," Mary pointed out. I nodded agreement and, on that thought, actually drew the pistol and hid it in my coat pocket.

Paranoid, probably. But better paranoid and armed then unarmed and dead.

The elevator arrived, empty. The entire building seemed pretty empty so far, but then it was an apartment building lobby in midwinter. Most of the people who lived there had probably gone elsewhere for the holidays.

The eighteenth floor was dead silent when we arrived. Apartment buildings like this had always creeped me out—I could see ten doors, all closed, and no audible sound came from any of them.

"This way," Mary told me, and led the way clockwise around the building. As we stepped around the corner, she stopped in shock, and I pulled the gun out of my pocket. The door to the third apartment down had been torn off its hinges. Somehow, I figured that was our destination.

As we approached the door, Mary produced an ugly-looking machine pistol I'd never seen before. It looked like a handgun with a magazine and a vented submachine-gun barrel tacked onto the end. Where the hell she'd been hiding it, I had no idea—probably under her coat, but I hadn't even thought to check to see if she was armed.

"I'll go first," she whispered. "I can survive being shot better than you."

She had a point, unless they were using silver. I nodded, and waved her forward while taking the safety off on my pistol. Mary looked at me, smiled, blinked, and her eyes were suddenly those of a cat.

For the first time, I saw her move with intent, and was stunned at the sheer silence of her motion. She stepped forward into the room, over the broken door, without making a single sound. I followed her, slowly and carefully, but I still crunched a bit on some fragments of wood.

It was a small apartment, and once we were inside, I heard whimpering coming from what I assumed was the living room. Mary sneaked forward, peeking around the corner. I don't know what she saw, because the next thing I knew, she'd stepped around the corner and opened fire.

By the time I'd made it the four steps to get into the living room and track what was going on, Mary had emptied the thirty-round clip in her machine pistol. Three men in the room had been thrown to the ground by the spray of bullets, and the rapidly healing wounds from the bullets that had hit marked them all as shifters.

A woman lay on the ground as well. She was tall, with long dark hair, and was probably very pretty when she wasn't bloodied and beaten in ruined clothes. Her shirt was torn to shreds, exposing her chest. Her pants were still on, but it looked like that had been a near-run thing.

One of the shifters started to stand again. I had enough time to recognize him as my "welcoming committee" from my first day in the city before I shot him in the head. Twice. The second got most of the way to his feet before I shot him, too.

The third, however, made it to his feet and *shifted*. Two hundred pounds of black wolf slammed into my chest, claws ripping into my arms. I felt skin tear, and I dropped the pistol in pain. Mary shouted, and my undamaged left hand burst into flame as I punched the wolf in the chest.

The fire around my hands burnt green and white and seared clean through him, carrying my fist with it. One moment, an enraged wolf was trying, very successfully, to rip me to pieces. The next, the corpse of a large fair-haired man with a hole burnt through his chest crumpled to the floor beside me.

I sprang back to my feet, facing the two Mary and I had both shot. One was already healed, though the one I'd shot in the head was still oozing from the bullet holes as he snarled at me.

My right hand was useless; I could *feel* that the tendons in my arm had been severed by the shifter's bite. The nimbus of green-and-white fire sparked around my left hand as I snarled back at the two shifters, and they charged me.

I blasted the one I'd met before across the room with a bolt of green flame. The other hit me in my right side, having changed into a large cougar along the way. Claws and teeth tore into my side, and I tried to twist to punch him with my useful hand.

The shifter and I rolled across the floor. His claws tore apart my jacket but bounced off the Queen's armor underneath, failing to seriously injure me. He still managed to keep me from managing to connect with him with my flaming fist.

Suddenly, the sound of more gunfire ripped through the apartment. One neat, short, controlled burst. Then a foot collided with the cougar on top of me, and the half-naked young lady whose apartment we were fighting in picked the big cat up by his throat and tore him off me.

The cougar bounced across the floor and came back up to all fours. He started to snarl, and then Mary put a second neat burst into his head. His flesh seared as the silver rounds from Mary's new magazine ripped into him and tore through his chest. He crumpled to the floor, his body returning to human as he died.

I rolled, slowly, back up to check on the third shifter. Mary's first burst had apparently taken him in the head. There was nothing left of the body above the neck.

26

"GO PUT A SHIRT ON," Mary told her friend, carefully laying her gun on a couch as she crossed to me, tearing a strip off her shirt to try and bandage my arm.

"I'll be fine," I told her. "I do heal."

"Not as fast as us, and you'll lose more blood than you can afford first," she said critically, ignoring my protest and pulling up my shirt to bind the wounds. "What the hell are you wearing?" she asked in a soft voice, running her fingers down the undamaged cloth of the vest under my shirt, now clearly exposed as most of my shirt and jacket had been ripped to shreds around it.

"Orichalcum-runed body armor," I admitted. "It's...a gift from a friend."

"You have impressive friends," Mary told me dryly, quickly tying the impromptu bandage around my shredded wrist. "And an impressive ability to get yourself mangled." She inspected my arm, and I winced at her touch. "You'll live," she added.

"I appreciate the vote of confidence," I said, levering myself to my feet with my left hand and retrieving my gun from the floor. "There's going to be police here any minute—someone will have called the cops."

"Bodies in my apartment aren't going to help me keep it," the young lady we'd come to rescue said, reentering the living room, now dressed in a black sweater. "But yes, the gunfire will have been heard. We need to leave."

"Do you have anything packed?" I asked.

"No time," she pointed out, and I had to nod in agreement.

"Jason, this is my friend Holly Fontaine," Mary introduced us. "Holly, this is my boyfriend Jason Kilkenny. He's a changeling."

"Fine, nice to meet you, can we get the hell *out of here*?" Holly snapped.

"One last thing," I told them. I stepped over to the closest dead shifter and focused on my hand. I called a carefully shaped burst of flame and turned the body to fine ash. That done, I moved on and ashed the other two bodies as well.

"Less evidence is better all around, I think," I told the girls as both of them stared at me. "Let's *go*."

I wasn't sure *why* my grandfather's gift was growing more and more powerful, but given that the ability to use faerie fire more and more effectively was probably the only reason I was still alive, I wasn't going to complain.

Visibly swallowing, Holly led the way out to the stairs. Halfway down the stairs, we heard footsteps coming up, rapidly, and we flattened ourselves against the wall, carefully concealing my blatantly damaged coat and clothes.

Four men clad head to toe in black body armor came charging up the stairs, the one in the lead gesturing us to the side with a brusque "Police, coming through!"

The armored officers kept going up, and we kept going down.

"They're going to stop us leaving," Holly whispered. "How are we going to get out?"

"You two can shift and sneak out, can't you?" I asked.

"I turn into a deer," Holly told me. "Not so useful for sneaking in the downtown."

"No," I drawled slowly as the thought sunk in. "But an awesome distraction to get us out."

She nodded. "Point. All right."

We reached the main floor, carefully peering out around the lobby. The lobby was mostly unoccupied, but we could see the police cars, the caution tape and the black SWAT van lined up outside. Four people in normal streetwear had been corralled to the side by uniformed officers.

"We'll open the door, and then you bolt out," Mary suggested to Holly, who nodded as her eyes went slightly unfocused.

"Go," she told us, her voice thickening as her body began to *flow*.

Mary and I walked to the front door. She did her best to shield the shredded side of my coat from view with her body until we popped the door and stepped out. A uniformed police officer intercepted us almost instantly.

"Sir, ma'am, we're going to have to ask you to step over here with us for the moment," he told us. "There's been an incident in the building and we will have some questions to ask..." He stopped, almost in mid-word, as an absolutely gorgeous white-tailed deer with black highlights through her fur bounded through the door between Mary and me.

"Shit, she's going to get hit!" were the next words out of the officer's mouth, and was clearly torn between trying to save the deer and keep us contained.

"Over there, right?" I said helpfully, pointing at where the other civilians were gathered, and then Mary and I started toward the group.

The officer gave me a thankful nod and then joined four of his comrades in trying to corral Holly while a sixth officer pulled out a cellphone and started trying to call Animal Services.

As soon as they were all thoroughly distracted, we turned in the opposite direction and slipped quietly around the corner to where we'd parked the car. A minute or so later, Holly joined us, brushing snow off her jacket.

"Let's get back to my place," I told the girls. "Get some hot chocolate and maybe something stronger into Holly."

AN HOUR LATER, whiskey-fortified hot chocolates were being passed around, and the shock had finally caught up with Holly, who was cradling the mug and kind of curled into herself. Mary sat down next to her on my cheap couch and wrapped an arm around the dark-haired woman.

"What the hell is going on?" I finally asked.

"Darius Fontaine has gone fucking insane," Holly said harshly as tears began to leak out. "Those men were *Clan,* they were supposed to be like *brothers* to me—and they were going to rape and murder me on his orders."

"Why?" Mary asked, gently stroking her friend's hair.

"Because we're the ones behind the fucking bombs and the attacks," Holly admitted. "Darius's inner circle is the ones doing it, and they're trying to keep it secret even in the Clan. I found out we bombed the Tenerim Den, and demanded answers—by right, an Alpha's supposed to answer questions from the Clan.

"He told me to keep my mouth shut or he'd shut it for me," she finished, shivering.

"I take it you didn't," I asked quietly, and she shook her head.

"I told someone I thought was a friend that I was going to go to Clan Council, that he couldn't do this without the vote of the Clan," she admitted, and I glanced questioningly at Mary.

"Fontaine are one of the largest Clans—Calgary is just one branch," she told me. "They were founded by refugees from Ireland and have one of the most authoritarian structures of any Clan—but they also have the Clan Council that stands above the Alphas and holds authority over them."

"Did you get to this Clan Council?" I asked, and Holly shook her head again.

"I told Mary I was being threatened," she continued, nodding to my girlfriend. "I was planning on contacting them once I was safe, but then those...men arrived. They told me that Darius had ordered me killed for talking too much, but they were going to have some 'fun' first." Her entire body shook now, and Mary pulled her closer.

"Darius is up to his neck in this mess with the Enforcers," I said quietly, meeting Mary's eyes. She nodded silently, holding her friend as she sobbed.

"Can you contact the Council now?" I asked Holly, who shook her head.

"The first things those fuckers did was break my phone," she told us. "Without the protocols from it, I can't reach them."

We sat there in quiet for a long time, Mary holding and comforting her friend while I tried to solve our growing puzzle. Darius had his part in this plot—a seizure of power? As Speaker, he could take the Clan out of the incipient war, leave it a clash between the Enforcers and the Court.

That would leave the Court weak enough that assassination would appear to have been a likely choice. If McDonald died then, with the Clan stepped aside and the Court fighting alone, the Wizards would descend on us like a hurricane. They would *probably* accept Oberis's death alone to save the Court, but that would gut us, leaving either Talus or Laurie in charge. A new Covenant would be negotiated, likely including the cabal, with the Enforcers as a power in their own right.

Even if I'd guessed the plan correctly, though, I didn't see a way to stop it. So many gears were in motion, grinding toward catastrophe. I needed a way to slow some of them. If I could stop one or two, maybe we could bring the whole thing crashing down.

"Holly," I asked slowly, thinking aloud. "What happens if you show up to the Speaker election and accuse Darius of all of this? Bear witness against him in public, before the Clans?"

"He'd be called to account, allowed to defend himself," Mary said slowly.

"It'd be his word against mine," Holly said quietly.

"In a room full of Alphas," I reminded them. "They can't force *him* to tell the truth, but they can know that *you* aren't lying."

Holly raised her head from Mary's shoulder, brushing away tears as she looked at me.

"I know it's a huge thing to ask," I told her. "But we could stop him becoming Speaker at least, couldn't we?"

"Stop him being Speaker?" she said harshly. "He ordered the

murder of a Clanswoman—if he can't prove his innocence, Clan Fontaine will tear him to shreds."

The anger in her voice led me to suspect she wasn't being at all metaphorical.

"The election will be at Tarvers's funeral," Mary said quietly, and a shiver ran down my spine.

Tarvers's funeral would see the largest gathering of supernaturals in the city since I'd arrived. He'd been a signatory to the city's Covenants, the voice for the shifters, a solid ally of peace—everyone had respected him. Every fae, every shifter, and most of the independent inhumans would be there. Every inhuman in the city—all five hundred-ish of us—would be gathered there.

At Tarvers's funeral, a new Speaker would be elected for the Clans. At Tarvers's funeral, Oberis's deadline would run out, and he intended to ask the Clans for help in waging war upon the Tower and the Enforcers. At Tarvers's funeral, Talus wanted to present incontrovertible proof of the vampires' presence. Everything was gathering at that funeral, to take place before the assembled inhuman populace of the city.

"That's going to be a big day," I said simply. "We need to keep you safe until then, Holly." I paused, eyeing my girlfriend. "I'd like you to stay with her, Mary," I told her, "but I need somewhere to hide you."

"Ask Shelly," Mary suggested. "If she runs Talus's properties, I bet anything she knows where there's a safehouse or three that no one else knows anything about."

As usual, my new girlfriend was demonstrating a better ability to think of allies than me. "You're right," I admitted. "Thanks."

I pulled out my phone and dialed the lawyer's number. She answered almost instantly.

"Hi, Jason, I was just about to call you—I've finished my digging for places to check out," she told me.

"That's good," I said quickly. "Can I ask you a huge favor first?"

"We're working together," Shelly said slowly. "What do you need?"

"I have some information tied into our mess that we're trying to deal with, and also the whole fight going on with the shifters," I told her. "I have a young lady we *need* to get to the funeral to accuse certain people, but I don't know if I can keep her safe in my place. Do you have a safehouse we can hide her in?"

"Place to hide, out of sight, concealed, guarded?" Shelly quickly reeled off the criteria.

"Only guarded if they're people we can absolutely trust," I said carefully.

"What do you know about goblins?" she responded.

"Goblins? They *exist*?" I asked, confused by the apparent change of topic.

"They're rare. Mainly because they're short, weak, ugly and prone to petty theft," Shelly said bluntly. "But once they give their loyalty, they hold to it to the death. Talus rescued a Clan of them out of the Vietnam War, and they swore undying fealty to him. I don't know if even Oberis knows they're here, to be honest, but they are completely reliable."

"What are you suggesting?"

"If you want to check out the sites I've picked out, I can swing by your place and pick up your witness," she offered. "There's an apartment building, much like yours, in the northeast that we bought for the goblins and they take care of for us. There are three empty units there that they keep maintained for if we need a safehouse.

"There are few safer places in the city—no one is getting into those apartments without fighting through forty or fifty goblins...all trained by Vietnam War veterans," she said simply.

"Okay," I agreed. "Where do you want me to check out?"

"Two places showed up when I went digging," she explained. "There's a hotel that was shut down a few years ago and is right by the big homeless shelter downtown. There's also a condemned office building in the same area—the previous owners didn't maintain it worth shit, and now it's about ready to fall down in on itself, but that won't bother vampires. They're both on the east end of downtown; I'll text you the addresses, if that helps."

"It does," I agreed. "I can't check them out tonight, though," I admitted. "I got rather badly torn up earlier and it's going to take me until morning to heal up."

"How badly?" she asked, concern in her voice.

"Well, I may need to heal every tendon in my right hand," I admitted.

"You can *do* that by morning?" she asked, sounding shocked.

"Um. Yes," I confirmed. I forgot, sometimes, that while my healing abilities were slow by fae standards and absolutely *glacial* by shifter standards, they were still lightning fast by human standards.

"We still have a couple of days," Shelly told me. "Talus will be bringing his team into Calgary early: Friday lunchtime. He's planning to move in Friday evening or Saturday morning, so we have tomorrow evening still to check them out. I can't see it being anywhere other than the hotel or that office unless they're way outside the profile Karl gave us."

"I'll check them out tomorrow, after work," I promised.

"Good enough," she said swiftly. "I'll still come by and collect your wayward witness tonight. In about an hour sound good?"

"Perfect," I told her. "Thank you."

I hung up and turned to the girls. "Shelly will be by to pick you up in about an hour," I told them. "She's got a safehouse in the middle of a goblin colony loyal to Talus that should be completely safe."

"Goblins?" Holly said uncertainly.

"They stand by their loyalties," Mary said quietly, confirming what Shelly had said. "That's the reputation, anyway—I've never actually met one."

"Well, now you'll have the opportunity," I told her with a forced grin.

27

SHELLY ARRIVED ALMOST PRECISELY one hour later, buzzing to be let in. She came down to my apartment, and must have come directly from work as she was still dressed in a prim black suit. She greeted Mary with a nod and handshake, and looked Holly over.

"So, you're our mystery witness?" she asked, and the shifter nodded. Shelly looked over at me. "Do I want to know what we're keeping her safe to say?"

"One of the Alphas is playing very dirty," I told her. "Pretty sure he's tied into our mess, so I want to make sure he doesn't end up as Speaker."

"Makes sense to me," Shelly agreed with a nod. "I'm Shelly," she introduced herself to Holly, and I mentally kicked myself for not doing so. "I work for one of the fae. Did he tell you what arrangements I've made?"

"Goblins," Holly said quietly.

"They're a lot nicer than you may think," the lawyer told her gently. "I've worked with this group for over ten years; they are amazing people. Think Hutterites, but ugly." She paused reflectively. "Really ugly."

"I'd like to go with her, if that works?" Mary asked. "An extra level of protection."

"Of course," Shelly agreed with a nod. "We should get going," she added, "it's getting late, and while I've warned them we're coming, they don't like visitors late at night."

Mary gave me a quick kiss goodbye, and I walked the trio of ladies out. Mary and Holly got into Shelly's powder blue SUV and drove off with a quick wave, and, shivering against the cold, I dove back into my apartment.

There I found I had a text message from Michael. ASKING AROUND. NO ONE CLAIMS TO HAVE HEARD FROM K WITHIN THE LAST WEEK EXCEPT SOME OF THE SENIORS. WILL BE IN TOUCH TOMORROW OR IF I LEARN MORE.

———

WORK the next day was a madhouse. With everything going on in the inhuman political world, I'd completely missed the approach of Christmas in the mortal world. With only a couple of weeks left, the business level at courier companies like ours was rapidly ratcheting up.

The good side of working in a madhouse is that the days pass quickly, and this Thursday was no exception to that rule. Before I knew it, most of the orders had been picked up, dropped off, or packed up for tomorrow's delivery, and Bill was chivvying everyone out of the office. We'd worked an extra hour today, and according to our boss, that was a mortal, unforgiveable sin. Mostly on his part.

Unfortunately, that hour later left me struggling into downtown, by bus, during rush hour. It was an experience. I'd been in cities with worse traffic problems, but I don't think anywhere with more than five people is fun to travel through downtown at rush hour.

In the end, it took me half an hour to get into downtown and to the somewhat run-down east end, where both of the buildings I was intending to check out lay. The first of the two possible dens was the abandoned office building. It wasn't much of an office building and would never have qualified as a skyscraper. Eight stories tall and largely brick with few windows, it clashed with the collection of modern glass-and-steel skyscrapers to the west of it, all of them brightly silhouetted against the giant under-construction tower that dwarfed them all and shone brightly with workmen's lights. Even the Wizard's Tower paled into insignificance against that edifice of glass and light.

Despite the glittering core, there were a number of low brick buildings like my destination in the blocks around it, however. It looked like an older portion of the downtown, and snow-covered cranes and scaffolding showed that the entire area was in the process of being rebuilt.

My candidate, however, had no scaffolding or cranes around it. Unlike the other buildings, which someone had apparently decided to repair and rebuild, this one had clearly been written off as a lost cause. An eight-foot-tall orange plastic fence surrounded it, and neatly lettered official signs declared the building condemned.

A quick wander around the building revealed one obvious issue with the vampires using this building as a hiding place—there wasn't any way through the fence. It looked like part of the fence could be rolled back, but it didn't look nearly easy enough to be done as a regular thing, and the snow around that part didn't look disturbed at all.

There could be other ways in as well, though. Karl had implied that they'd use sewers for travel, and I was pretty sure I'd seen a manhole inside the fence. I took a quick glance around to make sure no one was watching, and then quickly climbed up and over the fence, dropping lightly onto the untouched snow inside the fence.

With the exception of my own footprints, the snow inside the fence was fresh, touched only by the wind. Peeling my ears for the sound of anyone else moving around, I carefully approached one of the side doors to the building.

I listened at the door for a moment and heard nothing. I was pretty sure that the vampires weren't there now—night was starting to fall; if they were there, they'd be moving around. The untouched snow was a good sign as well.

However, I had to be certain, so with a deep breath and a flick of faerie flame, I melted the deadbolt holding the door closed. The door creaked loudly as I pushed it open, the sound echoing out into the office building's corridors.

I slipped quickly inside the door, drawing my pistol from under my coat. Anyone realizing I'd been carrying it on the bus would have had me arrested instantly, but I wasn't planning on facing vampires without being armed. Unlike last night when dealing in shifter politics, I'd loaded it with the triple-kill rounds the Queen had provided— silver, cold iron, distilled garlic.

No one came running to investigate the creaking door, so I moved deeper into the building. None of the lights were working, but enough light drifted in from the windows to allow me to see. Dust had gathered on the floor, and as I entered the main lobby I saw why the building had been condemned: at some point, a crane had been mounted on the roof for some form of repair, and the roof had given way.

The twisted wreckage of the machine lay untended in the middle of the old lobby, covered in a drift of snow that had fallen down through the hole that stretched through all eight floors. While much of the outer rooms and offices of the building were still intact, its central core was the eight-story path of the falling crane—clean into the basement.

Nothing moved in the building, and the only sound was the wind and my feet crunching on the snow. The vampires weren't there, and I'd just wasted half an hour. It was now fully dark, and the light filtering in was from the streetlights outside.

I carefully retraced my steps to the outside of the building, stowing the pistol back in its concealed holster as I did. It was generally a bad idea to walk around a Canadian city, waving firearms everywhere. The building creaked in the wind around me, and I started to worry more about the damn thing coming down on top of me than a vampire surprising me!

Thankfully, I made it out of the condemned building without incident and set off further east—to the old hotel Shelly had picked out as the other likely target. Even though it was dark, the sidewalks were still full enough that I didn't stand out, which helped soothe my rampant paranoia that I was being watched until I reached the hotel.

Silent and unlit, the long blue building looked amazingly creepy in the dim light cast by the streetlights. It looked like an old barn, and light reflected off an unlit neon sign on the roof. I stopped across the street from it, closer to the homeless shelter to the north, and studied the building.

Many of the windows were boarded up, and the others looked to have been covered by dust cloths. I didn't think a normal human could have picked that out, at least not at night, and it would serve double purpose to a vampire—blocking light leaking out at night, or leaking in during the day.

On the other hand, if someone was working on internal renovations —turning the place into low-cost housing, as appeared to be the rumor around town, for example—they'd do much the same. Scaffolding was set up around the front entrance, concealing any scuffing done in the snow there while also lending evidence to the renovations possibility.

From the outside, there was no way I was going to be sure. I was actually going to have to enter the building I had every reason to believe was a vampire lair. With a sigh, I crossed the street to inspect the scaffolding. It looked sturdy enough for being covered in snow and reached up to the top of the three-story building. A small ladder provided a way for workmen to reach the upper levels.

I quickly, and as quietly as possible, climbed to the second level of the scaffolding. For my efforts, I discovered a window just large enough for me—if I could get it open. Luckily, it wasn't one of the ones boarded shut, but the lock was obviously on the other side.

Wishing, once again, for the telekinetic powers of stronger fae, I snuck a tendril of fire through and cut the lock, allowing the window to swing free. I opened it a tiny crack and listened for a moment. The other side was silent, so I pulled the window all the way open and slipped inside.

The room on the other side was small and completely empty. It had clearly once been a hotel room—there were indentations in the carpet where a bed had stood for longer than I'd been alive.

A sound rustled behind me, and I spun to point the pistol at a large rodent that squeaked in horror and dived for a nearby hole in the wall. I stood stock-still for a moment, trying to control my rapid breathing as I realized I'd nearly blown everything because of a rat—the pistol wasn't silenced, and if I'd shot the rat, anyone in the building would have known I was there.

My heart still beating quickly, I stowed the pistol. If I ended up having to shoot someone or something, I'd already screwed up pretty badly. I carefully stepped over to the door and checked it out. At some point, it had been locked from this side and never unlocked.

Carefully, I unlocked the door and opened it, peering out into the corridor. It was empty, and I moved out into it. A piece of wooden debris shoved in to make sure the door didn't close and lock behind me, and I was ready to move on.

There wasn't a lot of dust in the hallway, and what there was showed signs of being disturbed. People had been moving through these corridors—recently, and quite a bit. A number of the doors were broken down, showing empty rooms beyond; but other doors were closed, the handles showing recent wear.

Breathing shallowly, I slowly opened one of those doors. There was a bed in the room beyond, and a pair of suitcases. The room was empty, but the suitcases held clothes and the bed had been slept in recently. From the looks of the room, I'd only missed the occupant by an hour or so.

Sleeping during the day wasn't an absolute guarantee of vampirism, but sleeping during the day in an abandoned building was a pretty good sign. I was pretty certain I'd found our nest now, but I didn't want to unleash Talus and a squad of fae troops with shoot-to-kill orders if it turned out to just be a bunch of bums who'd found a sheltered place to hide.

I moved down the hallway, listening and watching for any sign I could use to judge further. I was halfway down the hotel and had checked two more rooms with very similar contents to the first, before I heard the whimpering. It sounded like a woman or child.

The logical, sensible part of me told me I knew what I needed to know and it was time to get out. There was nothing I could do for anyone in this nest. Even if someone was trapped there, they were better served by waiting until I could come back with Talus and his men.

Even as I was telling myself that, I was pinpointing the door the whimpering was coming from behind and crossing to it. Unlike the other doors, this one was locked. I needed a key to get in from the outside, and Powers alone knew who had that.

I was about to give up, but the whimpering continued. I had no subtle way through a door, but I didn't have it in me to walk away from that sound, however much it might have been the correct decision.

With a slash of faerie flame, I cut the deadbolts and let the door swing open under its own weight. The whimpering stopped, choked off in a heart-wrenching sob as I stepped into the room.

The girl on the bed was human. No matter how adapted her eyes were to the dark, all she could see of me was a silhouette, likely that of her tormenter in her mind. My vision was much better, so I could take in the whole sight.

The girl was a ragged-looking blonde, probably either a runaway or a prostitute. She couldn't have been more than fifteen. Her clothes were intact, so she probably hadn't been raped, which was a very small mercy. Her hands were tied behind her back, and trails of dried blood ran up her chest to a series of bite wounds on her neck and upper chest.

She'd been fed on. Repeatedly. She watched me in a horrified silence, lacking even the energy to struggle. Not only was she suffering from massive blood loss, a vampire bite was mildly poisonous. With one bite, it acted as a sedative, subduing the victim. With this number of bites, it was massively weakening—and potentially fatal.

I watched the girl stiffen as I approached the bed, and rage boiled within me as I knelt beside her. Karl's comments about the lack of choice feeders had had left me feeling a little sympathetic to them, but this was beyond choice. A vampire had to have some control to feed without killing the victim once, let alone more than half a dozen times. This was sadistic cruelty, nothing more.

"I'm not here to hurt you," I whispered to the girl. "I'm not one of them."

"Lies," she whimpered. "Only monsters left. Only monsters."

"No," I told her, trying to fill the word with as much conviction as I could. "Not just monsters."

28

"WHAT'S YOUR NAME?" I asked the girl.

"Jill," she said, her voice still choked with sobs as she forced out the single word.

"Jill," I repeated. "If I cut you free, do you think you can walk?"

She turned away from me. "Is this your new torture?" she demanded.

I didn't know what to say to that, so I cut her free instead. I wasn't carrying much in terms of blades, but even my little pocketknife was sharp enough to cut through normal rope with changeling muscle behind it.

Jill stayed perfectly still, clearly still utterly terrified and unsure if this was real.

"Are you a TV fan, Jill?" I asked quietly, hoping for something to break her fugue. The girl jerked in surprise and turned to look at me for the first time.

"What?!" she demanded.

"'If you can't run, you walk,'" I quoted to her. "'If you can't walk, you crawl,'" I continued, sliding my arms under her before she could resist. "'And if you can't crawl,'" I finished, "'you find someone to carry you."

I left the knife, hoping that it would throw some confusion into what had happened. If one of the vampires had left it within her reach, she would theoretically have been able to escape on her own.

The *Firefly* quote seemed to have done the trick, as Jill went limp in my arms, clinging to me as I gently and carefully carried her out of the room. I could hear footsteps on the floor now and moved in the opposite direction—back toward my open window.

I made it to the room I'd entered through before the owner of the footsteps rounded the corner, and gently shoved the door closed with my foot.

Eyeing the window and feeling the cold draft coming from it, I eyed my rescuee. She was still in shock from being suddenly rescued, and weak from her ordeal. She couldn't take the cold. I could.

I removed my heavy winter coat—a new-bought replacement for the one the shifter had shredded last night—and wrapped the girl in it before she could protest.

"Hold on to me," I instructed quietly. "I am going to carry you to safety; do you understand? Whatever happens, do not let go."

The pale blonde nodded, wrapping her arms around my neck again as I tightened the coat around her and then carried her out into the cold. There was no way I was climbing down the ladder with ninety-odd pounds of underfed, blood-drained teenager in my arms, so I took a deep breath and jumped.

I think if she'd had the energy, Jill would have screamed fit to raise an army. As it was, she almost choked me before we hit the ground, the snow and a perfect landing on my part reducing the impact to a "DAMN, that hurts" to my legs.

Two people stared at me in complete shock and I gave them a calm "I know what I'm doing" nod, and then dashed around the corner, out of sight from the hotel.

My apartment was too far away to carry this girl, and right now, I had no idea who I could trust outside of a select few in this city. Carefully putting the girl down and keeping a spare hand on her to reassure her, I called Shelly.

"Shelly, it's Jason," I told her when she picked up. "I found our nest, but I have a little problem."

She sighed. "I'm not here to solve all your problems, Jason," she told me bluntly. "What happened?"

"They had a living victim in the hotel," I replied. "I brought her out with me, but I have nowhere to take her."

There was silence on the other end of the line. "Shelly?" I asked after easily ten seconds had lapsed.

"Your hero complex is worse than Talus's," she said quietly. "You are both going to get yourselves killed. And yet I can't blame you." She paused. "I can't get away just now. Where are you? I'll have someone pick you up."

I told her the street intersection and alley I was hidden in.

"All right," Shelly said. "Keep her warm, I'll make a call and you should have a pickup shortly."

Shelly hung up on me, and I turned to explain what was going on to Jill, to realize she'd slumped against my shoulder as I spoke on the phone. My momentary fear she'd died on me quickly faded as I realized she was breathing.

Safe and warm for the first time since she'd been kidnapped, the girl had passed out. I laid her gently on the ground, shivering against the cold myself. I'd barely managed to start thinking about using faerie flame to warm myself though when a bright orange Honda pulled up beside me.

The driver rolled the window down and looked at me quizzically.

"Kilkenny?" he asked.

"Yeah," I confirmed, looking over the small man in the passenger seat. He wore a scarf that covered his lower face, but something seemed slightly off about him.

"Put her in back," the driver told me. "Take you to colony."

I obeyed, laying Jill down in the passenger side of the backseat and then slipping into the front passenger seat myself, discreetly observing our driver.

He was perhaps five feet tall, fully clad in winter wear, and the scarf covered his lower face but still revealed his eyes. It was the eyes that gave it away—he was wearing contacts, and when he blinked at me, one slid aside, revealing a lizard like split pupil. That, combined with the mention of the "colony" and the odd accent, led to a simple conclusion.

"You're one of Talus's goblins," I said aloud, eyeing the creature.

"Am," he confirmed. "Name Krich. Swore to Talus. He save us from—" The goblin lapsed into another language for a few seconds. I realized it was Vietnamese just as he dropped into silence, realizing I didn't understand him.

"Bad men," he finished, and returned to silence as he drove us onward. Realizing I wasn't going to get much more from the man, I leaned back in my seat and closed my eyes. Just to rest them. It had been a busy day.

————

THE NEXT THING I KNEW, Mary and Holly were waking me up and helping me out of the car. In front of us stood a quartet of brownstone buildings standing around a central courtyard. Five or six short people, their gender and species concealed by bulky winter clothing, were with them, helping move the still completely unconscious Jill from the back seat of the Honda.

Mary wrapped her arms around me and kissed me fiercely.

"Shelly called and let us know what had happened—Krich was apparently right there, thank the Powers," she told me. Speaking of the old goblin, I looked around for him, only to catch him vanishing into one of the buildings.

"I didn't even get to say thank you," I said, watching the door close behind him.

"He wouldn't want you to," one of the goblins told me, his English perfect. "My grandfather is one of those who negotiated our travel here," he continued. "He remembers our debt to Talus and your Court very well." The goblin offered his hand to me. "I am Theino, grandson of Krich, son of Lorn, current Speaker to Outsiders for our clan." I shook his hand, and he smiled. The smile shifted his scarf, and for the first time I saw why they all wore them—inch-long ivory-white tusks protruded from each corner of the goblin's mouth.

"Please," he said, "come inside so we can attend to your ward."

"Do you have a doctor?" I asked.

"Not one versed in human physiology, I must admit," Theino told me as he led us into a different apartment building than his father had entered. "Your lady here called her brother, however, and Dr. Clementine is on his way."

I nodded as I followed the goblin and the two girls inside. "That's good. She's lost a lot of blood and is poisoned."

"I thought vampires always killed when they fed?" Holly asked as the door closed behind us.

"Only the newly turned ones," I said grimly. "The older ones have the self-control not to—they don't need to. So, instead, one of them decided to keep this poor girl around as a portable blood bank."

"We will take good care of her," Theino promised. "Dr. Clementine will have all the help we can provide."

"Thank you," I told the goblin, bowing my head slightly. It wasn't, after all, him I was angry at.

Theino wandered off, leaving the three of us with our privacy. With one of those cryptic exchanges of glances no male would ever understand, Holly and Mary decided that Holly would follow him, leaving me alone with my girlfriend.

"What are you going to do?" she asked quietly.

"Wait for Talus to get back into town with his hit squad," I told her slowly. "Then we are going to kill every last fucking one of them."

––––––––

SHELLY ARRIVED SHORTLY AFTER CLEMENTINE. Where Clementine just nodded to me and then asked the goblins where the girl was, Shelly settled down into a chair in the neatly furnished living room in the apartment suite the girls were living in.

"I repeat what I said earlier," she told me. "You are going to get yourself killed. They're going to know someone rescued the girl."

"So far as they know," I drawled to her, my composure mostly recovered by now, "no one knows they're there. Which seems more likely to you: someone finds your secret sanctum, breaks in without you noticing, rescues a single victim, and leaves without anyone seeing them; or someone dropped a knife by accident in the room and the girl escaped?"

Shelly sighed. "You have a point, and it's not like I can really blame you," she admitted. "You're sure they're in the hotel, then?"

"Most of the rooms on the upper floor were occupied, but had only recently been left—within the last hour," I told her. "There wasn't enough dust on the floor for the hotel to be unoccupied. Plus, the girl is a pretty damn good sign."

"Good enough for me," Shelly nodded. "I'm going to step outside and call Talus; I'll let you know what the plan is beyond 'kill them all'."

Mary and I sat on the couch, waiting silently. She held my hand, and I appreciated her letting me think. Enough shit had gone down in the last few days to last me a lifetime, and we were nowhere near done yet.

Talus was back in town tomorrow, and Tarvers Tenerim's funeral was the day after. At the funeral, Holly would give her evidence against Darius Fontaine, throwing out everyone's prediction of how the election would break down. Oberis's deadline to MacDonald would run out. Talus and I would hopefully have evidence to prove the existence of vampires—in all honesty, Jill was likely enough evidence on her own.

But oh, I wanted to bring more evidence. I wanted to bring the burnt and mangled bodies of the vampires and throw them before the court. I'd disliked vampires before, fought and killed them since coming to Calgary, but the fate of that one poor girl put just what they were in perspective.

"Talus agrees with us," Shelly told me, coming back into the room. "He'll be bringing his team—three gentry and three greater fae, he said —into town tomorrow afternoon. They'll meet up with you and move in while there's still some daylight left."

"Good," I replied grimly. "I'm looking forward to it."

"He said," she added, "that they could pick you up from work."

That stopped my thoughts in their tracks. With everything else going, I had completely forgotten that I had to go back to work tomorrow.

———

THE DAY at work passed in a blur of busy work and angry customers, none of which fazed me. It turned out, to my mild entertainment that I could hardly explain to my coworkers, that the prospect of walking into a firefight after work made facing the normal issues of a work day completely dismissible.

I walked out of work at the end of the day, Bill having kicked everyone out on time with "It's Friday; get out of my damned building," to find a black sedan waiting for me. The tinted window rolled down as I approached, and Talus wordlessly gestured for me to get into the back.

I obeyed, joining a dark skinned older woman in a conservative black pants suit. She wore a headscarf but her features were very much Greek, not Arabic. Talus, dressed in a plain black long sweatshirt and slacks, gestured toward her as the driver took off.

"Jason, be known to Celine Mattas," he told me, and the lady bowed her head to me. "She's a Fury. Our driver is George O'Malley, one of the gentry."

"Howdy," the ginger-haired driver told me in a thick Texan drawl. "Nice to meetcha."

"We're going to swing by your apartment so you can grab anything you need," Talus told me, "and then meet up with the rest of the team at a property of mine near the target."

"Sounds good," I confirmed.

I lived close enough to my work that I'd barely finished saying that before O'Malley pulled us up to the curb by my house. I had left everything I would need on the table in the morning, so it was a quick trip. I was already wearing the Queen's armor, so all I picked up were the pistol and the Micro Uzi, strapping one concealed holster under each arm and the clips for both weapons into special pouches on my belt.

"I'm ready," I told the others, returning to the vehicle.

We drove south, opposite rush-hour traffic until we'd pulled into downtown. O'Malley wove us through the traffic with consummate ease, eventually pulling us into a tiny parking lot behind a small apartment building on the south side of downtown.

"I own all four of the ground-floor apartments," Talus told us, leading us into the back rooms. "Normally, three are rented out to cover what's in the fourth, but I'd ordered renovations this month, so they're all empty. Convenient for us."

"What's in the fourth?" I asked, and Talus smirked.

"Take a look," he told me, opening the first door inside the plainly decorated apartment building.

For a moment, I got the impression of a normal-ish apartment. Same brown carpeting as the apartment building corridors outside. Plain white drywall. A single table, some chairs.

Then I stepped farther in and realized that as soon as you were out of the front hallway, that impression vanished. All of the internal walls of the apartment except the one in front of the main door were gone. It had been turned into one large spartan room with the single table at the left side.

The rest was filled with three rows of back-to-back floor-to-ceiling cabinets, clearly mounted straight down into the concrete under the carpet. If you blew up the building, those heavy metal cabinets would probably still be standing there, undamaged.

"I know you have armor," Talus told me, "but throw a flak vest over top of it, will you? I prefer my people over protected to under, and, bluntly, you're the weakest of us here."

As I obeyed, Celine silently following me to the cabinets to help me pick out and fit a suitable jacket, I surveyed the other four people in the room. Shelly sat at the table, pointing out details in a low voice I couldn't make out on what looked like a set of blueprints. Two men with the eerily perfect features of gentry passed a cigar back and forth between themselves and a woman with skin black as night, a tiny flicker of red flame glittering over her skin to my eyes.

"John MacDougall and Kyle Lawrence, gentry, and Tamara Roxeville, nightmare," Talus introduced them to me. "Meet Jason Kilkenny, our scout on this operation and a trusted friend of mine —changeling."

The noble glanced around. "Where's Frankie?" he asked.

"Right here," a voice said from right next to me, and the air next to where I was strapping on the flak jacket blurred, like a mirage, and a tall man suddenly stood there, dressed in camouflage greens.

He offered me his hand with a grin as I jumped in surprise at his sudden appearance.

"Frankie Mckenny," he introduced himself. "I'm what you call a green man; I blend in with everything. You'll want this," he finished, handing me a black cylinder sized to go on the barrel of my Uzi—a sound and flash suppressor.

"All right, now we're done playing games," Talus said repressively, "can we all gather around?"

The three men, three women and I gathered around Talus and Shelly at the table. I could see that the papers were, in fact, blueprints of the hotel. Two floors and a basement: it wasn't much of a building.

"This is our target," Talus told us, gesturing at the plans. "There are a limited number of exits and entrances, and it appears that the vampires are using the front door, here." He pointed at the lobby of the hotel. "There are secondary exits that they can likely use here, here and here." He indicated each one in turn.

"My biggest worry at this point is keeping the feeders bottled up," he explained. "I see that we can position snipers opposite this door and this door"—he pointed at the two in question—"and cover all the exits. O'Malley and MacDougall, that's your role in this mess," he told the two gentry. Both of them had already acquired large, ugly-looking rifles from the cabinets around them.

"The rest of us go in through the front entrance—we sweep the building, post a guard—probably you, Tamara—at the stairs here, where you can cover both sets on this side of the building." He pointed to a spot at the end of the lobby.

"There is an access on the second floor," I noted, touching the spot on the map. "I used it to sneak in," I explained.

Talus nodded. "That's a good point, and useful." He considered the map for a moment. "Okay, Tamara, you, Frankie, Celine and Kyle will go in the front door and sweep the building, still leaving you as a guard in the lobby. Jason and I will go in through the second-floor window and sweep the top floor. We meet here"—he stabbed at the old bar at the opposite end of the hotel—"and then head downstairs. Most likely, the basement is where we will meet the heaviest resistance, so we'll want to concentrate there.

"Any questions?"

29

WE ALL LOADED our weapons and gear into a van, more to conceal the fact that we were all wearing bulky body armor than any issue with walking the dozen or so blocks to the hotel. Shelly kissed Talus goodbye and wished us all luck before returning to the armory slash safehouse to secure it against accidental intrusion.

After the few minutes it took us to get there, Talus maneuvered the van into the parking area of the construction lot across the street from the hotel and parked. He took a moment to look back at all of us.

"Remember, there may be more prisoners in the building," he told us, "so watch for them, and try to rescue them. But remember—I don't want any vampires escaping alive. Kill every last one of them."

The sound that echoed in the van was too...animal to call anything but a snarl. Talus's comment was definitely one we could all agree with.

"O'Malley, MacDougall." The noble gestured to the two men who'd slung heavy sniper rifles. "Think you can get up on those roofs?" He pointed through the window. Both men nodded instantly. "We'll give you five minutes to get in position," Talus told them, "then we'll start moving in. Radio if there's a problem."

The two gentry didn't even respond before slipping out the back of the van. I watched them for a moment, somehow weaving their way through the sparse crowds while concealing the long weapons they held under their coats.

Talus looked over at me, his expression concerned.

"Jason, you can still back out if you want," he told me. "You're the only one here who isn't a greater or noble fae; you're not really in the weight class for this fight," he reminded me quietly. "You did more than enough by showing us where to strike."

I needed to be along as the Queen's eyes and ears on the ground, to see and remember the proof for Her as much as for myself. Talus knew I was a Vassal after our accidental mind-sharing, but his men didn't—and weren't supposed to know, either. I took a moment to think of how to explain to him, without saying the part we both knew.

"After what I saw last night," I said even more slowly than my usual drawl. "That poor girl. I want to help—I want to kill these bastards with my own hands."

"Fair enough," Talus grunted. "I won't mind the second gun hand and set of eyes upstairs." He checked the watch. "Let's move."

Tamara led the way out of the van, the flicker of flame on her skin concealed by a silk scarf wrapped around her face. The rest of us followed, keeping our weapons concealed. I know I walked with my hand on the grip of the Micro Uzi under my coat, and I doubted the others were any less paranoid.

Talus led us toward the hotel, stopping by the scaffolding to look around at the group of fae.

"Jason and I will go up here," he said simply. "Give us a minute, and then go through the front. We'll see you in a few minutes."

The fae noble was up the ladder so fast, I barely saw him move. I followed him up at a more sedate pace, joining him on the scaffolding as he opened the window I'd permanently unlocked the previous night. He held back, drawing his own machine pistol and waving me forward.

Taking the invitation, I drew the Micro Uzi and stepped through into the empty room. Nothing had changed from the last time I'd been in there, though weak sunlight still leaked in today, illuminating the dust and the scuffed-up track from my and Jill's escape last night.

"Clear," I whispered, knowing that Talus would hear me. One advantage to sneaking around when you knew your companions had superhuman hearing.

Talus ducked in, and we paused to attach the suppressors to our Uzis now that concealment was less of a factor than noise and light. The fae noble drew an ancient-looking short sword, its blade covered in black oil of some kind, and held it in his left hand.

"You have a knife?" he asked quietly. "Better than shooting them if they're still sleeping from the sun."

When I shook my head, he tucked the short sword into the same hand as his Uzi for a moment and produced a US Marine Corps combat knife from the small of his back, the blade pitch black.

"Nothing special about it; it's just black to conceal it," he whispered. "Sever the spinal cord, they'll survive anything else."

I nodded jerkily as I took the knife in my free hand. For all my anger at the vampires last night, the thought of knifing them in their sleep made me acutely uncomfortable. Given that the feeders were just as fast and strong as me, and some of them had blood magic as well, it made sense. I just didn't like it.

"You go left," the noble instructed, pointing as he stepped to the right. "Come if you hear me shoot."

With a swift exchange of nods, I headed left. More of the doors were shut tonight than last night, presumably closed on occupants asleep against the sun. The first one was locked, but we really didn't need to worry about people coming through after us and seeing evidence, so I burnt the deadbolt out with a quick slash of flame and stepped inside.

Two people were asleep on the bed, and I hesitated as I stepped inside. It was hard to consider killing someone in their sleep. Then I got closer and saw the state of the bed. It was half-covered in blood, as were the two vampires. The blood came from a man who looked to have been in his mid-thirties but aged another twenty years by drugs and alcohol. For all that, he hadn't deserved to be dragged up there and have his throat torn out to feed their thirst.

The male—I refused to think of the vampire as a man—was the first and, in some ways, the hardest. I very carefully positioned the *very* sharp knife at the base of his neck, then, with a deep breath, stabbed home.

A human might have failed to cleanly sever the spinal cord, but a changeling like me stood at the peak of human abilities. The knife slipped between the vertebrae perfectly, with a sickening popping feel, and the vampire just...stopped.

He wasn't really breathing and didn't have much of a heartbeat before, so it was hard to say exactly how I knew he was dead. But I did. Quickly, realizing I was probably moving much slower than Talus was expecting, I took a deep breath and repeated the exercise with the second vampire.

Then I regretted the deep breaths as, without the focus of needing to kill, the full stink of rotting blood and flesh in the room struck home and I gagged against it. Careful to breathe shallowly, I fled the room, forcing myself to move on to the next closed door.

Two more vampires died silently, in their sleep. The fourth room was much cleaner than the first three, no scattered blood, no bodies. The bed had been made up neatly around the figure sleeping in it, and the closet had been cleaned out and a number of dry-cleaning bags containing suits and what might have been black robes had been hung up in it.

I crossed to the bed and started to place the knife against the vampire's throat when his eyes flicked open and he grabbed for the knife just as it touched his skin. Panicked, I tried to level the gun at him, but he swiftly knocked it out of my hand.

Quickly, I grabbed the knife with both hands and started forcing it toward him. With a snarl, he tried to punch me, only to allow the knife to slip forward and gouge his half-dead flesh. He jerked sideways, half-opening his throat and falling out of the bed.

He rolled to his feet and we faced each other across the bed. I held the knife, and he opened his mouth to shout for help.

To both of our surprise, all that emerged was a hoarse croak. I'd managed to sever his windpipe and vocal cords, rendering him unable to make any real noise. Where a human would have been spurting blood, however, he only oozed a thick brown liquid it took me a moment to realize was half-congealed blood. An injury that would have been quickly if not instantly fatal to many inhumans, let alone humans, was a mild inconvenience.

He snarled soundlessly at me and dove for the closet. I met him halfway there, trying to slash at his throat with the knife. He parried the blow and punched me in the stomach, sending me stumbling back a few paces as he reached the closet and produced what he was looking for: a sawed-off pump-action shotgun.

I didn't even bother going for my gun—I didn't have time. By the time he'd finished pumping the first round into the chamber, I was in his face, stabbing down into his right arm. Tendons snapped and bone cracked under the strike, and the pistol grip of the shotgun slipped from his nerveless fingers.

His other hand was still intact, though, and he used it to slam the gun broadside on into my face. I felt my nose break and was shoved back a step. I blinked away stars, and then blinked again when I saw what he was doing.

The vampire's left hand still held the shotgun by its pump, but the pistol grip was now lifting again—held in a living simulacrum of a hand, formed from the brown ooze of the vampire's blood. I was fighting a blood mage.

For a moment, I was staring down the barrel of a shotgun, convinced I was going to die. Then fear and anger hit me, and I remembered *fire*. The same whip of flame I'd first conjured when fighting Laurie suddenly flashed into existence in my hand and I lashed out.

The whip wrapped around his left hand, and I *pulled*. Just as the gun was about to fire, I tore off the vampire's functioning hand with a tendril of flame, and he opened his mouth in a hoarse, creepily quiet scream of pain as the shotgun collapsed to the ground, his attention broken.

Taking advantage of his distraction, I wrapped the tendril around his neck. The vampire mage had enough time to realize what was about to happen and start to gesture his useless right hand at me to conjure some form of blood magic.

Then I burnt the fucker's head off.

———

I HELD my breath for a moment as the vampiric blood mage's body crumpled to the floor, half-expecting a horde of angry vampires, roused by our desperate struggle, to come charging through the door guns blazing.

When said horde failed to materialize, I allowed myself to slowly begin to breathe again, and picked up my knife and submachine gun. I had two more rooms to check before I reached the end of the floor, and I hoped that the others were just normal vampires. Because that wasn't a contradiction in terms.

I had just slipped the door to the next room open when everything went to hell. To my ears, the sound of a suppressed submachine gun might as well be cracking thunder, and three of them opened up simultaneously beneath me.

Vampiric hearing wasn't as good as mine, but it was good enough that the gunfire clearly woke up the vampire in the room I was entering. I never gave him a chance to do more than come to his feet, raising the Micro Uzi and putting a neat burst into his head. Even vampires die when they don't have a head anymore.

I kicked the next door open, not bothering with subtlety. Kicking hinges out hurts, but it's more effective than trying to break through the door directly. The cracking sound of a pistol firing echoed through the hotel as a heavy bullet barely missed me.

Diving through the door, I rolled under a second bullet and came to my feet to find two vampires in the room. Both were naked. The girl was rushing for the closet, presumably for some kind of weapon, while the man was bringing a very large revolver, a Dirty Harry gun, to bear on me as he fired again.

I threw my knife first, catching the female vampire in the leg as I jumped sideways to avoid a fourth bullet. I fired back while ducking under the bed, not so much intending to hit anyone as to keep the gunman down.

Two more bullets ripped into the bed, tearing apart the mattress and shattering the cheap wooden frame. That was six bullets, though, and revolvers were called six-shooters for a reason.

I leapt over the bed, one hand on the remnants of the frame, and landed in a perfect two-handed shooter's stance. My second burst was not intended to keep anyone down, and three rounds slammed into the girl's chest with bloody precision. For a moment, I thought I hadn't done anything, as the congealed black goo that was vampire blood began to ooze from the holes—and then her blood caught fire and the vampire screamed for a moment.

I knew that the bullets had been coated in garlic oil. I knew garlic was bad for vampires. I *hadn't* known that concentrated garlic oil ignited the blood of a living vampire like a match to gasoline. The girl's body burned up from the inside out, and I watched in horrified surprise.

Which almost killed me, as the other vampire slammed a single heavy cartridge into the cylinder and pointed the gun at me. At this range, with no cover, he couldn't possibly miss. If he hit me somewhere non-vital, I'd heal, but I'd be out of this fight. If I was lucky, he'd hit me somewhere really non-vital.

I didn't feel lucky, and the barrel of the gun was *huge*. And then it wasn't there anymore, as a half-seen, half-sensed, telekinetic blow smashed the vampire's spine to pieces. The shattered corpse collapsed, and Talus stood behind him. The noble's hand still glowed to my eyes with the force he'd used to destroy the vampire.

Gunfire continued to echo downstairs, and the suppressed submachine guns I knew were our companions were now being interspersed with the tearing sound of very real and very un-suppressed automatic weapons.

"Let's go," Talus ordered, and I followed him out.

The stairs at the rear of the hotel echoed with the gunfight going on below. With the top floor clear of vampires, Talus and I went down the stairs as quietly as we could, doing our best to work out where the fight was.

Halfway down the stairs, I gagged as a draft carried a suddenly intense smell of formaldehyde and rot up the stairwell. Talus and I exchanged questioning glances and he shrugged, clearly not having any more idea than I did.

The stairs exited into what had once been the hotel's bar but now was the source of the smell of preserved rot. The remaining tables and chairs had been haphazardly tossed aside, clearing space for several neat rows of bodies. All of the bodies showed the telltale neck wounds of being killed by vampires, and all had been, from the smell, soaked in some kind of preservative. Three rows of ten bodies filed the room, and Talus looked at them with horror on his face.

"What?" I whispered. "What the hell is this for?"

He shook himself. "I don't know," he said uncertainly. "It can't possibly be..." The fae noble trailed off, and the approaching sound of gunfire distracted us.

Whoever had the automatic weapons and was firing at our friends was getting closer. Talus gestured toward the bar and we took cover behind it. The only door out of the room other than the exit and the two leading deeper into the hotel was back there with us, and I kept one eye on it, just in case.

The gunfire grew louder, and four vampires walked backward into the bar, firing back down the hallways to keep the other fae's heads down. Talus and I waited for them to fully enter into the room, and then he gestured roughly to me and rose up to fire over the bar.

I hit the closest vampire with five or six bullets, and he crumpled in silent agony as his blood burst into flame inside him. The second one I fired at managed to turn and shoot at me before I hit him, but he went down after a single shot.

Talus's pair went down even faster, and the hotel was silent for a long moment until the others slowly appeared in the doors from the hotel. Tamara led the way, her face wrap gone somewhere along the way after she'd ignored the plan for her to stand guard at the other end of the hotel, and fire glittering across her black skin as she offered us a thumb-up.

"The rest will be in the basement," Talus said quietly, pointing at the door behind us. "Let's move in together."

Tamara and the other two fae crossed the room toward us, holding their weapons carefully as they stepped around the bodies. The nightmare opened her mouth to say something and then let out a surprisingly feminine shriek of surprise as one of the bodies moved and grabbed her ankle.

She opened fire at it, spraying the corpse with garlic-coated bullets. It ignored them, yanking her to the ground as several more of the bodies began to move. Tamara's shriek turned to silence, and a gout of flame flashed out from her black skin, burning the corpse's hand to ash.

"Shoot them," Talus barked, and I obeyed.

All of the corpses were getting up now, moving for the closest person. I emptied a clip almost instantly into the nearest, to no apparent effect beyond the impact of the bullets. The garlic did nothing, and the body kept coming, grabbing the Uzi as I tried to reload.

Another moving corpse grabbed at me, and I let the Uzi go to fend off the grasping hands. Then I had two sets of grasping hands grabbing me with inhuman strength. I struggled, but they were stronger than me. My world shrank down to me and two super-strong, somehow mobile corpses trying to tear me apart.

In a panic, I called faerie flame. Green fire coated my wrists, and the smell of burning meat wafted up as they held on, despite the fire. With a grunt of focused effort, I managed to burn one of the creatures' hands entirely to ash, and it tottered against the bar, trying to reach me still with its teeth and charred stumps.

The other let go of my arms and went for my throat while I was distracted. I missed stopping it, and its hands closed around my neck with that insane strength. I struggled as it cut off my breathing, and for a moment, I thought it was all over.

Then Talus's ancient short sword slashed down like an ax, severing both of the creature's arms with a single strike. A second strike decapitated the creature, and a third cleaved it apart just above the pelvis. Even as the corpse fell apart into pieces, the large bits still struggled to move.

"Go," Tamara shouted as I looked up. Talus had chopped apart three of the corpses by us, but Tamara, Celine and Frankie stood in the middle of a swarming crowd. They'd abandoned guns now for large knives. It took near-full dismemberment to stop the things. "We'll hold them," the nightmare insisted, "*Go.*"

Talus grabbed my arm and dragged me with him through the door into the basement, pulled it shut behind us just as another pair of corpses slammed into it.

30

"WHAT THE HELL ARE THOSE THINGS?" I asked, and felt a warmth on my skin under his hand in answer.

Blood-thralls, his voice said inside my head. *Keep quiet; we must let them think we're all trapped upstairs.*

Blood-what? I asked as I followed him down the stairs. I'd never heard of such a thing.

They're fucking zombies, Talus explained bluntly. *Corpses animated by the blood in their veins, powered by the will of a blood mage adept.* He paused. *Jason, there aren't supposed to be any blood adepts left. They were supposedly wiped out a decade ago. But nothing less than an adept could raise that many thralls.*

So, we have a problem?

We have a problem, he confirmed. *You lost your gun; still armed?*

I have a pistol. Just one clip, I warned, after checking my ammunition and realizing one of the thralls had managed to tear off my ammo pouch. *They're triple-kill rounds the Queen gave me—garlic, silver, cold iron.*

Damn, Talus replied, leading the way slowly down the stairs, keeping quiet and keeping his hand on my arm. *Hold on to those unless I tell you to shoot, okay?*

What happens if we face something you don't want me to use them on?

Stay behind me, he instructed, and I groaned as quietly as I could. I'd been afraid of that response.

We reached the bottom of the staircase into the basement, and Talus crept forward, motioning for me to wait behind him. After a moment, he gestured me forward and moved on himself.

The basement was plain concrete. The stairs opened into an empty storage room long devoid of the food and booze it had once held for the bar upstairs. A doorway exited on the north and south sides of the room. Talus investigated the north door for a few moments while I chafed impatiently—every moment we waited was a moment that the people we'd left behind had to fight for their lives against a horde of nearly unkillable zombies.

Talus obviously felt the same way, as he abandoned the north door after a quick inspection and led me to the south door. He listened at it for a moment and then opened the door, covering the hallway beyond with his gun.

He then touched my arm again. *North door hasn't been used, but there are tracks in the dust leading this way. Too much of a mess for me to say how many. Be ready for anything.*

I followed him through the door, and we made our way down the hall, listening at each door. We'd passed the first set of doors when a very familiar raised voice echoed down the hallway.

"What is the meaning of this, Madrigal?" the hag Laurie, left hand of the fae lord of Calgary demanded...in the heart of the vampire's lair.

"I," a soft, sibilant voice hissed, "was about to ask you the same question. About the fae hit squad that just *murdered my children.*" The hiss turned to a shriek, and the crack of a hard-delivered slap carried through the door.

"What?" Laurie demanded. "I would have known of such a thing!"

"So you said," Madrigal, presumably, hissed. "So you *promised.* You *swore* you would be able to warn us of any attack by the fae, and yet my children lie dead above us. Half and more of my brood—slaughtered by your brothers!"

"I didn't know," the hag said loudly as the whip-crack of Power echoed between the two women we couldn't see. "I swore I would warn you, and I warned you of every act, every move. Why would I stop now?! Winters would have my head!"

"Winters is *not* who you should be worried about," the vampire snarled. "A half dozen greater fae and gentry, led by that fool of a noble, have assaulted my den. My apprentices and children have been slaughtered. Now tell me, you fae bitch, why you should not die with them."

"I have not failed you yet," Laurie replied. "Talus must have brought soldiers from outside the city—without telling me. They must suspect something!"

"Well, then maybe I should leave you to them?" Madrigal suggested, her voice suddenly sickly sweet. "A peace offering, maybe —the traitor who sold them out?"

I realized that Talus was about to break through the door, and grabbed his arm. *Wait*, I told him. *We need to know more.*

"My thralls have trapped them," Madrigal continued. "They have murdered my children, but my toys are proving more than they can handle."

"I did not fail you," Laurie insisted.

"That does not mean I am not thoroughly fucking *pissed*," the vampire snapped. "My children are dead, and *your* kind did it."

We need Laurie alive, Talus said in my head through the link. *One of your rounds won't kill her but will disable her—I can't fight her and the adept and any other vampires in the room.*

"A few more days, and you will have the right to make more," Laurie told the vampire. "As a signed member of the new Covenants."

Can you fight them all? I asked.

New Covenants? Talus queried back, and then shook his head. *Not the adept, not if she has any other mages with her.*

So, shoot Laurie once and then dump the rest of the clip into whoever she's talking to?

"Do I suggest that *your* children are replaceable?" Madrigal said sharply, her voice back to being a sibilant hiss. "Your kind will pay for this murder."

That'll work, Talus agreed. The noble took a deep breath and then nodded me toward the door. *Now!*

With a flick of his wrist and a burst of Power, Talus shattered the door between us and the traitor and vampire. I charged through first, picking up a quick sight picture of the room as I raised the Jericho.

Laurie and a dark-haired woman in a rose-pink skirt suit stood in the center of the room, glaring at each other. Three men and two women, two of the men in black robes and the rest in street clothes, stood along the walls, all with bared fangs reacting to the destruction of the door. Another woman who I recognized from Court as a shade—a minor Unseelie fae—stood just behind Laurie, her hand on a concealed weapon.

The room had started life as some sort of storage cellar, but it had been converted to a twisted cross between a chapel, a formal dining room, and a butcher's workroom. A black stone plinth with an inverted pentacle in wrought gold hanging over it dominated one end of the room, the plinth carved with blood channels clearly visible in dried fluids from the other end of the room.

A heavy oak table, sized to fit over a dozen people, was perpendicular to the room in the middle, between the door and the altar. Madrigal and Laurie stood between us and the table, but Madrigal's vampire minions were behind it.

Heavy black drapes covered up the concrete walls, giving an impression of dark gothic elegance to the whole affair, with horror added by the pair of freshly bled bodies just barely visible beside the altar.

The entire impression of the room snapped into my mind as I trained the small pistol on Laurie, and flashed into the back of my head as I fired. The hag was barely beginning to react, drawing on her Power, when the mixed silver-and-cold-iron bullet slammed into her gut.

The Power flickering through her only accentuated the effect of the cold iron, and Laurie screamed as the bullet fractured inside her, the bane of our kind seeping into her blood. Her keening wail echoed through the room as Talus followed me into the room.

He took in the same picture as I had, and gestured once. The heavy oak table flew backward, slamming the vampires behind it to the ground as I turned to fire at Madrigal.

My first round missed as the vampire slipped sideways, alerted by the attack on Laurie. While I wasn't as fast as she was and couldn't possibly have kept up with her if I'd been trying to fight her hand to hand, I could track across the room faster than she could move. My second and third shots slammed into the blood mage, catching her mid-dodge and throwing her away from me. Light flickered around her as the garlic burned in her blood, but the blood mage *controlled* the fire, using it to fuel her Power.

My fourth shot missed again, and the fifth slammed into her hip as she paused, gesturing toward me. Power flared in the room, and a dark red mist burst into existence around her hand. The mist flashed out and knocked aside my last three rounds as I emptied the clip.

For a moment, I thought I was dead. The mist started to extend out from her hand as she slashed it toward me, and I had no illusions about my ability to stop that attack. But we both had forgotten about Talus, who had been busy throwing the furniture around.

The mist whipped out toward my face, and the fae noble calmly stepped up to the blood mage from behind her and ran her through with his sword. The mist broke apart, inches from my skin, and Madrigal ripped the blade out as she spun to face Talus.

"*You,*" she hissed.

"Me," he agreed calmly—and decapitated her. The mist that had started to flow out from her hands toward him dispersed instantly as the imitation of life that sustained her long-dead corpse fled. Screams of rage echoed through the tiny chamber, and the heavy table Talus had thrown onto the vampires was sent flying back at us.

Apparently, two of the still-living vampires were blood mages as well, and blood-driven telekinesis turned the heavy table into a weapon as it crossed the room. I ducked, hitting the ground as the table's progress was delayed by bouncing off Laurie's still-whimpering form with the shiver-worthy sound of bones breaking.

It stopped a yard or so from me, shattering into hundreds of pieces as Talus hit it with an even stronger and less spread-out blast of telekinetic force. The other fae who'd been with Laurie took advantage of my distraction, charging me with a machine pistol identical to the one I'd left somewhere upstairs in the hands of Madrigal's blood thralls.

Somewhere along the way, conjuring that whip of flame and controlling it had become a lot more instinctual, because I didn't even consciously think about it before I used it to tear the gun out of her hand in a flash of green faerie flame.

She responded by conjuring shadow out of thin air, a blade of darkness taking form around her arm as she slashed at me. I dodged, rolling to my feet as I moved away from the shadow, feeling a wave of cold as the shadow passed by me.

I flicked the whip of faerie flame at her, trying to wrap it around her as I'd done with the blood mage upstairs. The shade's shadow blade cut across the line of fire, shattering it into sparks that scattered all around us.

I was left holding about a foot of faerie flame as she came at me again with the shadow. Unthinkingly, I parried her shadow with the fire in my hand, and to my surprise, it worked. The fire broke the shadow apart in the same way the shadow had shattered my fire whip a moment before.

For a few seconds, we slashed back and forth at each other, quickly discovering that neither of us could conjure a blade of our element that the other couldn't break. She'd strike at me with shadow, and I'd block it with flame, and then I'd return the attack and she'd block mine.

After a several fruitless exchanges, she changed tactics, bounding away from me with the perfect grace of the true fae and *throwing* a bolt of shadowstuff at me. I almost managed to dodge it, but it clipped me on my shoulder.

The force tossed me backward even as a horrific chill began to rapidly radiate out from the wound. It felt *frozen*, not cut, and in moments, my left arm was frozen into uselessness. The shade smiled and advanced back toward me, the blade of shadow on her hand darkening as the cold stole my ability to conjure flame.

I've never seen a pretty girl look quite so ugly when smiling as the shade did as she advanced on me. Chill shivers tore through my body, dropping me back to my knees as I tried to stand, the cold rippling through me. Her smile was even colder, darkness shrouding her as the Unseelie drew her hand back to finish me off.

Somehow, some way, I reached through the chills wracking my

body and touched the fire at my core that fueled my Power. Something inside me *clicked*, and warmth shot out, radiating through my body, driving the chill from my flesh. The world froze, and I called faerie flame in the same way I had when fighting Sigridsen. My right hand flew out, palm first, to block the strike of her shadowblade.

The gout of green fire that blasted from my palm shattered the shade's blade and took her hand off at the wrist, cauterizing the wound as it burned its way past. She screamed, and the sound echoed horribly in the small concrete room as she conjured shadow with her other hand and threw it at me.

I stopped the bolt of shadowstuff with another burst of flame. The ball of shadow disappeared within the green-white flames, which continued on to take the Unseelie killer in the upper chest. She was pitched backwards, flying across the room to slam into the concrete wall with a very final impact.

My own opponent defeated, I turned to check on Talus. One of the blood mages and both of the female vampires were down, their unlife cut short by the fae noble's blade and Power. The remaining blood mage was using tendrils of red mist to manipulate the larger chunks of table. Talus kept dodging the pieces as they rushed at him with lethal force.

The other vampire was adding to the distraction, dodging in and out of the noble's reach, trying to stab him with a long obsidian dagger. All three of them were very focused on each other as I picked up the shade's Uzi.

Something warned the blood mage, who was starting to turn his head towards me as I opened fire. Moments later, the tendrils of mist vanished and the remnants of the table crashed to the ground as the Uzi's slugs ripped apart his head and upper chest.

Without the distraction of the blood mage, the other vampire met Talus's sword head on as he tried to stab the fae. His headless corpse crumpled on top of the shattered remnants of the table, leaving Talus and me the only people standing in the room.

––––––

LAURIE WHIMPERED as Talus crossed the room to her, her body crippled by the cold iron in her flesh and blood. From somewhere, he produced a pair of handcuffs and roughly bound her hands together before focusing healing energy into her.

Her whimpers slowly faded, though from the drawn expression on her face, I suspect Talus left more than a little cold iron in her system, weakening her enough she could not possibly be a threat to us.

"Laurie O'Donnell," he said finally, looking down on her as I slowly walked over to join him. "As a noble of Lord Oberis's Court, I place you under arrest for betrayal of race and Court and Covenant."

She was silent as Talus and I dragged her to her feet. The hag stumbled along with us as we retraced our steps out of the basement of the hotel, back up the stairs to the wreckage of the hotel bar.

Bodies and bits of bodies were scattered everywhere. Many of Madrigal's thralls had been hacked to pieces, but at least half appeared to have simply collapsed when the adept had died. Frankie lay away from them, his clothes and skin having faded to a light brown. His head was twisted at an angle that told a silent but explicit story.

Tamara and Celine stood next to him, Celine kneeling by the green man's corpse, while Tamara leaned against a wall, carefully tying torn strips of her jacket around several slowly oozing wounds. The nightmare spotted us and Laurie first, and stopped tying her wounds to produce her gun from under her torn jacket.

"What's *she* doing here?" the wounded fae demanded.

"She was with the vampires," Talus said simply. "I will be bringing her to my uncle."

Tamara nodded sharply, glaring at the hag. "The adept is dead," she stated. It wasn't really a question, given the state of the thralls all around us.

"She is," Talus confirmed. "O'Malley and MacDougall?"

"Not sure," Celine said, rising to her feet from where she'd finished laying Frankie's jacket over his head. "I tried to call them once the zombies went down—figured that was the end of it. Neither is answering their radio or cellphone."

For a moment, the idea of the two men we'd left outside as snipers answering their cellphones seemed ridiculous, and then I remembered the headset radio gear some of the team had was of a much cheaper grade than a mortal military team might have. Our cellphones were probably more reliable.

"No one went out by either entrance we saw," Tamara told Talus, still glaring at Laurie.

"There was an exit in the basement," I told the two women. "And a ritual chamber of some kind. Probably for these things," I realized aloud, gesturing at the bodies of the thralls.

"I'll check on the boys," Talus said quietly. "Can you walk?" he asked Tamara, who nodded. "You three move Frankie and Laurie out to the street; I don't want any of us here when someone decides to investigate the gunfire."

I nodded and took the traitor from him. I'd barely grabbed Laurie's cuffs before the fae noble slipped out the door. I looked at the two women from our team.

"Can you two carry Frankie?" I asked.

In answer, Celine threw the dead fae's body over her shoulders in a fireman's carry. The ease with which the Fury moved the body suggested that my question was more than a little laughable.

Tamara was clearly unneeded, and she slipped over to stand on the other side of Laurie as I began to guide our prisoner out to the street. The nightmare leaned in to whisper in the hag's ear, and I only barely caught what she said.

"Talus and Jason may have settled for cuffing your arms," she said softly, her voice sounding gentle, "but I know you. If you try and run, I will burn your legs off. Get me, bitch?"

Laurie nodded, roughly, still silent as we manhandled her out the door and across the street into a dark alley. Thankfully, it didn't look like anyone had been close enough to hear the gunshots, and no one saw us moving a prisoner and a body away from the hotel.

The alley was completely empty, though garbage littered the ground, mixed inextricably with snow and mud and ice. Celine took one look at the ground and kept Frankie's body over her shoulder. I was a little less polite to Laurie, shoving her against the wall and leaving whether she stayed on her feet or not entirely up to her.

At the very least, the death of the two Cunninghams was entirely at her feet. On top of that, her assistance in allowing the vampires to evade the efforts to bring them to justice had allowed dozens of murders to take place—and led quite directly to Tarvers's murder.

The traitor remained completely silent, though I could *feel* the cold iron still circulating through her body from my bullet. The sensation of cold iron near me was one I associated with a reason to get the hell out of wherever I was, which probably contributed to my now-violent antipathy to the hag.

We'd been in the alley for a few minutes and the cold was starting to seep past the adrenaline when a shadow came between us and the nearby streetlight. My attempt to go for a gun at that point was the first I realized that I'd left both weapons I'd started the evening with in the hotel.

Before I could start to summon Faerie flame, however, Talus landed next to us. He was supporting O'Malley, who was covered in blood from an ugly bullet wound clean through his left lung. It looked like the delay had been Talus healing him enough to keep him alive.

MacDougall was less lucky, and his corpse, slowly leaking from multiple bullet wounds, floated behind Talus until Tamara gently took him into her arms.

"I have him stabilized," Talus said quietly, "but I need somewhere warm and sterile to make sure he makes it."

"The colony?" I asked. I knew there was a doctor among the goblins who paid allegiance to Talus there, but he shook his head.

"With your girlfriend and our witness on the Clan mess there, I don't want to draw attention to them," he told us. "With her a traitor" —he pointed at Laurie—"I don't know who I can trust in the Court."

The answer was obvious to me after a moment's thought, and I shook my head at Talus.

"Eric," I suggested.

"I'm not even sure of him," Talus replied, and I shook my head at him again.

"Eric is like me," I reminded him. "His loyalty is neither to the Court nor breakable." Many Keepers bore fealty, *just* like a Vassal, though not hereditary like a Vassal, to the Queen or another member of the High Court.

In Eric's case, his fealty was to Queen Mabona, the same as me. His loyalty could not be broken without killing him.

While my comment earned me confused looks from Celine and Tamara, it bought an instant relieved smile of acknowledgement from Talus, who nodded. "Call him," he ordered me, and turned his attention back to O'Malley.

Obedient to a fault, I pulled out my own cellphone and started to dial.

31

THE BACKGROUND NOISE when Eric answered his phone was loud, the burbling chaos of Friday night at a bar. The sound of a band playing was almost lost under the dull roar of conversation.

"What's going on, Jason?" he asked abruptly. "I'm busy—I have a full house here."

"We need help," I told him. "Talus and I went after the vampire den —we have dead and wounded and a prisoner."

For a moment or so, all I could hear on the line was the background noise. "A prisoner?" he asked finally.

"One of ours was with them," I said simply. "She'd betrayed us and was helping them evade our ops. We have no transport and Talus can't heal our wounded in an alley covered in snow."

"Where are you?" the Keeper asked, and I told him the name of the hotel. "I'll be there," he promised, and hung up.

We spent what seemed like forever but probably was less than fifteen minutes waiting in the cold as Talus, the only one of us with any healing abilities, struggled to keep O'Malley alive in the horrendously adverse conditions.

Then an old Volkswagen minibus—the stereotypical hippie van, though this one was woodlands camouflage–colored, not tie-dyed—

whipped around the corner and skidded to a halt at the end of the alley.

The back door of the bus popped open, and Tarva, the blond nymph waitress from the Manor, jumped out. She wore a long black coat that covered her from neck to toe, probably because she was still wearing the nothing that passed for a uniform at her job underneath. The boxy bullpup assault rifle she carried with consummate professionalism held my attention more than memories of her in tightly scandalous clothing.

"Come on, let's get you all in out of the cold," she said quietly.

I started to move to help the others with the wounded, but Talus simply gestured. The two bodies floated into the van under his Power. He supported O'Malley and Celine helped Tamara into the van while Tarva and I took up the rear. I pushed Laurie in front of me, and Tarva eyed the hag, clearly wondering why she was bound.

"Everyone in?" Eric asked as I closed the door.

"Yes," I replied shortly, and looked forward to see the gnome look into his mirror. At the sight of Laurie, his jaw dropped.

"She's the traitor?" he demanded incredulously.

"Yes," Talus answered flatly. "Now, I have to focus if I'm going to save George's life, so if everyone can be quiet, I think we'd all appreciate it."

The drive back to the Manor passed in silence with Talus bent over O'Malley, fully focused on saving the older gentry's life. The rest of his team sprawled in their seats in various levels of exhaustion. I kept an eye on Laurie, who was being way too calmly docile and creepily silent for my peace of mind.

When we got back to the Manor, Eric maneuvered the minivan in behind the motel and turned it off, looking back at the rest of us.

"Rooms 114 through 118 never get rented," he told us. "They aren't actually rooms; it's a small office and storage space." He tossed me a key and paused. "There's also access to a morgue-style freezer under the space," he said quietly. That shocked me—though it made sense, seeing as how fae bodies would be problematic if a human coroner got his or her hands on one.

"Tarva and I have to get back to the bar," Eric continued. "Can you lot take care of yourselves for a few hours?"

"Yes, we can," Talus said quickly. "Thank you, Eric. I owe you a boon."

The gnome nodded sharply in acknowledgement of the formal debt Talus was offering, and exited the van. With a smile and nod all around, Tarva opened the back door and followed him.

"Let's get George inside," Talus instructed.

"I've got Frankie and MacDougall," Celine said softly, the Fury scooping up the two bodies as she said so. "Is the way clear?"

"I'll go grab the door," I volunteered. Leaving Laurie with Tamara, I got out of the truck, checking the badly lit alley and making sure no one was standing at the transit station across the street, watching us.

The motel parking lot was dark and quiet except for Eric's bar on the other side of it, and no one seemed to be coming in or out of the bar right now.

I opened the door to room 118, the closest of the four Eric had pointed out, and shouted back toward the van. "The door is open; bring them over."

Celine was first, the dead bodies of our friends sadly being the most noticeable and attention-grabbing portion of our group. Talus followed, supporting O'Malley, who was now at least semiconscious and paying attention to things around him.

Tamara and Laurie stepped out of the van, but as the nightmare was stepping down from the van, Laurie finally acted.

Her hands still cuffed together, she joined them into a double fist and slammed it into Tamara's leg before the other fae could react. Standing by the door to the motel, almost twenty feet away, I heard Tamara's thighbone snapping.

The dark-skinned fae crumpled, falling from the minivan to the concrete of the parking lot as Laurie bolted. She timed it perfectly, as a c-train started to come rumbling up to the platform as I dropped the key to take off after her.

With cold iron running through her veins, she had no powers, but she was still fast. I was faster, just barely, and starting from much farther behind. None of the others could react at all, tied down with wounded and dead, so it was all up to me.

If she escaped, we would probably never catch her again. Certainly not in time to help stop the coming catastrophe looming over the city. I put on an extra burst of speed, trying desperately to catch her.

I knew it wasn't going to be enough, and then a sudden flash of cold came over me. Between one breath and the next, my world was even colder than the frozen street I was running across. When it passed, and I breathed again, Laurie was inches from me—within arm's reach.

I hooked her legs out from underneath her before she processed that I was that close, and she went flying face first into the pavement. Before she could try to get up, I was on top of her. I grabbed her cuffed hands to immobilize them and drove a knee into her shoulder, pinning her to the ground.

"Stay down," I ordered, and she looked up at me in surprise.

"Damn you, Hunter," she gasped. "Who are you, truly?"

"Jason Kilkenny," I snapped. "Vassal of Queen Mabona," I finished, and a horrified understanding filled her eyes. "You aren't going anywhere."

I roughly manhandled her to her feet, pushing her before me with a hand on the chain of her handcuffs as I delivered her back to the motel rooms Eric had turned into a sanctuary. Celine, her burdens delivered to the basement, was waiting for me, her eyes glowing with black fire.

"We need her alive," I told the Fury roughly.

"I'm not going to kill her," Celine promised.

"Just lock her in a closet or something," I ordered. To my surprise, the Fury—who could easily have taken me apart—obeyed instantly. She dialed down the black fire in her eyes and took the hag in care with a rough but not damaging grip.

Tamara had made it into the sanctuary and Talus had helped her into a chair from which she watched as the fae noble laid George O'Malley flat on top of a desk.

The room had very obviously started as the motel room it once had been. Where the beds had once been had been replaced with four desks, and the bathroom had been torn out and replaced with a storage closet that Celine was now removing boxes of weapons from so she could lock Laurie in it. A door on the right side led into the other converted rooms, and a door by the closet, still slightly ajar, presumably led to the basement and its refrigerated morgue.

"You never told us he was a Vassal," Celine told Talus, somewhat accusingly.

"I take it everyone heard that," I realized aloud, remembering just how good the hearing of gentry and greater fae could be. I should never have said anything. Laurie didn't need to know, and neither did anyone else here.

"Yes, we did," Talus confirmed, drawing a blanket over O'Malley and stepping back from the now stable and mostly healed gentry. "And I didn't tell you," he said to Celine and Tamara, "because one huge advantage that Jason has as a changeling and a Vassal is that no one expects one of the High Court to hold a changeling's fealty."

"I'd prefer it if it stayed that way," I admitted, pulling up a chair and trying to calm my breathing and loosen my muscles. "The idea of painting a giant 'shoot here' sign on my head for the Queen's enemies doesn't appeal to me."

"We live in Fort McMurray," Celine told me dryly as she finished barring the closet door shut behind Laurie. "Who are we going to tell?"

"Heartstone flows from the oil sands," Talus said quietly. "Power flows from the heartstone. For all that it's the backwater of the world in almost every sense; Fort McMurray is the center of a lot of things both mortal and inhuman. Hell, the Fort is probably at least half the reason for the chaos here."

"So, what happens now?" Tamara asked, carefully shifting her leg to make sure it didn't heal crooked overnight.

"Tarvers's funeral," I told them. "The shifter clans will elect a new Speaker afterwards, and then Lord Oberis will request that Speaker's aid in waging war against Magus MacDonald."

"So far, so good," Tamara pointed out. "The Enforcers caused this whole mess; kicking their ass sounds good to me."

"The whole thing is a trap," I explained slowly, trying to lay out the pieces I'd uncovered so that the others would understand. "Oberis isn't going to kill MacDonald—force him to leave, yes, but not kill—

firstly because he probably *can't,* but secondly because if you kill one Wizard, three more descend to destroy you and anyone associated with you. It's how they protect their own when they're so scattered.

"But while the war is going on, Winters is going to kill the Magus."

Talus had worked it out, I knew, but clearly, he hadn't explained the whole situation to his people, as both Celine and Tamara stared at me in shock.

"The Alpha of Clan Fontaine is creating chaos and violence to undermine the other candidates for Speaker," I continued. "Right now, Darius Fontaine is the most likely Speaker for the Clans—and as either Speaker or a high-level Alpha, he can and will accuse Oberis of ordering the murder. The Wizards would destroy the Court and place Winters, as MacDonald's former right-hand man, in charge of the city in their name—and in charge of the heartstone."

"The vampires' role in this is done," Talus realized aloud, picking a point out of the whole mess that I'd actually missed. "All we've done is made it so that Winters doesn't have to include them in his new Covenant in payment."

"So, we have to stop the war," I told them all quietly. "We have witnesses who know what Fontaine was up to, so we *should* be able to stop him being elected. I'm hoping that Laurie can tell us enough of the truth to get Oberis to call it off."

"Why don't we interrogate her now?" Celine asked, with a toss of her head toward the closet we'd locked the traitor in.

The door to the outside opened before Talus could answer, and then slammed shut behind Eric as the gnome slipped into the room.

"Because she's protected against truth magic," the Keeper told us as he took a seat on one of the desks, looking around at us all. "Sorry," he continued, "I've been eavesdropping on you all—I figured I'd need to be up to date on what's going on and with whatever we're planning."

"Laurie, like Talus here and other fae who serve at that high a level in the Court, is shielded from truth magic by Oberis," Eric explained. "Only Oberis himself can force her to tell him everything and not lie."

"Damn," the Fury said quietly. "So, what do we do?"

"We air *all* the dirty laundry," I told them all. "We drag Laurie into the center of everything and throw her at Oberis's feet. We have our witnesses condemn Darius Fontaine before his clan and the other Alphas. We stop the war before it even starts."

Tamara inhaled sharply, looking at me with a tilt to her head. "Sounds simpler than it is," she observed. "What do you have planned for an encore?"

I took a deep breath and turned to look Talus in the eyes. Of anyone there, he was the one who had to understand just what *my* orders were in all of this.

"I fulfill my mission from the Queen—and rescue the Wizard from his own Tower."

Talus nodded, once, silently communicating his understanding to me. Not a promise of help, nothing like that, but it was an acceptance that he knew what I had to do.

"We're going to have a busy morning," he told everyone. "I am going to call Shelly and let her know to bring Mary and Holly. We will bring Laurie. Eric, can you keep an eye on our prisoner?"

Eric nodded. "I'll call a couple of friends I can completely trust," he promised. "I'll make sure she's still here. There are beds still in here for you to rest on," he continued. "It's probably best if you all stay here till the funeral."

That was about all the encouragement I needed. Celine and I helped Tamara—already healing from the break Laurie had given her —through to one of the beds, and then took others for ourselves.

Tomorrow was going to be a very big day.

32

THAT DAY STARTED, as odd as it sounds, with clothes-shopping. With the exception of Talus, who lived at least part-time in Calgary, none of us had full formal wear. Even if I hadn't been inclined to dress up to show respect to Tarvers, Talus made it clear to us all that we were to dress appropriately.

By morning, George O'Malley was mobile again. His own healing abilities and Talus's Power had fully dealt with his injuries, and the four of us headed downtown as Talus vanished to deal with his own preparations for the funeral—taking Laurie with him.

The fae noble had handed Celine a credit card before he left, and the Fury had promptly decided to find the most expensive fancy-dress store in the city. This, of course, was buried inside the core and relatively quiet on a Saturday morning.

One of Eric's "friends I can completely trust" had picked up the van we'd left at Talus's hidden apartment armory near downtown and delivered it to the motel, so we had transportation.

Celine drove us downtown like she owned the road, and walked into the store with about the same level of ownership vibe. I watched with more than a little fascination as the Fury—probably among the three or four most dangerous females I currently knew, *including* the

Queen—managed to corral four staff members and point one of them at each of us. She kept the manager, I noticed, to herself as she started audibly gleeing over a certain color of coat.

"And what is sir's style choice for the day?" the somewhat shell-shocked staff member asked me.

I answered with the long-standing conversational placeholder of choice: "Umm.

"I'm headed to a funeral in about two hours," I continued slowly, thinking carefully. "I want something appropriate, but still...easy to move in—I won't have to time to change afterward and I have a bunch of errands to do."

That seemed more acceptable in my ears—and apparently to the young "fashion consultant"—than "I'm going to a funeral, which will be followed by an election and a political negotiation, either or both of which may turn to violence at a moment's notice."

"We do have a new line of 'athletic dress shirts,'" the girl said after a moment. "They're designed so you can go right from the office to a golf game..."

I paid some attention to the girl's sales pitch, but mostly just nodded whenever she grabbed an item of clothing. Twenty minutes and a mind-boggling price tag later, I was dressed in a neat black suit with almost-invisible burgundy pinstripes. Both the suit and the shirt underneath it had a surprising degree of flexibility and flow, hopefully enough for me to fight in them if I had to.

O'Malley was finished before me, sitting in a plain charcoal-gray suit by the front entrance while we waited for the girls. Tamara joined us a few minutes after I finished, in a prim suit tied to a long skirt whose multiple layers concealed the fact that it was slit almost all the way up to the hip for ease of movement.

Celine took another hour on top of all of us. By the time she was done, the manager had three of the staff running relays of clothes in and out of the changing room. Finally, however, she emerged to join us —in much the same style of skirt suit as Tamara had picked out in half an hour.

We paid and left the store, heading for the van.

"What took so long?" I finally asked.

The Fury shrugged. "I didn't see a reason not to make sure I didn't get the perfect outfit on a noble's credit," she answered. "I didn't go over time—we have plenty of time to get to the funeral. And now I'm ready, and you're all ready, and you've spent the last hour being annoyed at me instead of nervous about what's coming. Let's go."

With that, she strode ahead of the rest of us as I looked after her, knowing I was staring in open-mouthed surprise.

The Fury was *good*.

———

We returned to the van in our new formal wear, and Tamara promptly started pulling shoulder holsters and black metal-and-polymer pistols —Glock 18s, apparently—from a box in the back of the van and passed them around. They slipped easily under the suit jackets we all wore and belted into place.

Armed and dressed for the occasion, Celine took the wheel and drove us farther into the city's southwest quarter. The funeral was at a small Catholic church that was heavily supported by the Clan Tenerim —Tarvers himself had converted to Catholicism several centuries earlier, apparently.

The building was no cathedral, but it was a fair-sized structure of concrete and wrought iron surrounded by easily two acres of land-scaped grounds, a tall and neatly trimmed hedge shielding the grounds from view.

A handful of "stray dogs" wandered around the perimeter, outside the hedge, with a precision and pattern that gave their true nature away almost instantly to those of us looking for the guards.

We pulled into the parking lot, slotting the black van in amidst the chaotic mix of vehicles. I recognized many of the cars from David and Elena's funeral—either shifters who'd known the two fae, or fae who were there to honor the leader of the shifters. Like us.

Mary texted me, asking me if I'd arrived yet, just as we were exiting the van. I excused myself from the group of fae and went to meet her and Holly. I found them standing just around the corner of the church, out of sight from the entrance.

Shelly stood with them, as did Theino, the young and well-spoken goblin who'd been organizing their care. All four were dressed in plain black formal clothes, though Theino also wore a plain white scarf wrapped around the lower half of his face to conceal his tusks.

Ignoring the fact that, even tucked out of view as we were, we were in public, I wrapped Mary in a tight embrace, feeling for a long moment like I would never let her go. She returned the embrace with full force for a moment and then gently extricated herself.

"Hey, what's going on with you?" she asked. "*I'm* not the one who tried to get killed last night—I should be the one freaking out over you."

"Yes, but you're not going to," I told her, trying to keep my voice reasonable and somewhat flippant. "So, I have to do it for both of us."

My shifter shook her head, pressed a kiss to my forehead, and cast a look around. "Shelly told us about Laurie," she said very quietly. "What are you going to do?"

"For now?" I shrugged, nodding toward Shelly. "Follow Talus's lead. I trust his sense of melodrama to provide the right timing to introduce Laurie."

"He's noble fae," Shelly said, nodding. "Melodrama runs in his blood."

"Shelly, melodrama runs in *all* fae blood," I told her, finding it easier to joke and smile now Mary was there. "What about you?" I asked, turning to Holly.

"I'm going to hide between you and Theino until the actual election starts," she said quietly, responding slightly to my smile and attempted good cheer. "Then I'm hoping you'll be between me and any of Darius's men who try to shut me up."

I nodded, laying a reassuring hand on her shoulder and glancing over at the goblin. In answer to my unspoken question, so that Holly wasn't aware of it, he opened his jacket just enough for me to see the black metal of some sort of firearm in a shoulder rig.

Both of us were armed, so with me on one side of the girl and Theino on the other, no one was getting to her without paying a heavier price than they expected. Mary saw the exchange as well and leaned in to kiss me. She grabbed my hand as she did and put it inside her jacket.

It looked like a cuddling, possibly somewhat indecent gesture to everyone else. I realized she'd put my hand on the grip of the same ugly-looking little submachine gun she'd produced in Holly's apartment.

There was a very real chance no one in this church was unarmed, and unlike most of them, *I* knew how ugly this could get.

"The Fontaines are in," Shelly told us quietly, having glanced around the corner. "We should head in. We don't want to miss the service."

I nodded at her comment, taking a deep breath as the *real* reason for today sank in. With everything else going on, I'd almost forgotten we were there to mourn a man who'd proven himself worthy of my respect in the short time I'd known him.

A man who hadn't deserved to die.

––––––––

THE CHURCH WAS VERY quiet inside, despite the several hundred people already in the building. A piano stood, untouched, by an empty choir stage. The seats were mostly full, and the empty ones rapidly filled around us as we slid into chairs in the back row.

It was a plain building, inside as well as out, but well maintained and sturdy. My quick eyeball suggested that extra chairs had been added, wrapping around the normal pews, allowing space for probably around six hundred people.

By five minutes after we'd sat down, every seat was full. A handful of people leaned against the back wall, but they were the final stragglers. There weren't six hundred supernaturals in the city, period, but there were apparently at least a few dozen humans who'd known who Tarvers Tenerim actually was.

Most of the attendees were shifters—there were probably less than a dozen shifters in the city who *weren't* there—but a fair number of fae and other inhumans filled out the rest of the chairs.

The shuffling slowed and eventually stopped as people either found seats or comfortable leaning places for the fifty or so people who there just weren't seats for. Almost before the movement stopped, the priest, clad in his black-and-white vestments, strode confidently toward the podium at the front of the church.

A closed casket rested just in front of the podium, a picture of Tarvers in his prime set upon it. The priest looked around at everyone and said a short benediction in Latin that went right over my head.

"Welcome," he said finally in a language I understood. "We have all come here today to honor and celebrate the life of an amazing man, who lived a life of service for over three hundred years."

He then launched into a sermon on public service. For a speech given by a Catholic priest, it was light on the religious symbolism and lacked even one parable from the Bible—probably in consideration to the fact that many of the shifters and almost *all* of the fae and other inhumans were the literal definition of pagans—unsaved and unin-clined to be saved by the stories of a mortal man when we had the very real Powers to look to for salvation.

For all that he started with a sermon, the service was short. It was also very clear that the priest had known Tarvers. He spoke to the man's virtues—many—and vices—anger, pride—and then passed the podium to the old Alpha's sons.

The two men, both carrying the bulk and menace of werebears, stood side by side at the podium and spoke, in voices that broke with every sentence, of growing up the children of a man who'd seen a city rise from nothing. They spoke of being raised to be shifters by the greatest shifter of all.

In there, subtly, although I doubt anyone missed it, was the announcement that the older brother—Michael—would succeed Tarvers as Alpha Tenerim. From the quiet sigh that Mary swallowed beside me, I took it that even *that* hadn't been certain. I squeezed her hand, knowing without even looking that she was quietly weeping as the sons continued to speak about their father.

I don't think there were many people in the hall that weren't crying to one extent or another. There was tension in the church—everyone knew what would follow the service—but at this moment, we mourned one of the greatest of our own.

The speeches done, the two brothers each took one end of the casket and slowly carried it from the church. We all followed them out into the chill and snowy air, row by row, in quiet grief.

It was possibly the quietest group of people of that size I've ever seen, and I was silent with them as we made it out into the small graveyard behind the church. There, I stood at the back of the crowd, barely able to see as Tarvers Tenerim was slowly lowered into the earth of the city he'd seen grow from nothing to a major center.

His sons took up shovels, and the other Alphas joined them. The crowd of over six hundred watched in silence as nine men slowly and carefully, for all the massive strength and speed available to them, filled in the grave.

Finally, the priest sprinkled water over the grave and spoke some more Latin I thought I recognized as the last rites.

His task done, the priest bowed to the Alphas and withdrew into the Church. The entire mood of the crowd shifted as he did so, and the tension ratcheted up a notch. Wordlessly, the eight Alphas walked in a group, leaving Tarvers's younger son kneeling by his father's grave until he joined the rest of the crowd.

We followed the Alphas to find a pair of large marquee tents had been set up to create a huge assembly hall. Propane heaters occupied each corner, but they didn't look nearly large enough to provide the comfortable warmth that filled the tents. I suspected the small beaver-fur fetishes hung above each heater had more to do with it. There was Power at work.

A long table was set up at the front of the table, and the eight Alphas each took a seat. I recognized Enli, the old Native American cougar shifter, Michael Tenerim—and Darius Fontaine. The others were familiar by face but not by name.

I was about to try and grab another back row set of seats, but Holly took charge as we entered the tent. "Follow me," she ordered in a whisper, and confidently strode right up the center of the hall to take a front row seat, directly across from Darius Fontaine. The young Fontaine deer shifter met her Alpha's gaze calmly, daring him to challenge her, to admit that he'd tried to have her killed.

He didn't take the bait, turning away to glance around the room as Enli stood, gesturing for people to hurry up and sit.

We'd shed a hundred or so people—most of the fae and other non-shifters who really didn't have a say or interest in the shifter election. Sitting at the front now, I saw Lord Oberis also in the front row, in one of the corners. He looked concerned, but that was likely due to the lack of both Talus *and* Laurie, though when he caught sight of me, the old fae looked somewhat relieved—probably presuming, correctly, that if I was there, Talus must be okay.

"Everyone here knows who I am," Enli said as the rustling continued. The old Alpha spoke quietly, but the entire tent heard him and quieted down. "We are gathered here to remember Tarvers Tenerim," he continued, "which does not stop because he is buried."

"But," Enli said with a deep sigh, "we must also now choose his successor. Today, here, of the Alphas of Calgary, we must choose a new Speaker, to lead us and to speak for us to the Covenants of this city."

A rumbling of noise and argument almost immediately erupted from the crowd, people shouting the names of Clans and Alphas they supported or would refuse to see elected. Several of the Alphas at the head table got in on the shouting as well, with one Alpha I didn't recognize banging on the table in a vain attempt to be recognized and heard.

"*Silence*," Enli bellowed, and I think the sheer shock of the kindly old native Grandfather shouting quelled the shifter Clans to silence.

"The custom is and has always been that the Alphas select one from among their number," he reminded everyone, his voice instantly calm and soft again. "If you have an opinion here, you should have raised it with your Alpha before now."

The chair beside me scraped across the grass, and I quietly shifted so I could readily reach the gun under my jacket as Holly stood. Few among the shifters had the gumption to interrupt Grandfather while he was speaking, and her presumption kept the inevitable shouting down.

"There is something I have to say before you vote," she said quietly, but the silence in the tent allowed her to be heard. "An Alpha has acted against his Clan and broken his oaths."

"Holly Fontaine, be seated," Darius barked. "This is not a place for grievances amongst Clan members."

"My grievance is *not* merely that of Clanswoman against Alpha," she responded. "We all know that someone has waged a campaign of violence amongst our numbers—trying to weaken Clans, distract others. This campaign has been waged to influence *this* election, and I know who waged it."

She paused as the crowd around her exploded. Shifters were on their feet, people were moving—and two were very clearly headed toward Holly. I stood, taking a place at one side of her as Theino rose on her other side and Mary slipped neatly in behind us.

Without even looking, I knew that Tamara, Celine and O'Malley were moving closer, making sure they were in a place to cover us if things got worse. The tension ratcheted in the air as the shouting continued, accusations and counter-accusations flying all around us.

"*BE SEATED*," Grandfather bellowed a second time, and this time, every ounce of energy and command and Power the old Alpha had cracked through his voice. A pointed, wrinkled finger silenced Darius before he could speak, and he turned back to Holly.

"I would hear the girl speak," he continued. "Will you approach the table and face the gaze of the Alphas?"

I could almost *feel* the fear in the girl. Darius had tried to kill her in the past, indirectly, and the Alphas were the strongest of her kind, any one of them able to kill her with a single swipe. Nonetheless, she squared her shoulders and walked forward, holding Enli's gaze every step of the way. The old shifter gave her an approving nod as she stopped directly in front of the table, facing Grandfather as a way to avoid looking at Darius.

"Speak, child," Enli said quietly.

"I overheard two of the men I knew were close to Darius talking," she began without pre-amble. "They spoke of the bombing of the Tenerim Den—with perfect knowledge of what had happened. They thought they were alone and so did not conceal that *they* had been the ones to attack the Den—on his orders.

"I thought they must have been mistaken, that my Alpha could never order such an action, so I demanded Clan right of truth of him,"

Holly told the assembled Alphas. "He told me to keep my mouth shut or I would be silenced."

"This is ridic—" Darius began, but the massed glares of the other Alphas silenced him in mid-sentence before Enli gestured for Holly to continue.

With a deep breath, and a swallow I could hear from where I stood half a dozen feet behind, she did. "I intended to take my fears to the Clan Council of Fontaine, and I mentioned this to another Clan member," she said softly.

"That evening, I was attacked in my home by several warriors of my Clan," Holly continued, her voice very small, yet carrying to every corner of the tent. "They told me Darius had sent them to silence me— told me they were going to rape me and murder me to carry out his orders.

"A friend from Clan Tenerim and another from the fae Court saved me," she told Enli, gaining some strength as she continued bravely. "They sheltered me where no Fontaine could find me, so I could speak here today.

"I accuse Darius Fontaine," she finished, her voice harsh, "of the murder of shifters in time of peace between Clans. Of the firebombing of a Den. Of ordering the murder of his own Clansmen. I name him oath-breaker and call upon Clan Fontaine to strip him of rank and authority."

"This is ridiculous; why would you believe this claptrap?" Darius demanded, rising to his feet. "This woman is clearly insane," he told the crowd. "Please, Grandfather, let me have my people take her home to rest."

Wordlessly, to forestall any further action on anyone's part, I stepped forward to stand by Holly's side. I didn't draw a weapon, but I didn't have to.

"She is speaking the truth," Enli said flatly. "But all she has heard is second-hand—the words of other men to your actions, Darius Fontaine."

"I am innocent of this slander!" the Alpha growled.

"If you are innocent," Michael Tenerim said sweetly, "then you will lower your defenses and allow the Alphas to See the truth of your side of this story. This sort of accusation cannot be left unanswered when the Speaker is elected."

"This is preposterous," Darius told Michael. "Clearly, my Clanswoman has been deceived by those who wish to steal this election. What possible reason would I have for this kind of violence?"

"Why don't we ask someone who was working with you on it?" A quiet voice cut through the tent as a chill wind blasted through the suddenly open tent flap.

I turned, and everyone else turned with me, to face the tent entrance. Talus, noble of the Joint Court of the fae, stood in the chill wind, the handcuffed Laurie held easily in front of him with a single hand.

"This woman, high in our trust," Talus continued as he walked through the crowd, all eyes on him and his prisoner, "betrayed us to work with part of a conspiracy to undermine the peace of this city. I think if we ask *her* about Alpha Fontaine's actions, she will be most illuminating."

I glanced back at Darius as Talus spoke, and the Alpha's face was terrifying. Before anyone could respond to the noble's words, the Alpha jerked his hand at Talus, and suddenly everything went to hell.

Someone in the crowd near Talus pulled a gun and opened fire on him. Someone *else*—either Celine or Tamara I suspected—opened fire on *them*. The crowd went crazy, some people diving for cover, other shifters trying to either put down the original gunman or protect him and create more chaos.

I dove forward, grabbing Holly by the shoulder and pulling her backward. Mary was beside me in a moment, grabbing Holly's other shoulder as we tried to protect the deer shifter from the chaos in the crowd.

We were watching for the wrong threat. I don't know what warned me, but the hairs on my neck all stood up and I looked up as an animal roar tore through the tent. Unthinkingly, I stepped between the sound and Mary and Holly, shielding the two women with my body.

The world seemed to slow around me as I looked up and realized that my body was about all the protection I could give them. Darius Fontaine had *shifted*, and a huge, magnificent polar bear, larger than even Tarvers in his other form, charged at me. I hadn't drawn a weapon, and my faerie flame would be nothing against the sheer brute power of an enraged shifter Alpha. In that moment, I knew that Fontaine was going to kill me.

Then, as his claws were slashing toward my face, there was a burst of light, and the claws were gone. The polar bear flew back a good ten feet, shattering the table, and Lord Oberis was suddenly in front of me. His hand was still extended in the open-palm strike that had thrown the shifter back, and the strange dark light of the Between scattered from him as he strode forward.

Darius tried to charge him again, and Oberis caught him with a cross-strike that blurred faster than even fae eyes could see. The bear Alpha lurched sideways, and the entire tent stopped as the Fontaine followers brave, stupid or loyal enough to try and fight, and everyone else, at this point realized what was happening.

Sluggish, lurching from the blow, the massive polar bear tried to circle around to go for Holly again. I don't know what was running through his head at that point—maybe he thought if he destroyed the evidence by killing her, he would somehow at least be able to walk free.

It didn't work. Oberis blocked him again, and this time, one of the polar bear's massive legs broke, the crash of shattering bone as the fae lord smashed Darius's foreleg aside clearly audible through the tent.

"Yield," the Lord of the Court ordered. "I do not wish to kill you."

Darius *roared* in response and charged, his broken leg already healed. The ground shook under the impact and force of the bear's charge. Somewhere in the middle of it, Oberis struck.

The sword suddenly in the fae lord's hand was a thing of glamor and Power, not steel or silver—but it may as well have been of the shifter's ancient bane. With a single slash of the shimmering blade he conjured from nowhere, Oberis cleaved through Darius Fontaine. The big shifter's charge ended with him returning to human form—in pieces that crashed into the ground with tremendous force.

33

Calm and silence descended on the tent as the remaining Fontaine loyalists surrendered their arms after their Alpha's death. Seven or eight bodies were slowly removed from the chaos as the crowd of shifters slowly moved away from the area around Talus.

The fae noble looked uninjured, as did Laurie. After a moment, I realized that the slight shimmering around him was a telekinetic barrier—serving the double purpose of containing Laurie and protecting them from bullets.

Talus let the barrier fall and strode forward again, half-pushing, half-leading Laurie with him until he stopped before his uncle.

Oberis had let the glamor-forged sword pass back into nothingness and stepped aside from the fallen body of the Fontaine Alpha, allowing two of the shifters to remove the body to where they were improvising a cover for the bodies from a tablecloth. Despite the lack of sword, he still stood ramrod straight, and every eye in the room could see the power crackle off of him.

"I am afraid," he said softly, projecting his voice to every corner of the room as he bowed to the Alphas, "that I have stolen justice from you, my lords."

There was a series of wordless glances and small nods amongst the Alphas, and then Enli spoke for them all.

"You did what was necessary," he said simply. "You defended one of our daughters from a traitor amongst those who *should* have defended her. We thank you."

Oberis bowed, ever so slightly, and started to move toward where Talus was bringing Laurie forward.

"If we may beg a boon, Lord Oberis," Enli said quietly, "I would ask that we all hear what this woman has to say."

I held my breath for a moment. If we were right, Laurie's testimony would break open the whole situation, expose everything and allow us to find the root of the problem. If Oberis insisted on interrogating her in private, we'd get our information, but I wasn't sure if it would have the same impact.

Oberis was a fae lord, however, and I probably shouldn't have worried. Melodrama is bred into our species' bones, after all, and he nodded agreement almost before I'd finished worrying, gesturing Talus to bring his prisoner forward.

"Laurie of the Unseelie," he said formally, in that same quiet, projected, terrible voice. "You stand accused of treason against the Court and are so stripped of the defenses I gave you against truth Sight."

I *felt* the quiet Power that moved with his words. It was a subtle thing, a thing of thought and word, but it tore through barriers I hadn't even *sensed* like they were paper, somehow baring Laurie's soul to the eyes of her erstwhile master.

"What do you have to say?" he asked.

"I see it in your eyes," she told him hoarsely. "You have condemned me already. What purpose is there for me to speak? I know what the law lays out for my crimes."

"There are ways to die and ways to die," Oberis told her gently. "The law prescribes the Cold Death—no warmth, no life, no breath, left Between to die."

His words hit the air like falling tombstones, and I shivered at my memory of the chill cold when I stood Between with the Queen. To be left there? Without the Gift to walk that path yourself, it was, as Oberis named it, a death sentence. A horrible one.

"Your service has earned you mercy, if not clemency," Oberis told Laurie, his voice still so terrifyingly soft. "Do me one more service and tell me what was planned here, and I will grant you a gentle death. It is all I can offer."

"*Service*," Laurie spat. "That's all I ever was to you—a *servant*, the dirty Unseelie you used when it suited you. *Years* together, and never a friend, never more."

"I was always your friend," Oberis told her, and I was close enough to him to hear the choke in his voice. I don't think anyone else except maybe Holly and Mary were. "And if I never saw you as a woman, I'm sorry," he continued, "but I never saw any woman that way. If you never knew that, you were as blind as I was for thirty years to miss how you felt, and I am sorry."

"And it changes nothing," she whispered, and the lord shook his head.

"You are responsible for the deaths of two fae I know of," he said gently but coldly. "I don't know how many humans or others the vampires killed that can be directly or indirectly laid at your feet. You have betrayed Court and race and Covenant, and I have offered all the mercy I can.

"Tell me everything," he ordered. Tearfully, kneeling at his feet, Laurie nodded.

"Winters came to me a year ago," she told Oberis, oblivious to the rest of us now. "He must have been watching for a while, learning who was...discontent. He offered me a place in a plan that would make me Lady in Calgary, and an increase in our heartstone supply to allow me to buy the support of other Courts.

"My initial role was just to keep him in the loop of all of our plans," she continued. "I helped him bring Madrigal and her vampires into the city—*I* found Professor Sigridsen and learned of her proclivities as a hunter and her disease. *I* confirmed that conversion to a vampire would cure her." Even while describing her crimes, there was pride in her voice at what she'd done.

"After that, my job—and Darius's," she added, glancing up at the

Alphas, acknowledging someone other than Oberis for the first time, "was to allow the vampires to wreak havoc. We were to deflect investigations, warn of raids, and help ratchet up the tensions. We were to point to the Enforcers, whose job it was to stop the vampires.

"It was our job to start the war," she said simply.

"Tarvers's death was planned for from the beginning, to allow Darius to seize control of the Clans," she told Oberis. "We needed that control for when the real plan took place."

"What real plan?" Oberis demanded.

"By now, MacDonald is restrained," she explained. "He doesn't have the power to do anything to Winters anymore—he's made his Chief Enforcer immune to his own Power. He is bound in silver and iron, unable to wield magic.

"When the war reached an appropriate peak, MacDonald would be murdered," Laurie said finally. "Winters would have to do the task himself, but he has a gnome-forged warblade to do it with—to lay the blame at the foot of the Court. Darius would then distance himself from the Court, claiming lack of knowledge when the Order sent their Wizards to avenge him.

"With the Court blamed and no way to prove the guilt of a specific member or innocence of us all, the Wizards would be prepared to destroy the entire Court, as is their way," she said softly. "You would then sacrifice yourself, taking responsibility and allowing the Wizards to destroy you to protect your Court.

"The Wizards would enforce peace but would not stay. Winters would control the Enforcers, now a power in the city in their own right, and establish a new Covenant—including Madrigal and her vampires, under the usual rules for a Covenant-bound cabal. Darius would control the Clans. I would take control of the Court, leaving Talus in Fort McMurray."

Her spiel finished, Laurie fell silent. Every gaze was on her, all of us shocked. I'd put together most of it myself, but it was still a bit disturbing to hear it all laid out in step-by-step detail.

"Do you know why Winters started this?" Oberis asked, finally. "If he had that kind of lust for power, MacDonald would never have raised him as high as he did. What's in it for him?"

"He never said," Laurie admitted. "I have told you all I know."

Oberis knelt by her and placed his hands on her shoulders.

"So you have," he accepted. "I owe you one last service, then. Rest, Laurie," he told her, gently laying her unresisting form down on the floor. "Sleep, and may your dreams be merciful on you."

Slowly, the hag's eyes fluttering shut under his soothing words, his hands on her shoulders. She passed into sleep under the eyes of us all, her breathing shallow. And then, peacefully, without so much as a spasm, her breathing stopped.

———

SOMEHOW, that quiet, utterly cold-blooded execution hit me harder than the violent deaths I'd seen and inflicted over the last few weeks. It put those deaths in perspective, and I barely heard Michael Tenerim speaking, addressing Enli.

I squeezed Mary's hand and released it, making my way outside as quietly as I could as shivers of shock ran through me.

When I'd come to this city, I'd never killed anyone in my life. Now? I'd *lost track*. Like it wasn't important. Like the vampires and shifters whose bodies I'd left behind me hadn't mattered.

Laurie's death suddenly put everything in perspective. The death of someone I knew reminded me that everyone I'd killed along the way had friends, even the vampires. The shifters I'd killed to save Holly had been vicious men, plotting rape and murder, but they'd had family. Loyalties. It was their loyalty to Darius Fontaine that had thrown them into conflict with me.

I threw up. I barely managed to make it out of the tent and out of the view of most before I did it, too. Collapsing to my knees in the snow, I emptied my stomach onto the ground. I'd come to this city weak, seeking a normal, mortal life. Where had everything gone so wrong?

Suddenly, I was a killer. The powers I'd wielded all my life had taken on new strengths, new intensities that terrified me. I'd become stronger than I'd ever dreamed and had seen more violence than I'd ever feared, and it had snuck up on me somehow.

"Are you okay?" I heard Mary ask behind me, but another voice answered her before I could.

"No, he isn't," Eric told her quietly. "You may not want to be here, girl," he continued. "This isn't pretty."

"I'm not leaving until I know he's okay," she answered fiercely, and I felt her step up behind me and place her hands on my shoulders.

"Just hit you, didn't it?" Eric asked me gruffly. "The things you've done for fealty. She changed you, and you didn't even realize until afterwards."

"What have I become?" I asked, looking up at the gnome as he passed Mary a warm wet cloth to clean my face with. "So much has happened here."

"You have become a Vassal of the Queen," Eric said simply. I felt Mary's hands tremble as she gently cleaned my face. By now, I was sure she'd known I was more than I'd admitted to, but it was something entirely different, I knew, to hear it all confirmed.

"Your fealty shields you from the impact of much of what you do," he told me. "Be grateful for it—it's not like you can go visit a therapist for it."

"Do I even get a fucking choice?" I demanded. I'd wanted a normal life—I still *did*. I wanted to drive a courier truck, be with Mary, and barely scrape by in the mortal lower class. Sad as it sounds, I wanted that mundanity so badly right then, I could taste it.

"No," the Keeper said bluntly. "You were born to this, Jason Kilkenny. Fate and blood and race and fealty command it, you have no choice. But remember this," he told me. "I did."

I reached up to squeeze Mary's hand as I looked up at the old gnome in question, and he nodded as I met his gaze.

"I was many things in my youth, much of which I regret," he told me. "I saw...much that I would not see again. I *chose* to swear fealty to the Queen and take up a Keeper's role. The Vassals of the Queen—and the rest of the High Court—keep the peace amongst our kind. They shield the mortals from the excesses of our race and the other inhuman races. There are darker sides," he admitted, "and we are bound to Her will, but by and large, Her will is to keep our people safe."

"I feel so much...less than I should be," I confessed. "What I feel at

Laurie's death—shouldn't I feel that for the others I saw die? What is so different about her?"

"You knew her," Mary said simply from behind me, and Eric nodded. "While she wasn't a friend, you knew her, and that always hits home harder. And every other death you've seen has been in battle —with them trying to kill you. Those *shouldn't* impact you as much. Self-defense is a necessary evil."

I squeezed her hand again and slowly stood up again with her help. "In the end, I don't have much choice, do I?" I asked Eric, and the Keeper shook his head.

"You were born to a Vassal bloodline," he said sadly. "Once She claimed you, you were Hers. Forever."

I had just finished nodding my—somewhat grudging—acceptance of this fact when a burning car came careening around the corner outside the church and smashed through the gate.

34

THE VEHICLE TRAILED flames and pieces as it spun across the parking lot, flipped up on its side and skidded another ten feet before finally coming to a stop. With the dramatic entrance finished, I recognized the silver sedan—it was Michael's car. The Enforcer who said he'd be in touch every day—who I now realized I hadn't heard from since Thursday.

"Fire extinguisher," Eric said quickly, pulling one from thin air and passing it to me before extracting another from nowhere.

Unlike in the movies, thankfully, real cars don't explode shortly after being set on fire. Eric started at one end of the car and I started at the other, and we quickly had the flames mostly doused. The last few stubborn flames revealed the source of it—the car had actually been sprayed with some sort of burning liquid. Someone had attacked the vehicle with a flamethrower.

Two of the shifter guards arrived just as we got the flames out and help Eric and me tear the roof off the car so we could get the driver out. Others emerged from the tent to make certain the continuing discussions were safe.

I was completely unsurprised to see Michael in the car. His state, however, was horrifying. Whoever had used the flamethrower had managed to get the burning napalm *inside* the vehicle. He was only barely responsive and all but screamed as we removed his hands from the steering wheel—they'd literally melted into the rubber coating.

"We need a healer," I said desperately, looking up to the guards. That was also when I realized that Mary had already left us. I looked around for her and spotted her leaving the pavilion, with Talus and Lord Oberis in tow. Her quick thinking gave Michael the only chance he had.

The two fae nobles reached us moments later, taking in the scene instantly and deciding, with some communication none of the rest could interpret, who would do what. Lord Oberis knelt by Michael's half-incinerated form, white light flowing from his hands as he moved them over the Enforcer's body.

Talus turned to me.

"Who is he?"

"One of the Enforcers," I explained. "He was investigating the truth of what was going on—promised he'd keep me informed, but with all the chaos, I hadn't realized he didn't contact me. He may know something."

"Well, someone seriously didn't want him telling us whatever he knows," the noble observed, eyeing the burnt remnants of the silver car. The napalm from the flamethrower had only been the final indignity visited on the car I realized. It had been sprayed with bullets from a high-caliber weapon first.

"Jason," a voice croaked, and Talus and I both turned to look at the Enforcer.

"Rest," Oberis murmured at him. "This isn't as easy as it looks."

"Have to," Michael forced himself to speak. It *looked* painful for him to be speaking. "Winters—killing Enforcers."

Killing Enforcers? Why would Winters be killing his own people? I knelt beside Oberis, focusing on the badly injured man he was trying to heal.

"MacDonald...is in chains," Michael forced out. "We tried...to free him. Honor...our oaths." He coughed, spewing blood over Oberis's white suit. The fae lord ignored it—ignored everything around him.

The white light shining between his hands and Michael grew stronger, and strain lines began to appear on the old Seelie's face.

"No chance," the Enforcer concluded. "Any who won't join...he kills. Can't...stop him. Can't...kill him... MacDonald...forged his own...doom."

Michael's gaze locked on mine, his eyes clear and his voice suddenly unbroken for a moment.

"Stop him," he pleaded. "I have fai..."

The light from Oberis's hands faded as the badly burnt Enforcer slumped back on the grass. I looked at the Seelie Lord. Lines were drawn deep in his ancient face, and for the first time since I'd met him, Oberis showed every year of his centuries of life as he shook his head in silence.

"I have to go," I told him simply. "The Queen commanded."

"We all have to go," another voice interjected, and I looked up to see Enli join us, the other Alphas walking behind him. "My fellows have pleaded and elected for me to be our new Speaker," Grandfather told us.

"As Speaker, it is my duty to uphold the Covenant," he continued. "And our Covenant is with *Kenneth MacDonald*, not the Enforcers—and Kenneth MacDonald is in danger. We must act."

Oberis rose to his feet once more, the strain lines dropping from his face as he did. By the time the fae lord reached his full height, every hint of a mar in the perfection of his ancient and ageless face was gone.

"Winters is no easy foe," he said quietly. "MacDonald bound many magics into that man—he is more of a construct than a man now, and no mortal weapon can harm him."

"No shifter can face him," Enli agreed simply. "But we can rescue the Enforcers in danger, eliminate the remaining vampires—we can clear the way."

"I am the only man who can face Winters," Oberis told us all. "Eric may be able to help," he continued, and pointed at me, "and this one has no choice about coming.

"If your shifters can deal with the situation outside Kenneth's Tower," he said to Enli, "my Court and I will deal with the Tower itself —and *I* will deal with Gerard Winters."

The old shifter Speaker considered for a moment, and then nodded. "Done and done," he said simply. "Let's go."

———

THE NEXT FEW minutes descended into an apparent chaos as Enli promptly took charge, organizing the shifters into hunting packs. Oberis and Talus spent most of the same time frame on their cell phones, calling and coordinating the few gentry and greater fae of the city who weren't already there.

After about fifteen minutes, Mary made a point of rejoining me where I stood by the two noble fae. She smiled and slipped into my arms, pressing a quick kiss to my lips.

"We're splitting up and heading out," she told me. "I'm a pretty good tracker, so I'm going with the team that's hitting up downtown to see if we can follow the vampires from where you guys ran them off."

"They may have fled through the sewers," I warned her. "They had tunnels leading into them."

Mary smiled sadly at me. "Unfortunately, that only means following them will smell much worse. I can track through that."

I kissed her.

"Be careful," I told her. "And good luck."

"*You* be careful," she responded. "I have big nasty shifters with me; vampires aren't going to be an issue. You're going to the Tower and hunting down Winters."

"I have Oberis," I told her, glancing over at the fae lord. "And no choice."

"Yeah, that last is the part I have an issue with," she replied, and sighed as an SUV rolled up beside us. "I have to go. Be safe, stay alive," she ordered.

"I will," I promised her, and watched her jump into the green truck before it shot away onto the back streets. I turned back to Oberis and Talus to see that Eric and the handful of other fae had joined them. More cars made their way out behind me as Calgary's shifter Clans scattered to hunt down the feeders in the city.

"Everyone is heading for the Tower," Talus said quietly. "It's time we did the same."

"You need a better weapon," Oberis told me as I rejoined the group. "Eric," he said sharply to the Keeper.

"What are you looking at me for?" the gnome protested as I followed Tamara back toward her car.

"You were a War Smith before you were a Keeper," the fae lord told him dryly. "You have something in your portable closet."

The gnome Keeper rolled his eyes and reached into thin air, producing a weapon that I thought was a rifle for a moment, until I realized it was way too bulky. A large magazine protruded halfway down its length, and the almost visibly sawed-off barrel led me to realize it was actually a shotgun of some kind. Orichalcum runes were traced over its remaining barrel and stock, glittering in the winter sunlight.

"This started life as an Italian SPAS-15 automatic shotgun," Eric told me as he passed me the weapon. "Modified to fire full spread, no choke. Infrared laser sight—you can see it, but mundanes like the Enforcers shouldn't. Enchanted to reduce weight, absorb recoil, and pull ammo from a pocket storage space."

"It pulls ammo from *where*?" I asked as I hefted the weapon. If the gnome's magic was reducing its weight significantly, I'm not sure I wanted to have to heft the weapon without it—it was easily ten pounds as it was.

"That ammo box is linked to a storage space like the one I carry with me," Eric told me, offhandedly explaining how he kept pulling objects from thin air. "It's not infinite ammo, but if you manage to use up the two thousand twelve-gauge shells I shoved in there when I built the gun, you have bigger issues than needing to reload. The gun is disgustingly illegal in Canada; don't be seen with it," he finished.

"Good, thank you, Eric," Oberis said briskly. "Talus, can you ride with Tamara and coordinate everyone else by phone? Jason, Eric, you're with me."

At this point, I joined the Keeper in following Oberis to his vehicle: a shining silver Lexus SUV. We were apparently the only ones riding with the lord.

Eric and I had barely finished getting into the car before Oberis floored the accelerator, glancing over at me once we hit the road.

"You two are both Vassals of the Queen," he said bluntly. "I know She has given you orders, and your fealty requires you to fulfill them by saving MacDonald. I intend to save him, and you two are here to bear witness."

The fae lord pulled a blatantly illegal left-hand turn on a red light, neatly slipping into the traffic going perpendicular to us without a scratch, though several dozen horns sounded.

"I am the only person in this city with a chance at facing Gerard Winters," he said simply. "What Talus knows without my saying, and what no one else will hopefully realize, is that every other greater fae and gentry in the city will basically be a distraction—*we* are the real attack.

"You two must make sure I make it to Winters," he told us. "He is unlikely to be far from MacDonald, so once he and I are tied up, I expect you to rescue the Wizard. However Winters has prevented the Magus from destroying him once he acted on his treachery, I hope it is removable—if I fail, allowing the Magus to deal with his own garbage is our only hope."

"How do you plan to pull this off?" Eric asked, voicing my thoughts. "Even if Winters killed half the Enforcers, he still has over a hundred armed men in the Tower, all carrying orichalcum runes. The building is blocked against walking Between, I'm sure!"

"What Gerard Winters doesn't know," Oberis said grimly as we drew into downtown and ever closer to the Tower, "is that there is one spot in the building that *isn't* blocked against Between. There were times MacDonald wanted things done without going through his people, and he came to me—and having a secret access to his tower has had...other advantages."

"We're going to walk right into the heart of the Wizard's Tower and save his millennial ass from his own prodigal creation," the fae lord told us. He pulled the Lexus into a dark alleyway, two blocks away from the glittering skyscraper our world knew as the Wizard's Tower.

Eric grabbed my shoulder as I was about to leave the car to join Oberis. "Jason," he said quickly. "You should probably use the Queen's gift. You are never going to be as out of your league as you are tonight."

For a moment, I had no idea what the old gnome was referring to, and then I remembered the tiny black pottery vial Niamh had given me at Queen Mabona's insistence—the vial of quicksilver that still rested inside the runic armored vest I wore under my dress shirt.

I took the vial and its leather thong out from around my neck and studied it in the anemic winter sunlight leaking down into the alley-way. The cork was sealed in tightly, and it took a moment of real effort to pop it out.

The tiny mouth of the vial seemed to glow in the sunlight sneaking into the vial, and a spicy scent of cinnamon wafted out into the alley. I breathed deeply of the oddly comforting smell, and then slugged back the tiny dose of the drug.

Nothing seemed to happen for a moment, and then a deep golden warmth began to spread out from my midsection. Everything felt a lot lighter, including the heavy auto-shotgun in my hands. With a surge of confidence, I stepped over to join Oberis, who gave me a questioning look, then shrugged.

"Both of you, stand with me," he instructed. Once Eric and I were standing on either side of him, he reached out and grabbed our arms, then *stepped*.

35

THE COLD CHILL that ran over my flesh felt familiar. Bone-chilling but somehow familiar—from my exposure to it by Mabona and previous, shorter trips with Oberis, I assumed. Everything around us faded to dim shadows of the world we'd left behind, intermixed with clouds and shadows of something *else*.

"Hold on," the fae lord murmured. "If you lose touch with me here, I may not be able to retrieve you in time—and the Cold Death is our worst punishment for a reason."

Remembering how Laurie's defiance had shattered when presented with that possible fate, I shivered—and made very sure to keep my arm in Lord Oberis's hand. For an interminable and cold moment, we stood there, Between, and did nothing.

Then we moved. There was no stepping, no physical action, just a thought from Oberis, and we were heading up through the mists. After a few moments, the void we moved through felt even more oppressive, somehow, and I knew we'd entered into the area barred on the other side. MacDonald's magic prevented us from crossing over back into the real world there.

Somehow, I could feel the barrier. Feel its strength. Feel its weakness. And I could tell, before Oberis even shifted his direction, where we would exit. There was a softness to it my quicksilver-fueled senses could feel, a room clear for the fae lord to enter.

Stepping back into the real world brought a surge of warmth almost equal to the quicksilver. It still felt strange for a moment, and then I realized that the drug was letting me feel the barriers erected against the Between—I could *feel* that other world that stood beside our normal one.

The room we'd entered was very plain. A couch occupied one wall, with a desk and chair on the opposite of the room. It was large, the size of an executive office, but with no windows to either the outside or the rest of the building.

Lord Oberis clearly knew the room well, better than I expected, even. He was heading toward the single door even before Eric and I had our bearings. Careful to keep the muzzle of the shotgun Eric had given me pointing away from the fae lord, I followed him.

We stepped out of the room into an empty corridor. On the inner side of the building was a solid concrete core sporting a number of closed doors, where the outer walls of the corridor were glass windows looking out onto a sunken atrium. Sunlight filtered through the outside wall of the tower, lighting up the downtown core that spread out beneath us—we were at least fifty stories up.

The view, sunlight and atrium distracted me for just long enough to miss several of the closed doors leading deeper into the tower opening. Quicksilver-fueled intuition caused me to dive for the floor as the shooting started regardless.

The Enforcer squad had traded in their standard black suits for full-body SWAT gear in black and gold, orichalcum runes traced over the surface of the well-made mundane equipment. Box-like bullpup assault rifles sprayed bullets in our direction as all three of us scattered out of the line of fire.

I could *feel* the cold iron in the rounds—the quicksilver sharpened my sense enough I could even say that it was every third bullet. I rode the quicksilver, letting it fuel my motion as I hit the ground, rolled, and came up facing the nearest of the half dozen Enforcers now in the hallway with us.

The heavy auto-shotgun roared, spraying heavy buckshot into the body armored guard. His armor and its enchantments stopped any of the rounds from penetrating but didn't do anything against the kinetic force of the overloaded shell. The impact flung him back, *through* the wall behind him, shattering bones and leaving him possibly dead and definitely out of the fight.

With the heartstone-and-mercury mix singing in my veins, I had tracked to the next Enforcer before the SPAS-15 had finished cycling. He tried to turn his rifle toward me before I fired, but his chamber clicked empty, his magazine drained, as the weapon bore on me. This time, the buckshot slammed into his head, ending his involvement in the fight with a very definitive snapping sound.

Oberis's response to the Enforcers was less advanced, possibly more elegant, and with the power of a fae lord behind it, much more effective. As the second Enforcer I'd shot dropped, he was lowering the last of the other four to the ground, having just scythed through them with the same glamor-blade he'd used to kill Darius Fontaine.

"They're expecting us," he said simply, not even panting from exertion. "MacDonald is that way," he continued, pointing. I didn't question how he knew where the Wizard was; I simply obeyed the implicit order, heading clockwise around the top floor of the Tower.

This floor, I realized, must have been MacDonald's actual residence. The open doors we passed showed a kitchen, an astonishingly comfortable-looking living room—whose furniture was probably worth more than my apartment—and the various other rooms and necessities of a home. The entire floor was wrapped in a circular atrium that filled the space that would have been an office cubicle farm in most of the buildings downtown at this height.

There was no sign of conflict or violence on the floor except the remnants of the squad of Enforcers that had tried to jump us. The floor was as silent as death as we ran, following Oberis toward MacDonald.

We'd rounded almost half of the tower when Oberis slowed, gesturing toward a pair of closed double doors. "In there," he murmured.

Eric and I stepped up to the doors, readying our weapons, as Oberis took a deep breath. With a firm nod to both of us, he *blurred* forward, shattering the door and crashing into the room.

I followed him through, riding the rush of the quicksilver as I searched for any Enforcers in the room with the Wizard. It was apparently MacDonald's bedroom, an opulent throwback to Victorian fantasies of Indian sultans. A giant four-poster bed occupied the center of the room, with heavy drapes and curtains over every wall, and piles of cushions.

MacDonald, wrapped in chains that glittered in silver and gold and cold iron, had been tied upright to one of the posts of the heavy bed. His eyes and mouth were bound, and the nearly immortal Wizard looked old—and terrified.

For a moment, I'm sure the three of us looked absolutely ridiculous. Eric and I were sweeping the room with the muzzles of our shotguns, and Oberis stood just out of reach from MacDonald in a low combat stance, a glowing blade of Power in his hand.

Then the glamor blade shattered into a million pieces as a black iron sword slashed through it, breaking the power that held it together. *None* of us saw Winters before he attacked, and even Oberis, ridiculously fast as he was, only barely managed to block the strike that followed his initial blow.

But he only had his bare hands to do it with, and the cold iron burnt his flesh. I could see it and smell it from across the room, as well as feel the cold iron, now that whatever had shielded Winters before he attacked was gone.

Winters had a head of height and forty pounds on Oberis's whip-thin build. With most mortals, it shouldn't have mattered, as Oberis had the speed and strength of his inhuman nature. Gerard Winters had long since moved past human, and as the fae lord stumbled back, white light flaring around his hands as he tried to heal and defend himself with Power, Winters used every inch of his height and reach to attack.

The black cold iron blade flashed across the room, dimly reflecting the sunlight trickling through the shattered doors, and embedded itself in Lord Oberis's torso, stabbing clean through his sternum and neatly pinning the fae lord to a post of the giant bed, next to the Magus.

"Drop the guns," Winters ordered Eric and me. "You can't hurt me with them."

I shot him. I knew he was correct about not being able to hurt him, but I was riding the quicksilver high and had just watched him impale Oberis. Obeying him was just not going to happen. Plus, I figured the same force that had bowled over the heavily armored Enforcers would work on him, too.

I was wrong. Three times I managed to cycle the heavy automatic shotgun. Three times I hit the Enforcer with the full blast of the buckshot. Three times the shot simply *bounced* off of him.

Then he broke the shotgun with a bladed hand strike—the stereotypical karate chop. From him, it sheared the rune-encrusted metal of the barrel in two, destroying the weapon.

"It's over, Winters," I told him as I dropped the ruined metal and stood there, facing a man I knew could destroy me in a moment. If guns weren't going to work, Eric wouldn't be any help here. He was a smith, not a warrior.

"Madrigal and her cabal are broken and being hunted down. Darius Fontaine is dead. Laurie confessed everything—your plan has failed."

He laughed and stepped away from me, looking at Oberis. The fae lord was desperately trying to get a grip on the sword impaling him, but the cold iron hilt kept defeating him.

"It's a sad love story we have here, isn't it?" he asked the lord, ignoring me like I was useless. "The brave Lord Oberis, coming to rescue the ex-lover who wronged him so. It's a little untraditional, but that's how the world works these days, isn't it."

Well, that helped explain why there was an access to MacDonald's personal quarters that Oberis was the only person in the city who could use.

"Did you really think, my lord, that the Magus's head of security didn't know about your tryst?" he demanded of the dying Lord. "Or that I wasn't expecting you after Michael escaped?"

"You *know* you've failed," I realized aloud. "You can never seize power here now. It's *over*."

Finally, he turned back to me, though he was still speaking to Oberis, I think.

"It's a shame that this love story ends in a tragedy," he told us. "But that is the fate of those who create monsters, isn't it? They die at the hands of their creations." He met my eyes and, for the first time, actually spoke to me.

"You've heard it said, haven't you, changeling?" he asked softly. "That Gerard Winters is a construct now, not a man—a monster forged by the power and arrogance of the Wizard MacDonald. He took a loyal man—and he made me into *nothing*.

"You think I've lost," he told me, "but you assume the real plan was to seize power. This was *always about MacDonald*. And now I know I gain nothing by killing him later, I see no reason not to kill him now," Winters spat.

A heavy automatic pistol appeared in his hand, and he turned toward the Wizard. Everything we'd done would implode when he pulled the trigger, and I would both fail in the charge given me under fealty and watch an innocent man be murdered.

With or without the chains of fealty, I could not let that happen. Knowing that angering Winters was suicide. Knowing that I could not face him. Knowing that I could not watch the Wizard die. I took a deep breath and annihilated the pistol with a bolt of green faerie flame.

"I think," I told him quietly, striving to put some semblance of calm in my voice, "that I have an objection to that plan."

———

THERE'S that sinking moment in this sort of situation where you realize that you're David, the other guy's Goliath, and the only available equivalent to God is trussed up and chained to his bed. The first time Winters hit me was that moment.

I barely saw him move between my blasting the gun out of his hand and him hitting me, but the blow knocked me clean through the wall, out into the corridor around the outside of the Tower. If there was ever a warning that I was even more out of my "weight class" than usual, this was it.

With the quicksilver in my veins, and aware that he was coming at me, I barely managed to dodge the next blow. Blocking or attacking was out of the question as the Enforcer came after me. Finally, I failed to dodge another blow.

Glass shattered around me as I was pitched clean through the *next* wall and into the atrium, crashing through several decorative trees and bushes before landing in some kind of fern. Winters casually hopped through the shattered glass and came after me. He'd acquired another black cold iron sword from somewhere, and my quicksilver-heightened speed of thought allowed me to wonder just how many weapons he had on him.

Again I found myself dodging his attacks, barely forcing misses from the deadly cold iron. I danced back out of his reach and managed to find enough of a breather to draw the Glock 18 Tamara had given me at the start of the morning.

The Glock 18 is almost unique among light handguns in having a burst-fire setting. *Tamara's* Glock 18s had been modified to fire full auto. Of course, with only the easily concealable ten-round magazine, full auto empties the weapon in slightly more than a second.

Throwing the pistol at Winters after I emptied it at him appeared to have about equal effect. The bullets *bounced*, scattering away from the tattooed man's skin as he advanced on me like a freight train, drawing the sword back.

"You can't hurt me, changeling," he told me. "Surrender, and I'll make it quick."

Apparently, I hadn't been upgraded to *threat*—just *annoyance*. Which was fair, as that was about where I was classifying myself.

He'd backed me against the window, and I suddenly realized I was trapped between two giant pots holding evergreen trees. An evil smile crossed the Enforcer's face, and I tried to dodge forward, past him, as he stabbed toward me.

Something *clicked* in my head, and the world went cold. For a moment, I thought he'd killed me, and then I recognized the cold. I was Between. How the hell was I Between?!

Then I *stepped* out of Between and was back in the room with Eric and Oberis, the gnome staring at me in shock from where he'd been desperately trying to wrap enough cloth around Winters's sword to allow him to pull it out of Oberis.

"You can't walk Between in here!" he said, astonished.

"*I* can't walk Between at all," I replied, equally astonished. Of course, I then realized that if we hadn't said anything, I might have managed to remain undiscovered.

"Go," Oberis groaned. "MacDonald's Order is..." he gasped around the sword, "...already sending help. You can't...save us. If you can walk...Between...take Eric and GO!"

I didn't let Eric try and argue. Hoping that it would work, I grabbed the gnome's arm and tried to *step*.

It was like pushing into putty. Somehow, I could tell we got halfway across but then were catapulted back, and the gnome gasped for breath, shaking his head at me.

"The quicksilver lets you cross over, but it's not enough to take two," he told me.

"We have to get back to the entrance. Run," I ordered, "I'll keep him distracted."

At that moment, Winters charged back into the room, heading for the gnome and me with that black and deadly blade.

With a deep breath, I focused on that mental click, the barrier I felt around us, and *stepped*. A flash of cold later, I was *behind* Gerard Winters and punched him in the back of the head.

I've punched walls with more effect. Hitting the Enforcer *hurt*, and it told him I was there. He turned, flashing around in a deadly spin with the sword cutting at neck height. I *stepped* out of the way, dropping into Between.

This time, I stopped in Between for a moment to capture my breath. I could breathe there. I'd always been there with someone else; I'd never been able to breathe there on my own before. The quicksilver was more impressive than I thought.

With that thought on my mind, I *stepped* back into reality. Winters had Eric in his grip, lifting the gnome off the ground with the sword in his other hand. It looked more threatening than actually lethal, but I didn't like the look of it anyway.

I hit Winters with another blast of Faerie flame. Fueled by my fear and the quicksilver, it was a lethal blast of flame that continued around his head and hit the wall behind him. Concrete and steel exploded above us, but Winters didn't even have singed hair as he turned back toward me, dropping Eric.

The gnome scuttled out of the room as Winters and I glared at each other.

"You're starting to *annoy* me, changeling," he told me. "All you're doing is drawing things out. You will change nothing."

I dodged backward as he slashed at me, retreating out of the room with my face to him. For a moment, I almost hoped he wouldn't follow —but if he hadn't, I knew I'd have had to find a way to make him.

Said following, however, took the form of a blurringly fast charge I barely dodged by bouncing through Between to the corner of the building. Missing me as I stepped into another reality, Winters crashed into the glass window, sending glass shards careening through the greenery.

He turned to glare at me, and giving in to an unknown impulse, I gave him a cheery wave and *stepped* again. This time, I emerged amidst the bodies of the Enforcers who'd ambushed us when we arrived, and by the time Winters came charging around the corner, I'd engaged in another moment of stupidity and picked up two of the boxy bullpup assault rifles.

The weapons were light enough and manageable enough that I could hold two. Even aim two. *Firing* two, as I discovered, was a different matter. With the quicksilver in my veins, I was easily strong enough and fast enough to do so and absorb the recoil.

But strength didn't do much for the fact that I'm almost skinny enough for a light breeze to blow me away. Without the mass to help absorb the recoil, the two guns quickly climbed for the roof and threw me.

Like every other time I'd shot him, the small high-velocity bullets bounced off of Winters, and then he was in my face. I was too close to dodge, too distracted to step Between. The first punch broke several ribs and drove me to the ground. The second shattered my left shoulder. The follow-up kick tossed me into the room we'd entered from.

I hit Eric and carried the gnome to the ground before bouncing further. There was no barrier there—I could feel it. I could walk Between there, save both myself and Eric from *this* room. Then I tried to stand, and the warmth and heat of the quicksilver faded almost instantly from my body as I realized I'd broken my leg when I landed.

Winters walked into the room slowly, his grin a terrible thing as he saw my injury. Ignoring Eric, the gnome lying where he'd fallen, he advanced on me as I struggled to get into some kind of position to fight back. Without the quicksilver in my veins, I didn't stand a chance at evading him. I barely managed to lurch to a kneeling position as he approached me, to die with some semblance of dignity.

The Enforcer stepped within reach of me, and then Eric shouted at me.

"Remember, under it all, *he's still mortal.*"

There must have been some quicksilver left in me, because time seemed to slow as Winters's sword arm drew back to end me.

He's still mortal. How was that relevant? There was enough magic woven into Winters's tattoos to protect him from any weapon, magic or attack I could come up with. It didn't matter if beneath those protections, he was still mortal.

He was still mortal. There are places mortals can't go, I remembered. Places no mortal could survive—not because it attacked them, but because the place was inherently hostile to them. Places no one except the fae could walk and live.

Knowing that if I failed, I died, I managed to half-lurch forward. I grabbed Winters's leg and *stepped.*

THE SWORD DIDN'T COME with us. That was the first thing I realized— cold iron can't go Between any more than non-fae can do it without a fae with the gift.

The lack of a sword saved my life, and I jerked away from Winters, abandoning him in the cold as he tried to strike at me with his bare hands. There, despite my broken leg, I could move and stand by thought, and I faced him squarely.

"What is this?" he demanded, and then clutched his throat as the last of his air left.

"This is Between," I told him, and then something swept through me, and words that were not mine issued from my lips.

"Gerard Winters," I found myself saying, my voice harsh and cold on my own tongue, "for breaking oath and trust and Covenant, you are sentenced to the Cold Death."

Winters's tattoos slowly turned black under the cold, and his skin blue around them. Gasping desperately for air, for any kind of breath at all, he looked at me in mute horror as he fell to his knees and mouthed a single word. I could make it out easily. *Mercy.*

"I'm sorry," I told him quietly. "There's no air here—no warmth, no life. No mortal, however shielded, can survive here. I can no more give you mercy than I could have let you kill MacDonald."

I knelt, just out of reach of the dying man.

"You chose this road," I said. "MacDonald only gave you power; you chose what to do with it. If you are a monster, it is because you chose to be.

"May some Power have mercy on you," I murmured as he slipped to the "ground" of this strange place. "I cannot."

I stayed there with him, outside the world, until it was over. It was a bad enough death. No one deserved to face it alone.

36

When I returned to the world, the room was empty. Slowly, weary with conflicting emotions and using the chair from the desk as a crutch, I retraced our earlier steps to MacDonald's bedroom. Below me, echoing up from the ground floors of the Tower, I could hear gunfire. The rest of the Court was there, fighting with the Enforcers defending an already-dead master.

Eric had used the time well, managing to use some of the drapes from the wall to pull the cold iron sword out of Oberis before it finally managed to kill him. The fae lord sat on the bed with his eyes closed, a faint light glowing around his midsection as he slowly healed himself with whatever Power was left to him.

Eric had removed the gag and blindfold from MacDonald and was busy breaking the chains with the strange powers gnomes had over metal. The last chain fell to the ground as I entered, and MacDonald finally stepped free of his bondage. The Wizard looked around the room slowly, carefully, once, and then gestured.

The sound of gunfire below us stopped.

"My Enforcers are now sealed in the parking garage beneath this building," he said quietly, passing a phone to Oberis. "If you could call off your Court, my old friend."

Oberis opened his eyes and nodded, taking the phone from the Wizard's hand.

"Talus," he said into it after a moment. "It's done. Get our people out before mortal authorities get there." He waited a moment for acknowledgement and then closed the phone.

"Thank you," MacDonald said simply. He reached over and touched Oberis. The gesture was gentle, caressing. A surge of Power flowed through it, and Oberis's wound healed. The Wizard turned to me.

"Where is Gerard?" he asked sadly.

"Between," I said simply, and he winced. "The Cold Death was the only way I could hurt him."

"A Hunter's changeling, I see," MacDonald said quietly. "I thank you, Jason Kilkenny. I will miss him and regret what happened, but you did what needed to be done. Any Boon you ask of me, I will grant."

As he said this, he laid his hand on my shoulder where I was leaning on the chair. That shoulder seemed like the only unbroken piece of my body, until another surge of Power flowed from the old Wizard. For a moment, my various broken bones seemed to *burn*, and then they flowed together as if I'd never been injured.

"I have no idea what I would ask for, Lord Magus," I said quietly.

He nodded and pulled a small black gem out of thin air and pressed it into my hand.

"Keep this, then," he told me. "You cannot lose it, and when you know what Boon you need, use it to call me. A Boon from such as I is best well thought on."

"I was sent to help," I admitted. "I am a Vassal of Queen Mabona."

I barely finished the words before the room warmed and the world shifted.

"And you have performed well," Mabona said, appearing from nothingness. Not even Between, I don't think. She was just suddenly there, as if summoned by her name.

"You are not supposed to be here without permission," MacDonald observed drily.

"I did not think you would mind," She replied, and the Wizard gave a weak attempt at a smile.

"Your action is noted," he told Her. "But I hold, and have always held, that the Boon is owed to the actor and not those who sent him to act. The thought is appreciated, though.

"Now, I dislike to be rude, but I would prefer this conversation be carried on somewhere other than my bedroom," MacDonald told us all. "I do have several hundred soon-to-be-ex-employees of mine to deal with as well, so would it be possible for us to reconvene—and bring the new Speaker of the Clans in as well—this evening?"

"What will happen to the Enforcers?" Oberis demanded. "They followed Winters—people have died for their actions."

"I will strip them of the power they were granted," MacDonald said coldly. "And then I will strip them of any memory of their time with me, and any knowledge of the supernatural. They will live the rest of their lives with a nagging feeling they were once part of something incredible and they threw it away. I will have no more death in our city; do you understand?"

Oberis nodded.

"I will meet you all in the lobby in four hours," the Magus continued. "We have much to establish as to where we go from here. I have apologies to make, and this city will change. Hopefully for the better."

"Walk with me," Mabona instructed the three of us fae. We obeyed, and in a moment, we were elsewhere.

IT TOOK me a moment to recognize the inside of the hotel that functioned as the fae Court in Calgary. The scent of life and greenery all through the enchanted building helped relax me, but the memory of letting Winters suffocate to death in front of me stuck in my head. Peace was going to be a while in coming.

"You are going to be well, Lord Oberis?" Mabona asked. The fae lord bowed his head.

"MacDonald...knows me well enough to do a perfect job of healing," he confirmed. "I am well. Concerned for my Court, so if you will excuse me?"

"Of course," she allowed. "I wish to speak with my Vassal in private, in any circumstance."

Eric took the hint and followed Lord Oberis out of the Court's grand hall, leaving me and my Queen alone. She gestured, and the moss quickly grew into a simple approximation of chairs. She took one and patted the other.

"Sit, my dear boy," she told me. "You have done well, far beyond my hopes."

"It was not by choice," I reminded her, and she nodded.

"Indeed," she agreed. "And as you have done so well, I will do as the Wizard did—for your superb actions here, I owe you a Boon. Name your reward, child."

It was almost harder to know what to ask the Queen for than it had been to know what to ask MacDonald for. On the other hand, She knew things about me that he did not.

"Tell me who my father was," I asked.

She sighed, deeply.

"What I can tell you will cost no Boon," She told me. "Your father was a Hunter—you must have realized that when you walked Between, for only the riders of the Wild Hunt can pass that gift onto their changelings.

"He was also noble fae, as you must have also realized since he was my Vassal," She told me.

"I thought the walking Between was from the quicksilver," I admitted.

"Quicksilver only makes you stronger," the Queen explained. "It does not give you any gifts you would not wield normally. I will ask Oberis to teach you more of the Between and its paths—I will likely not have time."

"But what about my father?" I asked again, not willing to let this go yet.

"I cannot tell you more," She admitted. "It would be no kindness to you if I did—it could easily cost your life. Your father had many enemies, and you remain concealed from them as long as your blood is not spoken of aloud. I will not tell you his name."

I wasn't sure how to take that, and I was silent for a moment as I considered.

"What," I said slowly, allowing my drawl to slow the words as I considered something else worth a Power's boon, "if I were to ask to be released from my fealty to you?"

"I would be displeased," She answered, equally slowly. "But I would be forced to grant the Boon. Think before you ask for such things, however, as the costs are many."

"To escaping slavery?" I asked.

"You are not a slave, Jason Kilkenny," my raven-haired Queen told me. "You are a Vassal. This relationship has obligations and rights both ways. As my Vassal, you hold diplomatic immunity across all fae Courts. From me you will receive aid and information to help keep the peace and fight evil. Think what would have happened here"—She gestured around us—"if I had not tasked you to seek out the plot on MacDonald's life."

Taking my silence as a sign, She explained quietly.

"Truths that are now unveiled would be secret. Many would be dead who now live. A war would have started, and Winters would have succeeded," she said bluntly. "Oberis would be dead. MacDonald would be dead. Many would have fallen prey to the vampires. You stopped all this."

"Not alone," I disagreed. "I worked with others, had help—I often just watched."

"And yet you were the catalyst to so much—because you were my Vassal and served the task I gave you," She reminded me. "Without you, this city would have burned. Without my aid, you would have died.

"You are your father's son—it is not in you to stand aside from evil," Mabona told me. "As my Vassal, you will have the aid and authority to fight it. And while I do not often offer Boons, there are many rewards in my service."

I touched the collar of the rune-encrusted bulletproof vest I wore under my shirt. Without that gift from Her, I would have been dead.

She was right in that, at least. And She was right that I wasn't willing to stand by and let harm come to the people around me. Stupid of me, but She was right.

"I will hold the Boon," I said slowly. "And I will hold you to your promise to release me if I call on that Boon."

"Done and done and done," She confirmed, repeating three times to prove She would honor the promise. "I want your service, not your unthinking obedience.

"There is something I want in return, though," She told me. She waited for me to respond, and I gestured for Her to continue. She'd already thrice-bound herself, which made it unlikely what She wanted would be too strenuous.

"I want you to swear fealty to me in your own voice and by your own choice, as well as fealty by your father's blood," She said simply.

I sat there on that moss chair in the Court for at least a minute in silence. She waited—I guess when you've lived longer than any human could dream of, waiting a few minutes isn't a big deal.

By my own voice and my own choice. The words were like tombstones—while the boon I held gave me an escape clause if I swore fealty to Her, I would no longer be able to say I'd been forced into this. I would *choose* to follow the Queen, to accept Her orders, to obey.

I would be a volunteer, not a conscript, which would change...everything. And nothing. I would serve either way. She would release me from my fealty if I invoked the boon either way. It just changed...context. It made it *my* choice to be a Vassal, because I could claim the Boon now and walk away.

But She was right. I didn't have it in me to walk away from need. And Her aid had kept me alive this far, and She was right that I would have died without it. I wasn't so sure the city would have burned without me, but I did seem to have been in the middle.

Finally, I made up my mind. I stood from the moss chair and knelt before Her as She rose to Her own feet. Alone on that mossy floor, we faced each other, and the words were in my mind—like I'd always known what they were.

"I, Jason Kilkenny, offer You my fealty," I said simply. "To serve with honor, to obey with fidelity, to answer with truth. Your foes are my foes. Your allies are my allies. Your will is my will. I am Your Vassal."

"I, Mabona, accept your fealty," She responded. "To reward honor with honor, fidelity with trust, truth with truth. While I am your Lady, you will never be without aid or reward or allies. Those who speak against you speak against me—as my foes and allies are yours, so your foes and allies are mine.

"Fealty flows both ways. I am your Queen; you are my Vassal."

———

I CALLED Mary from outside the hotel. After the phone had rung three times, my heart started to quicken with worry, and then she finally picked up.

"You're okay?" she asked, right off the bat.

"I am," I confirmed. "You?"

"In desperate need of a shower, but unhurt," she told me. "There weren't enough of the feeders in any group we found to be a threat. What *happened* in the Tower?"

"I killed Winters," I told her simply. "MacDonald ended the fight and is dealing with the Enforcers. The Queen is here and there's a giant conference at the Tower tonight—MacDonald wants to try and sort out where we go from here."

"I'd heard Winters was dead—why didn't you call me sooner?" she asked. "I was worried."

"I've been tied up with the Queen," I said. "We were...discussing things. I think we've settled on terms of service I can live with."

"You're seriously the Vassal of a Power?" Mary asked. "I know Eric said you were, but no one else has said anything about it."

"We're keeping it quiet," I explained. "Being a Vassal normally includes a large bull's-eye, and I'm not up to the usual weight class of Vassals."

"I haven't told anyone, and I won't," she promised. "I don't know if I'm supposed to be at this conference; it sounds like Enli is just bringing a small escort."

"Can you come for me?" I asked. "The Queen is going to need at least some people around Her so She doesn't *look* outnumbered."

Though, with the exception of MacDonald, my Queen had everyone else in the city outnumbered.

"And I want to see you," I admitted.

"I'll meet you there," she promised. "But I definitely need to shower and find another set of dress clothes."

"I will see you there," I agreed, and we hung up. Her closing words caused me to look down at the state of the expensive suit Talus had paid for this morning.

Blood spattered it, a good portion of it mine. Tears and rips in the cloth revealed the healed skin beneath. I needed to change.

Almost as I finished the thought, however, Mabona reappeared from wherever She'd vanished to and handed me a suit bag.

"Wear this," She instructed. "The people at this meeting are the ones in this city we *want* to know you're my Vassal—they're the ones who have to honor your diplomatic immunity."

I opened the suit bag and for a moment wished I could just show up in my tattered suit. Swallowing, I slowly dressed in the perfectly fitted black-and-gold uniform. Any real soldier would have laughed at the amount of braid, and then been silenced when he saw how easily I could move in it.

The long purple cape, however, I drew the line at. When I pulled it out of the suit bag, I looked up at Mabona.

"You cannot be serious," I told Her.

"The cape is the only part of the uniform of my retainers that has never changed," She told me. "There is a long and illustrious tradition behind it. It's also one of the more powerful shields against Power you will ever wear."

With a sigh, I slung the long cape around my shoulders and stood straight. A nearby hotel mirror showed me just how ridiculous I looked, but it was what my Queen wanted. I'd made my choice.

———

THERE WAS no sign that there had ever been anything resembling a battle when we arrived at the ground floor of MacDonald's tower in a black SUV borrowed from Lord Oberis. Other cars were also arriving, and neatly dressed valets directed people inside and took the vehicles.

The valet that met us didn't even finish his first sentence before I realized it was little more than a recording. The "valets" were illusions wrapped around energy constructs, preprogrammed extensions of MacDonald's will.

I passed the keys to the construct and felt my flesh shiver as the illusion brushed my flesh. It took over the vehicle, and I preceded my Queen with an abortive attempt at the stylistic flick of the cape you see in old movies.

Mary was waiting by the front door, and Enli stood with her. I inclined my head to the new Speaker and pointed him out to Mabona.

"My Queen, this is Speaker Enli of Clan Enli, leader of Calgary's shifter Clans," I introduced him to her. "Speaker Enli, this is my Lady, Queen Mabona."

Enli bowed, deeply, to the Queen.

"Mary told me that You would be here, Your Majesty," he greeted her. "I wanted to see You with my own eyes. It is rare that we are graced here by one of the Old Powers."

"We do not like to meddle in the affairs of other Powers," Mabona reminded him. "I am here by request, as I had an involvement in resolving the situation."

"So I am told," Enli said, and bowed slightly to me. "We owe Jason a large debt, which will not be forgotten." His words were addressed to my Queen, but his eyes were on me.

"I would like to offer the services of Mary Tenerim, one of the old Speaker's Clan, as an additional escort and guide to our city," he continued smoothly. "She and your Vassal have some experience working together."

Mary and I both blushed. For all the high-minded and formal speech they were wrapping around the offer, the twinkle in both Enli's and—I was sure—Mabona's eyes showed they both knew exactly why Mary was joining the Queen's party.

Given that, I shrugged, stepped forward and swept my girlfriend into a tight embrace, kissing her fiercely. Despite everything that had happened, we had survived. The city had survived.

And I was going to make sure that it *kept* surviving. As we walked into that conference, as retainers to an Old Power of the world, I fully accepted what I had decided earlier. I accepted what I had become.

My name is Jason Kilkenny. I am a Vassal of the Queen of the Fae, and Calgary is *my* city. It is under my protection, and through me, the protection of my Queen.

You have been warned.

JOIN THE MAILING LIST

Love Glynn Stewart's books? Join the mailing list at

GLYNNSTEWART.COM/MAILING-LIST/

to know as soon as new books are released, special announcements, and a chance to win free paperbacks.

ABOUT THE AUTHOR

Glynn Stewart is the author of *Starship's Mage,* a bestselling science fiction and fantasy series where faster-than-light travel is possible–but only because of magic. His other works include science fiction series *Duchy of Terra, Castle Federation* and *Vigilante,* as well as the urban fantasy series *ONSET* and *Changeling Blood.*

Writing managed to liberate Glynn from a bleak future as an accountant. With his personality and hope for a high-tech future intact, he lives in Kitchener, Ontario with his partner, their cats, and an unstoppable writing habit.

VISIT GLYNNSTEWART.COM FOR NEW RELEASE
UPDATES

[f] facebook.com/glynnstewartauthor

OTHER BOOKS
BY GLYNN STEWART

For release announcements join the
mailing list or visit **GlynnStewart.com**

STARSHIP'S MAGE
Starship's Mage
Hand of Mars
Voice of Mars
Alien Arcana
Judgment of Mars
UnArcana Stars
Sword of Mars
Mountain of Mars
The Service of Mars
A Darker Magic
Mage-Commander (upcoming)

Starship's Mage: Red Falcon
Interstellar Mage
Mage-Provocateur
Agents of Mars

Pulsar Race: A Starship's Mage Universe Novella

DUCHY OF TERRA
The Terran Privateer
Duchess of Terra
Terra and Imperium
Darkness Beyond
Shield of Terra
Imperium Defiant
Relics of Eternity
Shadows of the Fall
Eyes of Tomorrow

SCATTERED STARS

Scattered Stars: Conviction

Conviction

Deception

Equilibrium

Fortitude (upcoming)

PEACEKEEPERS OF SOL

Raven's Peace

The Peacekeeper Initiative

Raven's Course

Drifter's Folly (upcoming)

EXILE

Exile

Refuge

Crusade

Ashen Stars: An Exile Novella

CASTLE FEDERATION

Space Carrier Avalon

Stellar Fox

Battle Group Avalon

Q-Ship Chameleon

Rimward Stars

Operation Medusa

A Question of Faith: A Castle Federation Novella

SCIENCE FICTION STAND ALONE NOVELLA

Excalibur Lost

VIGILANTE
(WITH TERRY MIXON)
Heart of Vengeance
Oath of Vengeance

**Bound By Stars: A Vigilante Series
(With Terry Mixon)**
Bound By Law
Bound by Honor
Bound by Blood

TEER AND KARD
Wardtown
Blood Ward

CHANGELING BLOOD
Changeling's Fealty
Hunter's Oath
Noble's Honor
Fae, Flames & Fedoras: A Changeling Blood Novella

ONSET
ONSET: To Serve and Protect
ONSET: My Enemy's Enemy
ONSET: Blood of the Innocent
ONSET: Stay of Execution
Murder by Magic: An ONSET Novella

FANTASY STAND ALONE NOVELS
Children of Prophecy
City in the Sky

Printed in Great Britain
by Amazon